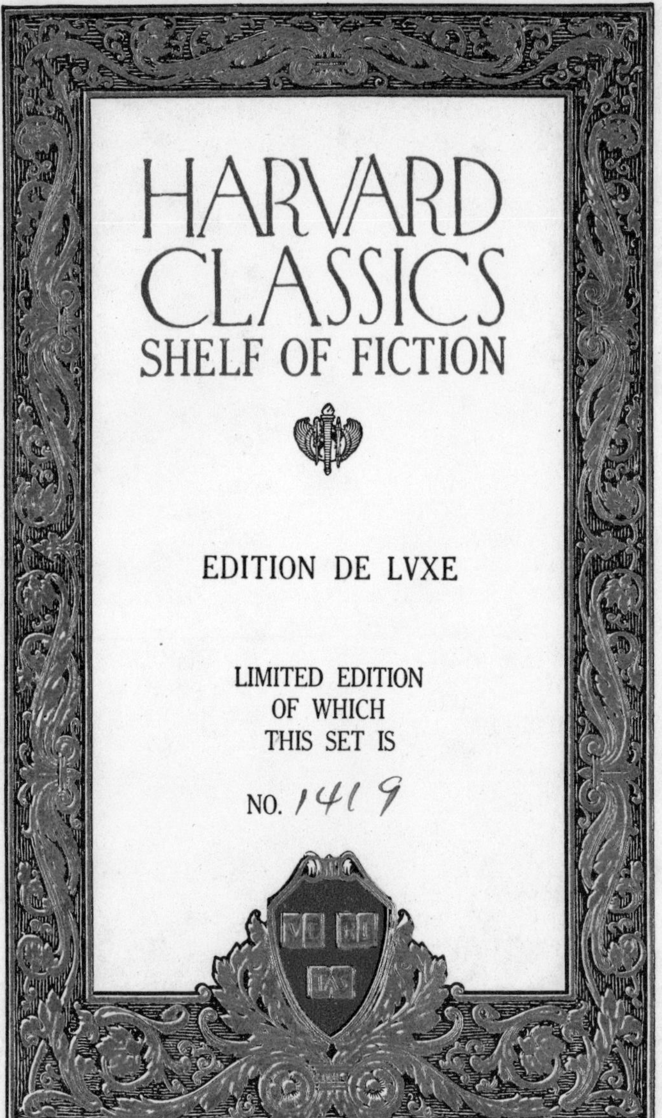

HARVARD CLASSICS
SHELF OF FICTION

EDITION DE LVXE

LIMITED EDITION
OF WHICH
THIS SET IS

NO. 1419

THE HARVARD CLASSICS
SHELF OF FICTION
SELECTED BY CHARLES W ELIOT LL D

PEPITA JIMENEZ

BY

JUAN VALERA

A HAPPY BOY

BY

BJORNSTJERNE BJORNSON

SKIPPER WORSE

BY

ALEXANDER L. KIELLAND

EDITED WITH NOTES AND INTRODUCTIONS
BY WILLIAM ALLAN NEILSON PH D

P F COLLIER & SON COMPANY
NEW YORK

Published under special arrangement with
The Macmillan Company

MANUFACTURED IN U. S. A.

CONTENTS

THE NOVEL IN SPAIN

THE three modern Spanish novels, "Pepita Jiménez," by Juan Valera; "The Fourth Estate," by Armando Palacio Valdés; and "Doña Perfecta," by Benito Pérez Galdós, are typical of the life of Spain, seen from various points of view—but all Spanish points of view—of to-day. They are not only artistic books of fiction, but sociological and psychological documents of the greatest value. Of the three, "Pepita Jiménez" is the most charming and characteristic; and it, of the three, is least touched by the French influence of the naturalistic school. Yet, if one compares the masterpiece of Fernan Caballero, which is "The Sea Gull," with a novel like "The Swan of Villamorta," by her successor, Madame Pardo Bazán, one finds that there is something in the genius of Spanish literature itself not unrelated to the less "scientific" and less repellent form of naturalism. Both in "Pepita Jiménez" and "The Fourth Estate" there is that "complete synthesis of gravity of matter and gaiety of manner," which, as Coventry Patmore says, "is the glittering crown of art, and which out of Spanish literature is to be found only in Shakespeare, and even in him in a far less obvious degree." Valera's masterpiece is a masterpiece of exquisite, cheerful, sensuous, but not sensual, art. It is difficult to find words to express its high value, and no words can express the nameless charm of personality which permeates its style and which is not lost in our colder English.

Of these three typical novelists, the author of "Pepita Jiménez" is the most joyously in love with life. In "Doña Perfecta," Galdós, as in all his best-known works, is almost dangerously in love with his thesis—less so, perhaps, in "Doña Perfecta" than in his more ponderous novel "Gloria," and the gaiety of the manner of Valdés sometimes leaves the English-speaking reader in doubt as to whether he takes life seriously. The realism of Galdós is more philosophical than that of Valdés, more abstract, and not impartial at all. In fact, the "tendency" with Galdós sometimes almost obliterates the "novel" quality, and we hear the preacher through the thin veil of fiction. On the other hand, the opponent to his doctrine, though his colleague in manner, Padre Coloma, is even more gloomy in his realism than Galdós. The hopelessness of "Currita," Coloma's masterpiece, is even deeper than that of "Doña Perfecta," where one feels the coming of the storm from the very beginning. Neither Coloma, the defender of the faith as held by the orthodox Spaniard, nor Galdós, the iconoclast, looks on Spain with cheerful eyes. If in "Currita" the society of Madrid is depicted as holding only male and female rakes, in "Doña Perfecta" the society of the provinces is composed of bigots without hearts and even without common sense.

"The Fourth Estate" is the best example of Spanish realism extant. Valdés knows the sea—witness "The Joy of Captain Ribot"—and the land by the sea as well. The town of Sarrio we can not see with our eyes, we can not know the color of its walls, nor touch the furniture of its clubs, but we know it in reality as well as we know Anthony Trollope's "Barchester," George Eliot's "Middlemarch," Mrs. Gaskell's "Cranford," Mrs. Oliphant's "Carlingford," or Mrs. Deland's "Old Chester"—as well as we know Father Goriot's boarding-house, or the interior of Mr. Squeers's school. Valdés owes much to Balzac, but here, too, when we speak of "influences," we must allow greatly for a certain Spanish quality, frequent in Calderon and Cervantes, which is not the realism of Balzac, but different from it because it is not self-conscious. Now, Galdós is often self-conscious, and Madame Pardo Bazán always is so; Valdés makes his picture with a light and cheerful touch, inexorably true, but with no constant assertion that he paints for the sake of truth.

The tragedy of "The Fourth Estate" is as inexorable as that of "Doña Perfecta," but it is not the main thing. All the life in the book is not subservient to this tragedy. There is, as in life, much comedy and many sidelights from the sun. And the ending of Gonzalo, his refusal to live after the loss of a woman he loved, whom he ought to have hated, is brought about by the processes of his soul, and not by any vulgar use of machinery. The end is, as Robert Louis Stevenson once said in regard to a story of his own, "inevitable" —it could not have been otherwise. And, after all, this is the only excuse for a tragedy in a novel—even in a novel of Continental realism, which differs as much from our realism as gray from complete black. The plain speaking of Valdés has no pruriency in it. It is the plain speaking of Calderon, not the self-conscious analysis of Bourget or the deliberate pruriency of Zola, in which the roots of life, which are in the mud, are exposed at the expense of the splendid blooms that open to heaven. Valdés, in "The Fourth Estate," is less religious than Valera, in "Pepita Jiménez"; but one feels that he is writing of a people who, as René Bazin says of the English, "still penetrated with Christianity, conserve, from their traditions, a divine ideal mingled with all human appetities."

"Let us take, for instance, the central figure in "The Fourth Estate," Cecilia. She is purity itself, though she loves Gonzalo with all her heart, even after his marriage with her sister. Christianity, working in one of the highest types of womanhood, could alone have produced such a creature. Don Rosendo and his wife, Doña Paula, are most carefully done—touch by touch their characters are painted until they stand before us, as if we saw them.

Doña Paula's progress from the costume of the cigarette-maker to the gloves and hat of the great lady, and its effect on the conservative minds of Sarrio, is shown to us rather than told. "Whenever Doña Paula appeared in public with the abhorred hat upon her head, or with any other departure from her old attire, she was always greeted with a murmur of disapproval. The fault of the matter lay in her never having resented, in public or in private, or even in the sanctum of her own feelings, this malignant treatment of her fellow townsfolk. She considered it natural and reasonable, and it never occurred to her that it ought not to have been; her ideas of conventionality had never prompted her to rebel against the tyranny of public opinion. She believed in all good faith that in adopting the gloves, the mantilla, or the hat, she had committed a breach of laws both human and divine, and that the murmurs and mocking glances were the just retribution for the infraction."

Doña Paula, married to a man much above her in rank, ardently desiring the prerogatives of her new class, and foolishly wretched when she acquires them, develops, as the story goes on, until we forget her frivolities and follies and learn to respect her. Don Rosendo, the rich, sentimental, and vain philanthropist, is a man who could only have existed in a Latin country, and in a town like Sarrio. The triumph of the character drawing of Valdés is in Venturita, the younger sister—charming, beautiful, seductive—who allured Gonzalo from his duty and his contentment. In the figure of the Duke, the egotistic, sensual, esthetic, and *blasé* man of the old nobility, it is easy to recognize a modern type presented often by the pessimist, Padre Coloma; but Valdés makes him individual and novel. One of the steps that lead to the end is the noteworthy scene of the picture. It is not reticently done—the process of the unveiling of the husband's eyes is not discreetly softened, as it is in the case of Rawdon Crawley by Thackeray. Nothing is left in doubt, though the end is different. Rawdon Crawley did not love his wife as Gonzalo loved Venturita, nor had he surrendered honor itself for her, and he would not die because, though she had treacherously betrayed him, he could live without her.

Cecilia makes the greatest sacrifice a woman can make, that of her good name—not to save her sister, but to save the man she loves from the madness she knows will come upon him should he learn the truth. And, in this episode, the fineness of the art of Valdés is shown. It is an old situation—as old as the earliest Italian romance; it reeks with the smell of gas and the orange-peel of the melodramas of the nineteenth century. Many ladies in the theatre and in the novels exist only that, at the right moment, they should put themselves innocently in an equivocal position, to thrill the reader with their heroism. But the art of Valdés makes it new, and deprives it both of stupidity and indecency. About the central persons of the tragedy walk, talk, laugh, grieve, love, and hate the burghers of the town of Sarrio—

this town of the fourth estate; no two are alike; the smallest person of the crowd is distinct and differentiated.

The minor characters in "Pepita Jiménez" are admirably drawn, too, but there are fewer of them; by comparison, one can not help wishing that Valdés had more of Valera's cheerful tolerance. He is sometimes relentlessly pitiless, as in the case of Galino Maza, the retired naval officer, of M. Delaunay, the Belgian engineer, and of the eager agitator, Sinforoso Suarez; and this is the more remarkable as there are occasions of great seriousness when he is almost absurdly gay. These passages have the effect on the reader that the reply of an amiable Tagalog, in Philippine "store" clothes, had on the grave clergyman who asked him what his neighbors would do to the public school teachers when these devoted folk should go among them. "Kill them, of course," the ingenuous savage replied, with a fetching and happy smile. One forgives Valdés because there are only a few flies of this kind in the amber.

There is nothing to forgive in "Pepita Jiménez"—the style and the fable go well together. Here, as Coventry Patmore says, "there is no sense of dislocation or incompatibility between the natural and spiritual." To the Puritan mind, Pepita is very shocking, and the means by which she awakens the mistaken young acolyte from his dreams of an impossible mysticism as horrible as the subterfuge of Marianna in "Measure for Measure." But the wise old ecclesiastic, who knows that the perfection of celibacy is not for all, watches the case, smiles, and forgives. English taste and English morals require that Don Luis—in fiction—should kill himself after the manner of Lucretia; but Valera is less exacting, and more true to life. The preface to "Pepita Jiménez" is one of the most delicious pieces of writing in any language. To the English mind the story represents the failure of the ideal to overcome the material—a failing which, under the circumstances, was necessary. To the Spanish mind, imbued with the principles of Catholicism, the motive is entirely different; Don Luis, the false mystic, does not fall essentially; he rises to a knowledge of his own nature, and he is happy because he, in time to save himself, recognizes in time its limitations and its true vocation. It would be a bold man who would excuse the grave Don Luis and the pious Pepita; let us leave them, as Valera leaves them, very charitably and gaily.

There is very little cheerfulness in "Doña Perfecta." There is, however, great power of description and terrible intensity of bitterness. One leaves Sarrio with regret; one even wants to go back to the spot where agonized Gonzalo dropped into the sea, to observe Cecilia, with his children, praying in the church; but one does not care to return to the town of Orbajosa, with all its dignities. Galdós's Rosarito is sweet, innocent, lovely, the Lucy of Lammermoor or the Ophelia of modern Spanish literature; she is more like Lucy and less like Ophelia. Pepe is a conceited young fellow, of good intentions and fine talent, who has neither common sense nor tact. The town is full of prejudices. Pepe, fresh from the scientific schools of Madrid, outrages them all. In spite of this, he has our sympathies, for all the world loves a lover. Doña Perfecta, proud, cold, unscrupulous, mistakes bigotry for spirituality and the exterior form for the sacred heart beneath the symbols of religion. She is beloved in the town because she seems to be serenely good—and she is good when no human being crosses her will. Galdós seems to hate her from the first moment she enters; she is to point his moral that religion—of the formal sort—destroys the law rather than fulfils it. And she does point it with a vengeance.

Rosarito, her daughter of pearl, of alabaster, compact of soft sighs and tender fears, and devotion to the things of Heaven, loves Pepe. And he, as his father intends, loves her. But Doña Perfecta and all the country about conspire against him—all, according to their own point of view, for the love of God. They are too blind to see that, under the "scientific" bumptiousness of Pepe, there is a faith in God as strong and more simple than their own. Doña Perfecta draws out the evil from those around her, that Pepe, who has outraged all her beliefs, opinions, and prejudices, may be forced back to Madrid. Hypocrisy and hatred spring up wherever she moves, seemingly as pure and kind as the Lady in Milton's "Comus." Rosarito's love awakens depth in what seems surface shallowness, and she stakes all on her faith in Pepe. The intense scene at the foot of the crucifix is the great moment of the novel; and, after that, Pepe's awful dread grows on him. It is the dread of a soul in the dark, surrounded by avenging forms. Rosarito fails him through weakness, and the end comes; but the real tragedy is not for them that die, but for them that live. "Doña Perfecta" is a realistic novel, not of detail, or analysis, not of physiology, but of psychology. Its thesis is modern—of the time of the beginning of Darwinism—but its pathos and humanity are of all time. It would have been better if the thesis were not so evident, for then Doña Perfecta might have been permitted to have one moment of womanly weakness, and this would have redeemed her. With all its bitterness and didacticism, "Doña Perfecta" deserves, as a sociological study, a place in this trilogy representing the modern novels of Spain. More than that, there are passages of such luminous atmosphere that only an author with more genius than talent could have written them.

MAURICE FRANCIS EGAN

BIOGRAPHICAL NOTE

DON JUAN VALERA Y ALCALÁ GALIANO was born on October 18, 1824, at Cabra, Cordova, Spain. His father was an admiral, his mother a marchioness in her own right, and his sister became Duchess of Malakoff. He studied at Malaga and the University of Granada, at the latter of which he took a degree in law. After a boisterous youth he entered the diplomatic service, and was attached to the Spanish embassies at Naples, Lisbon, Rio de Janeiro, Dresden, and St. Petersburg. In 1858 he published a volume of poems, and the next year he returned to Spain and entered politics, taking his seat in the Cortes as an advanced liberal, and writing for the press. For a short time he was Minister of Agriculture and Trade, and later was appointed Minister at Frankfort. Meantime he did not abandon literature. His contributions to periodicals won him election to the Spanish Academy in 1861. In 1864 appeared three volumes of criticism, which were followed by translations from the Greek and German.

After the revolution in 1868 Valera held high office during the short reign of Amadeo of Savoy, but withdrew when the republic was set up.

When, at the age of fifty, he published his first novel, "Pepita Jiménez," his political and intellectual prominence insured it attention; but the book met with a success that raised his reputation to a much higher level. It at once took rank as "the principal, the typical Spanish novel of our days." "'Pepita Jiménez'," says the author himself, "was written when Spain was agitated to its center and everything thrown out of its regular course by a radical revolution that at the same time shook to their foundations the throne and religious unity. It was written when everything was in fusion, like molten metal, might readily amalgamate, and be molded into new forms. It was written when the strife was raging fiercest between ancient and modern ideals; and, finally, it was written in all the plenitude of my powers, when my soul was sanest and most joyful in the possession of an enviable optimism and an all-embracing love and sympathy for humanity, which, to my misfortune, can never again find place within my breast." He followed up his success with three other novels, "The Illusions of Doctor Faustino" (1876), "Commander Mendoza" (1877), and "Doña Luz" (1878), and a volume of "Dramatic Experiments."

Meantime the Bourbon dynasty had been restored, and in 1881 Valera reentered diplomacy as minister at Lisbon. From 1884 to 1886 he represented his country at Washington, and later at Brussels and Vienna, finally retiring in 1896. After some years of private life, he died on April 18, 1905. His later works include some highly laudatory criticisms of Spanish American literature and a volume of "Tales, Dialogues, and Fancies."

Valera's inexperience in the writing of novels at the date at which he produced "Pepita Jiménez" is shown by its somewhat amateurish construction, but the extraordinary merits of the work have more than compensated for structural flaws. A translation cannot convey a just impression of the beauty of the Spanish style of the original, but neither can it disguise the vividness and lifelikeness of the character drawing. The four chief figures of the story compare with the creations of masters of the art of fiction in the illusion of reality which they produce and in the subtlety of the psychology employed in portraying them. In the treatment of the delicate theme of the novel Valera shows an agility and tact that are truly marvelous. Though issued at a time of passionate controversy, he succeeded in handling the issue between the church and the world without offending either party. And in doing this he has presented the foreign reader with a picture of Spain—"Spain with its fervor, its sensual piety, its rhetoric and hyperbole, its superficial passion, its mysticism, its graceful extravagance."

W. A. N.

CRITICISM AND INTERPRETATION

By Coventry Patmore

IN this work of Juan Valera we find that complete synthesis of gravity of matter and gaiety of manner which is the glittering crown of art, and which out of Spanish literature is to be found only in Shakespeare, and even in him in a far less obvious degree. It is only in Spanish literature, with the one exception of Dante, that religion and art are discovered to be not necessarily hostile powers; and it is in Spanish literature only, and without any exception, that gaiety of life is made to appear as being not only compatible with, but the very flower of that root which in the best works of other literatures hides itself in the earth, and only sends its concealed sap through stem and leaf of human duty and desire. The reason of this great and admirable singularity seems mainly to have been the singular aspect of most of the best Spanish minds toward religion. With them, religion has been, as it was meant to be, a human passion; they have regarded dogma as the form of realisable, and, by them, realised experience; and the natural instincts of humanity as the outlines of the lineaments of the Divinity—"very God and very man." Witness the writings of their greatest saints and theologians, in which dogma is, as it was, fused in, and becomes psychology, instead of remaining, as it has done with us, a rock, indeed of refuge to many, but a rock of stumbling and offence to many more, and of these especially such as have been endowed with the artistic temperament.

"Pepita Jiménez" is essentially a "religious novel," none the less so because it represents the failure of a good young aspirant to the priesthood to attain a degree of sanctity to which he was not called, and depicts the working in his aspirations of a pride so subtle as to be very venial, though, in some degree, disastrous. One of the many points in which Catholic philosophy shows itself superior to the philosophy of Protestant religionists in the knowledge of the human mind is its distinct recognition of the fact that there are as many degrees of human capacity for holiness as for any other kind of eminence, and that for most men a very moderate degree of spirituality is the utmost for which they are entitled to hope. An ardent Protestant, misinterpreting the words, "Be ye perfect as I am perfect," is apt to think that he is nothing if not a saint, whereas Juan Valera knew that to be a saint, as to be a poet, is to be about one in twenty millions, and he has made a very amusing as well as a very useful book out of the vain strivings of his hero for—

> "Heroic good, target for which the young
> Dream in their dreams that every bow is strung;"

and the course of experience by which he is brought to conclude—

> "That less than highest is good, and may be high."

In consequence of the characteristics I have endeavoured to indicate, this novel, though expressly "religious" in its main theme and most of its details, is as "natural," concrete, and wholesomely human and humanly interesting as one of Sir Walter Scott's. There is in it no sense of dislocation or incompatibility between the natural and the spiritual. From the dainty, naïve, innocently coquettish, and passionate Pepita, who is enraged by her lover's pretensions to a piety which, though she is devoted to her beautifully adorned "Infant Jesus," she cannot understand, and in which she sees only an obstacle to the fulfilment of her love for him, to the saintly ecclesiastic, who, almost from the first, sees the incapacity of his pupil, Don Luis, for the celibate heights to which he aspires, but who understands life in all its grades too well to look upon his strivings and his "fall," as Don Luis at first esteems it, with other than a good-humoured smile, all is upon one easy ascending plane and has an intelligible unity.—From "A Spanish Novelette," in "Religio Poetæ" (1893).

LIST OF CHARACTERS

DON LUIS DE VARGAS, an aspirant to the priesthood.

DON PEDRO, his father.

THE DEAN, his uncle.

DOÑA CASILDA, his aunt.

CURRITO, his cousin.

PEPITA JIMÉNEZ, a beautiful young heiress, widow of

DON GUMERSINDO, her uncle.

ANTOÑONA, her nurse and housekeeper.

The husband of Antoñona.

The Vicar.

The Notary.

The Apothecary.

THE COUNT OF GENAZAHAR, former suitor to Pepita.

A Captain of cavalry.

AUTHOR'S PREFACE TO THE FIRST AMERICAN EDITION

To the MESSRS. APPLETON:

Gentlemen:—

IT was my intention to write a preface for the purpose of authorizing the edition you are about to publish in English of "Pepita Jiménez"; but, on thinking the matter over, I was deterred by the recollection of an anecdote that I heard in my young days.

A certain gallant, wishing to be presented at the house of a rich man who was about to give a magnificent ball, availed himself for that purpose of the services of a friend, who boasted of his familiarity with the great man, and of the favor he enjoyed with him. They proceeded to the great man's house, and the gallant got his introduction; but the great man said to him who had introduced the other: "And you, who is to introduce you, for I am not acquainted with you?" As I entertain a profound respect and affection for this country, and have not, besides, the assurance that such an occasion would require, it would not do for me to say what the introducer of my story is said to have answered: "I need no one to introduce or to recommend me, for I am just now going away."

I infer from my story, as its evident moral, that I ought to refrain from addressing the public of the United States, to which I am entirely unknown as an author, notwithstanding the fact of my having maintained pleasant and friendly relations with its Government as the representative of my own.

The most judicious and prudent course I can adopt, then, is to limit myself to returning you earnest thanks for asking from me an authorization of which you did not stand in need, either by law or by treaty, for wishing to make known to your countrymen the least insipid of the products of my unfruitful genius, and for your generous purpose of conceding to me author's rights.

This, however, does not preclude the fact that, in thus expressing my thanks to you publicly, I incur a responsibility which I did not assume on any other occasion, either in Germany, Italy, or any other country where my works have been translated; for then, if they failed to please the public, although the fact might pain me, I could still shrug my shoulders, and throw the blame of failure on the translator, or the publisher; but in this case I make myself your accomplice, and share or rather receive, all the disgrace of failure, if failure there should be.

"Pepita Jiménez" has enjoyed a wide celebrity, not only in Spain, but in every other Spanish-speaking country. I am very far from thinking that we Spaniards of the present day are either more easily satisfied, less cultured than, or possessed of an inferior literary taste to, the inhabitants of any other region of the globe; but this does not suffice to dispel my misgivings that my novel may be received with indifference or with censure by a public somewhat prejudiced against Spain by fanciful and injurious preconceptions.

My novel, both in essence and form, is distinctively national and classic. Its merits—supposing it to have such—consist in the language and the style, and not in the incidents, which are of the most commonplace, or in the plot, which, if it can be said to have any, is of the simplest.

The characters are not wanting, as I think, in individuality, or in such truth to human nature as makes them seem like living beings; but, the action being so slight, this is brought out and made manifest by means of a subtle analysis, and by the language chosen to express the emotions, both of which may in the translation be lost. There is, besides, in my novel a certain irony, good-humored and frank, and a certain humor, resembling rather the humor of the English than the *esprit* of the French, which qualities, although happily they do not depend upon puns, or a play upon words, but are in the subject itself, require, in order that they may appear in the translation, that this should be made with extreme care.

In conclusion, the chief cause of the extraordinary favor with which "Pepita Jiménez" was received in Spain is something that may fail to be noticed here by careless readers.

I am an advocate of art for art's sake. I think it is very bad taste, always impertinent, and often pedantic, to attempt to prove theses by writing stories. For such a purpose dissertations or books purely and severely didactic should be written. The object of a novel should be to charm, through a faithful representation of human actions and human passions, and to create by this fidelity to nature a beautiful work. The object of art is the creation of the beautiful, and whoever applies it to any other end, of however great utility this end may be, debases it. But it may chance, through a conjunction of favorable circumstances, by a happy inspiration—because in a given moment everything is disposed as by enchantment, or by supernatural influences—that an author's soul may become like a clear and magic mirror wherein are reflected all the ideas and all the sentiments that animate the eclectic spirit of his country, and in which these ideas and these sentiments lose their discordance, and group and combine themselves in pleasing agreement and harmony.

Herein is the explanation of the interest of "Pepita Jiménez." It was written when Spain was agitated to its centre, and everything was thrown out of its regular course by a radical revolution that at the same time shook to their foundations the throne and religious unity. It was written when everything in fusion, like molten metal, might readily amalgamate, and be molded into new forms. It was written when the strife raged fiercest between ancient and modern ideals; and, finally, it was written in all the plenitude of my powers, when my soul was sanest and most joyful in the possession of an enviable optimism and an all-embracing love and sympathy for humanity that, to my misfortune, can never again find place within my breast.

If I had endeavored by dialectics and by reasoning to conciliate opinions and beliefs, the disapprobation would have been general; but, as the conciliating and syncretic spirit manifested itself naturally in a diverting story, even one accepted and approved it, each one drawing from my book the conclusions that best suited himself. Thus it was that, from the most orthodox Jesuit father down to the most rabid revolutionist, and from the ultra-Catholic who cherishes the dream of restoring the Inquisition, to the rationalist who is the irreconcilable enemy of every religion, all were pleased with "Pepita Jiménez."

It would be curious, and not inopportune, to explain here how it came about that I succeeded in pleasing every one without intending it, without knowing it, and, as it were, by chance.

There was in Spain, some years ago, a conservative minister who had sent a godson of his to study philosophy in Germany. By rare good fortune this godson, who was called Julian Sanz del Rio, was a man of clear and profound intelligence, of unwearied application, and endowed with all the qualities necessary to make of him a sort of apostle. He studied, he formulated his system, he obtained the chair of metaphysics in the University of Madrid, and he founded a school, from which has since issued a brilliant pleiad of philosophers and statesmen, and of men illustrious for their learning, their eloquence, and their virtues. Chief among them are Nicolas Salmeron, Francisco Giner, Gumersindo Azcarate, Frederico de Castro, and Urbano Gonzalez Serrano.

The clerical party soon began to stir up strife against the master, the scholars, and the doctrines taught by them. They accused them of mystical pantheism.

I, who had ridiculed, at times, the confused terms, the pomp of words, and the method which the new philosophers made use of, regarded these philosophers, nevertheless, with admiration, and took up their defense—an almost solitary champion—in periodicals and reviews.

I had already maintained, before this, that our great dogmatic theologians, and especially the celebrated Domingo de Soto, were more liberal than the liberal rationalists of the present day, affirming, as they do, the sovereignty of the people by divine right; for if, as St. Paul declares, all authority proceeds from God, it does so through the medium of the people whom God inspires to found it; and because the only authority that proceeds directly from God is that of the Church.

I then set myself to demonstrate that, if Sanz del Rio and his followers were pantheists, our mystical theologians of the sixteenth and seventeenth centuries were pantheists also; and that, if the former had for predecessors Fichte, Schelling, Hegel, and Krause, St. Theresa, St. John de la Cruz, and the inspired and ecstatic Father Miguel de la Fuente followed, as their model, Tauler and others of the Germans. In saying this, however, it was not my intention to deny the claims of any of these mystical writers as founders of their school in Spain, but only to recognize, in this unbroken transmission of doctrine, the progressive continuity of European civilization.

For the purpose of carrying forward my undertaking, I read and studied with ardor every Spanish book on devotion, asceticism, and mysticism that fell into my hands, growing every day more charmed with the richness of our literature in such works; with the treasures of poetry contained in them; with the boldness and independence of their authors; with the profound and delicate observation, in which they excel the Scottish school, that they display in examining the faculties of the soul; and with their power of entering into themselves, of penetrating to the very centre of the mind, in order there to behold God, and to unite themselves with God, not therefore losing their own personality, or their capacity for an active life, but issuing from the ecstasies and ravishments of divine love more apt than before for every work that can benefit the human species, as the steel is more finely tempered, polished, and bright after it has burned in the fires of the forge.

Of all this, on its most poetic and easily understood side, I wished to give a specimen to the Spanish public of to-day, who had forgotten it; but, as I was a man of my epoch, a layman, not very exemplary as regards penitential practises, and had the reputation of a freethinker, I did not venture to undertake doing this in my own name, and I created a theological student who should do it in his. I then fancied that I could paint with more vividness the ideas and the feelings of this student by contrasting them with an earthly love; and this was the origin of "Pepita Jiménez." Thus, when it was farthest from my thoughts, did I become a novelist. My novel had, therefore, the freshness and the spontaneity of the unpremeditated.

The novels I wrote afterward, with premeditation, are inferior to this one.

"Pepita Jiménez" pleased the public, also, as I have said, by its transcendentalism.

The rationalists supposed that I had rejected the old ideals, as my hero casts off the clerical garb. And the believers, with greater unanimity and truth, compared me with the false prophet who went forth to curse the people of Israel, and without intending it exalted and blessed them. What is certain is that, if it be allowable to draw any conclusion from a story, the inference that may be deduced from mine is, that faith in an all-seeing and personal God, and in the love of this God, who is present in the depths of the soul, even when we refuse to follow the higher vocation to which He would persuade and solicit us—even were we carried away by the violence of mundane passions to commit, like Don Luis, almost all the capital sins in a single day—elevates the soul, purifies the other emotions, sustains human dignity, and lends poetry, nobility, and holiness to the commonest state, condition, and manner of life.

Such is, in my opinion, the novel you are now about to present to the American public; for I repeat that I have not the right to make the presentation.

Perhaps, independent of its transcendentalism, my novel may serve to interest and amuse your public for a couple of hours, and may obtain some favor with it; for it is a public that reads a great deal, that is indulgent, and that differs from the English public—which is eminently exclusive in its tastes—by its generous and cosmopolitan spirit.

I have always regarded as a delusion of national vanity the belief that there is, or the hope that there ever will be, anything that, with legitimate and candid independence, may be called American literature. Greece diffused herself through the world in flourishing colonies, and, after the conquests of Alexander, founded powerful states in Egypt, in Syria, and even in Bactriana, among peoples who, unlike the American Indians, possessed a high civilization of their own. But, notwithstanding this dispersion, and this political severance from the mother-country, the literature of Syracuse, of Antioch, and of Alexandria was as much Greek literature as was the literature of Athens. In my opinion, then, and for the same reason, the literature of New York and Boston will continue to be as much English literature as the literature of London and Edinburgh; the literature of Mexico and Buenos Ayres will continue to be as much Spanish literature as the literature of Madrid; the literature of Rio Janeiro will be as much Portuguese literature as the literature of Lisbon. Political union may be severed, but, between peoples of the same tongue and the same race, the ties of spiritual fraternity are indissoluble, so long as their common civilization lasts. There are immortal kings or emperors who reign and rule in America by true divine right, and against whom no Washington or Bolivar shall prevail—no Franklin succeed in plucking from them their sceptre. These tyrants are called Miguel de Cervantes, William Shakespeare, and Luiz de Camöens.

All this does not prevent the new nation from bringing to the common fund, and *pro indiviso,* of the culture of their race, rich elements, fine traits of character, and perhaps even higher qualities. Thus it is that I observe, in this American literature, of English origin and language, a certain largeness of views, a certain cosmopolitanism and affectionate comprehension of what is foreign, broad as the continent itself which the Americans inhabit, and which forms a contrast to the narrow exclusivism of the insular English. It is because of these qualities that I venture to hope now for a favorable reception of my little book; and it is in these qualities that I found my hope that the fruits of Spanish genius in general will, in future, be better known and more highly esteemed here than in Great Britain.

Already, to some extent, Irving, Prescott, Ticknor, Longfellow, Howells, and others have contributed, with judgment and discretion, translating, criticizing and eulogizing our authors, to the realization of this hope.

Forgive my wearying you with this letter, and believe me to be sincerely yours,

JUAN VALERA.

NEW YORK, *April 18, 1886.*

PEPITA JIMÉNEZ

DISCOVERY OF THE MANUSCRIPT

"Nescit Labi Virtus"

THE reverend Dean of the Cathedral of ——, deceased a few years since, left among his papers a bundle of manuscript, tied together, which, passing from hand to hand, finally fell into mine, without, by some strange chance, having lost a single one of the documents contained in it. Inscribed on this manuscript were the Latin words I use above as a motto, but without the addition of the woman's name I now prefix to it as its title; and this inscription has probably contributed to the preservation of the papers, since, thinking them, no doubt, to be sermons, or other theological matter, no one before me had made any attempt to untie the string of the package, or to read a single page of it.

The manuscript is in three parts. The first is entitled "Letters from my Nephew"; the second, "Paralipomena"; and the third, "Epilogue—Letters from my Brother."

All three are in the same handwriting, which, it may be inferred, is that of the reverend Dean; and as taken together they form something like a novel, I at first thought that perhaps the reverend Dean wished to exercise his genius in composing one in his leisure hours; but, looking at the matter more closely, and observing the natural simplicity of the style, I am inclined to think now that it is no novel at all, but that the letters are copies of genuine epistles which the reverend Dean tore up, burned, or returned to their owners, and that the narrative part only, designated by the pedantic title of "Paralipomena," is the work of the reverend Dean, added for the purpose of completing the story with incidents not related in the letters.

However this may be, I confess that I did not find the reading of these papers tiresome; I found them, indeed, rather interesting than otherwise; and as nowadays everything is published, I have decided to publish them too, without further investigation, changing only the proper names, so that if those who bear them be still living they may not find themselves figuring in a book without desiring or consenting to it.

The letters contained in the first part seem to have been written by a very young man, with some theoretical but no practical knowledge of the world, whose life was passed in the house of the reverend Dean, his uncle, and in the seminary, and who was imbued with an exalted religious fervor and an earnest desire to be a priest.

We shall call this young man Don Luis de Vargas.

The aforesaid manuscript, faithfully transferred to print, is as follows.

PART I

LETTERS FROM MY NEPHEW

March 22d.

FOUR days ago I arrived in safety at this my native village, where I found my father, and the reverend vicar, as well as our friends and relations, all in good health. The happiness of seeing them and conversing with them has so completely occupied my time and thoughts that I have not been able to write to you until now.

You will pardon me for this.

Having left this place a mere child, and coming back a man, the impression produced upon me by all those objects that I had treasured up in my memory is a singular one. Everything appears to me more diminutive, much more diminutive, but also more pleasing to the eye, than my recollection of it. My father's house, which in my imagination was immense, is, indeed, the large house of a rich husbandman, but still much smaller than the seminary. What I now understand and appreciate better than formerly is the country around here. The orchards, above all, are delightful. What charming paths there are through them! On one side, and sometimes on both, crystal waters flow with a pleasant murmur. The banks of these streams are covered with odorous herbs and flowers of a thousand different hues. In a few minutes one may gather a large bunch of violets. The paths are shaded by majestic trees, chiefly walnut and fig trees; and the hedges are formed of blackberry bushes, roses, pomegranates, and honeysuckle.

The multitude of birds that enliven grove and field is marvelous.

I am enchanted with the orchards, and I spend a couple of hours walking in them every afternoon.

My father wishes to take me to see his olive plantations, his vineyards, his farmhouses; but of all this we have as yet seen nothing. I have not been outside of the village and the charming orchards that surround it.

It is true, indeed, that the numerous visits I receive do not leave me a moment to myself.

Five different women have come to see me, all of whom were my nurses, and have embraced and kissed me.

Every one gives me the diminutive "Luisito," or "Don Pedro's boy," although I have passed my twenty-second birthday; and every one inquires of my father for "the boy," when I am not present.

I imagine I shall make but little use of the books I have brought with me to read, as I am not left alone for a single instant.

The dignity of squire, which I supposed to be a matter for jest, is, on the contrary, a serious matter. My father is the squire of the village.

There is hardly any one here who can understand what they call my caprice of entering the priesthood, and these good people tell me, with rustic candor, that I ought to throw aside the clerical garb; that to be a priest is very well for a poor young man; but that I, who am to be a rich man's heir, should marry, and console the old age of my father by giving him half a dozen handsome and robust grandchildren.

In order to flatter my father and myself, both men and women declare that I am a splendid fellow, that I am of an angelic disposition, that I have a very roguish pair of eyes, and other stupid things of a like kind, that annoy, disgust, and humiliate me, although I am not very modest, and am too well acquainted with the meanness and folly of the world to be shocked or frightened at anything.

The only defect they find in me is that I am too thin through overstudy. In order to have me grow fat they propose not to allow me either to study or even to look at a book while I remain here; and, besides this, to make me eat of as many choice dishes of meats and confectionery as they know how to concoct in the village.

It is quite clear—I am to be stall-fed. There is not a single family of our acquaintance that has not sent me some token of regard. Now it is a sponge-cake, now a meat-salad, now a pyramid of sweetmeats, now a jug of syrup. And these presents, which they send to the house, are not the only attentions they show me. I have also been invited to dinner by three or four of the principal persons of the village.

To-morrow I am to dine at the house of the famous Pepita Jiménez, of whom you have doubtless heard. No one here is ignorant of the fact that my father is paying her his addresses.

My father, notwithstanding his fifty-five years, is so well preserved that the finest young men of the village might feel envious of him. He possesses, besides, the powerful attraction, irresistible to some women, of his past conquests, of his celebrity, of his—of course exaggerated—reputation as a modern rival to that national rake, Don Juan Tenorio.

I have not yet made the acquaintance of Pepita Jiménez. Every one says she is very beautiful. I suspect she will turn out to be a village beauty, and somewhat rustic. From what I have heard of her I can not quite decide whether, ethically speaking, she is good or bad; but I am quite certain that she is possessed of great natural intelligence. Pepita is about twenty years old, and a widow; her married life lasted only three years. She was the daughter of Doña Francisca Galvez, the widow, as you know, of a retired captain,

> "Who left her at his death,
> As sole inheritance, his honorable sword,"

as the poet says. Until her sixteenth year Pepita lived with her mother in very straitened circumstances—bordering, indeed, upon absolute want.

She had an uncle called Don Gumersindo, the possessor of a small entailed estate, one of those petty estates that, in olden times, owed their foundation to a foolish vanity. Any ordinary person, with the income derived from this estate, would have lived in continual difficulties, burdened by debts, and altogether cut off from the display and ceremony proper to his rank. But Don Gumersindo was an extraordinary person—the very genius of economy. It could not be said of him that he created wealth himself, but he was endowed with a wonderful faculty of absorption with respect to the wealth of others; and in regard to dispensing, it would be difficult to find any one on the face of the globe with whose maintenance, preservation, and comfort, Mother Nature and human industry ever had less reason to trouble themselves. No one knows how he lived; but the fact is that he reached the age of eighty, saving his entire income, and adding to his capital by lending money on unquestionable security. No one here speaks of him as a usurer; on the contrary, he is considered to have been of a charitable disposition, because, being moderate in all things, he was so even in usury, and would ask only ten per cent a year, while throughout the district they ask twenty and even thirty per cent, and still think it little.

In the practise of this species of industry and economy, and with thoughts dwelling constantly on increasing instead of diminishing his capital, indulging neither in the luxury of matrimony and of having a family, nor even of smoking, Don Gumersindo arrived at the age I have mentioned, the possessor of a fortune considerable anywhere, and here regarded as enormous, thanks to the poverty of these villages, and to the habit of exaggeration natural to the Andalusians.

Don Gumersindo, always extremely neat and clean in his person, was an old man who did not inspire repugnance.

The articles of his modest wardrobe were somewhat worn, but carefully brushed and without a stain; although from time immemorial he had always been seen with the same cloak, the same jacket, and the same trousers and waistcoat. People sometimes asked each other in vain if any one had ever seen him wear a new garment.

With all these defects, which here and elsewhere many regard as virtues, though virtues in excess, Don Gumersindo possessed excellent qualities; he was affable, obliging, compassionate; and did his utmost to please and to be of service to everybody, no matter what trouble, anxiety, or fatigue it might cost him, provided only it did not cost him money. Of a cheerful disposition, and fond of fun and joking, he was to be found at every feast and merry-making around that was not got up at his expense, which he enlivened by the amenity of his manners, and by his discreet although not very Attic conversation. He had never had any tender inclination for any one woman in particular, but, innocently and without malice, he loved them all; and was the most given to complimenting the girls, and making them laugh, of any old man for ten leagues around.

I have already said that he was the uncle of Pepita. When he was nearing his eightieth year she was about to complete her sixteenth. He was rich; she, poor and friendless.

Her mother was a vulgar woman of limited intelligence and coarse instincts. She worshiped her daughter, yet lamented continually and with bitterness the sacrifices she made for her, the privations she suffered, and the disconsolate old age and melancholy end that awaited her in the midst of her poverty. She had, besides, a son, older than Pepita, who had a well-deserved reputation in the village as a gambler and a quarrelsome fellow, and for whom, after many difficulties, she had succeeded in obtaining an insignificant employment in Havana; thus finding herself rid of him, and with the sea between them. After he had been a few years in Havana, however, he lost his situation on account of his bad conduct, and thereupon began to shower letters upon his mother, containing demands for money. The latter, who had scarcely enough for herself and for Pepita, grew desperate at this, broke out into abuse, cursed herself and her destiny with a perseverance but little resembling the theological virtue, and ended by fixing all her hopes upon settling her daughter well, as the only way of getting out of her difficulties.

In this distressing situation Don Gumersindo began to frequent the house of Pepita and her mother, and to pay attentions to the former with more ardor and persistence than he had shown in his attentions to other girls. Nevertheless, to suppose that a man who had passed his eightieth year without wishing to marry, should think of committing such a folly, with one foot already in the grave, was so wild and improbable a notion that Pepita's mother, still less Pepita herself, never for a moment suspected the audacious intentions of Don Gumersindo.

Thus it was that both were struck one day with amazement when, after a good many compliments, between jest and earnest, Don Gumersindo, with the greatest seriousness and without the least hesitation, proposed the following categorical question:

"Pepita, will you marry me?"

Although the question came at the end of a great deal of joking, and might itself be taken for a joke, Pepita, who, inexperienced though she was in worldly matters, yet knew by a certain instinct of divination that is in all women, and especially in young girls, no matter how innocent they may be, that this was said in earnest, grew as red as a cherry and said nothing. Her mother answered in her stead:

"Child, don't be ill-bred; answer your uncle as you should: 'With much pleasure, uncle—whenever you wish.'"

This "with much pleasure, uncle—whenever you wish," came then, it is said, and many times afterward, almost mechanically from the trembling lips of Pepita, in obedience to the admonitions, the sermons, the complaints, and even the imperious mandate of her mother.

I see, however, that I am enlarging too much on this matter of Pepita Jiménez and her history; but she interests me, as I suppose she should interest you too, since, if what they affirm here be true, she is to be your sister-in-law and my stepmother.

I shall endeavor, notwithstanding, to avoid dwelling on details, and to relate briefly what perhaps you already know, though you have been away from here so long.

Pepita Jiménez was married to Don Gumersindo. The tongue of slander was let loose against her, both in the days preceding the wedding and for some months afterward.

In fact, from the point of view of morals, this marriage was a matter that will admit of discussion; but, so far as the girl herself is concerned, if we remember her mother's prayers, her complaints, and even her commands—if we take into consideration the fact that Pepita thought by this means to procure for her mother a comfortable old age, and to save her brother from dishonor and infamy, constituting herself his guardian angel and his earthly providence, we must confess that our condemnation will admit of some abatement. Besides, who shall penetrate into the recesses of the heart, into the hidden secrets of the immature mind of a young girl, brought up, probably, in the most absolute seclusion and ignorance of the world, in order to know what idea she might have formed to herself of marriage? Perhaps she thought that to marry this old man meant to devote her life to his service, to be his nurse, to soothe his old age, to save him from a solitude and abandonment embittered by his infirmities, and in which only mercenary hands should minister to him; in a word, to cheer and illumine his declining years with the glowing beams of her beauty and her youth, like an angel who has taken human form. If something of this, or all of this, was what the girl thought, and if she failed to perceive the full significance of her act, then its morality is placed beyond question.

However this may be, leaving aside psychological investigations that I have no authority for making, since I am not acquainted with Pepita Jiménez, it is quite certain that she lived in edifying harmony with the old man during three years, that she nursed him and waited upon him with admirable devotion, and that in his last painful and fatal sickness she ministered to him and watched over him with tender and unwearying affection, until he expired in her arms, leaving her heiress to a large fortune.

Although more than two years have passed since she lost her mother, and more than a year and a half since she was left a widow, Pepita still wears the deepest mourning. Her sedateness, her retired manner of living, and her melancholy, are such that one might suppose she lamented the death of her husband as much as though he had been a handsome young man. Perhaps there are some who imagine or suspect that Pepita's pride, and the certain knowledge she now has of the not very poetical means by which she has become rich, trouble her awakened and more than scrupulous conscience; and that, humiliated in her own eyes and in those of the world, she seeks, in austerity and retirement, consolation for the vexations of her mind, and balm for her wounded heart.

People here, as everywhere, have a great love of money. Perhaps I am wrong in saying, *as everywhere;* in populous cities, in the great centres of civilization, there are other distinctions which are prized as much as, or even more than, money, because they smooth the way to fortune, and give credit and consideration in the eyes of the world; but in smaller places, where neither literary nor scientific fame, nor, as a rule, distinction of manners, nor elegance, nor discretion and amenity in intercourse, are apt to be either valued or understood, there is no other way by which to adjust the social hierarchy than the possession of more or less money, or of something worth money. Pepita, then, in the possession of money, and beauty besides, and making a good use, as every one says, of her riches, is to-day respected and esteemed in an extraordinary degree. From this and the surrounding villages the most eligible suitors, the wealthiest young men, have crowded to pay their court to her. But, so far as as can be seen, she rejects them all, though with the utmost sweetness, for she wishes to make no one her enemy; and it is commonly supposed that her soul is filled with the most ardent devotion, and that it is her fixed intention to dedicate her life to practises of charity and religious piety.

My father, according to the general opinion, has not succeeded better than her other suitors; but Pepita, to fulfil the adage that "courtesy and candor are consistent with each other," takes the greatest pains to give him proofs of a frank, affectionate, and disinterested friendship. She is unremitting in her attentions to him, and when he tries to speak to her of love she brings him to a stop with a sermon delivered with the most winning sweetness, recalling to his memory his past faults, and endeavoring to undeceive him in regard to the world and its vain pomps.

I confess that I begin to have some curiosity to know this woman, so much do I hear her spoken of! nor do I think my curiosity is without foundation, or that there is anything in it either vain or sinful. I myself feel the truth of what Pepita says; I myself desire that my father, in his advanced years, should enter upon a better life; should forget, and not seek to renew, the agitations and passions of his youth; and should attain to the enjoyment of a tranquil, happy, and honorable old age. I differ from Pepita's way of thinking in one thing only: I believe my father would succeed in this rather by marrying a good and worthy woman who loved him, than by remaining without a wife. For this very reason I desire to become acquainted with Pepita, in order to know if she be this woman; for I am to a certain extent troubled—and perhaps there is in this feeling something of family pride, which, if it be wrong, I desire to cast out—by the disdain, however honeyed and gracious, of the young widow.

If my situation were other than it is, I should prefer my father to remain unmarried. Then, being the only child, I should inherit all his wealth, and, as one might say, nothing less than the position of squire of the village. But you already know how firm is the resolution I have taken. Humble and unworthy though I be, I feel myself called to the priesthood, and the possessions of this world have but little power over my mind. If there is anything in me of the ardor of youth, and the vehemence of the passions proper to that age, it shall all be employed in nourishing an active and fecund charity. Even the many books you have given me to read, and my knowledge of the history of the ancient civilizations of the peoples of Asia, contribute to unite within me scientific curiosity with the desire of propagating the faith, and invite and animate me to go forth as a missionary to the far East. As soon as I leave this village, where you, my dear uncle, have sent me to pass some time with my father, and am raised to the dignity of the priesthood, and, ignorant and sinner as I am, feel myself invested by free and supernatural gift, through the sovereign goodness of the Most High, with the power to absolve from sin, and with the mission to teach the peoples—as soon as I receive the perpetual and miraculous grace of handling with impure hands the very God made man, it is my purpose to leave Spain, and go forth to distant lands to preach the Gospel.

I am not actuated in this by vanity. I do not desire to believe myself superior to other men. The power of my faith, the constancy of which I feel myself capable, everything after the favor and grace of God, I owe to the judicious education, to the holy teaching, and to the good example I have received from you, my dear uncle.

There is something I hardly dare confess to myself, but which, against my will, presents itself with frequency to my mind; and, since it presents itself to my mind, it is my desire, it is my duty to confess it to you: it would be wrong for me to hide from you even my most secret and involuntary thoughts. You have taught me to analyse the feelings of the soul; to search for their origin, if it be good or evil; to make, in short, a scrupulous examination of conscience.

I have often reflected on two different methods of education: that of those who endeavor to keep the mind in innocence, confounding innocence with ignorance, and believing evil that is unknown to be avoided more easily than evil that is known; and that of those, on the other hand, who courageously, and as soon as the pupil has arrived at the age of reason, show him, with due regard for modesty, evil in all its hideous ugliness and repulsive nakedness, to the end that he may abhor and avoid it.

According to my way of thinking, it is necessary to know evil in order the better to comprehend the infinite Divine goodness, the ideal and unattainable end of every virtuously born desire. I am grateful to you that you have made me to know, with the honey and the butter of your teaching, as the Scripture says, both good and evil, to the end that I should aspire to the one and condemn the other, knowingly and with discreet ardor. I rejoice that I am no longer in a state of mere innocence, and that I shall go forward in the progress toward virtue, and, in so far as is permitted to humanity, toward perfection, with a knowledge of all the tribulations, all the asperities that there are in the pilgrimage we are called upon to make through this valley of tears; as I am not ignorant, on the other hand, of how smooth, how easy, how pleasant, how flowery the road is in appearance that leads to perdition and eternal death.

Another thing for which I feel bound to be grateful to you is the indulgence, the toleration—not condescending nor lax, but, on the contrary, serious and thoughtful—with which you have been able to inspire me for the errors and the sins of my fellow men.

I say all this to you because I wish to speak to you on a subject of so delicate a nature that I hardly find words in which to express myself concerning it. In short, I often ask myself whether the resolution I have adopted had not its origin, in part at least, in the character of my relations with my father. In the bottom of my heart have I been able to pardon him his conduct toward my poor mother, the victim of his errors?

I consider this matter carefully, and I can not find an atom of hatred in my breast. On the contrary, gratitude fills it entirely. My father has brought me up affectionately. He has tried to honor in me the memory of my mother, and one would have said that in my bringing up, in the care he took of me, in the indulgence with which he treated me, in his devotion to me as a child, he sought to appease her angry shade—if the shade, if the spirit of her who was on earth an angel of goodness and gentleness, could be capable of anger.

I repeat, then, that I am full of gratitude toward my father; he has acknowledged me, and, besides, he sent me at the age of ten years to you, to whom I owe all that I am.

If there is in my heart any germ of virtue, if there is in my mind any element of knowledge, if there is in my will any honorable and good purpose, to you it is I owe it.

My father's affection for me is extraordinary; the estimation in which he holds me is far superior to my merits. Perhaps vanity may have something to do with this. In paternal love there is something selfish; it is, as it were, a prolongation of selfishness. If I were possessed of any merit, my father would regard it all as a creation of his own, as if I were an emanation of his personality, as much in spirit as in body. Be this as it will, however, I believe that my father loves me, and that there is in his affection something self-sustaining, and superior to all this pardonable selfishness of which I have spoken.

I experience a great consolation, a profound tranquillity of conscience—and for this I return most fervent thanks to God—when I discern the fact that the power of blood, the tie of nature, that mysterious bond that unites us, leads me, without any consideration of duty, to love my father and to reverence him. It would be horrible not to love him thus—to be compelled to force myself to love in order to obey a Divine command. Nevertheless—and here comes back my doubt—does my purpose of becoming a priest or a friar, of not accepting, or of accepting only a very small part of, the immense fortune that will be mine by inheritance, and which I might enjoy even during my father's lifetime; does this proceed solely from my contempt of the things of this world, from a true vocation for a religious life, or does it not also proceed from pride, from hidden rancor, from resentment, from something in me that refuses to forgive what my mother herself, with sublime generosity, forgave? This doubt assails and torments me at times, but almost always I resolve it in my favor, and come to the conclusion that I have no feeling of pride toward my father. I think I would accept from him all he has, if I were to need it, and I rejoice to be as grateful to him for little as for much.

Farewell, uncle. In future I will write to you often, and as much at length as you desire, if not quite so much so as to-day, lest I should appear prolix.

March 28th.

I BEGIN to be tired of my stay in this place, and every day the desire grows stronger within me to return to you and to receive my ordination. But my father wishes to accompany me. He wishes to be present at that solemn ceremony, and desires that I should remain here with him at least two months longer. He is so amiable, so affectionate with me, that it would be impossible for me not to gratify him in all his wishes. I shall remain here, therefore, for the time he desires. In order to give him pleasure I do violence to my feelings, and make an effort to seem interested in the amusements of the village, the country sports and even shooting, in all of which I am his companion. I try to appear gayer and more animated than I am by nature. As in the village, half in jest, half by way of eulogy, I am called "The Saint," I endeavor, through modesty, to avoid the appearance of sanctity, or to soften and humanize its manifestations with the virtue of moderation, displaying a serene and decent cheerfulness which was never yet opposed to holiness nor to the saints. I confess, nevertheless, that the merry-making and the sports of these people, with their coarse jokes and boisterous mirth, weary me. I do not want to fall into the sin of scandal, nor to speak ill of any one, though it be only to you and in confidence; but I often think that it would be a more difficult enterprise, as well as a more rational and meritorious one, to preach the Gospel to these people, and try to elevate their moral nature, than to go to India, Persia, or China, leaving so many of my country-people behind, who are, if not perverted, at least to some extent gone astray. Many, indeed, are of the opinion that modern ideas, that materialism and infidelity, are to blame for this. But if that be the case, if they it be that produce such evil effects, then it must be in some strange, diabolical, and miraculous manner, and not by natural means; since the fact is, that here the people read no books, either good or bad, so that I do not well see how they can be perverted by any evil doctrines the books in fashion may contain.

Can these evil doctrines be in the air, like a miasma or an epidemic? Perhaps—and I am sorry this thought, which I mention to you only, should occur to me—perhaps the clergy themselves are in fault? Are they, in Spain, equal to their mission? Do they go among the people, teaching and preaching to them? Are they all capable of this? Have those who consecrate themselves to a religious life and to the salvation of souls a true vocation for their calling? Or is it only a means of living, like any other, with this difference—that in our day only the poorest, only those who are without expectations and without means, devote themselves to it, for the very reason that this calling offers a less brilliant prospect than any other? Be that as it may, the very scarcity of virtuous and learned priests arouses all the more within me the desire to be a priest. I would not willingly let self-love deceive me. I recognize all my defects; but I feel within me a true vocation, and many of those defects it may still be possible, with the divine help, to correct.

The dinner at the house of Pepita Jiménez, which I mentioned to you, took place three days ago. As she leads so retired a life, I had not met her before; she seemed to me, in truth, as beautiful as she is said to be, and I noticed that her amiability with my father was such as to give him reason to hope, at least judging superficially, that she will yield to his wishes in the end, and accept his hand.

As there is a possibility of her becoming my stepmother, I have observed her with attention; she seems to me to be a remarkable woman, whose moral qualities I am not able to determine with exactitude. There is about her an air of calmness and serenity that may come either from coldness of heart and spirit, with great self-control and power of calculating effects, accompanied by little or no sensibility; or that may, on the other hand, proceed from the tranquillity of her conscience and the purity of her aspirations, united to the purpose of fulfilling in this life the duties imposed upon her by society, while her hopes are fixed, meantime, upon loftier things, as their proper goal. What is certain is that, either because with this woman everything is the result of calculation, without any effort to elevate her mind to a higher sphere, or, it may be, because she blends in perfect harmony the prose of daily life with the poetry of her illusions, there is nothing discernible in her out of tone with her surroundings, although she possesses a natural distinction of manner that elevates her above and separates her from them all. She does not affect the dress of a provincial, nor does she, on the other hand, follow blindly the fashions of the city; she unites both these styles in her mode of dress in such a manner as to appear like a lady, but still a lady country-born and country-bred. She disguises to a great extent, as I think, the care she takes of her person. There is nothing about her to betray the use of cosmetics or the arts of the toilet. But the whiteness of her hands, the color and polish of her nails, and the grace and neatness of her attire denote a greater regard for such matters than might be looked for in one who lives in a village, and who is said, besides, to despise the vanities of this world and to think only of heavenly things.

Her house is exquisitely clean, and everything in it reveals the most perfect order. The furniture is neither artistic nor elegant, nor is it, on the other hand, either pretentious or in bad taste. To give a poetic air to her surroundings, she keeps in the rooms and passages, as well as in the garden, a multitude of plants and flowers. There is not, indeed, among them any rare plant or exotic, but her plants and flowers, of the commonest species here, are tended with extraordinary care.

Canaries in gilded cages enliven the whole house with their songs. Its mistress, it is obvious, has need of living creatures on which to bestow some of her affection; and besides several maid-servants, that one would suppose she had selected with care, since it can not be by mere chance that they are all pretty, she has, after the fashion of old maids, various animals to keep her company—a parrot, a little dog, whose coat is of the whitest, and two or three cats, so tame and sociable that they jump up on one in the most friendly manner.

At one end of the principal saloon is a species of oratory, whose chief ornament is an *Infant Jesus,* carved in wood, with red and white cheeks and blue eyes, and altogether quite handsome. The dress is of white satin, with a blue cloak full of little golden stars; and the image is completely covered with jewels and trinkets. The little altar on which the figure is placed is adorned with flowers, and around it are set pots of broom and bay; and on the altar itself, which is furnished with steps, a great many wax tapers are kept burning. When I behold all this I know not what to think, but for the most part I am inclined to believe that the widow loves herself above all things, and that it is for her recreation, and for the purpose of furnishing her with occasions for the effusion of this love, that she keeps the cats, the canaries, the flowers, and even the *Infant Jesus* itself, which in her secret soul, perhaps does not occupy a place very much higher than the canaries and the cats.

It can not be denied that Pepita Jiménez is possessed of discretion. No silly jest, no impertinent question in regard to my vocation, and, above all, in regard to my approaching ordination, has crossed her lips. She conversed with me on matters relating to the village, about agriculture, the last crop of grapes and olives, and the means of improving the methods of making wine, expressing herself always with modesty and naturalness and without manifesting any desire of appearing to know more than others.

My father was at his best; he seemed to have grown younger, and his pressing attentions to the lady of his thoughts were received, if not with love, at least with gratitude.

There were present at dinner, the doctor, the notary, and the reverend vicar, who is a great friend of the house and the spiritual father of Pepita.

The reverend vicar must have a very high opinion of her, for on several occasions he spoke to me apart of her charity, of the many alms she bestows, of her compassion and goodness to every one. In a word, he declared her to be a saint.

In view of what the vicar has told me, and relying on his judgment, I can do no less than wish that my father may marry Pepita. As my father is not fitted for a life of penance, in this way only could he hope to change his mode of life, that up to the present has been so dissipated, and settle down to a well-ordered and quiet, if not exemplary, old age.

When we reached our house, after leaving that of Pepita Jiménez, my father spoke to me seriously of his projects. He told me that in his time he had been very wild, that he had led a very bad life, and that he saw no way of reforming, notwithstanding his years, unless Pepita were to fall in love with and marry him.

Taking for granted, of course, that she would do so, my father then spoke about money matters. He told me that he was very rich, and would leave me amply provided for in his will, even though he should have other children. I answered him that for my plans and purposes in life I needed very little money, and that my greatest satisfaction would always consist in knowing him to be happy with wife and children, his former evil ways forgotten.

My father then spoke to me of his tender hopes with a candor and eagerness that might make one suppose me to be the father and the old man, and he a youth of my age, or younger. In order to enhance the merit of his mistress and the difficulties of his conquest, he recounted to me the accomplishments and the excellences of the fifteen or twenty suitors who had already presented themselves to Pepita, and who had all been rejected. As for himself, as he explained to me, the same lot, to a certain extent, had been his also; but he flattered himself that this want of success was not final, since Pepita showed him so many kindnesses, and an affection so great that, if it were not love, it might easily, with time and the persistent homage he dedicated to her, be converted into love.

There was, besides, in my father's opinion, something fantastic and fallacious in the cause of Pepita's coldness, that must in the end wear away. Pepita did not wish to retire to a convent, nor did she incline to a penitential life. Notwithstanding her seclusion and her piety, it was easy to see that she took delight in pleasing. Her daintiness and dress and the care she bestowed upon her person indeed exhibited little of the conventual. The cause of her coldness, then, my father declared to be, without a doubt, her pride—a pride to a certain extent well founded. She is naturally elegant and distinguished in appearance; both by her force of character and by her intelligence she is superior to those who surround her, no matter how she may seek, through modesty, to disguise it. How, then, should she bestow her hand upon any of the rustics who up to the present time have been her suitors? She imagines that her soul is filled with a mystic love of God, and that God only can satisfy it, because thus far no mortal has crossed her path intelligent enough and agreeable enough to make her forget even her image of the *Infant Jesus.* "Although it may seem conceited on my part," added my father, "I flatter myself that I am the happy man."

Such, dear uncle, are the occupations and the projects of my father here, and such the matters, so foreign to my nature, and to my aims and thoughts, of which he speaks to me with frequency, and on which he requires me to give an opinion.

It would almost seem as if your too indulgent opinion of my judgment had extended itself to the people here, for they all tell me their troubles, and ask my advice as to the course they should adopt. Even the reverend vicar, exposing himself to the risk of betraying what might be called secrets of confession, has already come to consult me in regard to several cases of conscience that have presented themselves to him in the confessional.

One of these cases—related, like all the others, with much mystery, and without revealing the name of the person concerned—has greatly interested me.

The reverend vicar tells me that a certain penitent of his is troubled by scruples of conscience, because, while she feels herself irresistibly attracted toward a solitary and contemplative life, she yet fears at times that this devout fervor is not accompanied by a true humility, but that it is in part excited by, and has its source in, the demon of pride himself.

To love God in all things, to seek Him in the inmost recesses of the soul wherein He dwells, to purify ourselves from all earthly passions and affections, in order to unite ourselves to Him—these are, in truth, pious aspirations and virtuous inclinations; but the doubt arises in determining whether the source of these aspirations and inclinations be not an exaggerated self-love. "Have they their origin," the penitent, it seems, asks herself, "in the thought that I, although unworthy and a sinner, presume my soul to be of more value than the souls of my fellow-mortals—that the interior beauty of my mind and of my will would be dimmed by harboring affection for the human beings by whom I am surrounded, and whom I deem unworthy of me? Do I love God above all things, infinitely, or only more than the little things that I know, and that I scorn and despise, that can not satisfy my heart?" If my piety is founded upon this feeling, then there are in it two great defects: the first, that it is not based upon a pure love of God, full of humility and charity, but on pride; and the second, that this piety, because it is thus without foundation, is unstable and inefficacious. For who can be certain that the soul will not forget the love of its Creator, when it does not love Him infinitely, but only because there is no other being whom it deems worthy of endowing with its love?

It is concerning this case of conscience, refined and subtle enough thus to exercise the mind of a simple rustic, that the reverend vicar has come to consult me. I would have excused myself from saying anything in the matter, alleging, as a reason for doing so, my youth and inexperience; but the reverend vicar has shown himself so persistent in the matter that I could do no less than discuss the question with him. I said—and it would rejoice me greatly should you concur in my opinion—that what this troubled penitent requires is to regard those who surround her with greater benevolence; to try to throw the cloak of charity over their faults, instead of analysing and dissecting them with the scalpel of criticism, bringing into relief and dwelling upon their good qualities, to the end that she may esteem and love them; to endeavor, in fact, to behold in every human being an object worthy of her love, a true fellow-creature, her equal, a soul wherein there is a treasure of good qualities and virtues—a being made, in short, in the image and likeness of God. Entertaining this exalted view of our surroundings, loving and esteeming others for what they are, and as more than they are, striving not to hold ourselves superior to them in anything, but, on the contrary, searching courageously in the depths of our own consciousness for the purpose of discovering all our faults and sins, and thus acquiring a devout humility and contempt of self—standing upon such a principle as this, the heart will feel itself full of human affection, and, instead of despising, will value highly the worth of things and of persons. Then, if afterward, Divine love should, with irresistible power, erect itself upon and tower above this foundation, there can be no fear but that such a love has its origin, not in an exaggerated self-esteem, in pride, or in an unjust contempt for our neighbor, but in a pure and holy contemplation of Infinite Beauty and Goodness.

If, as I suspect, it be Pepita Jiménez who has consulted the reverend vicar in regard to these doubts and tribulations, I think my father can not yet flatter himself with being very dear to her; but if the vicar should resolve on giving her my advice, and she accepts it and acts upon it, then she will either become a sort of Maria de Agreda, a self-conscious recluse, or, what is more probable, she will cast away mysticism and coldness altogether, and will consent to accept, without further caviling, the hand and heart of my father, who is in no respect her inferior.

April 4th.

MY life in this place begins, from its monotony, to be wearisome; and not because it is, physically, less active here than it was elsewhere; on the contrary, I walk and ride a great deal, and make excursions into the country, and, to please my father, visit the club-house and go to parties; in short, my life and my surroundings are quite uncongenial to me. For my intellectual life is a blank; I read nothing, and there is hardly a moment left me in which to reflect and meditate with tranquillity; and, as reflection and meditation were what constituted the chief charm of my existence, my life without them seems to me monotonous. Thanks to the patience which you have recommended to me for every occasion, I am able to endure it.

Another thing that prevents my spirit from being completely at rest is the longing, that becomes every day more ardent within me, to embrace that life to which I have for years been so earnestly inclined. It seems to me that, in those moments when I feel myself so near to the realization of the constant dream of my life, it is something like a profanation to allow my mind to be distracted by other objects. So much does this idea torment me, and to so many doubts does it give rise within me, that my admiration for the beauty of things created; of the heavens, so full of stars in these serene nights of spring, and in this favored region of Andalusia; of these smiling fields, now covered with verdure; of these cool and pleasant gardens, abounding in shady and delightful walks, in gently flowing streams and rivulets, in sequestered nooks, in birds that enliven them with song, and in flowers and odorous herbs—this admiration and enthusiasm, I repeat, which formerly seemed to me in perfect harmony with the religious feeling that filled my soul, animating and exalting it, instead of weakening it, seems to me now almost a sinful distraction, and an unpardonable forgetfulness of the eternal for the temporal, of the uncreated and the spiritual for the material and created.

Although I have made but little progress in virtue, although my mind is never free from the phantasms of the imagination; although the interior man is never exempt in me from the influence of external impressions, and from the need of employing in meditation the fatiguing argumentative method; although I can not, by an effort of love, withdraw myself to the very centre of pure intelligence, to the loftiest sphere of thought, in order to behold there goodness and truth divested of images and forms; though this is all true, yet I confess to you that the method of mental prayer, unrestricted by set forms, makes me afraid. Even rational meditation inspires me with distrust. I do not want to employ a process of reasoning in order to know God, nor to adduce arguments for loving, in order to love Him. I desire, by a single effort of the will, to elevate myself to and be absorbed in the Divine contemplation. Oh that I had the wings of a dove, to fly to the bosom of Him whom my soul loveth! But what and where are my merits? Where the mortifications, the extended prayers, and the fasting? What have I done, oh my God, that Thou shouldst favor me?

I know that the ungodly of the present day accuse—though without any foundation whatever—our holy religion of inciting souls to abhor the things of this world, to despise or to contemn Nature, perhaps to fear it also, as if there were in it something diabolical, placing all their affections on what these ungodly call the monstrous egotism of Divine love, for they say that the soul loves herself in loving God; I know, too, that this is not the case; that the Divine love is charity, and that to love God is to love all things, for all things are in God, in a supreme and ineffable manner. I know that I commit no sin in loving material things for the love of God, which is to love them for themselves, righteously; for what are material things but the manifestation, the creation, of the love of God? Yet I often feel some undefinable fear, some unwonted scruple, some vague and scarcely perceptible remorse tormenting me even at the moment when I am experiencing an effusion of tenderness, a sort of ecstasy of enthusiasm, on penetrating into a leafy grove; on hearing the song of the nightingale, or the twittering of the swallows, or the tender cooing of the dove; on looking at the flowers; on beholding the stars.

I imagine, at times, that there is in all this something of sensual pleasure, a something that makes me forget, for the moment at least, more lofty aspirations. I do not desire that in me the spirit should sin against the flesh; but neither do I desire, on the other hand, that the beauty of the material world—that its delights, even those most delicate, subtle, and ethereal ones that are perceived rather by the spirit than by the senses, such as the soft sigh of the zephyr, laden with rural scents, the song of the birds, the peaceful and majestic silence of the night in these gardens and orchards—that these delights should distract me from the contemplation of higher beauty, or weaken, even for a moment, my love toward Him who has created this harmonious fabric of the world.

I know that all these material things are like the letters of a book, the signs and characters in which the soul, eager for knowledge, may find a hidden meaning, and decipher and discover the beauty of God, which is shadowed forth in them, though but dimly, and of which they are the pictures, or rather emblems, because they do not represent, but only symbolize that beauty. On this distinction I dwell at times to fortify my spirit and mortify the flesh. For, I consider, if I love the beauty of earthly things for itself, it is idolatry; I ought to love this beauty as a sign and symbol of a beauty occult and divine and infinitely superior to it.

A few days ago I completed my twenty-second year. Heretofore my religious fervor has been such that I have felt no other love than the immaculate love of God Himself and of His holy religion, which I desire to diffuse and see triumphant in all the regions of the earth.

But I must needs confess that something of a profane sentiment has mingled itself with this purity of affection. You are aware of this; I have told it to you many times, and you, regarding me with your accustomed indulgence, have answered me that man is not an angel, and that even to aspire to so great a degree of perfection is pride; that I should endeavor to moderate these sentiments rather than seek to eradicate them entirely. Love of knowledge, a desire for the reputation which is founded on the possession of knowledge, even a not unfavorable opinion of one's own merits—these, even when kept within just bounds, though guarded and moderated by Christian humility, and directed toward a good end, have in them, doubtless, something of selfishness, but they may serve as a stimulus and a support to the noblest and most constant resolutions. The scruples that trouble my conscience now, therefore, have not their source in pride, in an overweening self-confidence, in a desire for worldly fame, or in a too great love of knowledge. Nothing of this nature it is that troubles me; nothing bearing any relation to self-conceit, but, in a certain sense, something entirely opposed to it. I feel a lassitude, a debility and abandonment of the will so great that it almost makes me afraid: I am too ready to weep for tenderness when I see a little flower, or when I contemplate the ray, mysterious, slender, and swift, of a remote star.

Tell me what you think of these things; and if there be not something morbid in this disposition of my mind.

April 8th.

THE amusements of the country, in which, very much against my will, I am compelled to take part, still go on.

My father has taken me to see almost all his plantations, and he and his friends are astonished to find me not altogether ignorant in matters pertaining to the country. It would seem as if, in their eyes, the study of theology, to which I have dedicated myself, were incompatible with a familiarity with Nature. How much have they not wondered at my knowledge, on seeing me discriminate, among the vines that have only just begun to sprout, the common from the choice varieties! How much have they not wondered, too, at my being able to distinguish, among the young plants in the fields, the shoots of the barley from those of the bean; at my being familiar with many fruit and shade trees; at my knowing the names of many plants, even, that grow spontaneously in the woods, as well as something of their properties and virtues!

Pepita Jiménez, who has heard through my father of the delight I take in the gardens here, has invited me to visit one that she owns at a short distance from the village, and eat the early strawberries that grow there. This caprice of Pepita's to show so many little attentions to my father, while at the same time she declines his addresses, seems to me at times to partake somewhat of coquetry, and to be worthy of reprobation. But whenever I see her, and find her so natural, so frank, and so simple, this bad opinion is dispelled, and I can not believe her to have any other end in view than to maintain the friendly relations that exist between her and our family.

Be this as it may, yesterday afternoon we went to Pepita's garden. It is charmingly situated, and as delightful and picturesque a place as one can imagine. The river, that by means of innumerable drains waters almost all these gardens, falls into a deep ravine, bordered on both sides by white and black poplars, willows, flowering oleanders, and other leafy trees. The waterfall, clear and transparent, precipitates itself into this ravine, sending up a cloud of spray, and then follows its tortuous course by a channel formed for it by Nature herself, enameling its banks with a thousand plants and flowers, and just now covering them with a multitude of violets. The declivity at the end of the garden is full of walnut, hazel, fig, and other fruit trees; and in the level portion are beds planted with strawberries and vegetables, tomatoes, potatoes, beans, and peppers. There is also a little flower-garden, with a great abundance of flowers, of the kinds most commonly cultivated here. Roses especially abound, and of these there are innumerable varieties. The gardener's house is prettier and cleaner than the houses of its class that one is accustomed to see in this part of the country; and near it there is another, smaller building, dedicated to the use of the mistress of the place, where Pepita regaled us with a sumptuous collation. The pretext for this collation was the strawberries, to eat which was the chief purpose of our visit. The quantity of strawberries, considering the earliness of the season, was astonishing. They were served with the milk of goats, which belonged likewise to Pepita.

There were present at this banquet the doctor, the notary, my aunt Casilda, my father, and myself, and of course the indispensable vicar, spiritual father, and, more than spiritual father, admirer and perpetual eulogist of Pepita.

By a sort of Sybaritic refinement, it was not by the gardener, nor his wife, nor the son of the gardener, nor by any other rustic, that we were served at this banquet, but by two lovely girls, confidential servants, in a manner, of Pepita's, dressed like peasants, but with the greatest neatness and even elegance. They wore gowns of gay-colored cotton, short and confined at the waist, and around their shoulders silk handkerchiefs. Their lustrous and abundant black hair, without covering, was braided and arranged in a knot behind; and in front they wore curls confined to the head by large hairpins, here called *Caracols*. Above the knot, or *chignon,* they each displayed a bunch of fresh roses.

Pepita's attire, except that it was black and of rich material, was equally unpretending. Her merino gown, made in the same style as those of her maids, without being short, was yet not long enough to catch the dust of the ground. A modest handkerchief of black silk covered also, according to the usage of the country, her shoulders and bosom; and on her head she wore no other ornament, either flower or jewel, than that of her own blond tresses.

The only particular, with respect to Pepita, in which I observed a certain fastidiousness, and in which she departed from the customs of the country people, was in wearing gloves. It is evident that she takes great care of her hands, and is, perhaps, to a certain extent, vain of their beauty and whiteness, as well as of her rose-colored and polished nails; but if this be so, it is to be pardoned to the weakness of the flesh; and indeed, if I remember aright, I think that St. Theresa, in her youth, had this same species of vanity, which did not prevent her, however, from becoming a great saint.

In truth, I can understand, even though I do not excuse, this little piece of vanity. It is so distinguished, so aristocratic, to possess a beautiful hand! I even think, at times, that there is something symbolic in it. The hand is the instrument by which we execute our works, the sign of our nobility, the means by which the intellect gives form and shape to its artistic conceptions, by which it gives reality to the mandates of its will, by which it exercises the dominion that God conceded to man over all other creatures. The rough, strong, sinewy, horny hand—it may be, of a laborer, a workman—testifies nobly to this dominion, but on its rudest and least intellectual side. The hands of Pepita, on the contrary, transparent almost, like alabaster, but rosy-hued, and in which one can almost see the pure and subtle blood circulate that gives to the veins their faint bluish tinge—these hands, I say, with their tapering fingers and unrivaled purity of outline, seem the symbol of the magic power, the mysterious dominion, that the human spirit holds and exercises, without the intervention of material force, over all those visible things that are the creation of God by a direct act of His will, and which man, as the instrument of God, improves and completes. It would be impossible to suppose that any one with hands like Pepita's should have an impure thought, a gross desire, an unworthy purpose at variance with the purity of her hands that would be called upon to put them into effect.

It is unnecessary to say that my father appeared as much charmed with Pepita, and she as attentive and affectionate toward him, as always; though her affection seemed, perhaps, of a character more filial than he could have wished. The fact is, that my father, notwithstanding the reputation he has of being in general but little respectful or reverent toward women, treats this one woman with such respect and consideration that not even Amadis, in the most devoted period of his wooing, showed greater toward Oriana. Not a single word that might shock the ear, no indelicate or inopportune compliment, no coarse jest, of the kind the Andalusians permit themselves so frequently to employ, does he ever indulge in. Hardly does he dare say to Pepita, "What beautiful eyes you have!" and, indeed, should he say so, he would only speak the truth, for Pepita's eyes are large, green as those of Circe, expressive, and well-shaped. And what enhances their beauty is that she seems unaware of all this, for there is not to be detected in her the slightest wish to please or attract any one by the sweetness of her glances.

One would say she thought eyes were only made to see with, and for no other purpose—the contrary of what I suppose to be the opinion, according to what I have heard, of the greater number of young and pretty women, who use their eyes as a weapon of offense, or as a sort of electric battery, by means of which to subdue hearts and captivate them. Not like those, indeed, are Pepita's eyes, wherein dwell a peace and a serenity as of heaven. And yet it can not be said that there is anything of coldness in their glance. Her eyes are full of charity and sweetness. They rest with tenderness on a ray of light, on a flower, on the commonest object in Nature; but with greater tenderness still, with signs of a softer feeling, more human and benign, do they rest on her fellow man, without his daring to imagine in that tranquil and serene glance, however young or handsome or conceited he may happen to be, anything more than charity and love toward a fellow man, or, at most, a friendly preference.

I sometimes wonder if all this can be studied, and if Pepita be, in truth, an accomplished actress; but the acting would be so perfect, and so purposeless the play, that it seems to me, after all, impossible that this should be the case. Nature herself it is, then, who serves as teacher and as type for that glance and for those eyes. First, Pepita loved her mother; then circumstances led her to love Don Gumersindo through duty, as the companion of her existence; and then, doubtless, all passion that any earthly object could inspire was extinguished in her breast, and she loved God, and loved material objects for the love of God; and so arrived at last at a peaceful and even enviable condition of spirit, in which, if there be anything to censure, it is perhaps a certain vanity of which she is herself unconscious. It is very convenient to love in this mild fashion, without allowing ourselves to be disturbed by our feelings, to have no passion to combat, to make of our love and affection for others an addition to, and, as it were, the complement of self-love.

I ask myself at times if, when I censure this state of mind in Pepita, it be not myself I censure. How do I know what passes in the soul of this woman that I should censure her? Perhaps, in thinking I behold her soul, it is my own soul that I behold. I never had, nor have I now, any passion to conquer. All my virtuous inclinations, all my instincts, good or bad, tend, thanks to your wise teachings, without obstacle or impediment, to the furtherance of the one purpose. In the fulfilment of this purpose, I should satisfy not only my noble and disinterested desires, but my selfish ones also—my love for distinction, my desire for knowledge, my curiosity to see distant lands, my longing for name and fame. All these are centred in the completing of the career upon which I have entered. I fancy at times that, in this respect, I am more worthy of censure than Pepita, supposing her even to deserve censure at all.

As regards this career, I have already begun it. I have cast out from my soul the vanities of the world; I have received the tonsure; I have consecrated myself to the service of the altar. I have a future full of ambition before me, and

I dwell with pleasure on the thought that this future is within my reach. I please myself in thinking that the conditions I possess for it are real and efficacious, though I call humility to my aid, at times, to save me from an overweening self-confidence.

To what, on the other hand, does this woman aspire, and what are her hopes? I censure her for the care she takes of her hands, for regarding her beauty, perhaps, with complacency; I almost censure her for her neatness, for the attention she bestows on her dress; for a certain indefinable coquetry there is in the very modesty and simplicity of her attire. But must virtue be slovenly? Must holiness be unclean? Can not a pure and clean soul rejoice in the cleanliness and purity of the body also? Is there not something reprehensible in the displeasure with which I regard the neatness and purity of Pepita? Is this displeasure, perchance, because she is to be my stepmother? But perhaps she does not wish to be my stepmother. Perhaps she does not love my father! It is true, indeed, that women are incomprehensible. It may be that in her secret heart she already feels inclined to return my father's affection, and marry him, though, in accordance with the saying that "what is worth much costs much," she chooses first to torment him with her affected coldness, to reduce him to unquestioning submission, to put his constancy to the proof, and then means to end by quietly saying Yes. We shall see.

What there is no question about is, that our garden party was decorously merry. We talked of flowers, of fruit, of grafts, of planting, and of innumerable other things relating to husbandry, Pepita displaying her knowledge of agriculture in rivalry with my father, with myself, and with the reverend vicar, who listens with open mouth to every word she utters, and declares that in the seventy odd years of his life, and during his many wanderings, in the course of which he has traversed almost the whole of Andalusia, he has never known a woman more discreet or more judicious in all she thinks and says.

On returning home from any of these excursions, I renew my entreaties to my father to allow me to go back to you, in order that the wished-for moment may at last arrive in which I shall see myself elevated to the priesthood. But my father is so pleased to have me with him, he is so happy here in the village, taking care of his plantations, exercising the judicial and executive authority of squire, paying homage to Pepita, and consulting her in everything as his Egeria, that he always finds, and will find perhaps for months to come, some plausible pretext to keep me here. Now he has to clarify the wine of I know not how many casks; now he has to bottle more wine still; now it is necessary to hoe around the vines; now to plow the olive groves and dig around the roots of the olives; in short, he keeps me here against my wishes—though I should not say "against my wishes," for it gives me great pleasure to be with my father, who is so good to me.

The evil is that, with this way of life, I fear I shall grow too material. I am conscious in my devotions of a certain aridity of spirit. My religious fervor diminishes; common life begins to penetrate, to infiltrate my nature. When I pray, I suffer distractions; in my solitary meditations, when the soul should raise itself up to God, I can no longer concentrate my thought as formerly. My sensibility of heart, on the other hand, which refuses to occupy itself with any worthy object, or employ and consume itself on its legitimate ends, wells forth, and, as it were, overflows at times for objects and under circumstances which are almost puerile, which seem to me ridiculous, and of which I am ashamed. If I awaken in the silence of the night, and hear by chance some lovelorn rustic singing, to the sound of his badly played guitar, a verse of a song, neither very original nor very poetical, nor very delicate, I am wont to be affected as if I were listening to some celestial melody.

A feeling of pity, childish, even absurd, comes over me at times. The other day the children of my father's overseer stole a nestful of young sparrows, and on seeing the little birds, not yet fledged, torn thus violently from their tender mother, I felt a sudden pang of anguish, and I confess I could not restrain my tears. A few days before this a peasant had brought in from the fields a calf that had broken its leg. He was about to carry it to the slaughter-house, and came to ask my father what part he wished for his table.

My father answered, "The head and the feet, and a few pounds of the flesh." I was touched by compassion on seeing the calf, and but that shame prevented me, would have bought it from the man, in the hope of curing and keeping it alive. In short, my dear uncle, nothing less than the confidence I have in you would make me recount to you these signs of an extravagant and restless emotion, so that you may judge by them how necessary it is that I should return to my former way of life, to my studies, to my lofty speculations, and be at last elevated to the priesthood, in order to provide with its fit and proper aliment the fire that consumes my soul.

April 14th.

I CONTINUE to lead the same life as usual, and am detained here still by my father's entreaties.

The greatest pleasure I enjoy, after that of being with him, is my intercourse and conversation with the reverend vicar, with whom I am in the habit of taking long walks. It seems incredible that a man of his age—for he must be near eighty—should be so strong and active, and so good a walker. I grow tired sooner than he; and there is no rough road, no wild place, no rugged hilltop in the neighborhood where we have not been.

The reverend vicar is reconciling me in a great degree with the Spanish clergy, whom I have stigmatized at times, in speaking to you, as but little enlightened. How much more to be admired, I often say to myself, is this man, so full of candor and benevolence, so simple and affectionate, than one who may have read many books, but in whose soul the flame of charity, fed by the purest and sincerest faith, burns less brightly than it does in his! Do not suppose from this that the understanding of the reverend vicar is a limited one; his is a spirit uncultured, indeed, but clear and sagacious. At times I fancy that the good opinion I entertain of him may be due to the attention with which he listens to me; but if this be not the case, it seems to me that he reasons on every subject with remarkable perspicacity, and that he knows how to unite an ardent love of our holy religion with an appreciation of all the good things that modern civilization has brought us. I am charmed, above all, by the simplicity, the sobriety, of sentiment, the naturalness, in short, with which the reverend vicar performs the most disagreeable works of charity. There is no misfortune he does not seek to alleviate, no suffering he does not strive to console, no error he does not endeavor to repair, no necessity which he does not hasten solicitously to relieve.

In all this, it must be confessed, he has a powerful auxiliary in Pepita, whose piety and compassionate disposition he is always extolling.

This species of homage which the vicar pays to Pepita is founded upon, and goes side by side with, the practise of a thousand good works—the giving of alms, prayer, public worship, and the care of the poor. Pepita not only gives alms for the poor, but also gives money for special prayers, sermons, and other observances of the Church. If the altars of the parish are gay at times with beautiful flowers, these flowers are due to the bounty of Pepita, who has sent them from her garden. If Our Lady of Sorrows, instead of her old worn cloak, wears to-day a resplendent and magnificent mantle of black velvet embroidered with silver, Pepita it is who has paid for it.

These and other similar acts of beneficence the vicar is always extolling and magnifying. Thus it is, when I am not speaking of my own aims, of my vocation, of my studies, to hear about which gives the reverend vicar great delight, and keeps him hanging upon my words, that, after a thousand turns, he always ends by speaking of Pepita Jiménez. And of whom, indeed, should the reverend vicar speak to me? His intercourse with the doctor, with the apothecary, with the rich husbandmen of the place, hardly gives ground for three words of conversation. As the reverend vicar possesses the very rare quality, in one bred in the country, of not being fond of scandal, or of meddling in other people's affairs, he has no one to speak of but Pepita, whom he visits frequently, and with whom, as may be gathered from what he says, he is in the habit of holding the most familiar colloquies.

I know not what books Pepita Jiménez has read, nor what education she may have received, but from what the reverend vicar says it may be deduced that she possesses a restless soul and an inquiring spirit, to which a multiplicity of questions and problems present themselves that she longs to elucidate and resolve, bringing them for that purpose before the reverend vicar, whom she thus puts into a state of agreeable perplexity.

This man, educated in country fashion, a priest whose breviary is, as one may say, his library, possesses an understanding open to the light of truth, but is wanting in original power, and thus the problems and questions Pepita presents to him open before him new horizons and new paths, nebulous and vague indeed, and which he did not even imagine to exist, which he is not able to follow with exactitude, but whose vagueness, novelty, and mystery enchant him.

The vicar is not ignorant of the danger of all this, and that he and Pepita expose themselves to falling, without knowing it, into some heresy; but he tranquillizes his conscience with the thought that, although very far from being a great theologian, he has his Catechism at his fingers' ends, he has confidence in God that He will illuminate his spirit, and he hopes not to be led into error, and takes it for granted that Pepita will follow his counsels, and never deviate from the right path.

Thus do both form to themselves a thousand poetical conceptions, full of charm although vague, of all the mysteries of our religion and the articles of our faith. Great is the devotion they profess to the most Holy Virgin, and I am astonished to see how they are able to blend the popular idea or conception of the Virgin with some of the sublimest theological thoughts.

From what the vicar relates I can perceive that Pepita Jiménez's soul, in the midst of its apparent calmness and serenity, is transfixed by the sharp arrow of suffering; there is in it a love of purity in contradiction with her past life. Pepita loved Don Gumersindo as her companion, as her benefactor, as the man to whom she owed everything; but she is tortured, she is humiliated, by the recollection that Don Gumersindo was her husband.

In her devotion to the Virgin there may be detected a feeling of painful humiliation, of suffering, of sadness, produced by the recollection of her ignoble and childless marriage.

Even in her adoration of the *Infant Jesus,* in the beautiful carved image she has in her house, there is something of maternal love that lacks an object on which to expend its tenderness, of maternal love that seeks this object in a being not born of sin and impurity.

The vicar says that Pepita worships the *Infant Jesus* as her God, but that she also loves him with the maternal tenderness she would feel for a son, if she had one, and whom she had no cause to regard with any other feeling than affection. The vicar sees that Pepita, in her prayers to the Holy Virgin, and in her care of her beautiful image of the Child Jesus, has in her thoughts the ideal Mother and the ideal Son, both alike immaculate.

I confess that I know not what to think of all these singularities. I know so little of women! What the vicar tells me of Pepita surprises me; and yet, though on the whole I believe her to be good rather than the contrary, she inspires me at times with a certain fear on my father's account. Notwithstanding his fifty-five years, I believe that he is in love; and Pepita, although virtuous through conviction, may, without premeditating or intending it, be an instrument of the spirit of evil, may practise a species of coquetry, involuntary and instinctive, more irresistible, efficacious, and fatal than that which proceeds from premeditation, calculation, and reasoning.

Who knows, I say to myself at times, notwithstanding her prayers, her secluded and devout life, her alms and her gifts to the churches—on all which is based the affection that the vicar entertains for her—if there be not also an earthly spell, if there be not something of diabolical magic in the arts she practises, and with which she deludes and beguiles this simple vicar, so that he thinks and speaks only of her on all occasions?

The very influence that Pepita exercises over a man so incredulous as my father, a man whose nature is so vigorous and so little sentimental, has in it, in truth, something extraordinary.

Nor do the good works of Pepita suffice to explain the respect and affection with which she inspires these country people in general. On the rare occasions on which she leaves the house the little children run to meet her and kiss her hand; the young girls smile, and salute her with affection; and the men take off their hats as she passes, and incline themselves before her with the most spontaneous reverence and the most natural good feeling.

Pepita Jiménez, whom many of the villagers have known since she was born, and who, to the knowledge of every one here, lived in poverty with her mother until her marriage to the decrepit and avaricious Don Gumersindo, has caused all this to be forgotten, and is now looked upon as a wondrous being, a visitant, pure and radiant, from some distant land, from some higher sphere, and is regarded by her fellow townspeople with affectionate esteem, and something like loving admiration.

I see that I am inadvertently falling into the same fault that I censure in the reverend vicar, and that I speak to you of nothing but Pepita. But this is natural. Here no one speaks of anything else. One would suppose the whole place to be full of the spirit, of the thought, of the image of this singular woman, in regard to whom I have not been able to determine if she be an angel or an accomplished coquette, full of *instinctive astuteness,* although the words may seem to involve a contradiction. For I am fully convinced in my own mind that this woman does not play the coquette, nor seek to gain the good-will of others, in order to gratify her vanity.

Pepita's soul is full of candor and sincerity. One has only to see her to be convinced of this. Her dignified and graceful bearing, her slender figure, the smoothness and clearness of her forehead, the soft and pure light of her eyes, all blend into a fitting harmony, in which there is not a single discordant note.

How deeply I regret having come to this place, and having remained here so long! I had passed my life in your house, and in the seminary; I had seen and known no one but my companions and my teachers; I knew nothing of the world but through speculation and through theory; and suddenly I find myself thrown into the midst of this world, though it be only that of a village, and distracted from my studies, meditations, and prayers by a thousand profane objects.

April 20th.

YOUR last letters, dearest uncle, have been a welcome consolation to my soul. Benevolent, as always, you admonish and enlighten me with prudent and useful reflections.

It is true my impetuosity is worthy of reprobation. I wish to attain my aims without making use of the means requisite to their attainment; I wish to reach the journey's end without first treading, step by step, the rough and thorny path.

I complain of an aridity of spirit in prayer, of inability to fix my thoughts, of a proneness to dissipate my tenderness on childish objects; I desire to elevate myself to and be absorbed in God, to attain at once to the contemplation of essential being; and yet I disdain mental prayer and rational and discursive meditation. How, without attaining to its purity, how, without beholding its light, can I hope to enjoy the delights of divine love?

I am by nature arrogant, and I shall therefore endeavor to humiliate myself in my own eyes, in order that God may not suffer the spirit of evil, in punishment of my pride and presumption, to cover me with humiliation.

I do not believe that it would be easy for me to fall into a lapse from virtue so shameful and unexpected as the one you fear. I do not confide in myself; I confide in the mercy of God and in His grace; and I trust they will not fail me.

Nevertheless, you are altogether right in advising me to abstain from forming ties of friendship with Pepita Jiménez; I am far enough from being bound to her by any tie.

I am not ignorant that, when those holy men and saints, who should serve us as models and examples, were bound in close intimacy and affection with women, it was in their old age, or when they were already proved and disciplined by penitence; or when there existed a noticeable disproportion in years between them and the pious women they elected to be their friends, as is related of St. Jerome and St. Paulina, and of St. John of the Cross and St. Theresa. And even thus, even with a purely spiritual affection, I know it is possible to sin through excess; for God only should occupy the soul as Lord and Spouse, and any other being who dwells in it should do so but as the friend, the servant, the creation of the Spouse, and as one in whom the Spouse delights.

Do not think, however, that I vaunt myself on being invincible, that I despise danger, and defy and seek it. He who loves danger shall perish therein. And if the prophet-king, though so agreeable in the sight of God, and so favored of Him, and Solomon, notwithstanding his supernatural and God-given wisdom, were troubled and fell into sin because God turned His face away from them, what have not I to fear, miserable sinner that I am, so young, so inexperienced in the wiles of the devil, and so wavering and unpractised in the combats of virtue?

Filled with a salutary fear of God, and imbued with a fitting distrust of my own weakness, I shall not be forgetful of your counsels and your prudent admonitions; and I shall pray meantime with fervor, and meditate on holy things, in order to abhor the things of the world, in so far as they deserve abhorrence; but of this I may assure you, that, however deeply I penetrate into the depths of my conscience, however carefully I search its inmost recesses, I have thus far discovered nothing to make me share your fears.

If my former letters are full of encomiums on the virtue of Pepita, it is the fault of my father and of the reverend vicar, and not mine; for at first, far from being friendly to this woman, I was unjustly prejudiced against her.

As for the beauty and physical grace of Pepita, be assured that I have contemplated them with entire purity of thought, and, though it cost me something to say it, and may cost you a little to hear it, I confess that, if any cloud has arisen to dim the clear and serene image of Pepita in the mirror of my soul, it has been owing to your harsh suspicions, which for an instant have almost made me suspect myself.

But no; what thought have I ever entertained with regard to Pepita, what have I seen or praised in her that should lead any one to suppose me to have any other feeling for her than friendship, and the admiration, pure and innocent, that a work of art may inspire, the more especially if it be the work of the Supreme Artist, and nothing less than the temple wherein He dwells?

Besides, dear uncle, I shall have to live in the world, to hold intercourse with my fellow beings, to see them, and I can not, for that reason, pluck out my eyes. You have told me many times that you wish me to devote myself to a life of action, preaching the Divine law, and making it known in the world, rather than to a contemplative life in the midst of solitude and isolation. Well, then, this being so, how would you have me act in order to avoid seeing Pepita Jiménez? Unless I made myself ridiculous by closing my own eyes in her presence, how could I fail to notice the beauty of hers; the clearness, the roseate hue, and the purity of her complexion; the evenness and pearly whiteness of her teeth, which she discloses with frequency when she smiles; the fresh carmine of her lips, the serenity and smoothness of her brow, and a thousand other attractions with which Heaven has endowed her? It is true that for one who bears within his soul the germ of evil thoughts, the leaven of vice, any one of the impressions that Pepita produces might be the shock of the steel against the flint, kindling the spark that would set fire to and consume all around it; but, prepared for this danger, watching against it, and guarded with the shield of Christian prudence, I do not think I have anything to fear. Besides, if it be rash to seek danger, it is cowardly not to be able to face it, and to shun it when it presents itself.

Have no fear; I see in Pepita only a beautiful creation of God, and in God I love her as a sister. If I feel any predilection for her, it is because of the praises I hear spoken of her by my father, by the reverend vicar, and by almost every one here.

For my father's sake it would please me were Pepita to relinquish her inclination for a life of seclusion, and her purpose to lead it, and to marry him. But were it not for this—were I to see that my father had only a caprice and not a genuine passion for her—then I should be glad that

Pepita would remain resolute in her chaste widowhood; and when I should be far away from here—in India, or Japan, or some other yet more dangerous mission—I might find a consolation in writing to her of my wanderings and labors. Then, when I returned here in my old age it would be a great pleasure for me to be on friendly terms with her, who would also then be aged, and to hold spiritual colloquies with her, and chats of the same sort as those the father vicar now holds with her. At present, however, as I am but a young man, I see but little of Pepita; I hardly speak to her. I prefer to be thought bashful, shy, ill-bred, and rude, rather than give any one the least occasion for thinking that I feel toward her as I ought not to, or even for suspicion or for gossip.

As for Pepita herself, not even in the most remote degree do I share the apprehension which vaguely you express. What projects could she form in respect to a man who, in two or three months more, is to be a priest! She, who has treated so many others with disdain—why should she be attracted by me? I know myself well, and I know that, fortunately, I am not capable of inspiring a passion. They say I am not ill-looking, but I am awkward, dull, shy, wanting in amiability; I bear the stamp of what I am—a humble student. What am I, compared with the gallant if somewhat rustic youths who have paid court to Pepita—agile horsemen, discreet and agreeable in conversation, Nimrods in the chase, skilled in all bodily exercises, singers of renown in all the fairs of Andalusia, and graceful and accomplished in the dance? If Pepita has scorned all these, how should she now think of me, and conceive the diabolical desire, and the more than diabolical project, of troubling the peace of my soul, of making me abandon my vocation, perhaps of plunging me into perdition? No, it is not possible. Pepita I believe to be good, and myself—and I say it in all sincerity—insignificant; insignificant, be it understood, so far as inspiring her with love is concerned, but not too insignificant to be her friend, to merit her esteem, to be the object one day, in a certain sense, of her preference, when I shall have succeeded in making myself worthy of this preference by a holy and laborious life.

I ask you to forgive me if I have vindicated myself too warmly from certain half-expressed suspicions in your letter—suspicions that sound like accusations, or like prophetic warnings.

I do not complain of these suspicions: you have given me judicious advice, the greater part of which I accept and intend to follow; if you have gone a little beyond what is just in your suspicions, it is owing, without doubt, to the interest you take in me, and for which I am grateful to you with all my heart.

May 4th.

IT is strange that in so many days I should not have had time to write to you, but such is the fact. My father does not let me rest a moment, and I am besieged by visitors.

In large cities it is easy to avoid seeing visitors, to isolate one's self, to create for one's self a solitude, a Thebaid in the midst of the tumult; in an Andalusian village, and, above all, when one has the honor of being the son of the squire, it is necessary to live in public. Not only now to my study, but even to my bedroom, do the reverend vicar, the notary, my cousin Currito, the son of Doña Casilda, and a hundred others, penetrate without any one daring to oppose them, waken me if I am asleep, and carry me off with them wherever they wish.

The clubhouse here is not a place of amusement for the evening only, but for all the hours of the day. From eleven o'clock in the morning it is full of people, who chat, glance over a paper to learn the news, and play at *ombre,* which, I have come to the conclusion, is the Spaniard's favorite game of cards; there are persons here who spend ten or twelve hours a day at it. In short, there is as much enjoyment here as one could well desire. In order that this enjoyment may be uninterrupted there are a great many amusements. Besides *ombre,* there are many other games at cards. Draughts, chess, and dominoes are not neglected. And, finally, there is a decided passion for cock-fighting.

All this, together with making calls, going to the fields to inspect the work, settling accounts every night with the overseer, visiting the wine-vaults and cask-stores, superintending the clarifying, rebottling, and perfecting of the wines, treating with gipsies and horsedealers for the purchase, sale, or barter of horses, mules, and donkeys, or with dealers from Xeres who come to buy our wine in order to convert it into sherry, are here the daily occupation of the gentry, squirearchy, or whatever else they may choose to call themselves. On extraordinary occasions there are other tasks and amusements that give a greater appearance of animation to everything: as in harvest-time, at the vintage, and the gathering in of the olives; or when there is a fair or a bull-fight, either here or in a neighboring village; or when there is a pilgrimage to the sanctuary of some miraculous image of the Holy Virgin, where, if it be true that many go through curiosity, or to amuse themselves, and give to their sweethearts a fairing of a Cupid or a rosary, many more go through devotion, or in fulfilment of a vow or promise. One of these sanctuaries is situated at the top of a very high mountain, yet there is no lack of delicate women who, to reach it, will climb, with bare feet wounded by the stones and brambles, the steep and rugged path that leads to it.

There is a certain charm in the life here. For one who has no desire for fame, no ambition, I can understand that it might be a very easy and agreeable life. Even solitude may be obtained by an effort. As I am here only for a short time, I can neither make this effort, nor ought I to do so; but if I were settled here, I should find no difficulty in secluding myself—and that, too, without offending any one—for several hours, or for the whole day, if it were necessary, in order to devote myself to my studies and meditations.

Your last letter has troubled me a little. I see that you persist in your suspicions, and I know not what answer to make in order to justify myself but the answer I have already made you.

You say that the victory, in a certain kind of warfare, consists in flight; that to fly is to conquer. Why should I seek to deny what the Apostle and so many holy Fathers and Doctors of the Church have said? But you well know that, in this case, flight does not depend upon me. My father is resolved that I shall not go; he keeps me here against my will, and I must obey him. The victory must be gained by other means, then, than by flight.

To set your mind at rest, I repeat that matters have not gone so far as you think; that you see them in a much more advanced stage than they really are.

There is not the slightest sign that Pepita Jiménez loves me. And even did she love me, it would be in a different way from that in which these women loved whom you cite as a salutary warning to me. A lady of our times, virtuous and well brought up, is neither so susceptible nor so wanting in decorum as those matrons of whose adventures ancient history is full.

The passage you cite from St. John Chrysostom is indeed worthy of consideration; but it is not altogether applicable to the circumstances. The great lady who in On, Thebes, or Diospolis Magna, fell in love with the favorite son of Jacob, was in all probability extremely handsome. By such a supposition only can one comprehend the words of the saint, that it was a greater miracle that Joseph should have passed through this ordeal unscathed, than that the three young men whom Nebuchadnezzar caused to be placed in the fiery furnace were not reduced to ashes!

As far as beauty is concerned, I confess frankly that I can not think that the wife of the Egyptian prince, chamberlain of the palace of the Pharaohs, or whatever else may have been his title, was in any degree superior to Pepita Jiménez. But neither am I endowed with as many gifts and excellences as was Joseph, nor is Pepita a woman without religion and without decorum. And even were the circumstances such as he relates, were all those horrors true, I can only account for the exaggerated language of St. John Chrysostom by the fact that he lived in the corrupt capital, half Gentile still, of the Lower Empire, in the midst of that Court whose vices he so harshly censures, and where the Empress Eudoxia herself gave an example of scandal and corruption.

But in our day, when the morality taught in the Gospel has penetrated more deeply into the strata of society, it seems to me an exaggeration to think the chaste scorn of the son of Jacob any more miraculous than the material incombustibility of the three young men of Babylon.

There is one point on which you touch in your letter that encourages and pleases me greatly. You condemn, as is right, the exaggerated sentimentality, and the tendency to be easily moved and to weep from childish motives, from which I told you that I suffered at times; but since this disposition of soul, so necessary to combat, exists in me, you rejoice that it does not affect my prayers and meditations and contaminate them. You recognize and praise in me the virile energy that should animate the passions and the mind that seek to elevate themselves to God.

The intelligence that strives to comprehend Him must be a vigorous one; the will that submits itself entirely to Him must first have triumphed, fighting bravely against every appetite, and defeating and putting to flight every temptation over self. The very passion which, purified and ardent, has power, even in weak and miserable mortals, to exalt itself, by an ecstasy of love, to God Himself, attaining by a supernatural illumination to the knowledge of Him, is the offspring of a steadfast and upright character, as well as of the Divine grace. This languor, this debility of the will, this morbid tenderness have nothing in them in common with charity, with piety, or with Divine love. The former are the attributes of a nature less than feminine; the latter are passions, if passions they can be called, of angels rather than of men. God will be my surety, and with His help I will fight for my own salvation. But should I sink into perdition, not in disguise nor by capitulation shall the enemies of the soul and the sins of the flesh enter into the fortress of my conscience, but with banners flying, laying waste everything before them by fire and sword, and after a desperate conflict.

In the past few days I have had occasion to practise patience in an extreme degree, and to mortify my self-love in the most cruel manner. My father, wishing to return Pepita's compliment of the garden-party, invited her to visit his villa at the Pozo de la Solana. The excursion took place on the 22d of April. I shall not soon forget the date.

The Pozo de la Solana is about two leagues distant from the village, and the only road to it is a bridle-path. We all had to go on horseback. As I never learned to ride, I had on former occasions accompanied my father mounted on a pacing mule, gentle, and, according to the expression of Dientes the muleteer, as good as gold, and of easier motion than a carriage. On the journey to the Pozo de la Solana I went in the same manner.

My father, the notary, the apothecary, and my cousin Currito were mounted on good horses. My aunt, Doña Casilda, who weighs more than two hundred and fifty pounds, rode on a large and powerful donkey, seated in a commodious side-saddle. The reverend vicar rode a gentle and easy mule like mine.

As for Pepita Jiménez, who, I supposed, would go also mounted on a donkey, in the same sort of easy saddle as my aunt—for I was ignorant that she knew how to ride—she surprised me by making her appearance on a black and white horse full of fire and spirit. She wore a riding-habit, and managed her horse with admirable grace and skill.

I was pleased to see Pepita look so charming on horseback, but I soon began to foresee and to be mortified by the sorry part I would play, jogging on in the rear beside my corpulent aunt Casilda and the vicar, all three as quiet and tranquil as if we were seated in a carriage, while the gay cavalcade in front would caracole, gallop, trot, and make a thousand other displays of their horsemanship.

I fancied on the instant that there was something of compassion in Pepita's glance as she noted the pitiable appearance I no doubt presented, seated on my mule. My cousin Currito looked at me with a mocking smile, and immediately began to make fun of me and to tease me.

Confess that I deserve credit for my resignation and courage. I submitted to everything with a good grace, and Currito's jests soon ceased when he saw that I was invulnerable to them. But what did I not suffer in secret! The others, now trotting, now galloping, rode in advance of us, both in going and returning. The vicar and I, with Doña Casilda between us, rode on, tranquil as the mules we were seated upon, without hastening or retarding our pace.

I had not even the consolation of chatting with the vicar, in whose conversation I find so much pleasure, nor of wrapping myself up in my own thoughts and giving the rein to my fancy, nor of silently admiring the beauty of the scenery around us. Doña Casilda is gifted with an abominable loquacity, and we were obliged to listen to her. She told us all there is to be told of the gossip of the village; she recounted to us all her accomplishments; she told us how to make sausages, brain-puddings, pastry, and innumerable other dishes and delicacies. There is no one, according to herself, who can rival her in matters pertaining to the kitchen, or to the dressing of hogs, but Antoñona, Pepita's nurse, and now her housekeeper and general manager. I am already acquainted with this Antoñona, for she goes back and forth between her mistress's house and ours with messages, and is in truth extremely handy—as loquacious as Aunt Casilda, but a great deal more discreet.

The scenery on the road to the Pozo de la Solana is charming, but my mind was so disturbed during our journey that I could not enjoy it. When we arrived at the villa and dismounted, I was relieved of a great load, as if it had been I who carried the mule, and not the mule who carried me.

We then proceeded on foot through the estate, which is magnificent, of varied character and extensive. There are vines, old and newly planted, all on the same property, producing more than five hundred bushels of grapes; olive trees that yield to the same amount; and, finally, a grove of the most majestic oaks that are to be found in all Andalusia. The water of the Pozo de la Solana forms a clear and deep brook, at which all the birds of the neighborhood come to drink, and on whose borders they are caught by hundreds, by means of reeds smeared with bird-lime, or of nets, in the centre of which are fastened a cord and a decoy. All this carried my thoughts back to the sports of my childhood, and to the many times that I too had gone to catch birds in the same manner.

Following the course of the brook, and especially in the ravines, are many poplars and other tall trees, which, together with the bushes and the shrubs, form a dark and labyrinthine wood. A thousand fragrant wild flowers grow there spontaneously, and it would, in truth, be difficult to imagine anything more secluded and sylvan, more solitary, peaceful, and silent than this spot. Even in the fervor of noonday, when the sun pours down his light in torrents from a heaven without a cloud, the mind experiences the same mysterious terror as visits it at times in the silent hours of the night. One can understand here the manner of life of the patriarchs of old, and of the primitive shepherds and heroes; and the visions and apparitions that appeared to them of nymphs, of gods, and of angels, in the midst of the noonday brightness.

As we walked through this thicket, there arrived a moment in which, I know not how, Pepita and I found ourselves alone together. The others had remained behind.

I felt a sudden thrill pass through me. For the first time, and in a place so solitary, I found myself alone with this woman; while my thoughts were still dwelling on the noontide apparitions, now sinister, now gracious, but always supernatural, vouchsafed to the men of remote ages.

Pepita had left the long skirt of her riding-habit in the house, and now wore a short dress that did not interfere with the graceful ease of her movements. She had on her head a little Andalusian hat, which became her extremely. She carried in her hand her riding-whip, which I fancied to myself to be a magic wand by means of which this enchantress might cast her spells over me.

I am not afraid to transcribe here these eulogies of her beauty. In this sylvan scene she appeared to me more beautiful than ever. The precaution recommended in similar cases by ascetics, to think of her beauty defaced by sickness and old age, to picture her to myself dead, the prey of corruption and of the worm, presented itself, against my will, to my imagination; and I say *against my will,* for I do not concur in the necessity for such a precaution. No thought of the material, no suggestion of the evil spirit, troubled my reason or infected my will or my senses.

What did occur to me was an argument—at least to my mind—in disproof of the efficacy of this precaution. Beauty, the creation of a Sovereign and Divine Power, may indeed be frail and ephemeral, may vanish in an instant; but the idea of beauty is eternal, and, once perceived by the mind, it lives there an immortal life. The beauty of this woman, such as it manifests itself to-day, will disappear in a few short years; the graceful form, those charming contours, the noble head that raises itself so proudly above her shoulders: all will be food for loathsome worms; but—though the material must of necessity be transformed—its idea, the creative thought—abstract beauty, in a word—what shall destroy this? Does it not exist in the Divine Mind? Once perceived and known by me, must it not continue to live in my soul, triumphing over age and even over death?

I was meditating thus, striving to tranquilize my spirit and dissipate the doubts which you have succeeded in infusing into my mind, when Pepita and I encountered each other. I was pleased and at the same time troubled to find myself alone with her—hoping and yet fearing that the others would join us.

The silvery voice of Pepita broke the silence, and drew me from my meditations, saying:

"How silent you are, Don Luis, and how sad! I am pained to think that it is perhaps through my fault, or partly so at least, that your father has caused you to spend a disagreeable day in these solitudes, taking you away from a solitude more congenial, where there would be nothing to distract your attention from your prayers and pious books."

I know not what answer I made to this. It must have been something nonsensical, for my mind was troubled. I did not wish to flatter Pepita by paying her profane compliments, nor, on the other hand, did I wish to answer her rudely.

She continued:

"You must forgive me if I am wrong, but I fancy that, in addition to the annoyance of seeing yourself deprived to-day of your favorite occupation, there is something else that powerfully contributes to your ill-humor."

"And what is this something else?" I said; "since you have discovered it, or fancy you have done so."

"This something else," responded Pepita, "is a feeling not altogether becoming in one who is going to be a priest so soon, but very natural in a young man of twenty-two."

On hearing this I felt the blood mount to my face, and my face burn. I imagined a thousand absurdities; I thought myself beset by evil spirits; I fancied myself tempted by Pepita, who was doubtless about to let me understand that she knew I loved her. Then my timidity gave place to haughtiness, and I looked her steadily in the face. There must have been something laughable in my look, but either Pepita did not observe it, or, if she did, she concealed the fact with amiable discretion; for she exclaimed, in the most natural manner:

"Do not be offended because I find you are not without fault. This that I have observed seems to me a slight one. You are hurt by the jests of Currito, and by being compelled to play—speaking profanely—a not very dignified part, mounted, like the reverend vicar with his eighty years, on a placid mule, and not, as a youth of your age and condition should be, on a spirited horse. The fault is the reverend dean's, to whom it did not occur that you should learn to ride. To know how to manage a horse is not opposed to the career you intend to follow, and I think, now that you are here, that your father might in a few days give you the necessary instruction to enable you to do so. If you should go to Persia or to China, where there are no railroads yet, you will make but a sorry figure in those countries as a bad horseman. It is possible even that, by this oversight, the missionary himself may come to lose prestige in the eyes of those barbarians, which will make it all the more difficult for him to reap the fruits of his labors."

This and other arguments Pepita adduced in order to persuade me to learn to ride on horseback; and I was so convinced of the necessity of a missionary's being a good horseman that I promised her to learn at once, taking my father as a teacher.

"On the very next expedition we make," I said, "I shall ride the most spirited horse my father has, instead of the mule I am riding to-day."

"I shall be very glad if you do," responded Pepita, with a smile of indescribable sweetness.

At this moment we were joined by the rest of the party, at which I was secretly rejoiced, though for no other reason than the fear of not being able to sustain the conversation, and of saying a great many foolish things, on account of the little experience I have had in conversing with women.

After our walk my father's servants spread before us on the fresh grass, in the most charming spot beside the brook, a rural and abundant collation.

The conversation was very animated, and Pepita acquitted herself with much discretion and intelligence. My cousin Currito returned to his jests about my manner of riding and the meekness of my mule. He called me a theologian, and said that, seated on muleback, I looked as if I were dispensing blessings. This time, however, being now firmly resolved to learn to ride, I answered his jests with sarcastic indifference. I was silent, nevertheless, with respect to the promise I had just made Pepita. The latter, doubtless thinking as I did—although we had come to no understanding in the matter—that silence for the present was necessary to ensure the complete success of the surprise that I would create afterward by my knowledge of horsemanship, said nothing of our conversation. Thus it happened, naturally and in the simplest manner, that a secret existed between us; and it produced in my mind a singular effect.

Nothing else worth telling occurred during the day.

In the afternoon we returned to the village in the same manner in which we had left it. Yet, seated on my easy-going mule and at the side of my aunt Casilda, I did not experience the same fatigue or sadness as before.

During the whole journey I listened without weariness to my aunt's stories, amusing myself at times in conjuring up idle fancies. Nothing of what passes in my soul shall be concealed from you. I confess, then, that the figure of Pepita was, as it were, the centre, or rather the nucleus and focus, of these idle fancies.

The noonday vision in which she had appeared to me, in the shadiest and most sequestered part of the grove, brought to my memory all the visions, holy and unholy, of wondrous beings, of a condition superior to ours, that I had read of in sacred authors and in the profane classics. Pepita appeared to the eyes and on the stage of my fancy in the leafy seclusion of the grove, not as she rode before us on horseback, but in an ideal and ethereal fashion—as Venus to Æneas, as Minerva to Callimachus, as the sylph who afterward became the mother of Libusa to the Bohemian Kroco, as Diana to the son of Aristæus, as the angels in the valley of Mamre to the Patriarch, as the hippocentaur to St. Anthony in the solitude of the wilderness.

That the vision of Pepita should assume in my mind something of a supernatural character seems to me no more to be wondered at than any of these. For an instant, seeing the consistency of the illusion, I thought myself tempted by evil spirits; but I reflected that in the few moments during which I had been alone with Pepita near the brook of the Solana, nothing had occurred that was not natural and commonplace; that it was afterward as I rode along quietly on my mule, that some demon, hovering invisible around me, had suggested these extravagant fancies.

That night I told my father of my desire to learn to ride. I did not wish to conceal from him that it was Pepita who had suggested this desire. My father was greatly rejoiced; he embraced me, he kissed me, he said that now not you only would be my teacher, but that he also would have the pleasure of teaching me something. He ended by assuring me that in two or three weeks he would make me the best horseman of all Andalusia; able to go to Gibraltar for contraband goods, and come back laden with tobacco and cotton, after eluding the vigilance of the Custom-house officers; fit, in a word to astonish the riders who show off their horsemanship in the fairs of Seville and Mairena, and worthy to press the flanks of Babieca, Bucephalus, or even of the horses of the sun themselves, if they should by chance descend to earth, and I could catch them by the bridle.

I don't know what you will think of this notion of my learning to ride, but I take it for granted you will see nothing wrong in it.

If you could but see how happy my father is, and how he delights in teaching me! Since the day after the excursion I told you of, I take two lessons daily. There are days on which the lesson is continuous, for we are on horseback from morning till night. During the first week the lessons took place in the courtyard of the house, which is unpaved, and which served us as a riding-school.

We now ride out into the country, but manage so that no one shall see us. My father does not want me to show myself on horseback in public until I am able to astonish every one by my fine appearance in the saddle, as he says. If the vanity natural to a father does not deceive him, this, it seems, will be very soon, for I have a wonderful aptitude for riding.

"It is easy to see that you are my son!" my father exclaims with joy, as he watches my progress.

My father is so good that I hope you will pardon him the profane language and irreverent jests in which he indulges at times. I grieve for this at the bottom of my soul, but I endure it with patience. These constant and long-continued lessons have reduced me to a pitiable condition with blisters. My father enjoins me to write to you that they are caused by mortification of the flesh.

As he declares that within a few weeks I shall be an accomplished horseman, and he does not desire to be superannuated as a master, he proposes to teach me other accomplishments of a somewhat irregular character, and sufficiently unsuited to a future priest. At times he proposes to train me in bull-fighting, in order that he may take me afterward to Seville, where, with lance in hand, on the plains of Tablada, I shall make the braggarts and the bullies stare. Then he recalls his own youthful days, when he belonged to the bodyguard, and declares that he will look up his foils, gloves, and masks, and teach me to fence. And, finally, as my father flatters himself that he can wield the Sevillian dagger better than any one else, he has offered to teach me even this accomplishment also.

You can already imagine the answer I make to all this nonsense. My father replies that, in the good old times, not only the priests, but even the bishops themselves, rode about the country on horseback, putting infidels to the sword. I rejoin that this might happen in the Dark Ages, but that in our day the ministers of the Most High should know of no other weapons than those of persuasion.

"And what if persuasion be not enough?" says my father. "Do you think it would be amiss to reenforce argument with a few good blows of a cudgel?"

The complete missionary, according to my father's opinion, should know how, on occasion, to take recourse to these heroic measures, and as my father has read a great many tales and romances, he quotes various examples in support of his opinion.

He cites, in the first place, St. James, who on his white horse, without ceasing to be an apostle, put more Moors to the sword than he preached to or convinced. He cites a certain Señor de la Vera, who, being sent on an embassy to Boabdil by Ferdinand and Isabella, became entangled in a theological discussion with the Moors in the Court of the Lions, and, having exhausted his arguments, drew his sword and fell upon them with fury in order to complete their conversion. And he finally cites the Biscayan nobleman, Ignatius Loyola, who, in a controversy he had with a Moor regarding the purity of the Holy Virgin, growing weary at last of the impious and horrible blasphemies with which the aforesaid Moor contradicted him, fell upon him, sword in hand, and, if he had not taken to his heels, would have forced conviction upon his soul in a terrible fashion. In regard to the incident relating to St. Ignatius, I answer my father that this was before the saint became a priest; and in regard to the other examples, I answer that historians are not agreed.

In short, I defend myself as best I can against my father's jests, and I content myself with being a good horseman, without learning other accomplishments unsuited to the clergy, although my father assures me that not a few of the Spanish clergy understand and practise them with frequency in Spain, even in our own day, with a view to contributing to the triumph of the faith, and to the preservation or the restoration of the unity of the Church.

I am grieved to the soul by this levity of my father's, and that he should speak with irreverence and jestingly about the most serious things; but a respectful son is not called upon to go further than I do in repressing his somewhat Voltairean freedom of speech. I say *Voltairean,* because I am not able to describe it by any other word. At heart my father is a good Catholic, and this thought consoles me.

Yesterday was the Feast of the Cross, and the village presented a very animated appearance. In each street were six or seven May-crosses covered with flowers, but none of them was so beautiful as that placed by Pepita at the door of her house. It was adorned by a perfect cascade of flowers.

In the evening we went to an entertainment at the house of Pepita. The cross which had stood at the door was now placed in a large saloon on the ground floor, in which there is a piano, and Pepita presented us with a simple and poetic spectacle—one that I had seen when a child, but had since forgotten.

From the upper part of the cross hung down seven bands or broad ribbons, two white, two green, and three red, the symbolic colors of the theological virtues. Small children, five or six years old, representing the seven sacraments, and holding the seven ribbons that hung from the cross, performed with great skill a species of contra-dance. The sacrament of baptism was represented by a child wearing the white robe of a catechumen; ordination, by another child as a priest; confirmation, by a little bishop; extreme unction, by a pilgrim with staff and scrip, the latter filled with shells; marriage, by a bride and bridegroom; and penance, by a Nazarene with cross and crown of thorns.

The dance was a series of reverences, steps, evolutions, and genuflexions, rather than a dance, performed to the sound of very tolerable music, something like a march, which the organist played, not without skill, on the piano.

The little dancers, children of the servants or retainers of Pepita, after playing their parts, went away to bed loaded with gifts and caresses.

The entertainment, in the course of which we were served with refreshments, continued till twelve; the refreshments were syrup served in little cups, and afterward chocolate with spongecake, and meringues and sugared water.

Since the return of spring Pepita's seclusion and retirement are being gradually abandoned, at which my father is greatly rejoiced. In future Pepita will receive every night, and my father desires that I shall be one of the guests.

Pepita has left off mourning, and now appears, more lovely and attractive than ever, in the lighter fabrics appropriate to the season, which is almost summer. She still dresses, however, with extreme simplicity.

I cherish the hope that my father will not now detain me here beyond the end of this month at farthest. In June we shall both join you in the city, and you shall then see how, far from Pepita, to whom I am indifferent, and who will remember me neither kindly nor unkindly, I shall have the pleasure of embracing you, and attaining at last to the happiness of being ordained.

May 7th.

PEPITA, as I mentioned to you before, receives every evening, from nine to twelve.

Four or five married ladies of the village, and as many more unmarried ones, including Aunt Casilda, are frequent visitors; as well as six or seven young men, who play at forfeits with the girls. Three or four engagements are the natural result.

The sedate portion of the company are the same as usual. These are, as one may say, the high functionaries of the village—my father, who is the squire, the apothecary, the doctor, and the vicar.

Pepita plays *ombre* with my father and the vicar and a fourth player.

I am at a loss to know in which division to place myself. If I join the young people, my gravity proves a hindrance to their games and flirtations; if I stay with the elders, I must play the part of a looker-on in things I have no knowledge of. The only games of cards I know are simple and old-fashioned, and do not seem to be in vogue here, in polite society.

The best course for me to pursue would be to absent myself from the house altogether, but my father will not hear of this. By doing so, according to him, I should make myself ridiculous.

My father shows many signs of wonder when he sees my ignorance in certain things. That I should not know how to play even *ombre* fills him with astonishment.

"Your uncle has brought you up quite out of the world," he says to me, "cramming you with theology, and leaving you in the dark about everything else you ought to know. For the very reason that you are to be a priest, and can neither dance nor make love in society it is necessary that you should know how to play *ombre*. Otherwise how are you going to spend your time, unhappy boy?"

To these and other arguments of a like kind I have been obliged to yield, and my father is teaching me at home to play *ombre,* so that, as soon as I have learned it, I may play it at Pepita's. He wanted also, as I already told you, to teach me to fence, and afterward to smoke and shoot and throw the bar; but I have consented to nothing of all this.

"What a difference," my father exclaims, "between your youth and mine!"

And then he adds, laughing:

"In substance it is the same thing. I, too, had canonical hours in my regimental quarters: a cigar was the censer; a pack of cards, the hymn-book; and there were never wanting other devotions and exercises of a more or less spiritual character."

Although you had warned me of my father's levity of disposition, on account of which I have lived with you for twelve years of my life—from the age of ten to that of twenty-two—yet his sayings, altogether too free at times, perturb and mortify me. But what is to be done? Although I can not reprove him for making use of them, I do not, on the other hand, applaud or laugh at them. The strangest part of it is, that my father is altogether another person when he is in the house of Pepita. Never, even by chance, does he utter a single phrase, a single jest of the kind he is so prodigal of at other times. At Pepita's my father is propriety itself. He seems, too, to become every day more attached to her, and to cherish greater hopes of success.

My father continues greatly pleased with me as his pupil in horsemanship. He declares that in four or five days I shall have mastered the art, and that I shall then mount Lucero, a black horse bred from an Arab horse and a mare of the race of Guadalcazar, full of fire and spirit, and trained to all manner of curvetings.

"Whoever succeeds in getting on the back of Lucero," my father says to me, "may venture to compete in horsemanship with the centaurs themselves; and that you shall do very soon."

Although I spend the whole day out of doors on horseback, in the clubhouse, or at Pepita's, I yet steal a few hours from slumber, sometimes voluntarily, sometimes because I can not sleep, to meditate on my situation and to examine my conscience. The image of Pepita is always present to my mind. "Can this be love?" I ask myself.

The moral obligation I am under, the vow I have made to consecrate myself to the service of the altar, although not confirmed, is nevertheless in my eyes full and binding. If anything opposed to the fulfilment of this vow has entered into my soul, it must be combated.

I note, too—and you must not accuse me of arrogance because I mention this to you—that the empire of my will, which you have taught me to exercise, is complete over my senses. While Moses on the top of Mount Sinai conversed with God, the rebellious people on the plain below adored the golden calf. Notwithstanding my youth, my spirit has no fears of falling into a like rebelliousness. I might commune with God in full security, if the enemy did not come to attack me in the sanctuary itself. But the image of Pepita presents itself to my soul. It is a spirit that makes war against my spirit. It is the idea of her beauty, in all its spiritual purity, that stands before the sanctuary of the soul, where God resides, and prevents me from reaching Him.

I do not shut my eyes to the truth, however; I can see clearly; I can reason; I do not deceive myself.

Above and beyond this spiritual inclination that draws me to Pepita, is the love of the Infinite and of the Eternal. Although I represent Pepita to myself as an idea, as a poem, it is still the idea, the poetry of something finite, limited, concrete; while the love of God and the conception of God embrace everything. But notwithstanding all my efforts, I am unable to give form in my mind to this supreme conception—this object of the highest love—in order that it may combat the image, the memory of the frail and ephemeral reality that continually besets me.

Fervently do I implore Heaven to awaken within me the power of the imagination, that it may create a likeness, a symbol of this conception, that shall be all-embracing, and absorb and efface the image of Pepita. This highest conception, on which I desire to centre my love, is vague, shadowy, indescribable, like the blackness of darkness; while

Pepita's image presents itself to me in clearly defined outlines, bright, palpable, luminous with the subdued light that may be borne by the eyes of the spirit, not bright with the intense light that for the eyes of the spirit is as darkness.

Every other consideration, every other object, is of no avail to destroy her image. It rises up between the crucifix and me; between the most sacred image of the Virgin and me; I see it on the page of the religious book I am reading.

Yet I do not believe that my soul is invaded by what in the world is called love. And even if this were so, I would do battle against this love, and conquer in the end.

The daily sight of Pepita, the hearing her praises sounded continually, even by the reverend vicar, preoccupy me; they turn my spirit toward profane things, and withdraw it from its proper meditations. But no—I do not yet love Pepita; I will go away from here and forget her.

While I remain here I will battle valiantly. I will wrestle with the Lord in order to prevail with Him by love and submission. My cries shall reach Him like burning arrows, and shall break down the buckler wherewith He defends and hides Himself from the eyes of my soul. I will fight like Israel in the silence of the night and the Lord shall wound me in the thigh, and shall humble me in the conflict, in order that, being vanquished, I may become the victor.

May 12th.

BEFORE I had any intention of doing so, my dear uncle, my father persuaded me to ride Lucero. Yesterday, at six in the morning, I mounted the beautiful wild beast, as my father calls Lucero, and we set out for the country. My father rode a spirited chestnut.

I rode so well, I kept so firm a seat, and looked to such advantage on the superb animal, that my father could not resist the temptation of showing off his pupil; and about eleven in the morning, after resting at a farm he owns half a league distant from here, he insisted on our returning to the village and entering by the most frequented street, which we did, our horses' hoofs clattering loudly on the paving stones. It is needless to say that we rode by Pepita's house, who for some time past is to be seen occasionally at her window, and who was then seated at the grating of a lower window, behind the green shutter.

Hardly had Pepita heard the noise we made than, lifting up her eyes and seeing us, she rose, laid down the sewing she had in her hands, and set herself to observe us. Lucero, who has the habit, as I learned afterward, of prancing and curveting when he passes the house of Pepita, began to show off, and to rear and plunge. I tried to quiet him, but as there was something unfamiliar to him in the ways of his present rider, as well as in the rider himself, whom perhaps he regarded with contempt, he grew more and more unmanageable, and began to neigh and prance, and even to kick. But I remained firm and serene, showing him that I was his master, chastising him with the spur, touching his breast with the whip, and holding him in by the bridle. Lucero, who had almost stood up on his hind legs, now humbled himself so far as to bend his knees gently and make a reverence.

The crowd of idlers who had gathered around us broke into boisterous applause. My father called out to them:

"A good lesson that for our braggarts and blusterers!"

And, observing afterward that Currito—who has no other occupation than to amuse himself—was among the crowd, he addressed him in these words:

"Look at that, you rascal! Look at the theologian now, and see if you don't stare with wonder, instead of laughing at him!"

And, in fact, there Currito stood open-mouthed, stock-still with amazement, and unable to utter a word.

My triumph was great and assured, although unsuited to my character. The unfitness of the triumph covered me with confusion. Shame brought the blood to my cheeks. I must have turned as red as scarlet, or redder, when I saw that Pepita was applauding and saluting me graciously, while she smiled and clapped her beautiful hands.

In short, I have been adjudged a man of nerve and a horseman of the first rank.

My father could not be prouder or happier than he is. He declares that he is completing my education; that in me you have sent him a book full of wisdom, but uncorrected and unbound, and that he is now making a fair copy, and putting it between covers.

On two occasions I played *ombre* with Pepita. Learning *ombre,* if that be a part of the binding and the correcting, is also done with.

The night after my equestrian feat Pepita received me with enthusiasm, and—what she had never done before, nor perhaps desired to do—gave me her hand.

Do not suppose that I did not call to mind what so many moralists and ascetics recommend in like cases, but in my inmost thoughts I believed they exaggerated the danger. Those words of the Holy Spirit, that it is as dangerous to touch a woman as a scorpion, seem to me to have been said in another sense. In pious books, no doubt, many phrases and sentences of the Scriptures are, with the best intentions, interpreted harshly. How are we to understand otherwise the saying that the beauty of woman, this perfect work of God, is always the cause of perdition? Or how are we to understand, in a universal and invariable sense, that woman is more bitter than death? How are we to understand that he who touches a woman, on whatever occasion or with whatsoever thought, shall not escape without stain?

However, I made answer rapidly within my own mind to these and other similar counsels; I took the hand that Pepita kindly extended to me, and pressed it in mine. Its softness made me comprehend all the better the delicacy and beauty of the hand that until now I had known only by sight.

According to the usages of the world, the hand, once given, should always be given on entering a room and on taking leave. I hope that in this ceremony, in this evidence of friendship, in this manifestation of kindness, given and accepted in purity of heart, and without any mixture of levity, you will see nothing either evil or dangerous.

As my father is often obliged of an evening to see the overseer and others of the country people, and is seldom free until half-past ten or eleven, I take his place with Pepita at the card-table. The reverend vicar and the notary are generally the other partners, and we play for very small stakes, so that not more than a piastre or two changes hands.

As the game thus possesses but little serious interest, we interrupt it constantly with pleasant conversation, and even with discussions on matters foreign to the game itself, in all which Pepita displays such clearness of understanding, such liveliness of imagination, and such extraordinary grace of expression as to astonish me.

I find no sufficient motive to change my opinion with respect to what I have already said in answer to your suspicions that Pepita perhaps feels a certain liking for me. She manifests towards me the affection she would naturally entertain for the son of her suitor, Don Pedro de Vargas, and the timidity and shyness that would be inspired by a man in my position, who, though not yet a priest, is soon to become one.

Nevertheless, as I always speak to you in my letters as if I were kneeling before you in the confessional, I desire, as is my duty, to communicate to you a passing impression I have received on two or three occasions. This impression may be but a hallucination or a delusion, but I have none the less felt it.

I have already told you in my former letters that the eyes of Pepita, green as those of Circe, are frank and tranquil in their gaze; she does not seem to be conscious of their power, or to know that they serve for any other purpose than to see with. When she looks at one, the soft light of her glance is so clear, so candid, and so untroubled that, instead of giving rise to any evil thoughts, it seems to give birth to pure thoughts, and leaves innocent and chaste souls in untroubled repose, while it destroys every incitement to evil in souls that are not chaste. There is no trace of ardent passion, no fire to be discovered in Pepita's eyes. Their light is like the mild ray of the moon.

Well, then, notwithstanding all this, I fancied I detected, on two or three occasions, a sudden brightness, a gleam as of lightning, a swift, devouring flame in her eyes as they rested on me. Can this be the result of a ridiculous vanity, inspired by the arch fiend himself?

I think so. I believe it is, and I wish to believe it.

The swiftness, the fugitive nature of the impression make me conjecture that it had no external reality, that it was only an illusion.

The serenity of heaven, the coldness of indifference, tempered, indeed, with sweetness and charity—this is what I always discern in Pepita's eyes.

Nevertheless, this illusion, this vision of a strange and ardent glance, torments me.

My father affirms that in affairs of the heart it is the woman, not the man, who takes the first step; but that she takes it without thereby incurring any responsibility, and with the power to disavow or retract it whenever she desires to do so. According to my father, it is the woman who first declares her passion through the medium of furtive glances, which she afterward disavows to her own conscience if necessary, and of which he to whom they are directed divines, rather than reads, the significance. In this manner, by a species of electric shock, by means of a subtle and inexplicable intuition, he who is loved perceives that he is loved; and when at last he makes up his mind to declare himself, he can do so confidently, and in the full security that his passion is returned.

Perhaps it is these theories of my father, to which I have listened because I could not help it, that have heated my fancy and made me imagine what has no existence in reality.

Yet, after all, I say to myself at times, Is the thought so absurd, so incredible, that this illusion should have an existence in reality? And if it had, if I were pleasing in Pepita's eyes otherwise than as a friend, if the woman to whom my father is paying his addresses should fall in love with me, would not my position then be terrible?

But let us cast away these fears, the creation, no doubt, of vanity. Let us not make a Phædra of Pepita, or a Hippolytus of me.

What in reality begins to surprise me is my father's carelessness and complete consciousness of security. Pardon my pride, ask Heaven to pardon it; for at times this consciousness of security piques and offends me. What! I say to myself, is there something so absurd in the thought that it should not even occur to my father that, notwithstanding my supposed sanctity, or perhaps because of my supposed sanctity, I should, without wishing it, inspire Pepita with love?

There is an ingenious method of reasoning by which I explain to myself, without wounding my vanity, my father's carelessness in this important particular. My father, although he has no reason for doing so, regards himself already in the light of Pepita's husband, and shares that fatal blindness with which Asmodeus, or some other yet more malicious demon, afflicts husbands. Profane and ecclesiastical history is full of instances of this blindness, which God permits, no doubt, for providential purposes. The most remarkable example of it, perhaps, is that of the Emperor Marcus Aurelius, who had for his wife a woman so vile as Faustina, and though so wise a man and so great a philosopher, remained in ignorance to the end of his days of what was known to every one else in the Roman Empire; so that in the meditations, or memoirs, that he composed, he gives infinite thanks to the immortal gods for having bestowed upon him so faithful and so good a wife, thus provoking the smiles of his contemporaries and of future generations. Every day since that time we see examples of great men, and men of exalted rank, who make those who enjoy the favor of their wives their private secretaries, and bestow honors on them. Thus do I explain to myself my father's indifference, and his failure to suspect that, even against my will, I might become his rival.

Would it be a want of respect on my part, should I fall into the sin of presumption or insolence, if I were to warn my father of the danger which he himself does not see? But he gives me no opportunity to say anything to him. Besides, what could I say to him? That once or twice I fancy Pepita has looked at me in a way different from that in which she usually does? May not this be an illusion of mine? No; I have not the least proof that Pepita desires to play the coquette with me.

What, then, could I tell my father? Shall I say to him that it is I who am in love with Pepita, that I covet the treasure he already regards as his own? This is not the truth; and, above all, how could I tell this to my father, even if, to my misfortune and through my fault, it were the truth?

The best course I can adopt is to say nothing; to combat the temptation in silence, if it should indeed assail me, and to endeavor as soon as possible to leave this place and return to you.

May 19th.

I RETURN thanks to Heaven and to you for the letter and the counsels you have lately sent me. To-day I need them more than ever.

The mystical and learned St. Theresa is right in dwelling upon the suffering of timid souls that allow themselves to be disturbed by temptation; but a thousand times worse than that suffering is the awakening from error of those who, like me, have permitted themselves to indulge in arrogance and self-confidence.

Our bodies are the temples of the Holy Spirit; but when fire is set to the walls of the temple, though they do not burn, yet they are blackened.

The first evil thought is the head of the serpent; if we do not crush it with firm and courageous foot, then will the venomous reptile climb up and hide himself in our bosom.

The nectar of earthly joys, however innocent they be, is sweet indeed to the taste; but afterward it is converted into gall, and into the venom of the serpent.

It is true—I can no longer deny it to you—I ought not to have allowed my eyes to rest with so much complacency on this dangerous woman.

I do not deem myself lost; but I feel my soul troubled.

Even as the thirsty hart desires and seeks the water-brooks, so does my soul still seek God. To God does it turn that He may give it rest; it longs to drink at the torrent of His delights, whose gushing waters rejoice Paradise, and whose clear waves can wash us whiter than snow; but deep calleth unto deep, and my feet have stuck fast in the mire that is hidden in their abysses.

Yet have I still breath and voice to cry out with the psalmist: "Arise, my joy! If thou art on my side, who shall prevail against me?"

I say unto my sinful soul, full of the chimerical imaginings and sinful desires engendered by unlawful thoughts: "Oh, miserable daughter of Babylon! happy shall he be who shall give thee thy reward! Happy shall he be that dasheth thy little ones against the stones!"

Works of penance, fasting, prayer, and penance, are the weapons wherewith I shall arm myself to the combat, and, with the Divine help, to vanquish.

It was not a dream; it was not madness; it was the truth: she lets her eyes rest upon me at times with the ardent glance of which I have told you. There is in her glance an inexplicable magnetic attraction. It draws me on, it seduces me, and I can not withdraw my gaze from her. On such occasions my eyes must burn, like hers, with a fatal flame, as did those of Ammon when he turned them upon Tamar, as did those of the prince of Shechem when they were fixed upon Dinah.

When our glances thus meet, I forget even God. Her image rises up within my soul, the conqueror of everything. Her beauty outshines all other beauty; the joys of heaven seem to me less desirable than her affection. An eternity of suffering would be little in exchange for a moment of the infinite bliss with which one of those glances which pass like lightning inundates my soul.

When I return home, when I am alone in my room, in the silence of the night, I realize all the horror of my position, and I form good resolutions, only to break them again.

I resolve to feign sickness, to make use of any pretext so as not to go to Pepita's on the following night, and yet I go.

My father, confiding to the last degree, says to me when the hour arrives, without any suspicion of what is passing in my soul:

"Go to Pepita's; I will go later, when I have finished with the overseer."

No excuse occurs to me; I can find no pretext for not going, and instead of answering, "I can not go," I take my hat and depart.

On entering the room I shake hands with Pepita, and as our hands touch she casts a spell over me; my whole being is changed; a devouring fire penetrates my heart, and I think only of her. Moved by an irresistible impulse, I gaze at her with insane ardor, and at every instant I think I discover in her new perfections. Now it is the dimples in her cheeks when she smiles, now the roseate whiteness of her skin, now the straight outline of her nose, now the smallness of her ear, now the softness of contour and the admirable modeling of her throat.

I enter her house against my will, as though summoned there by a conjurer, and no sooner am I there than I fall under the spell of her enchantment. I see clearly that I am in the power of an enchantress whose fascination is irresistible.

Not only is she pleasing to my sight, but her words sound in my ears like the music of the spheres, revealing to my soul the harmony of the universe; and I even fancy that a subtle fragrance emanates from her, sweeter than the perfume of the mint that grows by the brookside, or the woodlike odor of the thyme that is found among the hills.

I know not how, in this state of exaltation, I am able to play *ombre,* or to converse rationally, or even to speak, so completely am I absorbed in her.

When our eyes meet, our souls rush forth in them and seem to join and interpenetrate each other. In that meeting a thousand feelings are communicated that in no other way could be made known; poems are recited that could be uttered in no human tongue, and songs are sung that no human voice could sing, and no guitar accompany.

Since the day I met Pepita by the Pozo de la Solana I have not seen her alone. Not a word has passed between us, yet we have told each other everything.

When I withdraw myself from this fascination, when I am again alone at night in my chamber, I set myself to examine coolly the situation in which I am placed; I see the abyss that is about to engulf me yawning before me; I feel my feet slip from under me, and that I am sinking into it.

You counsel me to reflect upon death—not on the death of this woman, but on my own. You counsel me to reflect on the instability, on the insecurity of our existence, and on what there is beyond it. But these considerations, these reflections neither terrify nor daunt me. Why should I, who desire to die, fear death? Love and death are brothers. A sentiment of self-abnegation springs to life within me, and tells me that my whole being should be consecrated to and annihilated in the beloved object. I long to merge myself in one of her glances; to diffuse and exhale my whole being in the ray of light shot forth from her eyes; to die while gazing on her, even though I should be eternally lost.

What is still to some extent efficacious with me against this love is not fear, but love itself. Superior to this deep-rooted love with which I now have the evidence that Pepita inspires me, Divine love exalts itself in my spirit in mighty uprising. Then everything is changed within me, and I feel that I may yet obtain the victory. The object of my higher love presents itself to my mental vision, as the sun that kindles and illuminates all things, and fills all space with light; and the object of my inferior love appears but as an atom of dust floating in the sunbeam. All her beauty, all her splendor, all her attractions are nothing but the reflection of this uncreated sun, the brilliant, transitory, fleeting spark that is cast off from that infinite and inexhaustible fire.

My soul, burning with love, would fain take to itself wings and rise to that flame, in order that all that is impure within it might be consumed therein.

My life, for some days past, is a constant struggle. I know not how it is that the malady from which I suffer does not betray itself in my countenance. I scarcely eat, I scarcely sleep; and if by chance sleep closes my eyelids, I awake in terror, as from a dream in which rebel angels are arrayed against good angels, and in which I am one of the combatants. In this conflict of light against darkness I do battle for the right, but I sometimes imagine that I have gone over to the enemy, that I am a vile deserter; and I hear a voice from Patmos saying, "And men loved darkness rather than light"; and then I am filled with terror, and I look upon myself as lost.

No resource is left me but flight. If, before the end of the month, my father does not go with me, or consent to my going alone, I shall steal away like a thief, without a word to any one.

May 23d.

I AM a vile worm, not a man; I am the opprobrium and disgrace of humanity. I am a hypocrite.

I have been encompassed by the pangs of death, and the waters of iniquity have passed over me.

I am ashamed to write to you, and yet I write. I desire to confess everything to you.

I can not turn away from evil. Far from abstaining from going to Pepita's, I go there each night earlier than the last. It would seem as if devils took me by the feet and carried me there against my will!

Happily, I never find Pepita alone; I do not desire to find her alone. I almost always find the excellent vicar there before me, who attributes our friendship to similarity of feeling in religious matters, and bases it on piety, like the pure and innocent friendship he himself entertains for her.

The progress of my malady is rapid. Like the stone that is loosened from the mountain-top and gathers force as it falls, so is it with my spirit.

When Pepita and I shake hands, it is not now as at first. Each one of us, by an effort of the will, transmits to the other, through the handclasp, every throb of the heart. It is as if, by some diabolical art, we had effected a transfusion and a blending together of the most subtle elements of our blood. She must feel my life circulate through her veins, as I feel hers in mine.

When I am near her, I love her; when I am away from her, I hate her. When I am in her presence she inspires me with love; she draws me to her; she subjugates me with gentleness; she lays upon me a very easy yoke.

But the recollection of her undoes me. When I dream of her, I dream that she is severing my head from my body, as Judith slew the captain of the Assyrians; or that she is driving a nail into my temple, as Jael did to Sisera. But when I am near her, she appears to me the Spouse of the

Song of Songs, and a voice within me calls to her and I bless her, and I regard her as a sealed fountain, as an enclosed garden, as the flower of the valley, as the lily of the fields, my dove and my sister.

I desire to free myself from her, and I can not. I abhor, yet I almost worship her. Her spirit enters into me and takes possession of me as soon as I behold her; it subjugates me, it abases me.

I leave her house each night, saying, "This is the last night I shall return here"; and I return there on the following night!

When she speaks, and I am near, my soul hangs, as it were, upon her words. When she smiles, I imagine that a ray of spiritual light enters into my heart and rejoices it.

It has happened, when playing *ombre,* that our knees have touched by chance, and then I have felt a thrill run through me impossible to describe.

Get me away from this place. Write to my father and ask him to let me return to you. If it be necessary, tell him everything. Help me! Be my refuge!

May 30th.

GOD has given me strength to resist, and I have resisted.

It is now many days since I have been in the house of Pepita, many days since I have seen her.

It is scarcely necessary that I should feign sickness, for I am in reality sick. I have lost my color, and dark circles begin to show themselves under my eyes; and my father asks me, full of affectionate anxiety, what the cause of my suffering is, and manifests the deepest concern.

The kingdom of Heaven is said to yield to violence, and I am resolved to conquer it. With violence I call at its gates that they may open to me.

With wormwood am I fed by the Lord, in order to prove me; and in vain do I supplicate Him to let this cup of bitterness pass away from me. But, as I have passed and still pass many nights in vigil, delivered up to prayer, a loving inspiration from the Supreme Consoler has come to sweeten the bitterness of my cup.

I have beheld with the eyes of the soul the new country; and the new song of the heavenly Jerusalem has resounded within the depths of my heart.

If in the end I should conquer, glorious will be the victory; but I shall owe it to the Queen of Angels, under whose protection I place myself. She is my refuge and my defense; the tower of the house of David, on whose walls hang innumerable shields and the armor of many valiant champions; the cedar of Lebanon, which puts the serpent to flight.

The woman who inspires me with an earthly love, on the contrary, I endeavor to despise and abase in my thoughts, remembering the words of the sage, and applying them to her.

"Thou art the snare of the hunter," I say of her; "thy heart is a net of deceit, and thy hands are bands that imprison; he who fears God will flee from thee, and the sinner shall be taken captive by thee."

In my meditations on love I find a thousand reasons for loving God, and against loving her.

I feel, in the depths of my heart, an indescribable enthusiasm that convinces me that for the love of God I would sacrifice all things—fame, honor, power, dominion. I feel myself capable of imitating Christ, and if the Tempter should carry me off to the mountain-top, and should there offer me all the kingdoms of the earth if I consented to bow the knee before him, yet would I not bend it. But were he to offer me this woman if I should do so, I feel that I should waver, that I could not reject his offer. Is this woman, then, worth more in my eyes than all the kingdoms of the earth? More than fame, honor, power, and dominion?

Is the virtue of love, I ask myself at times, always the same, even when applied to divers objects? Or are there two species and qualities of love? To love God seems to me to be the giving up of self and selfish interest. Loving Him, I desire to love, and I can love, all things through Him, and I am not troubled or jealous because of His love toward all things. I am not jealous of the saints, or of the martyrs, or of the blessed, or even of the seraphim. The greater I picture to myself to be the love of God for His creatures, and the graces and gifts He bestows upon them, the less am I troubled by jealousy; the more I love Him, the nearer to me do I feel Him to be, and the more loving and gracious does He seem toward me. My brotherhood, my more than brotherhood, with all creatures, stands forth then in a most pleasing light. It seems to me that I am one with all things, and that all things are bound together in the bonds of love through God and in God.

Very different is it when my thoughts dwell upon Pepita, and on the love with which she inspires me. This love is a love full of hatred, that separates me from everything but myself. I love her for myself, altogether for myself, and myself altogether for her. Even devotion to her, even sacrifices made for her sake, partake of the nature of selfishness. To die for her would be to die of despair at not being able to possess her in any other manner—from the fear of not enjoying her love completely, except by dying and commingling with her in an eternal embrace.

By these reflections I endeavor to render the love of Pepita hateful to me. I invest my love in my imagination with something diabolical and fatal; but, as if I possessed a double soul, a double understanding, a double will, and a double imagination, in contradiction to this thought, other feelings rise up within me in its train, and I then deny what I have just affirmed, and insanely endeavor to reconcile the two loves. Would it not be possible, I ask myself, to fly from Pepita, and yet continue to love her, without ceasing therefore to consecrate myself with fervor to the love of God? For, as the love of God does not exclude love of country, love of humanity, love of learning, love of beauty in Nature and in Art, neither should it exclude another love, if it be spiritual and immaculate. I will make of her, I say to myself, a symbol, an allegory, an image of all that is good, of all that is beautiful. She shall be to me, as Beatrice was to Dante, the image and the symbol of country, of knowledge, and of beauty.

This intention suggests to me a horrible fancy, a monstrous thought. In order to make of Pepita this symbol, this vaporous and ethereal image, this sign and epitome of all that I can love under God, in God, and subordinate to God, I picture her to myself dead, as Beatrice was dead when Dante made her the subject of his song.

If I picture her to myself among the living, then I am unable to convert her into a pure idea; and if I convert her into a pure idea, I kill her in my thoughts.

Then I weep; I am filled with horror at my crime, and I draw near to her in spirit, and with the warmth of my heart I bring her back to life again; and I behold her, not errant, diaphanous, floating in shadowy outline among roseate clouds and celestial flowers, as the stern Ghibelline beheld his beloved in the upper sphere of Purgatory; but coherent, solid, clearly defined in the pure and serene air, like the masterpieces of Greek art, like Galatea already animated by the love of Pygmalion, and descending from her pedestal of marble, full of fire, exhaling love, rich in youth and beauty.

Then I exclaim in the depths of my perturbed heart: "My virtue faints! My God, do not Thou forsake me! Hasten to my help; show Thy countenance, and I shall be saved!"

Thus do I recover strength to resist temptation. Thus again does the hope spring to life within me, that I shall regain my former tranquillity when I shall have left this place.

The Devil longs with ardor to swallow up the pure waters of Jordan, by which are symbolized the persons who are consecrated to God. Hell conspires against them, and lets loose all her monsters upon them. St. Bonaventure says: "We should not wonder that these persons have sinned, but rather that they have not sinned."

Notwithstanding, I shall be able to resist and not sin. The Lord will protect me.

June 6th.

PEPITA'S nurse—now her housekeeper—is, as my father says, a good bag of wrinkles; she is talkative, gay, and skilful, as few are. She married the son of Master Cencias, and has inherited from the father what the son did not inherit—a wonderful facility for the mechanical arts; with this difference: that while Master Cencias could set the screw of a wine-press, or repair the wheels of a wagon, or make a plow, this daughter-in-law of his knows how to make sweetmeats, conserves of honey, and other dainties. The father-in-law practised the useful arts; the daughter-in-law those that have for their object pleasure, though only innocent, or at least lawful pleasure.

Antoñona—for such is her name—is permitted, or assumes, the greatest familiarity with all the gentry here. She goes in and out of every house as if it were her own. She uses the familiar "thou" to all young people of Pepita's age, or four or five years older; she calls them "child," and treats them as if she had nursed them at her breast.

She behaves toward me in this way; she comes to visit me, enters my room unannounced, has asked me several times already why I no longer go to see her mistress, and has told me that I am wrong in not going.

My father, who has no suspicion of the truth, accuses me of eccentricity; he calls me an owl, and he, too, is determined that I shall resume my visits to Pepita. Last night I could no longer resist his repeated importunities, and I went to her house very early, as my father was about to settle his accounts with the overseer.

Would to God I had not gone!

Pepita was alone. When our glances met, when we saluted each other, we both turned red. We shook hands with timidity and in silence.

I did not press her hand, nor did she press mine, but for a moment we held them clasped together.

In Pepita's glance, as she looked at me, there was nothing of love; there was only friendship, sympathy, and a profound sadness.

She had divined the whole of my inward struggle; she was persuaded that Divine love had triumphed in my soul—that my resolution not to love her was firm and invincible.

She did not venture to complain of me; she had no reason to complain of me; she knew that right was on my side. A sigh, scarcely perceptible, that escaped from her dewy, parted lips, revealed to me the depth of her sorrow.

Her hand still lay in mine; we were both silent. How was I to tell her that she was not destined for me, nor I for her; that we must part forever?

But though my lips refused to tell her this in words, I told it to her with my eyes; my severe glance confirmed her fears; it convinced her of the irrevocableness of my decision.

All at once her gaze was troubled; her lovely countenance, pale with a translucent pallor, was full of a touching expression of melancholy. She looked like Our Lady of Sorrows. Two tears rose slowly to her eyes, and began to steal down her cheeks.

I know not what passed within me, nor how to describe it, even if I knew.

I bent toward her to kiss away her tears and our lips met.

Rapture unspeakable, a faintness full of peril, invaded us both. She would have fallen, but that I supported her in my arms.

Heaven willed that we should at this moment hear the step and cough of the reverend vicar, who was approaching, and we instantly drew apart.

Recovering myself, and summoning all the strength of my will, I brought to an end this terrible scene, that had been enacted in silence, with these words, which I pronounced in low and tense accents:

"The first and the last!"

I made allusion to our profane kiss; but, as if my words had been an invocation, there rose before me the vision of the Apocalypse in all its terrible majesty. I beheld Him who is indeed the First and the Last, and with the two-edged sword that proceeded from His mouth He pierced my soul, full of evil, of wickedness, and of sin.

All that evening I passed in a species of frenzy, an inward delirium, that I know not how I was able to conceal.

I withdrew from Pepita's house very early.

The anguish of my soul was yet more poignant in solitude.

When I recalled that kiss and those words of farewell, I compared myself with the traitor Judas, who made use of a kiss to betray; and with the sanguinary and treacherous assassin Joab, who plunged the sharp steel into the bowels of Amasa while in the act of kissing him.

I had committed a double treason; I had been guilty of a double perfidy. I had sinned against God and against her.

I am an execrable wretch.

June 11th.

EVERYTHING may still be remedied.

Pepita will in time forget her love and the weakness of which we were guilty.

Since that night I have not returned to her house. Antoñono has not made her appearance in ours.

By dint of entreaties I have obtained a formal promise from my father that we shall leave here on the 25th, the day after St. John's day, which is here celebrated with splendid feasts, and on the eve of which there is a great vigil.

Absent from Pepita, I began to recover my serenity and to think that this first beginning of love was a trial of my virtue.

All these nights I have prayed, I have watched, I have performed many acts of penance.

The persistence of my prayers, the deep contrition of my soul, have found favor with the Lord, who has manifested to me His great mercy.

The Lord, in the words of the prophet, has sent fire to the stronghold of my spirit; He has illuminated my understanding, He has kindled my resolution, and He has given me guidance.

The working of the Divine love which animates the Supreme Will has had power, at times, without my deserving it, to lead me to that condition of prayerful contemplation in which the soul enjoys repose. I have cast out from the lower faculties of my soul every image—even her image; and I am persuaded, if pride does not deceive me, that, in perfect peace of mind and heart I have known and enjoyed the Supreme Good that dwells within the depths of the soul.

Compared with this good all else is worthless—compared with this beauty all else is deformity—compared with these heights all else is vile. Who would not forget and scorn every other love for the love of God?

Yes; the profane image of this woman shall depart finally and forever from my soul. I shall make of my prayers and of my penance a sharp scourge, and with it I will expel her therefrom, as Christ expelled the money-lenders from the Temple.

June 18th.

THIS is the last letter I shall write to you. On the 25th I shall leave this place without fail.

I shall soon have the happiness of embracing you. Near you I shall be stronger. You will infuse courage into me, and lend me the energy in which I am wanting.

A tempest of conflicting emotions is now raging in my soul. The disorder of my ideas may be known by the disorder of what I write.

Twice I returned to the house of Pepita. I was cold and stern. I was as I ought to have been, but how much did it not cost me!

My father told me yesterday that Pepita was indisposed, and would not receive.

The thought at once assailed me that the cause of her indisposition might be her ill-requited love.

Why did I return her glances of fire? Why did I basely deceive her? Why did I make her believe I loved her? Why did my vile lips seek hers with ardor, and communicate the ardor of an unholy love to hers?

But no; my sin shall not be followed, as its unavoidable consequence, by another sin!

What has been, has been, and can not be undone; but a repetition of it may be avoided—shall be avoided in future.

On the 25th, I repeat, I shall depart from here without fail.

The impudent Antoñona has just come to see me. I hid this letter from her, as if it were a crime to write to you.

Antoñona remained here only for a moment.

I arose, and remained standing while I spoke to her, that the visit might be a short one.

During this short visit she gave utterance to a thousand mad speeches, which disturbed me greatly. Finally, as she was going away, she exclaimed, in her half-gipsy jargon:

"You deceiver! You villain! My curse upon you! You have made the child sick, and now you are killing her by your desertion. May witches fly away with you, body and bones!"

Having said this, the fiendish woman gave me, in a coarse vulgar fashion, six or seven ferocious pinches below the shoulders, as if she would like to tear the skin from my back in strips, and then went away, looking daggers at me.

I do not complain. I deserve this brutal jest, granting it to be a jest. I deserve that fiends should tear my flesh with red-hot pincers.

Grant, my God, that Pepita may forget me! Let her, if it be necessary, love another, and be happy with him!

Can I ask more than this of Thee, oh, my God?

My father knows nothing, suspects nothing. It is better thus.

Farewell for a few days, till we see and embrace each other again.

How changed will you find me! How full of bitterness my heart! How soiled my purity! How bruised and wounded my soul!

PART II

PARALIPOMENA

HERE end the letters of Don Luis de Vargas. We should therefore be left in ignorance of the subsequent fortunes of these lovers, if one familiar with all the circumstances had not communicated the following particulars:

No one in the village found anything strange in the fact of Pepita's being indisposed, or thought, still less, of attributing her indisposition to a cause of which only we, Pepita herself, Don Luis, the reverend dean, and the discreet Antoñona, are thus far cognizant.

They might rather have wondered at the life of gaiety that Pepita had been leading for some time past, at the daily gatherings at her house, and the excursions into the country in which she had joined. That Pepita should return to her habitual seclusion was quite natural.

Her secret and deeply rooted love for Don Luis was hidden from the searching glances of Doña Casilda, of Currito, and of all the other personages of the village of whom mention is made in the letters of Don Luis. Still less could the public know of it. It never entered into the head of any one, no one imagined for a moment, that the theologian, the "saint," as they called Don Luis, could become the rival of his father, or could have succeeded where the redoubtable and powerful Don Pedro de Vargas had failed—in winning the heart of the graceful, coy, and reserved young widow.

Notwithstanding the familiarity of the ladies of the village with their servants, Pepita had allowed none of hers to suspect anything. Only the lynx-eyed Antoñona, whom nothing could escape, and more especially nothing that concerned her young mistress, had penetrated the mystery.

Antoñona did not conceal her discovery from Pepita, nor could Pepita deny the truth to the woman who had nursed her, who idolized her, and who, if she delighted in finding out and gossiping about all that took place in the village, being, as she was, a model scandal-monger, was yet, in all that related to her mistress, reticent and loyal as but few are.

In this manner Antoñona made herself the confidante of Pepita; and Pepita found great consolation in unburdening her heart to one who, though she might be coarse in the frankness with which she expressed her sentiments, was not so either in the sentiments or the ideas that she expressed.

In this may be found the explanation of Antoñona's visits to Don Luis, as well as of her words, and even of the ferocious and disrespectful pinches, given in so ill-chosen a spot, with which she bruised his flesh and wounded his dignity on the occasion of her last visit to him.

Not only had Pepita not desired Antoñona to carry messages to Don Luis, but she did not even know that she had gone to see him. Antoñona had taken the initiative, and had interfered in the matter simply because she herself had wanted to do so.

As has already been said, she had with wonderful perspicacity discovered the state of affairs between her mistress and Don Luis.

While Pepita herself was still scarcely conscious of the fact that she loved Don Luis, Antoñona already knew it. Scarcely had Pepita begun to cast on him those furtive glances, ardent and involuntary, which had wrought such havoc—glances which had been intercepted by none of those present when they were given—when Antoñona, who was not present, had already spoken of them to Pepita. And no sooner had those glances been returned, than Antoñona knew that also.

There was but little left, then, for the mistress to confide to a servant of so much penetration, and so skilled in divining what passed in the inmost recesses of her breast.

Five days after the date of Don Luis's last letter our narrative begins:

June 23

CHAPTER I

IT was eleven o'clock in the morning. Pepita was in an apartment on an upper floor, contiguous to her bedroom and dressing-room, where no one ever entered without being summoned, save Antoñona.

The furniture of this apartment was simple, but comfortable and in good taste. The curtains and the covering of the easy-chairs, the sofas, and the armchairs, were of a flowered cotton fabric. On a mahogany table were writing materials and papers, and in a bookcase, also of mahogany, were many books of devotion and history. The walls were adorned with pictures- -engravings of religious subjects, but with this peculiarity in their selection—unheard-of, extraordinary, almost incredible in an Andalusian village—that, instead of being bad French lithographs, they were engravings in the best style of Spanish art, as the *Spasimo di Sicilia* of Raffael; the *St. Ildefonso* and the *Virgin,* the *Conception,* the *St. Bernard,* and the two *Lunettes* of Murillo.

On an antique oak table, supported by fluted columns, was a small writing-desk, or escritoire, inlaid with mother-of-pearl, ivory, and brass, and containing a great many little drawers, in which Pepita kept bills and other papers. On this table were also two porcelain vases filled with flowers; and, finally, hanging against the walls were several flower-pots of Seville Carthusian ware, containing ivy, geraniums, and other plants and three gilded cages, in which were canaries and larks.

This apartment was the retreat of Pepita, where no one entered during the daytime except the doctor and the reverend vicar; and in the evening only the overseer, to settle accounts. This apartment was called the study, and served the purpose of one.

Pepita was seated, half reclining on a sofa, before which stood a small table with some books upon it.

She had just risen, and was attired in a light summer

wrapper. Her blond hair, not yet arranged, looked even more beautiful in its disorder. Her countenance, somewhat pale, and showing dark circles under the eyes, still preserved its fresh and youthful aspect, and looked more beautiful than ever under the influence of the trouble which robbed it of color.

Pepita showed signs of impatience; she was expecting some one.

At last the person she was awaiting, who proved to be the reverend vicar, arrived, and entered without announcement.

After the usual salutations the vicar settled himself comfortably in an easy-chair, and the conversation thus began:

"I am very glad, my child, that you sent for me; but, even without your doing so, I was just coming to see you. How pale you are! What is it that ails you? Have you anything of importance to tell me?"

Pepita began her answer to this series of affectionate inquiries with a deep sigh; she then said:

"Do you not divine my malady? Have you not discovered the cause of my suffering?"

The vicar made a gesture of denial, and looked at Pepita with something like terror in his gaze; for he knew nothing of all that had taken place, and was struck by the vehemence with which she spoke.

Pepita continued:

"I ought not to have sent for you, father. I should have gone to the church myself instead, to speak with you in the confessional, and there confess my sins. But, unhappily, far from repenting of them, my heart has hardened itself in wickedness. I have neither the courage nor the desire to speak to the confessor, but only to the friend."

"What are you saying about sins and hardness of heart? Have you taken leave of your senses? What sins can you have committed, you who are so good?"

"No, father, I am wicked. I have been deceiving you; I have been deceiving myself; I have tried to deceive God."

"Come, come, calm yourself; speak with moderation and common sense, and don't talk foolishly."

"And how shall I avoid talking foolishly when the spirit of evil possesses me?"

"Holy Virgin! Don't talk nonsense, child; the demons most to be feared who take possession of the soul are three, and none of them, I am certain, can have dared to enter into yours. One is Leviathan, or the spirit of Pride; the other is Mammon, or the spirit of Avarice; and the other is Asmodeus, or the spirit of Unholy Love."

"Well, I am the victim of all three; all three hold dominion over me."

"This is dreadful! Calm yourself, I repeat. The real trouble with you is that you are delirious."

"Would to God it were so! The contrary, unhappily for me, is the case. I am avaricious, because I possess riches, and do not perform the works of charity I ought to perform; I am proud, because I scorn the addresses of my many suitors, not through virtue, not through modesty, but because I thought them unworthy of my love. God has punished me; God has permitted the third enemy you have named to take possession of me."

"How is this, child? What diabolical notion has entered into your mind! Have you by chance fallen in love? And, if you have, what harm is there in that? Are you not free? Get married, then, and stop talking nonsense. I am certain it is my friend Don Pedro de Vargas who has wrought the miracle. That same Don Pedro is the very Devil! I confess I am surprised. I did not think matters had gone quite so far as that already."

"But it is not Don Pedro de Vargas that I am in love with."

"And with whom, then?"

Pepita rose from her seat, went to the door, opened it, looked to see if any one was listening outside, drew near to the reverend vicar, and with signs of the deepest distress, in a trembling voice and with tears in her eyes, said, almost in the ear of the good old man:

"I am hopelessly in love with his son."

"With whose son?" cried the reverend vicar, who could not yet bring himself to believe what he had heard.

"With whose son should it be? I am hopelessly, desperately in love with Don Luis."

Consternation and dolorous surprise were depicted on the countenance of the kind and simple priest. There was a moment's pause; the vicar then said:

"But this is love without hope; a love not to be thought of. Don Luis will never love you."

A joyful light sparkled through the tears that clouded Pepita's beautiful eyes: her rosy, dewy lips, contracted by sorrow, parted in a smile, disclosing to view her pearly teeth.

"He loves me," said Pepita, with a faint and ill-concealed accent of satisfaction and triumph, which rose exultant over her sorrow and her scruples of conscience.

The consternation and astonishment of the reverend vicar here reached their highest pitch. If the saint of his most fervent devotions had been suddenly cast down from the altar before him, and had fallen, broken into a thousand fragments, at his feet, the reverend vicar could not have felt greater consternation. He still looked at Pepita with incredulity, as if doubting whether what she had said were true, or only a delusion of feminine vanity, so firmly did he believe in the holiness and mysticism of Don Luis.

"He loves me," Pepita repeated, in answer to his incredulous glance.

"Women are worse than the very Devil!" said the vicar. "You would set a snare for old Nick himself."

"Did I not tell you already that I was very wicked?"

"Come, come! calm yourself. The mercy of God is infinite. Tell me all that has happened."

"What should have happened? That he is dear to me; that I love him; that I adore him; that he loves me, too, although he strives to conquer his love, and in the end may succeed in doing so; and that you, without knowing it, are very much to blame for it all!"

"Well, this is too much! What do you mean by saying I am very much to blame?"

"With the extreme goodness which is characteristic of you, you have done nothing but praise Don Luis to me; and I am sure that you have pronounced still greater eulogies on me to him, although very much less deserved. What is the natural consequence? Am I of bronze? Have I not the passions of youth?"

"You are more than right; I am a dolt. I have contributed, in great part, to this work of Lucifer."

The reverend vicar was so truly good, and so full of humility, that, while pronouncing the preceding words, he showed as much confusion and remorse as if he were the culprit and Pepita the judge.

Pepita, conscious of her injustice and want of generosity in thus making the reverend vicar the accomplice, and scarcely less than the chief author of her fault, spoke to him thus:

"Don't torment yourself, father; for God's sake, don't torment yourself! You see now how perverse I am. I commit the greatest sins, and I want to throw the responsibility of them on the best and the most virtuous of men. It is not the praises you have recited to me of Don Luis that have been my ruin, but my own eyes, and my want of circumspection. Even though you had never spoken to me of the good qualities of Don Luis, I should still have discovered them all by hearing him speak; for after all, I am not so ignorant, nor so great a fool. And in any case, I myself have seen the grace of his person, the natural and untaught elegance of his manners, his eyes full of fire and intelligence—his whole self, in a word, which seems to me altogether amiable and desirable. Your eulogies of him have indeed pleased my vanity, but they did not awaken my inclinations. Your praises charmed me because they coincided with my own opinion, and were like the flattering echo—deadened, indeed, and faint—of my thoughts. The most eloquent encomium you have pronounced in my hearing on Don Luis was far from being equal to the encomiums that I, at each moment, at each instant, silently pronounced upon him in my own soul."

"Don't excite yourself, child," interrupted the reverend vicar.

Pepita continued, with still greater exaltation:

"But what a difference between your encomiums and my thoughts! For you, Don Luis was the exemplary model of the priest, the missionary, the apostle; now preaching the Gospel in distant lands, now endeavoring in Spain to elevate Christianity, so degraded in our day through the impiety of some, and the want of virtue, of charity, and of knowledge of others. I, on the contrary, pictured him to myself, handsome, loving, forgetting God for me, consecrating his life to me, giving me his soul, becoming my stay, my support, my sweet companion. I longed to commit a sacrilegious theft: I dreamed of stealing him from God and from His temple, like a thief, the enemy of Heaven, who robs the sacred monstrance of its most precious jewel. To commit such a theft I have put off the mourning garments of the widow and orphan, and have decked myself with profane adornments; I have abandoned my seclusion; I have sought company and gathered it around me; I have tried to make myself look beautiful; I have cared for every part of this miserable body, that must one day be lowered into the grave and be converted into dust, with an unholy devotion; and finally, I have looked at Don Luis with provoking glances, and on shaking hands with him I have sought to transmit from my veins to his the inextinguishable fire that is consuming me."

"Alas! my child, what grief it gives me to hear this! Who could have imagined it?" said the vicar.

"But there is still more," resumed Pepita. "I succeeded in making Don Luis love me. He declared it to me with his eyes. Yes, his love is as profound, as ardent as mine. His virtues, his aspirations toward heavenly things, his manly energy have all urged him to conquer this insensate passion. I sought to prevent this. Once, at the end of many days during which he had stayed away, he came to see me, and found me alone. When he gave me his hand, I wept; I could not speak; but hell inspired me with an accursed, mute eloquence that told him of my grief that he had scorned me, that he did not return my love, that he preferred another love—a love without a stain—to mine. Then he was unable to resist the temptation, and he approached his lips to my face to kiss away my tears. Our lips met. If God had not willed your approach at that moment, what would have become of me?"

"How shameful! My child, how shameful!" said the reverend vicar.

Pepita covered her face with both hands and began to sob like a Magdalen. Her hands were in truth beautiful, more beautiful even than Don Luis had described them to be in his letters: their whiteness, their pure transparency, the tapering form of the fingers, the roseate hue, the polish and the brilliancy of the pearl-like nails, all were such as might turn the head of any man.

The virtuous vicar, notwithstanding his eighty years, could understand the fall, or rather, the slip, of Don Luis.

"Child!" he exclaimed, "don't cry so! It breaks my heart to see you. Calm yourself; Don Luis has no doubt repented of his sin; do you repent likewise, and nothing more need be said. God will pardon you both, and make a couple of saints of you. Since Don Luis is going away the day after to-morrow, it is a sure sign that virtue has triumphed in him, and that he flees from you, as he should, that he may do penance for his sin, fulfil his vow, and return to his vocation."

"That is all very well," replied Pepita; "fulfil his vow, return to his vocation, after giving me my death-wound! Why did he love me, why did he encourage me, why did he deceive me? His kiss was a brand; it was as a hot iron with which he marked me and stamped me as his slave. Now that I am marked and enslaved, he abandons and betrays and destroys me. A good beginning to give to his missions, his preachings, and Gospel triumphs! It shall not be! By Heaven, it shall not be!"

This outbreak of anger and scorned love confounded the reverend vicar.

Pepita had risen. Her attitude, her gesture, had something in them of tragic animation. Her eyes gleamed like daggers; they shone like two suns. The vicar was silent, and regarded her almost with terror. She paced the apartment with hasty steps. She did not now seem like a timid gazel, but like an angry lioness.

"What!" she said, once more facing the vicar, "has he nothing to do but laugh at me, tear my heart to pieces, humiliate it, trample it under foot, after having cheated me out of it? He shall remember me! He shall pay me for this! If he is so holy, if he is so virtuous, why did he with his glance promise me everything? If he loves God so much, why does he seek to hurt one of God's poor creatures? Is this charity? Is this religion? No; it is pitiless selfishness."

Pepita's anger could not last long. After she had spoken

the last words, it turned to dejection. She sank into a chair, weeping more bitterly than ever, and abandoning herself to real anguish.

The vicar's heart was touched with pity; but he recovered himself on seeing that the enemy gave signs of yielding.

"Pepita, child," he said, "be reasonable; don't torment yourself in this way. Console yourself with the thought that it was not without a hard struggle he was able to conquer himself; that he has not deceived you; that he loves you with his whole soul, but that God and his duty come first. This life is short, and soon passes. In heaven you will be reunited, and will love each other as the angels love. God will accept your sacrifice; he will reward you, and repay you with interest. Even your self-love ought to be satisfied. How great must be your merit, when you have caused a man like Don Luis to waver in his resolution, and even to sin! How deep must be the wound you have made in his heart! Let this suffice you. Be generous, be courageous! Be his rival in firmness. Let him depart; cast out from your heart the fire of impure love; love him as your neighbor, for the love of God. Guard his image in your memory, but as that of the creature, reserving to the Creator the noblest part of your soul. I know not what I am saying to you, my child, for I am very much troubled; but you have a great deal of intelligence and a great deal of common sense, and you will understand what I mean. Besides, there are powerful worldly reasons against this absurd love, even if the vocation and the vow of Don Luis were not opposed to it. His father is your suitor. He aspires to your hand, even though you do not love him. Does it look well that the son should turn out now to be the rival of his father? Will not the father be displeased with the son for loving you? See how dreadful all this is, and control yourself, for the sake of Jesus and His blessed Mother!"

"How easy it is to give advice!" returned Pepita, becoming a little calmer. "How hard for me to follow it, when there is a fierce and unchained tempest, as it were, raging in my soul! I am afraid I shall go mad!"

"The advice I give you is for your own good. Let Don Luis depart. Absence is a great remedy for the malady of love. In giving himself up to his studies, and consecrating himself to the service of the altar, he will be cured of his passion. When he is far away you will recover your serenity by degrees, and will preserve in your memory only a grateful and melancholy recollection of him that will do you no harm. It will be like a beautiful poem, whose music will harmonize your existence. Even if all your desires could be fulfilled, earthly love lasts, after all, but a short time. The delight the imagination anticipates in its enjoyment—what is it in comparison with the bitter dregs. How much better is it that your love, hardly yet contaminated, hardly despoiled of its purity, should be dissipated, and exhale itself now, rising up to heaven like a cloud of incense, than that, after it is once satisfied, it should perish through satiety! Have the courage to put away from your lips the cup while you have hardly tasted of its contents. Make a libation of them and an offering to the Divine Redeemer. He will give you, in exchange, the draft He offered to the Samaritan—a draft that does not satiate, that quenches the thirst, and that gives eternal life!"

"How good you are, father! Your holy words lend me courage. I will control myself—I will conquer myself. It would be shameful—would it not?—that Don Luis should be able to control and conquer himself, and that I should not be able to do so? Let him depart. He is going away the day after to-morrow. Let him go, with God's blessing. See his card. He was here, with his father, to take leave of me, and I would not receive him. I will never see him again. I did not even want to preserve the poetical remembrance of him of which you speak. This love has been a nightmare; I will cast it way from me."

"Good—very good! It is thus that I want to see you—energetic, courageous."

"Ah, father, God has cast down my pride with this blow! I was insolent in my arrogance, and the scorn of this man was necessary to my self-abasement. Could I be more humbled or resigned than I am now? Don Luis is right—I am not worthy of him. However great the efforts I might make, I could not succeed in elevating myself to him and comprehending him, in putting my spirit into perfect communication with his. I am a rude country girl unlearned, uncultured;

and he—there is no science he does not understand, no secret of which he is ignorant, no region of the intellectual world, however exalted, to which he may not soar. Thither on the wings of his genius does he mount; and me he leaves behind in this lower sphere—poor, ignorant woman that I am—incapable of following him, even in my hopes or with my aspirations!"

"But, Pepita, for Heaven's sake, don't say such things, or think them! Don Luis does not scorn you because you are ignorant, or because you are incapable of comprehending him, or for any other of those absurd reasons that you are stringing together. He goes away because he must fulfil his obligation toward God; and you should rejoice that he is going away, for you will then get over your love for him, and God will reward you for the sacrifice you make."

Pepita, who had left off crying, and had dried her tears with her handkerchief, answered quietly:

"Very well, father. I shall be very glad of it; I am almost glad now that he is going away. I long for to-morrow to pass, and for the time to come when Antoñona shall say to me when I awake, 'Don Luis is gone.' You shall see then how peace and serenity will spring up again in my heart."

"God grant it may be so!" said the reverend vicar; and, convinced that he had wrought a miracle, and almost cured Pepita's malady, he took leave of her and went home, unable to repress a certain feeling of vanity at the thought of the influence he had exercised over the noble spirit of this charming woman.

CHAPTER II

PEPITA, who had risen as the reverend vicar was about to take his leave, after she had closed the door, stood for a moment motionless in the middle of the room—her gaze fixed on space, her eyes tearless. A poet or an artist, seeing her thus, would have been reminded of Ariadne, as Catullus describes her, after Theseus has abandoned her on the island of Naxos. All at once, as if she had but just succeeded in untying the knot of a cord that was strangling her, Pepita broke into heartrending sobs, let loose a torrent of tears, and threw herself down on the tiled floor of her apartment. There, her face buried in her hands, her hair loose, her dress disordered, she continued to sigh and moan.

She might have remained thus for an indefinite time if Antoñona had not come to her. Antoñona had heard her sobs from without, and hurried to her apartment. When she saw her mistress extended on the floor, Antoñona gave way to a thousand extravagant expressions of fury.

"Here's a pretty sight!" she cried; "that sneak, that blackguard, that old fool, what a way he has to console his friends! I shouldn't wonder if he has committed some piece of barbarity—given a couple of kicks to this poor child, perhaps; and now I suppose he has gone back to the church to get everything ready to sing the funeral chant, and sprinkle her with hyssop, and bury her out of sight without more ado."

Antoñona was about forty, and a hard worker—energetic, and stronger than many a laborer. She often lifted up, with scarcely more than the strength of her hand, a skin of oil or of wine weighing nearly ninety pounds, and placed it on the back of a mule, or carried a bag of wheat up to the garret where the grain was kept. Although Pepita was not a feather, Antoñona now lifted her up in her arms from the floor as if she had been one, and placed her carefully on the sofa, as though she were some delicate and precious piece of porcelain that she feared to break.

"What is the meaning of all this?" asked Antoñona. "I wager anything that drone of a vicar has been preaching you a sermon as bitter as aloes, and has left you now with your heart torn to pieces with grief."

Pepita continued to weep and sob without answering.

"Come, leave off crying, and tell me what is the matter. What has the vicar said to you?"

"He said nothing that could offend me," finally answered Pepita.

Then, seeing that Antoñona was waiting anxiously to hear her speak, and feeling the need of unburdening herself to some one who could sympathize more fully with her, and with more human feeling, Pepita spoke as follows:

"The reverend vicar has admonished me gently to repent of my sins; to allow Don Luis to go away; to rejoice at his departure; to forget him. I have said yes to everything; I have promised him to rejoice at Don Luis's departure; I have tried to forget him, and even to hate him. But, look you, Antoñona, I can not; it is an undertaking superior to my strength. While the vicar was here I thought I had strength for everything; but no sooner had he gone than, as if God had let go His hold of me, I lost my courage, and fell, crushed with sorrow, on the floor. I had dreamed of a happy life at the side of the man I love; I already saw myself elevated to him by the miraculous power of love—my poor mind in perfect communion with his sublime intellect, my will one with his, both thinking the same thought, our hearts beating in unison. And now God has taken him away from me, and I am left alone, without hope or consolation. Is this not frightful? The arguments of the reverend vicar are just and full of wisdom; for the time, they convinced me. But he has gone away, and all those arguments now seem to me worthless—a tissue of words, lies, entanglements, and sophistries. I love Don Luis, and this argument is more powerful than all other arguments put together. And if he loves me in return, why does he not leave everything and come to me, break the vows he has taken, and renounce the obligations he has contracted? I did not know what love was; now I know—there is nothing stronger on earth or in heaven. What would I not do for Don Luis? And he—he does nothing for me! Perhaps he does not love me. No; Don Luis does not love me. I have deceived myself; I was blinded by vanity. If Don Luis loved me, he would sacrifice his plans, his vows, his fame, his aspirations to be a saint and a light of the Church, he would sacrifice all to me. God forgive me, what I am about to say is horrible, but I feel it here in the depths of my heart, it burns here in my fevered brow: for him I would give even the salvation of my soul!"

"Holy Virgin!" exclaimed Antoñona.

"It is true; may our blessed Lady of Sorrows pardon me—I am mad—I know not what I say, I blaspheme!"

"Yes, child; you are talking indeed a little naughtily. Heaven help us! To think how this coxcomb of a theologian has turned your head! Well, if I were in your place, I would not take Heaven to task, which is in nowise to blame, but the jackanapes of a collegian, and I would have it out with him, or never again call myself Pepita Jiménez. I should like to go hunt him up, and bring him here to you by the ear, and make him beg your pardon and kiss your feet on his knees."

"No, Antoñona; I see that my madness is contagious, and that you are raving too. There is, in fact, nothing left for me to do but what the reverend vicar advises. And I will do it, even though it should cost me my life. If I die for him, he will then love me; he will cherish my image in his memory, my love in his heart; and God, who is so good, will permit me to see him again in Heaven with the eyes of the soul, and will let our spirits mingle together and love each other there."

Antoñona, although of a rugged nature, and not at all sentimental, on hearing these words felt the tears start to her eyes.

"Good gracious, child!" she said; "do you want to make me take out my handkerchief and begin to bellow like a calf? Calm yourself, and don't talk about dying, even in jest. I can see that your nerves are very much excited. Sha'n't I bring you a cup of fine flower tea?"

"No, thanks; leave me—you see how calm I am now."

"I shall close the window, then, to see if you can sleep. How should you feel well when you have not slept for days? The devil take that same Don Luis, with his fancy for making himself a priest! A nice price you are paying for it!"

Pepita had closed her eyes; she was calm and silent, weary now of her colloquy with Antoñona.

The latter, either thinking she was asleep, or hoping her to be so, bent over Pepita, imprinted a kiss softly and slowly on her white forehead, smoothed out the folds of her dress, arranged the windows so as to leave the room half dark, and went out on tiptoe, closing the door behind her, without making the slightest noise.

CHAPTER III

WHILE these things were taking place at the house of Pepita, Don Luis de Vargas was neither happier nor more tranquil in his.

His father, who scarcely let a day pass without riding out into the country, had to-day wished to take Don Luis with him; but he had excused himself, on the pretext of a headache, and Don Pedro had gone without him. Don Luis had spent the whole morning alone, delivered up to his melancholy thoughts, and continuing firm as a rock in his resolution of blotting from his soul the image of Pepita, and of consecrating himself wholly to God.

Let it not be supposed, however, that he did not love the young widow. We have already, in his letters, seen the proof of the vehemence of his passion for her, but he continued his efforts to curb it by means of the devout sentiments and elevated reflections of which he has given us in his letters so extended a specimen, and of which we may here omit a repetition, in order not to appear prolix.

Perhaps, if we examine into this matter closely, we shall find that the reasons which militated in the breast of Don Luis against his love for Pepita were not only his vow to himself—which, though unconfirmed, was binding in his eyes—or the love of God, or respect for his father, whose rival he did not wish to be; or, finally, the vocation which he felt himself to have for the priesthood. There were other reasons of a more doubtful character than these.

Don Luis was stubborn; he was obstinate; he had that quality of soul which, well directed, constitutes what is called firmness of character, and there was nothing that lowered him more in his own eyes than to feel himself obliged to change his opinions or his conduct. The purpose of his life—a purpose which he had declared and maintained on all occasions—his moral ideal, in a word, was that of an aspirant to holiness, of a man consecrated to God, of one imbued with the sublimest religious teachings. All this could not fall to earth, as it would fall if he allowed himself to be carried away by his love for Pepita, without great discredit. Although the price, indeed, was in this case incomparably higher, yet Don Luis felt that, should he yield to his passion, he would be following the example of Esau, selling his birthright, and bringing opprobrium on his name.

Men, as a rule, allow themselves to be the playthings of circumstances; they let themselves be carried along by the current of events, instead of devoting all their energies to one single aim. We do not choose our part in life, but accept and play the part allotted us, that which blind fortune assigns to us. The profession, the political faith, the entire life of many men, depend on chance circumstances, on what is fortuitous, on the caprice and the unexpected turns of fate.

Against all this the pride of Don Luis vigorously rebelled. What would be thought of him, and, above all, what would he think of himself, if the ideal of his life, the new man that he had created in his soul, if all his plans of virtue, of honor, and even of holy ambition, should vanish in an instant, should melt away in the warmth of a glance, at the fugitive flame of a pair of beautiful eyes, as the hoar-frost melts in the yet mild ray of the morning sun?

These and other egotistic reasons militated against the young widow, side by side with others more weighty and legitimate, but every argument clothed itself in the same religious garb, so that Don Luis himself was unable to recognize and distinguish between them, believing to be the love of God not only what was in truth the love of God, but also self-love. He recalled to mind, for instance, the examples of many saints who had resisted greater temptations than his, and he did not wish to be less than they. And he recalled to mind, above all, the notable firmness of St. Chrysostom, who was able to disregard the caresses of a good and tender mother, and her tears and gentle entreaties, and all the eloquent and touching words she spoke to him, in the very room where he was born, to the end that he might not abandon her and become a priest. And after reflecting on this, Don Luis could not tolerate in himself the weakness of being unable to reject the entreaties of a woman who was a stranger to him, whom he had known for so short a time, and of still wavering between his duty and the attractions of one who perhaps, after all, did not really love him, but was only a coquette.

Don Luis then reflected on the supreme position of the sacerdotal dignity to which he was called, regarding it in his thoughts as superior to all the dignities and unsatisfying honors of the world, since it was founded neither by any mortal man, nor by the caprice of the variable and servile populace, nor by the irruption or invasion of barbarians, nor by the violence of rebellious armies urged on by greed, nor by angel nor archangel, nor by any created power; but by the Paraclete Himself. How for a motive so unworthy, for a mere woman, for a tear or two, feigned perhaps, scorn that august dignity, that authority which was not conceded by God even to the archangels nearest to His throne? How should he descend to be one of the obscure people, become one of the flock—he, who had dreamed of being the shepherd, tying and untying on earth what God should tie and untie in Heaven, pardoning sins, regenerating the people by water and by the spirit, teaching them in the name of an infallible authority, pronouncing judgments that should be ratified and confirmed by the Lord of the heaven—he, the instructor and the minister in tremendous mysteries inscrutable by human reason, calling down from Heaven, not, like Elias, the flame that consumes the victim, but the Holy Spirit, the Word made flesh, the river of grace that purifies hearts and makes them clean like unalloyed gold?

When Don Luis let his mind dwell on these thoughts his spirit took wings and soared up above the clouds into the empyrean, and poor Pepita Jiménez remained below, far away, and hardly within sight.

But the wings of his imagination soon drooped, and the spirit of Don Luis touched earth again. Again he saw Pepita, so graceful, so young, so ingenuous, and so enamored. Pepita combated in his soul his firmest and most deep-seated resolutions, and Don Luis feared that in the end she would put them all to flight.

In this way was Don Luis allowing himself to be tormented by opposing thoughts, that make war on each other, when Currito, without asking leave or license, entered his room.

Currito, who had held his cousin in very slight esteem so long as he was only a student of theology, now regarded him with wonder and veneration, looking upon him, from the moment when he had seen him manage Lucero so skilfully, as something more than human.

To know theology and not know how to ride, had discredited Don Luis in the eyes of Currito; but when Currito saw that, in addition to his learning, and to all those other matters of which he himself knew nothing, although he supposed them to be difficult and perplexing, Don Luis could also keep his seat so admirably on the back of a fiery horse, his veneration and his affection for his cousin knew no bounds. Currito was an idler, a good-for-nothing, a very block of wood; but he had an affectionate and loyal heart.

To Don Luis, who was the idol of Currito, happened what happens with all superior natures when inferior persons take a liking to them. Don Luis permitted himself to be loved—that is to say, he was governed despotically—by Currito in matters of little importance. And as for men like Don Luis there are hardly any matters of importance in common daily life, the result was that Don Luis was led about by Currito like a little dog.

"I have come for you," the latter said, "to take you with me to the clubhouse, which is full of people to-day, and unusually gay. What is the use of sitting here alone gazing into vacancy, as if you were waiting to catch flies?"

Don Luis, without offering any resistance, took his hat and cane, as though the words were a command, and saying, "Let us go wherever you wish," followed Currito, who led the way, very well pleased with the influence he exercised over his cousin.

The clubhouse was full of people, owing to the festivities of the morrow, which was St. John's day. Besides the gentry of the village many strangers were there, who had come in from the neighboring villages to be present at the fair and the vigil in the evening.

The principal point of reunion was the courtyard, which was paved with marble. In its centre played a fountain, which was adorned with flower pots containing roses, pinks, sweet basil, and other flowers. Around this courtyard ran a corridor or gallery supported by marble columns, in which, as well as in the various saloons that opened into it, were tables for *ombre,* others with newspapers lying on them, others where coffee and other refreshments were served, and finally, lounges, benches, and several easy-chairs. The walls were like snow, from frequent whitening; nor were pictures wanting for their adornment. There were French colored lithographs, a minute explanation of the subject of each being written, both in French and in Spanish below. Some of them represented scenes in the life of Napoleon, from Toulon to St. Helena; others, the adventures of Matilda and Malek-Adel; others, incidents in love and war, in the lives of the Templar, Rebecca, Lady Rowena, and Ivanhoe; and others, the gallantries, the intrigues, the lapses and the conversions of Louis XIV. and Mademoiselle de la Vallière.

Currito took Don Luis, and Don Luis allowed himself to be taken, to the saloon where were gathered the cream of the fashion, the dandies and *cocodés* of the village and of the surrounding district. Prominent among these was the Count of Genazahar, of the neighboring city of —. The Count was an illustrious and much admired personage. He had made visits of great length to Madrid and Seville, and, whether as a country dandy or as a young nobleman, was always attired by the most fashionable tailors.

The Count of Genazahar was a little past thirty. He was good-looking, and he knew it; and could boast of his prowess in peace and in war, in duels and in love-making. The Count, however—and this notwithstanding the fact that he had been one of the most persistent suitors of Pepita—had received the sugar-coated pill of refusal that she was accustomed to bestow on those who paid their addresses to her and aspired to her hand.

The wound inflicted on his pride by this rejection had never quite healed. Love had turned into hatred, and the Count lost no occasion of giving utterance to his feelings, holding Pepita up on such occasions to ridicule as a prude.

The Count was engaged in this agreeable exercise when, by an evil chance, Don Luis and Currito approached and joined the crowd that was listening to the odd species of panegyric, which opened to receive them. Don Luis, as if the Devil himself had had the arrangement of the matter, found himself face to face with the Count, who was speaking as follows:

"She's a cunning one, this same Pepita Jiménez, with more fancies and whims than the Princess Micomicona. She wants to make us forget that she was born in poverty, and lived in poverty until she married that accursed usurer, Don Gumersindo, and took possession of his dollars. The only good action this same widow has performed in her life was to conspire with Satan to send the rogue quickly to hell, and free the earth from such a contamination and plague. Pepita now has a hobby for virtue and for chastity. All that may be very well; but how do we know that she has not a secret intrigue with some plow-boy, and is not deceiving the world as if she were Queen Artemisia herself?"

People of quiet tastes, who seldom take part in reunions of men only, may perhaps be scandalized by this language. It may appear to them indecent and brutal even to the point of incredibility; but those who know the world will confess that language like this is very generally employed in it, and that the most amiable and agreeable women, the most honorable matrons, if they chance to have an enemy, or even if they have none, are often made the subjects of accusations no less infamous and vile than those made by the Count against Pepita; for scandal, or, to speak more accurately, disrespect and insult are often indulged in for the purpose of showing wit and effrontery.

Don Luis had from childhood been accustomed to the consideration and respect of those around him, first, of the servants and dependents of his father, who gratified him in all his wishes, and then of every one in the seminary, not only because he was a nephew of the dean, but also on account of his own merits, and when he heard the insolent Count thus drag in the dust the name of the woman he loved, he felt as if a thunderbolt had fallen at his feet.

But how undertake her defense? He knew, indeed, that although he was neither husband, brother, nor other relative of Pepita's he might yet come forward in her defense as a man of honor; but he saw what scandal this would give rise to, since, far from saying a word in her favor, all the other persons present joined in applauding the wit of the Count. He, already the minister, almost, of a God of peace, could not be the one to give the lie to this ruffian, and thus expose himself to the risk of a quarrel.

Don Luis was on the point of departing in silence; but his heart would not consent to this, and striving to clothe himself with an authority which was justified neither by his years nor by his countenance, where the beard had scarcely begun to make its appearance, nor by his presence in that place, he began to speak with earnest eloquence in denunciation of all slanderers, and to reproach the Count, with the freedom of a Christian and in severe accents, with the vileness of his conduct.

This was to preach in the desert, or worse. The Count answered his homily with gibes and jests; the bystanders, among whom were many strangers, took the part of the jester, notwithstanding the fact that Don Luis was the son of the squire. Even Currito, who was of no account whatever, and who was, besides, a coward, although he did not laugh, yet made no effort to take the part of his friend, and the latter was obliged to withdraw, disturbed and humiliated by the ridicule he had drawn on himself.

CHAPTER IV

"THIS flower only was wanting to complete the nosegay," muttered poor Don Luis between his teeth when he had reached his house and shut himself up in his room, vexed and ill at ease because of the jeers of which he had been the butt. He exaggerated them to himself; they seemed unendurable. He threw himself into a chair, depressed and disheartened, and a thousand contradictory ideas assailed his mind.

The blood of his father, which boiled in his veins, incited him to anger, and urged him to throw aside the clerical garb, as he had in the beginning been advised to do in the village, and then give the Count his deserts; but the whole future he had planned for himself would be thus at a blow destroyed. He pictured to himself the dean disowning him; and even the Pope, who had already sent the pontifical dispensation permitting him to be ordained before the required age, and the bishop of the diocese, who had based the petition for the dispensation on his approved virtue and learning and on the firmness of his vocation—all appeared before him now to reproach him.

Then those other arguments, cited by his father, of which the apostle St. James, the bishops of the Middle Ages, and St. Ignatius Loyola had made use, occurred to his mind, and now seemed less preposterous than before, and he almost repented of not having put them into practise.

He then recalled the custom of a distinguished philosopher of Persia, of our own day, mentioned in a book recently written on that country—a custom which consisted in punishing with harsh words his hearers and pupils when they laughed at his teachings or could not understand them, and if this did not suffice, in descending from his chair, sabre in hand, and giving them all a beating. This method, as it appears, had proved efficacious, especially in controversy; although it had chanced that the said philosopher, coming across an opponent of the same way of thinking as himself, had received a severe wound in the face from him.

Don Luis, in the midst of his mortification and ill-humor, could not help laughing at the absurdity of this recollection. He thought philosophers were not wanting in Spain who would willingly adopt the Persian method, and if he himself did not put it into practise, it was certainly not through fear of the wounds he might receive, but through considerations of greater weight.

At last better thoughts returned and somewhat comforted his soul.

"I did very wrong in preaching there," he said to himself; "I should have remained silent. Our Lord Jesus Christ has said, 'Give not that which is holy to dogs, neither cast ye your pearls before swine, lest they trample them under their feet, and turn again and rend you.' "

"But, no; why should I complain? Why should I return evil for evil? Why should I allow myself to be vanquished by anger? Many holy fathers have said, 'Anger in a priest is even worse than lasciviousness.' The anger of priests has caused many tears to be shed, and has been the cause of terrible evils."

"It was anger—the terrible counselor—that at times persuaded them that it was necessary for the people to shed blood at the Divine command, and that brought before their sanguinary eyes the vision of Isaiah; they have then seen, and caused their fanatic followers to see, the meek Lamb converted into an inexorable avenger, descending from the summit of Edom, proud in the multitude of his strength, trampling the nations under foot, as the treader tramples the grapes in the wine-press, their garments raised, and covered with blood to the thighs. Ah, no. My God! I am about to become Thy minister. Thou art the God of peace, and my first duty should be meekness. Thou makest the sun to shine on the just and the unjust, and pourest down upon all alike the fertilizing rain of inexhaustible goodness. Thou art our Father, who dwellest in the heavens, and we should be perfect, even as Thou art perfect, pardoning those who have offended us, and asking Thee to pardon them, because they know not what they do. I should recall to mind the beatitudes of the Scripture: Blessed are ye when they revile you and persecute you, and say all manner of evil things against you. The minister of God, or he who is about to become His minister, must be humble, peaceable, lowly of heart; not like the oak that lifts itself up proudly until the thunderbolt strike it, but like the fragrant herbs of the woods and the modest flowers of the fields, that give sweeter and more graceful perfume after the rustic has trodden them under foot."

In these and other meditations of a like nature the hours passed until three o'clock, when Don Pedro, who had just returned from the country, entered his son's room to call him to dinner. The gay joviality of his father, his jests, his affectionate attentions during the meal, were all of no avail to draw Don Luis from his melancholy, or to give him an appetite; he ate little, and scarcely spoke while they were at table.

Although much troubled by the silent melancholy of his son, whose health, though indeed robust, might nevertheless suffer from it, Don Pedro—who rose with the dawn and had a busy time of it during the day—when he had finished his after-dinner cigar and taken his cup of coffee and his glass of anisette, felt fatigued, and went, according to his custom, to take a long nap.

Don Luis had been careful not to draw the attention of his father to the offense done him by the Count of Genazahar; for Don Pedro, who, for his part, was not preparing for the priesthood, and who, besides, was not of a very meek disposition, would otherwise have rushed instantly to wreak the vengeance his son had foregone.

When his father had retired the young man also left the dining-room, that he might give himself up undisturbed to his thoughts in the seclusion of his own apartment.

CHAPTER V

DON LUIS had been sunk in meditation for a long time, seated before his desk, with his elbows resting upon it, when he heard a noise close by. He raised his eyes and saw standing beside him the meddlesome Antoñona, who, although of such massive proportions, had entered like a shadow, and was now watching him attentively, with a mixture of pity and of anger.

Antoñona, taking advantage of the hour in which the servants dined and Don Pedro slept, had penetrated thus far without being observed, and had opened the door of the room and closed it behind her so gently that Don Luis, even if he had been less absorbed, would not have noticed it.

She had come resolved to hold a very serious conference with Don Luis, but she did not quite know what she was going to say to him. Nevertheless, she had asked heaven or hell, whichever of the two it may have been, to loosen her tongue and bestow upon her the gift of speech—not such grotesque and vulgar speech as she generally used, but correct, elegant, and adapted to the noble reflections and beautiful things she had in her mind and wanted to express.

When Don Luis saw Antoñona he frowned, and showed by his manner how much this visit displeased him, at the same time saying roughly:

"What do you want here? Go away!"

"I have come to call you to account about my young mistress," returned Antoñona, quietly, "and I shall not go away until you have answered me."

She then drew a chair toward the table and sat down in it, facing Don Luis with coolness and effrontery.

Don Luis, seeing there was no help for it, restrained his anger, armed himself with patience, and, in accents less harsh than before, exclaimed:

"Say what you have to say!"

"I have to say," resumed Antoñona, "that what you are plotting against my mistress is a piece of wickedness. You are behaving like a villain. You have bewitched her; you have given her some malignant potion. The poor angel is going to die; she neither eats nor sleeps, nor has a moment's peace, on account of you. To-day she has had two or three hysterical attacks at the bare thought of your going away. A good deed you have done before becoming a priest! Tell me, wretch, why did you not stay where you were, with your uncle, instead of coming here? She, who was so free, so completely mistress of her own will, enslaving that of others, and allowing her own to be taken captive by none, has fallen into your treacherous snares. Your hypocritical sanctity was doubtless the lure you employed. With your theologies and your pious humbug you have acted like the wily and cruel sportsman, who whistles to attract the silly thrushes only to catch them in his net."

"Antoñona," returned Don Luis, "leave me in peace. For God's sake, cease torturing me! I am a villain; I confess it. I ought not to have looked at your mistress; I ought not to have allowed her to believe that I loved her; but I loved her, and I love her still, with my whole heart; and I have given her no other potion or philtre than the love I have for her. It is my duty, nevertheless, to cast away, to forget this love. God commands me to do so. Do you imagine that the sacrifice I make will not be—is not already—a tremendous one? Pepita ought to arm herself with fortitude and make a similar sacrifice."

"You do not give even that consolation to the unhappy girl," replied Antoñona. "You sacrifice voluntarily, on the altar, this woman who loves you, who is already yours—your victim. But she—how do you belong to her that she should offer you up as a sacrifice? What is the precious jewel she is going to renounce, what the beautiful ornament she is going to cast into the flames, but an ill-requited love? How is she going to give to God what she does not possesss? Is she going to try to cheat God, and say to Him: 'My God, since he does not love me, here he is; I offer him up to you; I will not love him either.' God never laughs—if He did, He would laugh at such a present as that!"

Don Luis, confounded, did not know what answer to return to these arguments of Antoñona, more painful than her former pinches. Besides, it was repugnant to him to discuss the metaphysics of love with a servant.

"Let us leave aside," he said, "these idle discussions. I can not cure the malady of your mistress. What would you have me do?"

"What would I have you do?" replied Antoñona, more gently and with insinuating accents; "I will tell you what I would have you do. If you can not cure the malady of my mistress, you should at least alleviate it a little. Are you not saintly? Well, the saints are compassionate, and courageous besides. Don't run away like an ill-mannered coward, without saying good-by. Come to see my mistress, who is sick. Do this work of mercy."

"And what would be gained by such a visit? It would aggravate her malady, instead of curing it."

"It will not do so; you don't see the matter in its proper light. You shall go to see her, and, with your honeyed tongue and the gift of the gab that Nature has bestowed upon you, you will put some resignation into her soul, and leave her consoled for your departure; and if you tell her, in addition to this, that you love her, and that it is only for the sake of God you are leaving her, her woman's vanity, at least, will not be wounded."

"What you propose to me is to tempt God; it is dangerous both for her and for me."

"And why should it be to tempt God? Since God can see the rectitude and the purity of your intentions, will He not grant you His favor and His grace that you may not yield to temptation during the visit to her, which it is but justice you should make? Ought you not to fly to her to deliver her from despair, and bring her back to the right path? If she should die of grief at seeing herself scorned; or if, in a frenzy, she should seize a rope and hang herself to a beam, I tell you, your remorse would be harder to bear than the flames of pitch and sulphur that surround the caldrons of Lucifer."

"This is horrible! I would not have her grow desperate. I shall arm myself with courage—I will go to see her."

"May Heaven bless you! But my heart told me you would go. How good you are!"

"When do you wish me to go?"

"To-night, at ten o'clock precisely. I will be at the street-door waiting for you, and will take you to her."

"Does she know you have come to see me?"

"She does not—it was all my own idea; but I will prepare her cautiously, so that the surprise, the unexpected joy of your visit, may not be too much for her. You promise me to come?"

"I will go."

"Good-by. Don't fail to come. At ten o'clock precisely I shall be at the door."

And Antoñona hurried away, descended the steps two at a time, and so gained the street.

CHAPTER VI

IT can not be denied that Antoñona had displayed great prudence, and that her language had been so dignified and proper that some may think it apocryphal, if there were not the very best authority for all that is related here, and if we did not know, besides, the wonders a woman may work by her natural cleverness when she is spurred on by interest or by some strong passion.

Great, indeed, was the affection Antoñona entertained for her mistress, and, seeing her so much in love and in such desperate case, she could do no less than seek a remedy for her ills.

The consent she had succeeded in obtaining from Don Luis was an unexpected triumph; and in order to derive the greatest possible advantage from this triumph, she was obliged to make the most of her time, and to use all her worldly wisdom in preparing for the occasion.

Antoñona had suggested ten as the hour of Don Luis's visit, because this was the hour in which Don Luis and Pepita had been accustomed to see each other in the now abolished or suspended gatherings at the house of the latter. She had suggested this hour also in order to avoid giving rise to scandal or slander; for she had once heard a preacher say that, according to the Gospel, there is nothing so wicked as scandal, and that a scandal-monger ought to be flung into the sea with a millstone hung round his neck.

Antoñona then returned to the house of her mistress, very well satisfied with herself, and with the firm determination so to arrange matters that the remedy she had sought should not prove useless, or aggravate instead of curing Pepita's malady. She resolved to say nothing of the matter to Pepita herself until the last moment, when she would tell her that Don Luis had asked her of his own accord at what hour he might make a farewell visit, and that she had said ten.

In order to avoid giving rise to talk, she determined that Don Luis should not be seen to enter the house, and for this the hour and the internal arrangement of the house itself were alike propitious. At ten the street would be full of people, on account of the vigil, which would make it easier for Don Luis to reach the house without being observed. To enter the hall would be the work of a moment, and Antoñona, who would be waiting for him, could then take him to the library without any one seeing him.

All, or at least the greater part, of the handsome country-houses of Andalusia are built as double rather than single houses. Each of these double houses has its own door. The principal door leads to the courtyard, which is paved and surrounded by columns, to the parlors and the other apartments of the family. The other door leads to the inner yards, the stable, and coach-house, the kitchens, the mill, the wine-press, the granaries, the buildings where the oil, the must, the alcohol, the brandy, and the vinegar are kept in large jars, and also to the cask stores, or cellars, where the wine, new and old, is stored in pipes or barrels. This second house, or portion of a house, although it may be situated in the heart of a town of twenty or twenty-five thousand inhabitants, is called the "farmhouse." The overseer, the foreman, the muleteer, the principal workmen, and the domestics who have been longest in the service of the master are accustomed to gather here in the evenings, during the winter, around the enormous fireplace of a spacious kitchen, and in summer in the open air, or in some cool and well-ventilated apartment, and there chat or take their ease until the master's family are ready to retire.

Antoñona was of opinion that the colloquy or explanation which she desired should take place between her mistress and Don Luis must be absolutely undisturbed, and interrupted by no one; and she therefore determined that, as it was St. John's Eve, the maid-servants of Pepita should be to-night released from all their occupations, and should go to amuse themselves at the farmhouse, where, in union with the rustic laborers, they might get up impromptu amusements, to consist of the recitation of pretty verses, playing the castanets, and dancing jigs and fandangoes.

In this manner the dwelling-house—with no other occupants than Pepita and herself—would be silent and almost deserted, and therefore quiet enough for the interview she had planned, and on which perhaps—or rather to a certainty—depended the fate of two persons of such distinguished merit.

CHAPTER VII

WHILE Antoñona went about turning over and arranging in her mind all these things, Don Luis had no sooner been left alone than he repented of having proceeded with so much haste, and weakly consenting to the interview Antoñona had asked of him. As he reflected upon it it seemed to him full of peril. He saw before him all the danger to which he was exposing himself, and he could perceive no advantage whatever in thus making a visit to the beautiful widow in secret and by stealth.

To go and see her in order to succumb to her attractions and fall into her snares, making a mockery of his vows, and placing not only the bishop, who had endorsed his petition for a dispensation, but even the holy Pontiff, who had conceded it, in a false position, by relinquishing his purpose of becoming a priest, seemed to him very dishonorable. It was, besides, a treason against his father, who loved Pepita and desired to marry her; and to visit her in order to undeceive her in regard to his love for her, seemed to him a greater refinement of cruelty than to depart without saying anything.

Influenced by these considerations, the first thought of Don Luis was to fail, without excuse or warning, to keep his appointment, and leave Antoñona to wait in vain for him in the hall; but then, as Antoñona had, in all probability, already announced his visit to her mistress, he would, by failing to go, unpardonably offend, not only Antoñona, but Pepita herself.

He then resolved on writing Pepita a very affectionate and discreet letter, excusing himself from going to see her, justifying his conduct, consoling her, manifesting his tender sentiments toward her, while letting her see that duty and Heaven were before everything, and endeavoring to inspire her with the courage to make the same sacrifice as he himself was making.

He made four or five different attempts to write this letter. He blotted a great deal of paper which he afterward tore up, and could not, in the end, succeed in getting the letter to his taste. Now it was dry, cold, pedantic, like a poor sermon or a schoolmaster's discourse; now its contents betrayed a childish apprehension, as if Pepita were a monster lying in wait to devour him; now it had other faults not less serious. In fine, after wasting many sheets of paper in the attempt, the letter remained unwritten.

"There is no help for it," said Don Luis to himself; "the die is cast. I must summon up all my courage and go."

He comforted his spirit with the hope that his self-control would not forsake him during the coming interview, and that God would endow his lips with eloquence to persuade Pepita, who was so good, that it was she herself who, sacrificing her earthly love, urged him to fulfill his vocation, resembling in this those holy women, of whom there are not wanting examples, who not only renounced the society of a bridegroom or a lover, but even the companionship of a husband, as is narrated, for instance, in the life of St. Edward of England, whose queen lived with him as a sister.

Don Luis felt himself consoled and encouraged by this thought, and he already pictured himself as St. Edward, and Pepita as Queen Edith. And under the form and in the character of this virgin queen Pepita appeared to him, if possible, more graceful, charming, and romantic than ever.

Don Luis was not, however, altogether so secure of himself, or so tranquil; as he should have been, after forming the resolution of following the example of St. Edward. There seemed to him something almost criminal, which he could not well define, in the visit he was about to make to Pepita without his father's knowledge. He felt tempted to awaken him from his nap, and to reveal everything to him; two or three times he rose from his chair with this purpose, then he stopped, feeling that such a revelation would be dishonoring and a disgraceful exhibition of childishness. He might betray his own secrets, but to betray those of Pepita, in order to set himself right with his father, seemed to him contemptible enough. The baseness and ridiculous meanness of the action were still further increased in his eyes by the reflection that what prompted him to it was the fear of not being strong enough to resist temptation.

Don Luis kept silence, therefore, and revealed nothing to his father.

More than this, he did not even feel that he had the confidence and composure necessary to present himself before his father, with the consciousness of this secret interview interposing itself as a barrier between them. He was, indeed, so excited and so beside himself, under the influence of the contending emotions that disputed the possession of his soul, that he felt as if the room, though a large one, was too small to contain him. Starting to his feet, he paced with rapid strides up and down the floor, like some wild animal in his cage, impatient of confinement. At last, although—being summer—the window was open, he felt as if he could remain here no longer, lest he should suffocate for want of air; as if the roof pressed down upon his head; as if, to breathe, he needed the whole atmosphere; to walk, he required space without limits; to lift up his brow and exhale his sighs and elevate his thoughts, to have nothing less than the immeasurable vault of heaven above him.

Impelled by this necessity, he took his hat and cane and went out into the street. Thence, avoiding every one he knew, he passed on into the country, plunging into the leafiest and most sequestered recesses of the gardens and walks that encompass the village and make for a radius of more than half a league a paradise of its surroundings.

We have said but little, thus far, concerning the personal appearance of Don Luis. Be it known, then, that he was in every sense of the word a handsome fellow—tall, well-formed, with black hair, and eyes also black and full of fire and tenderness. His complexion was dark, his teeth were white, his lips delicate and curling slightly, which gave his countenance an appearance of disdain; his bearing was manly and bold, notwithstanding the reserve and meekness proper to the sacred calling of his election. The whole mien of Don Luis bore, in a word, that indescribable stamp of distinction and nobility that seems to be—though this is not always the case—the peculiar quality and exclusive privilege of aristocratic families.

On beholding Don Luis one could not but confess that Pepita Jiménez was esthetic by instinct.

Don Luis hurried on with precipitate steps in the course he had taken, jumping across brooks and hardly glancing at surrounding objects, almost as a bull stung by a hornet might do. The countrymen he met, the market-gardeners who saw him pass, very possibly took him for a madman.

Tired at last of walking on so aimlessly, he sat down at the foot of a stone cross near the ruins of an ancient convent of St. Francis de Paul, almost two miles from the village, and there plunged anew into meditation, but of so confused a character that he himself was scarcely conscious of what was passing in his mind.

The sound of the distant bells, calling the faithful to prayer, and reminding them of the salutation of the angel to the Most Holy Virgin, reached him in his solitude through the evening air, and at last drew Don Luis from his meditations, recalling him once more to the world of reality.

The sun had just sunk behind the gigantic peaks of the neighboring mountains, making their summits—in the shape of pyramids, needles, and broken obelisks—stand out in bold relief against a background of topaz and amethyst—for such was the appearance of the heavens, gilded by the beams of the setting sun. The shadows began to deepen over the plain, and on the mountains opposite to those behind which the sun was sinking the more elevated peaks shone like flaming gold or crystal.

The windows and the white walls of the distant sanctuary of the Virgin, patroness of the village, situated on the summit of a hill, and of another small temple or hermitage situated on a nearer hill called Calvary, still shone like two beacon lights touched by the oblique rays of the setting sun.

Nature exhaled a poetic melancholy, and all things seemed to intone a hymn to the Creator, with that silent music heard only by the spirit. The slow tolling of the bells, softened and almost lost in the distance, hardly disturbed the repose of the earth, and invited to prayer without distracting the senses by their noise. Don Luis uncovered his head, knelt down at the foot of the cross, the pedestal of which had served him as a seat, and repeated with profound devotion the *Angelus Domini.*

The shades of evening were gathering fast, but when Night unfolds her mantle, and spreads it over those favored regions, she delights to adorn it with the most luminous stars and with a still brighter moon. The vault of heaven did not exchange its cerulean hue for the blackness of night; it still retained it, though it had assumed a deeper shade. The atmosphere was so clear and pure that myriads of stars could be descried shining far into the limitless depths of space. The moon silvered the tops of the trees, and touched with its splendor the waters of the brooks that gleamed, luminous and transparent, with colors as changeful and iridescent as the opal. In the leafy groves the nightingales were singing. Herbs and flowers shed a rich perfume. Countless multitudes of glowworms shone like diamonds or carbuncles among the grass and wild flowers along the banks of the brooks. In this region the fire-fly is not found, but the common glowworm abounds, and sheds a most brilliant light. Fruit trees still in blossom, acacias, and roses without number perfumed the air with their rich fragrance.

Don Luis felt himself swayed, seduced, vanquished by this voluptuousness of Nature, and began to doubt himself. He felt compelled, however, to fulfil his promise and keep his appointment.

Deviating often from the straight path, hesitating at times whether he should not rather push forward to the source of the river, where, at the foot of a mountain and in the midst of the most enchanting surroundings, the crystal torrent that waters the neighboring gardens and orchards bursts from the living rock, he turned back, with slow and lingering step, in the direction of the village.

In proportion as he approached it, the terror inspired by the thought of what he was about to do increased. He plunged into the thickest of the wood, hoping there to behold some sign, some wonder, some warning, that should draw him back. He thought often of the student Lisardo, and wished that, like him, he might behold his own burial. But heaven smiled with her thousand lights, and invited to love; the stars twinkled at each other with love; the nightingales sang of love; even the crickets chirped their amorous serenade. All the earth, on this tranquil and beautiful night, seemed given up to love. All was life, peace, joy.

Where was his guardian angel now? Had he abandoned Don Luis as already lost; or, deeming that he ran no risk, did he make no effort to turn him from his purpose? Who can say? Perhaps from the danger that menaced him would in the end result a triumph? St. Edward and Queen Edith presented themselves again to the imagination of Don Luis, and the vision strengthened his resolution.

Engrossed in these meditations, he delayed his return, and was still some distance from the village when ten, the hour appointed for his interview with Pepita, struck from the parish clock. The ten strokes of the bell were ten blows that, falling on his heart, wounded it as with a physical pain—a pain in which dread and treacherous disquiet were blended with a ravishing sweetness.

Don Luis hastened his steps, that he might not be too late, and shortly found himself in the village.

The hamlet presented a most animated scene. Young girls flocked to wash their faces at the spring outside the village; those who had sweethearts, that their sweethearts might remain faithful to them; and those who had not, that they might obtain sweethearts. Here and there women and children were returning from the fields, with verbena, branches of rosemary, and other plants, which they had been gathering, to burn as a charm. Guitars tinkled on every side, words of love were to be overheard, and everywhere happy and tender couples were to be seen walking together. The vigil and the early morning of St. John's Day, although a Christian festival, still retain a certain savor of paganism and primitive naturalism. This may be because of the approximate concurrence of this festival and the summer solstice. In any case, the scene to-night was purely mundane and not religious. All was love and gallantry. In our old romances and legends the Moor always carries off the beautiful Christian princess, and the Christian knight receives the reward of his devotion to the Moorish princess on the eve or in the early morning of St. John's Day; and the traditionary custom of the old romances had been, to all appearances, preserved in the village.

The streets were full of people. The whole village was out of doors, in addition to the strangers from the surrounding country. Progress, thus rendered extremely difficult, was still further impeded by the multitude of little tables laden with almond sweetmeats, honey-cakes, and biscuits, with fruit-stalls, with booths for the sale of dolls and toys, and cake-shops, where gipsies, young and old, fried the dough —tainting the air with the odor of oil—weighed and served the cakes, responded with ready wit to the compliments of the gallants who passed by, and told fortunes.

Don Luis sought to avoid meeting any of his acquaintances and, when he caught sight by chance of one he knew, turned his steps in another direction. Thus, by degrees, he reached the entrance to Pepita's house without having been stopped or spoken to by any one. His heart now began to beat with violence, and he paused a moment to recover his serenity. He looked at his watch; it was almost half-past ten.

"Good heavens!" he exclaimed; "she has been waiting for me nearly half an hour."

He then hurried his pace and entered the hall. The lamp by which it was always lighted was burning dimly on this particular evening.

No sooner had Don Luis entered the hall than a hand, or rather a claw, seized him by the right arm. It belonged to Antoñona, who said to him under her breath:

"A pretty fellow you are, for a divinity student! Ingrate! Good-for-nothing! Vagabond! I began to think you were not coming. Where have you been, you idiot? How dare you delay, as if you had no interest in the matter, when the salt of the earth is melting for you, and the sun of beauty awaits you?"

While Antoñona was giving utterance to these complaints, she did not stand still, but continued to go forward, dragging after her by the arm the now cowed and silent collegian. They passed the grated door, which Antoñona closed carefully and noiselessly behind them. They crossed the courtyard, ascended the stairs, passed through some corridors and two sitting-rooms, and arrived at last at the door of the library, which was closed.

Profound silence reigned throughout the house. The library was situated in its interior, and was thus inaccessible to the noises of the street. The only sounds that reached it, dim and vague, were the clatter of castanets, the thrumming of a guitar, and the murmur of the voices of Pepita's servants, who were holding their impromptu dance in the farmhouse.

Antoñona opened the door of the library and pushed Don Luis toward it, at the same time announcing him in these words:

"Here is Don Luis, who has come to take leave of you."

This announcement being made with due ceremony, the discreet Antoñona withdrew, leaving the visitor and her mistress at their ease, and closing the door behind her.

CHAPTER VIII

AT this point in our narrative we can not refrain from calling attention to the character of authenticity that stamps the present history, and paying a tribute of admiration to the scrupulous exactness of the person who composed it. For, were the incidents related in these *paralipomena* fictitious, as in a novel, there is not the least doubt but that an interview so important and of such transcendent interest as that of Pepita and Don Luis would have been brought about by less vulgar means than those here employed.

Perhaps our hero and heroine, in the course of some new excursion into the country, might have been surprised by a sudden and frightful tempest, thus finding themselves obliged to take refuge in the ruins of some ancient castle or Moorish tower, with the reputation, of course, of being haunted by ghosts or other supernatural visitants. Perhaps our hero and heroine might have fallen into the power of a party of bandits, from whom they would have escaped, thanks to the presence of mind and courage of Don Luis; taking shelter afterward for the night—they two alone, and without the possibility of avoiding it—in a cavern or grotto. Or, finally, perhaps the author would have arranged the matter in such a way that Pepita and her vacillating admirer would have been obliged to make a journey by sea, and, although at the present day there are neither pirates nor Algerine corsairs, it is not difficult to invent a good shipwreck, during which Don Luis could have saved Pepita's life, taking refuge with her afterward on a desert island, or some other equally romantic and solitary place.

Any one of these devices would more artfully prepare the way for the tender colloquy of the lovers, and would better serve to exculpate Don Luis. We are of the opinion, nevertheless, that, instead of censuring the author for not having had recourse to such complications as those we have mentioned, we ought rather to thank him for his conscientiousness in sacrificing to the truth of his relation the marvelous effect he might have produced had he ventured to adorn it with incidents and episodes drawn from his own fancy.

If the means by which this interview was brought about were, in reality, only the officiousness and the skill of Antoñona, and the weakness with which Don Luis acceded to her request that he should grant it, why forge lies, and cause the two lovers to be impelled, as it were, by Fate, to see and speak with each other alone, to the great danger of the virtue and honor of both? Nothing of the kind! Whether Don Luis did well or ill in keeping his appointment, and whether Pepita Jiménez, whom Antoñona had already told that Don Luis was coming of his own accord to see her, did well or ill in rejoicing over that somewhat mysterious and untimely visit, let us not throw the blame on Fate, but on the personages themselves who figure in this history, and on the passions by which they are actuated. We confess to a great affection for Pepita; but the truth is before everything, and must be declared, even should it be to the prejudice of our heroine.

At eight o'clock, then, Antoñona had told her that Don Luis was coming, and Pepita, who had been talking of dying, whose eyes were red, and her eyelids slightly inflamed with weeping, and whose hair was in some disorder, thought of nothing from that moment but of adorning and dressing herself to receive Don Luis. She bathed her face with warm water, so that the ravages her tears had made might be effaced to the exact point of leaving her beauty unimpaired, while still allowing it to be seen that she had wept. She arranged her hair so as to display, rather than a studied care in its arrangement, a certain graceful and artistic carelessness, that fell short of disorder, however, which would have been indecorous; she polished her nails, and, as it was not fit that she should receive Don Luis in a wrapper, she put on a simple house-dress. In fine, she managed instinctively that all the details of her toilet should concur in heightening her beauty and grace, but without allowing any trace to be perceived of the art, the labor, and the time employed in the details. She would have it appear, on the contrary, as if all this beauty and grace were the free gift of Nature, something inherent in her person, no matter how she might, owing to the vehemence of her passions, neglect it on occasion.

Pepita, so far as we have been able to discover, spent more than an hour in these labors of the toilet, which were to be perceived only by their results. She then, with ill-concealed satisfaction, gave herself the final touch before the looking-glass. At last, at about half-past nine, taking a candle in her hand, she descended to the apartment in which was the *Infant Jesus.* She first lighted the altar candles, which had been extinguished; she saw with something of sorrow that the flowers were drooping; she asked pardon of the sacred Image for neglecting it so long, and, throwing herself on her knees before it, prayed in her solitude with her whole heart, and with that frankness and confidence that a guest inspires who has been so long an inmate of the house. Of a *Jesus of Nazareth* bearing the cross upon his shoulders, and crowned with thorns; of an *Ecco Homo,* insulted and scourged, with a reed for derisive sceptre, and his hands bound with a rough cord; of a *Christ Crucified,* bleeding and in the last throes of death, Pepita would not have dared to ask what she now asked of a Saviour, still a child, smiling, beautiful, untouched by suffering, and pleasing to the eye. Pepita asked him to leave her Don Luis; not to take him away from her, since he, who was so rich and so well provided with everything, might, without any great sacrifices, deny himself this one of his servants, and give him up to her.

Having completed these preparations, which we may classify as cosmetic, decorative, and religious, Pepita installed herself in the library, and there awaited the arrival of Don Luis with feverish impatience.

Antoñona had acted with prudence in not telling her mistress that Don Luis was coming to see her until a short time before the appointed hour. Even as it was, thanks to the delay of her gallant, poor Pepita, from the moment in which she had finished her prayers and supplications to the *Infant Jesus,* to that in which she beheld Don Luis standing in the library, was a prey to anguish and disquietude.

The visit began in the most grave and ceremonious manner. The customary salutations were mechanically interchanged, and Don Luis, at the invitation of Pepita, seated himself in an easy-chair, without laying aside his hat or cane, and at a short distance from her. Pepita was seated on the sofa; beside her was a little table on which were some books, and a candle, the light from which illuminated her countenance. On the desk also burned a lamp. Notwithstanding these two lights, however, the apartment, which was large, remained for the greater part in darkness. A large window, which looked out on an inner garden, was open on account of the heat; and although the grating of the window was covered with climbing roses and jasmine, the clear beams of the moon penetrated through the interlaced leaves and flowers, and struggled with the light of the lamp and candle. Through the open window came, too, the distant and confused sounds of the dance at the farmhouse, which was at the other extremity of the garden, the monotonous murmur of the fountain below, and the fragrance of the jasmine and roses that curtained the window, mingled with that of the mignonette, sweet-basil, and other plants that adorned the borders beneath.

There was a long pause—a silence as difficult to maintain as it was to break. Neither of the two interlocutors ventured to speak. The situation was, in truth, embarrassing. They found it as difficult to express themselves then as we find it now to reproduce their words; but there is nothing else for it than to make the effort. Let us allow them to speak for themselves, transcribing their words with exactitude.

CHAPTER IX

"SO you have finally condescended to come and take leave of me before your departure," said Pepita; "I had already given up the hope that you would do so."

The part Don Luis had to perform was a serious one; and, besides, in this kind of dialogue, the man, not only if he be a novice, but even when he is old in the business and an expert, is apt to begin with some piece of folly. Let us not too freely condemn Don Luis, therefore, because he began unwisely.

"Your complaint is unjust," he said. "I came here with my father to take leave of you, and, as we had not the pleasure of being received by you, we left cards. We were told that you were somewhat indisposed, and we have sent every day since to inquire about you. We were greatly pleased to learn that you were improving. I hope you are now much better."

"I am almost tempted to say I am no better," answered Pepita, "but, as I see that you have come as the ambassador of your father, and I do not want to distress so excellent a friend, it is but right that I should tell you, that you may repeat it to him, that I am much better now. But it is strange that you have come alone. Don Pedro must be very much occupied indeed, not to accompany you."

"My father did not accompany me, because he does not know that I have come to see you. I have preferred to come without him, because my farewell must be a serious, a solemn, perhaps a final one, and his would naturally be of a very different character. My father will return to the village in a few weeks; it is possible that I may never return to it, and, if I do, it will be in a very different condition from my present."

Pepita could not restrain herself. The happy future of which she had dreamed vanished into air. Her unalterable resolution to vanquish this man, at whatever cost, the only man she had loved in her life, the only one she felt herself capable of loving, seemed to have been made in vain. She felt herself condemned at twenty years of age, with all her beauty, to perpetual widowhood, to solitude, to an unrequited love—for to love any other man seemed impossible to her.

The character of Pepita, in whom obstacles only strengthened and rekindled her desires, with whom a determination, once taken, carried everything before it until it was fulfilled, showed itself now in all its violence and without restraint. She must conquer, or die in the attempt. Social considerations, the fixed habit of guarding and concealing the feelings, acquired in the great world, which serve as a restraint to the paroxysms of passion, and which veil in ambiguous phrases and circumlocution the most violent explosion of undisciplined emotion, had no power with Pepita. She had had but little intercourse with the world, she knew no middle way; her only rule of conduct hitherto had been to obey blindly her mother and her husband while they lived, and afterward to command despotically every other human being.

Thus it was that on this occasion Pepita spoke her thoughts and showed herself such as she really was. Her soul, with all the passion it contained, took form in her words; and her words, instead of serving to conceal her thoughts and her feelings, gave them substance. She did not speak as a woman of the world would have spoken, with circumlocutions and attenuations of expression, but with that idyllic frankness with which Chloe spoke to Daphnis, and with the humility and the complete self-abandonment with which the daughter-in-law of Naomi offered herself to Boaz.

"Do you persist in your purpose?" she asked. "Are you sure of your vocation? Are you not afraid of being a bad priest? Don Luis, I am going to make a supreme effort. I am going to forget that I am an uncultured girl; I am going to dispense with all sentiment, and to reason as coldly as if it were concerning the matter most indifferent to me. Things have taken place that may be explained in two ways; both explanations do you discredit. I will tell you what I think:

"If a woman who, with her coquetries—not very daring ones, in truth—almost without a word, and but a few days after seeing and speaking to you for the first time, has been able to provoke you, to move you to look at her with glances which reveal a profane love, and has even obtained from you such a proof of that love as would be a fault, a sin, in any one, but is so especially in a priest—if this woman be, as she indeed is, a simple country girl, without education, without talent, and without elegance, what may not be feared for you when in great cities you see and converse with other women a thousand times more dangerous? Your head will be turned when you are thrown into the society of the great ladies who dwell in palaces, who tread on soft carpets, who dazzle the eye with their diamonds and pearls, who are clad in silks and laces instead of muslin and cotton, who display their white and well-formed throat instead of covering it with a plebeian and modest handkerchief, who are adepts in all the arts of flirtation, and who, by reason of the very ostentation, luxury, and pomp that surround them, are all the more desirable for being apparently more inaccessible. Yes, these elegant and beautiful women discuss politics, philosophy, religion, and literature; they sing like canaries; they are enveloped, as it were, in clouds of incense, adoration, and homage, set upon a pedestal of triumphs and of victories, glorified by the prestige of an illustrious name, enthroned in gilded drawing-rooms, or secluded in voluptuous boudoirs; and there enter only the blessed ones of the earth, its titled ones, perhaps, who only to their most intimate friends are 'Pepita,' 'Antoñita,' or 'Angelita,' and to the rest of the world, 'Her Grace the Duchess,' or 'The Marchioness.'

"If you have yielded to the arts of a mere country girl when you were on the eve of being ordained, and in spite of all the enthusiasm for your calling that you may naturally be supposed to entertain—if you have thus yielded, urged by a passing impulse, am I not right in foreseeing that you will make an abominable priest, impure, worldly, and of evil influence, and that you will yield to temptation at every step?

"On such a supposition as this, believe me, Don Luis—and do not be offended with me for saying so—you are not even worthy to be the husband of an honest woman. If, with all the ardor and tenderness of the most passionate lover, you have pressed the hand of a woman, if you have looked at one with glances that foretold a heaven, an eternity of love; if you have even kissed a woman who inspired you with no other feeling than one that for me has no name—then go, in God's name and do not marry her! If she is virtuous, she will not desire you for a husband, nor even for a lover. But, for God's sake, do not become a priest either! The Church needs men more serious, more capable of resisting temptation, as ministers of the Most High.

"If, on the other hand, you have felt a noble passion for the woman of whom we are speaking, although she be of little worth, why abandon and deceive her so cruelly? However unworthy she may be, if she has inspired this great passion, do you not suppose that she must share it, and be the victim of it? For, when a love is great, elevated, and passionate, does it ever fail to make its power felt? Does it not irresistibly vanquish and subjugate the beloved object? By the extent of your love for her you may measure hers for you. How then can you avoid fearing for her, if you abandon her? Has she the masculine energy, the firmness of character produced by the wisdom learned from books, the attraction of fame, the multitude of splendid projects, and all the resources of your cultured and exalted intellect, to distract her mind, and turn her away without destructive violence, from every other earthly affection? Can you not see that she will die of grief, and that you, called by your destiny to offer up bloodless sacrifices, will begin by pitilessly sacrificing her who most loves you?"

"I too," returned Don Luis, endeavoring to conquer his emotion, and to speak with firmness—"I too am obliged to make a great effort in order to answer you with the calmness necessary to one who opposes argument to argument, as in a controversy; but your accusation is supported by so many reasons and you have invested those reasons—pardon me for saying so—with so specious an appearance of truth, that I have no choice left me but to disprove them by other reasons. I had no thought of being placed in the necessity of maintaining a discussion here, and of sharpening my poor wits for that purpose; but you compel me to do so, unless

I wish to pass for a monster. I am going to reply to the two extremes of the cruel dilemma in which you have placed me.

"Though it is true that my youth was passed in my uncle's house and in the seminary, where I saw nothing of women, do not therefore think me so ignorant, or possessed of so little imagination, that I can not picture to myself how lovely, how seductive they may be. My imagination, on the contrary, went far beyond the reality. Excited by the reading of the sacred writers and of profane poets, it pictured woman more charming, more graceful, more intelligent, than they are commonly to be found in real life. I knew then, and I even exaggerated to myself, the cost of the sacrifice I was making, when I renounced the love of those women for the purpose of elevating myself to the dignity of the priesthood. I know well how much the charms of a beautiful woman are enhanced by rich attire, by splendid jewels, by being surrounded with all the arts of refined civilization, all the objects of luxury produced by the indefatigable labor and the skill of man. I knew well, too, how much the natural cleverness of a woman is increased, how much her natural intelligence is sharpened, quickened and brightened by intercourse with learned men, by the reading of good books, even by the familiar spectacle of the wealth and splendor of great cities, and of the monuments of the past that they contain. All this I pictured to myself with so much vividness, my fancy painted it in such glowing colors, that you need have no doubt that, should I be thrown into the society of those women of whom you speak, far from feeling the adoration and the transports you prophesy, I shall rather experience a disenchantment on seeing how great a distance there is between what I dreamed of and the truth, between the living reality and the picture of it that my fancy drew."

"This is indeed specious reasoning," exclaimed Pepita. "How can I deny that what you have pictured in your imagination is, in truth, more beautiful than what exists in reality? But who will deny, either, that the real possesses a more seductive charm than that which exists only in the imagination? The vague and ethereal beauty of a phantasm, however great, can not compete with what is palpable and visible to the senses. I can understand that holy images might triumph over worldly dreams, but I fear they would scarcely be able to vanquish worldly realities."

"Have no such fear," returned Don Luis. "My fancy, by its own creations, has more power over my spirit than the whole universe—only excepting yourself—by what it transmits to it through the senses."

"And why except me? Such an exception gives room to another suspicion. The idea you have of me, the idea which you love, may be but the creation of this potent fancy of yours, and an illusion that resembles me in nothing."

"No, this is not the case. You may be assured that this idea resembles you in everything. It may be that it is innate in my soul, that it has existed in it since it was created by God, that it is a part of its essence, the best and purest part of its being, as the perfume is of the flower."

"This is what I had feared, and now you confess it to me. You do not love me. What you love is the essence, the fragrance, the purest part of your own soul, that has assumed a form resembling mine."

"No, Pepita; do not amuse yourself by tormenting me. What I love is you—and you such as you really are; but what I love is also so beautiful, so pure, so delicate that I can not understand how it should have reached my mind, in a material manner, through the senses. I take it for granted, then, and it is my firm belief, that it must have had an innate existence there. It is like the idea of God which is inborn in my soul, which has unfolded and developed itself within me, and which, nevertheless, has its counterpart in reality, superior, infinitely superior to the idea. As I believe that God exists, so do I believe that you exist, and that you are a thousand times superior to the idea that I have formed of you."

"Still, I have a doubt left. May it not be woman in general, and not I, solely and exclusively, that has awakened this idea?"

"No, Pepita; before I saw you, I had felt in imagination what might be the magic power, the fascination, of a woman beautiful of soul and graceful in person. There is no duchess or marchioness in Madrid, no empress in all the world, no queen or princess on the face of the globe, to be compared to the ideals and fantastic creations with whom I have lived.

"These were inhabitants of the castles and boudoirs, marvels of luxury and taste, that I pleased myself in boyhood by erecting in my fancy, and that I afterward gave as dwelling-places to my Lauras, Beatrices, Juliets, Marguerites, and Leonoras; to my Cynthias, Glyceras, and Lesbias. I crowned them in my imagination with coronets and Oriental diadems; I clothed them in mantles of purple and gold, and surrounded them with regal pomp like Esther and Vashti. I endowed them, like Rebecca and the Shulamite, with the bucolic simplicity of the patriarchal age; I bestowed on them the sweet humility and the devotion of Ruth; I listened to them discoursing like Aspasia, or Hypatia, mistresses of eloquence. I enthroned them in luxurious drawing-rooms, and cast over them the splendor of noble blood and illustrious lineage, as if they had been the proudest and noblest of patrician maidens of ancient Rome. I beheld them graceful, coquettish, gay, full of aristocratic ease and manner, like the ladies of the time of Louis XIV, in Versailles; and I adorned them, now with the modest *stola,* inspiring veneration and respect; now with diaphanous tunics and *peplums,* through whose airy folds were revealed all the plastic perfections of their graceful forms; now with the transparent *coa* of the beautiful courtezans of Athens and Corinth, showing the white and roseate hues of the finely molded forms that glowed beneath their vaporous covering.

"But what are the joys of the senses, what the glory and magnificence of the world, to a soul that burns and consumes itself in Divine love, as I believed mine, perhaps with too much arrogance, to burn and consume itself? As volcanic fires, when they burst into flame, send flying into air, shattered in a thousand fragments, the solid rocks, the mountainside itself, which obstruct their passage, so, or with even greater force, did my spirit cast from itself the whole weight of the universe and of created beauty that lay upon it and imprisoned it, preventing it from soaring up to God, as the centre of its aspirations.

"No; I have rejected no delight, no sweetness, no glory, through ignorance. I knew them all, and valued them all at more than their worth, when I rejected them all for a greater delight, a greater sweetness, a greater glory. The profane love of woman presented itself to my fancy, clothed, not only with all its own charms, but with the sovereign and almost irresistible charms of the most dangerous of all temptations—of that which the moralists call virginal temptation—when the mind, not yet undeceived by experience and by sin, pictures to itself in the transports of love a supreme and ineffable delight immeasurably superior to all reality.

"Ever since I reached manhood—that is to say, for many years past, for my youth was short—I have scorned those delights and that beauty that were but the shadow and the reflex of the archetypal beauty of which I was enamored, of the supreme delight for which I longed. I have sought to die to myself, in order to live in the beloved object; to free, not only my senses, but even my soul itself, from every earthly affection, from illusions and imaginings, in order to be able to say with truth that it is not I who live, but Christ who lives in me. Sometimes, no doubt, I sinned through arrogance and self-confidence, and God wished to chastise me; you came across my path, and tempted me and led me astray.

"Now you upbraid me, you deride me, you accuse me of levity and weakness; but in upbraiding me and deriding me you insult yourself, for you thus imply that any other woman might have had equal power over me. I do not wish, when I ought to be humble, to fall into the sin of pride, by trying to justify my fault. If God, in chastisement of my pride, has let me fall from His grace, it is possible that any temptation, however slight, might have made me waver and fall. Yet I confess that I do not think so. It may be that I err in my judgment that this is but the consequence of my undisciplined pride, but, I repeat, I do not think so. I can not succeed in persuading myself that the cause of my fall had in it anything either mean or base.

"Above all the dreams of my youthful imagination, the reality, such as I beheld it in you, enthroned itself. You towered above all the nymphs, queens, and goddesses of my fancy. Above the ruins of my ideal creations, overthrown and shattered by Divine love, there arose in my soul the faithful image, the exact reproduction of the living beauty which adorns and is the essence of that body and of that soul. There may be even something mysterious, something supernatural in this; for I loved you from the moment I first saw you—almost before I saw you. Long before I was conscious of loving you, I loved you. It would seem as if there were some fatality in this—that it was decreed, that it was predestination."

"And if it were predestined, if it be decreed," said Pepita, "why not submit to Fate, why still resist? Sacrifice your purpose to our love. Have not I sacrificed much? Am I not now sacrificing my pride, my modesty, my reserve, in supplicating you thus, in making this effort to overcome your scorn? I too believe that I loved you before I saw you. Now I love you with my whole heart, and without you there is no happiness for me. It is true indeed that in my humble intelligence you can find no rival so powerful as that which I have in yours. Neither with the understanding, nor the will, nor the affections, can I raise myself all at once up to God. Neither by nature nor by grace can I mount, or desire to mount, up to such exalted spheres. My soul, nevertheless, is full of religious devotion, and I know and love and adore God; but I only behold His omnipotence and admire His goodness in the works that have proceeded from His hands. Nor can I, with the imagination, weave those visions that you tell me of.

"Yet I too dreamed of some one nobler, more intelligent, more poetic, and more enamored than the men who have thus far sought my hand; of a lover more distinguished and accomplished than any of my adorers of this and the neighboring villages, who should love me, and whom I should love and to whose will I should blindly surrender mine. This some one was you. I had a presentiment of it when they told me that you had arrived at the village. When I saw you for the first time, I knew it. But, as my imagination is so sterile, the picture I had formed of you in my mind was not to be compared, even in the most remote degree, to the reality. I too have read something of romances and poetry. But from all that my memory retained of them, I was unable to form a picture that was not far inferior in merit to what I see and divine in you since I have known you. Thus it is that from the moment I saw you I was vanquished and undone.

"If love is, as you say, to die to self, in order to live in the beloved object, then is my love genuine and legitimate, for I have died to myself, and live only in you and for you. I have tried to cast this love away from me, deeming it ill-requited, and I have not been able to succeed in doing so. I have prayed to God with fervor to take away from me this love, or else to kill me, and God has not deigned to hear me. I have prayed to the Virgin Mary to blot your image from my soul, and my prayer has been in vain. I have made vows to my patron, Saint Joseph, to the end that he would enable me to think of you only as he thought of his blessed spouse, and my patron saint has not succored me.

"Seeing all this, I have had the audacity to ask of Heaven that you should allow yourself to be vanquished, that you should cease to desire to be a priest, that there might spring up in your soul a love as great as that which is in my heart.

"Don Luis, tell me frankly, has Heaven been deaf to this last prayer also? Or is it, perchance, that to subjugate a soul as weak, as wretched, and as petty as mine, a petty love is sufficient, while to master yours, protected and guarded as it is by vigorous and lofty thoughts, a more powerful love than mine is necessary, a love that I am neither worthy of inspiring, nor capable of sharing, nor even able to understand?"

"Pepita," returned Don Luis, "it is not that your soul is less than mine, but that it is free from obligations, and mine is not. The love you have inspired me with is profound, but my obligations, my vows, the purpose of my whole life so near to its realization, contend against it. Why should I not say it without fearing to offend you? If you succeed in making me love you, you do not humiliate yourself. If I succumb to your love, I both humiliate and abase myself. I leave the Creator for the creature. I renounce the unwavering purpose of my life, I break the image of Christ that was in my soul; and the new man, which I had created in myself at such cost, disappears, that the old man may come to life again. Intsead of my lowering myself to the earth, to the impurity of the world that I have hitherto despised, why do not you rather elevate yourself to me by virtue of that very love you entertain for me, freeing it from every earthly alloy? Why should we not love each other without shame, and without sin, and without dishonor? God penetrates holy souls with the pure and refulgent fire of His love, and so fills them with it that, as metal fresh from the forge, without ceasing to be a metal, shines and glitters and is all fire, these souls are filled with joy, and see God, in all things penetrated by God in every part, through the grace of the Divine love. These souls love and enjoy each other, as if they loved and enjoyed God, loving and enjoying Him in truth because they are God. Let us mount together in spirit this steep and mystical ladder. Let our souls ascend, side by side, to this bliss, which even in this mortal life is possible! But to do this we must separate in the body; it is essential that I should go whither I am called by my duty, my vow, and the voice of the Most High, who disposes of His servant, and has destined him to the service of His altar."

"Ah, Don Luis," replied Pepita, full of sorrow and contrition, "now indeed I see how vile is the metal I am made of, and how unworthy I am that the Divine fire should penetrate and transform me. I will confess everything, casting away even shame.

"I am a vile sinner; my rude and uncultured understanding can not grasp these subtleties, these distinctions, these refinements of love. My rebellious will refuses what you propose. I can not even conceive of you but as yourself. For me you are your mouth, your eyes, your dark locks that I desire to caress with my hands; your sweet voice, the pleasing sound of your words that fall upon my ears and charm them through the senses; your whole person, in a word, which charms and seduces me, and through which, and only through which, I perceive the invisible spirit, vague and full of mystery. My stubborn soul, incapable of these mystical raptures, will never be able to follow you to those regions whither you would take it. If you soar up to them, I shall remain alone, abandoned, plunged in the deepest affliction. I prefer to die; I deserve death; I desire it. It may be that after death my soul, loosening or breaking the vile bonds which chain it here, will be able to understand the love with which you desire we should be united.

"Kill me, then, in order that we may thus love each other; kill me, and my spirit, set free, will follow you whithersoever you may go, and will journey invisible by your side, watching over your steps, contemplating you with rapture, penetrating your most secret thoughts, beholding your soul as it is, without the intervention of the senses.

"But in this life it can not be. I love in you, not only the soul, but the body, and the shadow cast by the body, and the reflection of the body in the mirror and in the water, and the Christian name, and the surname, and the blood, and all that goes to make you such as you are, Don Luis de Vargas; the sound of your voice, your gesture, your gait, and I know not what else besides. I repeat that you must kill me. Kill me without compassion. No, I am not a Christian; I am a material idolater."

Here Pepita made a long pause. Don Luis knew not what to say, and was silent. Tears bathed the cheeks of Pepita, who continued, sobbing:

"I know it; you despise me, and you are right to despise me. By this just contempt you will kill me more surely than with a dagger, and without staining either your hands or your conscience with blood. Farewell! I am about to free you from my odious presence. Farewell forever!"

Having said this, Pepita rose from her seat, and, without looking at Don Luis, her face bathed with tears, beside herself, rushed toward the door that led to the inner apartment. An unconquerable tenderness, a fatal pity, took possession of Don Luis. He feared Pepita would die. He started forward to detain her, but it was too late. Pepita had crossed the threshold. Her form disappeared in the darkness within. Don Luis, impelled by a superhuman power, drawn as by an invisible hand, followed her into the unlighted chamber.

CHAPTER X

THE library remained deserted.

The servants' dance must have already terminated, for the only sound to be heard was the murmur of the fountain in the garden below.

Not even a breath of wind troubled the stillness of the night and the serenity of the air.

The perfume of the flowers and the light of the moon entered softly through the open window. After a long interval, Don Luis made his appearance, emerging from the darkness. Terror was depicted on his countenance, mingled with despair—such despair as Judas may have felt after he had betrayed his Master.

He dropped into a chair, and burying his face in his hands, with his elbows resting on his knees, he remained for more than half an hour plunged in a sea of bitter reflections.

To see him thus, one might have supposed that he had just murdered Pepita.

Pepita, nevertheless, at last made her appearance. With a slow step, and an air of the deepest melancholy, with bent head, and eyes directed to the floor, she approached Don Luis, and spoke.

"Now, indeed," said she, "though, alas! too late, I know all the vileness of my heart and the iniquity of my conduct. I have nothing to say in my own defense, but I would not have you think me more wicked than I am. You must not think I have used any arts—that I have laid any plans for your destruction. Yes; it is true that I have been guilty of an atrocious crime, but an unpremeditated one; a crime inspired, perhaps, by the spirit of evil that possesses me. Do not abandon yourself to despair, do not torture yourself, for God's sake! You are responsible for nothing. It was a frenzy, a madness, that took possession of your noble spirit. Your sin is a light one; mine is flagrant, shameful, horrible. Now I am less worthy of you than ever. It is I who now ask you to leave this place. Go; do penance. God will pardon you. Go; a priest will give you absolution. Once cleansed from sin, carry out your purpose, and become a minister of the Most High. Then, through the holiness of your life, through your ceaseless labors, not only will you efface from your soul the last traces of this fall, but you will obtain for me, when you have pardoned me the evil I have done you, the pardon of Heaven also. You are bound to me by no tie, and even if you were I should loosen or break it. You are free. Let it suffice me that I have taken captive by surprise the star of the morning. It is not my desire—I neither can nor ought to seek to keep him in my power. I divine it, I read it in your manner, I am convinced of it—you despise me more than before. And you are right in despising me; there is neither honor, nor virtue, nor shame in me!"

When she had thus spoken, Pepita, throwing herself on her knees, bowed her face till her forehead touched the floor. Don Luis continued in the same attitude as before. Thus, for some moments. they remained both silent with the silence of despair.

In a stifled voice, and without raising her face from the floor, Pepita after a time continued:

"Go, now, Don Luis, and do not, through an insulting pity, remain any longer at the side of so despicable a wretch as I. I shall have courage to bear your indifference, your forgetfulness, your contempt, for I have deserved them all. I shall always be your slave—but far from you, very far from you, in order that nothing may recall to your memory the infamy of this night!"

Pepita's voice, as she ended, was choked with sobs.

Don Luis could restrain himself no longer. He arose, approached Pepita, and, raising her in his arms from the floor, pressed her to his heart; then, putting aside from her face the blond tresses that fell in disorder over it, he covered it with passionate kisses.

"Soul of my soul," he said at last, "life of my life, treasure of my heart, light of my eyes, raise your dejected brow, and do not prostrate yourself any longer before me. The sinner, the vile wretch, he who has shown himself weak of purpose, who has made himself the butt of scorn and ridicule, is I, not you. Angels and devils alike must laugh at me and mock me. I have clothed myself with a false sanctity. I was not able to resist temptation, and to undeceive you in the beginning, as would have been right, and now I am equally unable to show myself a gentleman, a man of honor, or a tender lover who knows how to value the favors of his mistress. I can not understand what it was you saw in me to attract you. There never was in me any solid virtue—nothing but vain show and the pedantry of a student who has read pious books as one reads a novel, and on this foundation has based his foolish romance of a future devoted to converting the heathen and to solemn meditations. If there had been any real virtue in me I should have undeceived you in time, and neither you nor I would have sinned. True goodness is not so easily vanquished. Notwithstanding your beauty, notwithstanding your intelligence, notwithstanding your love for me, I should not have fallen if I had been really good. God, to whom all things are possible, would have bestowed His grace upon me. It would have needed nothing less than a miracle, or some other supernatural event, to have enabled me to resist your love, but God would have wrought the miracle, if I had been worthy of it and there was a motive sufficient for its being wrought. You are wrong to counsel me to become a priest. I know my own unworthiness. It was only pride that actuated me. It was a worldly ambition, like any other. What do I say—like any other? It was worse than any other; it was hypocritical, sacrilegious, simoniacal."

"Do not judge yourself so harshly," said Pepita, now more tranquil, and smiling through her tears. "I do not want you to judge yourself thus, not even for the purpose of making me appear less unworthy to be your companion. No; I would have you choose me through love—freely; not to repair a fault, not because you have fallen into the snare you perhaps think I have perfidiously spread for you. If you do not love me, if you distrust me, if you do not esteem me—then go. My lips shall not breathe a single complaint if you abandon me for ever, and never think of me again."

To answer this fittingly, our poor and beggarly human speech was insufficient for Don Luis. He cut short Pepita's words by pressing his lips to hers, and again clasping her to his heart.

CHAPTER XI

SOME time afterward, with much previous coughing and shuffling of the feet, Antoñona entered the library with the words:

"What a long talk you must have had! The sermon our student has been preaching this time can not have been that of the *seven words*—it came very near being that of the *forty hours.* It is time you should go now, Don Luis; it is almost two o'clock in the morning."

"Very well," answered Pepita; "he will go directly."

Antoñona left the library again, and waited outside.

Pepita was like one transformed. One might suppose that the joys she had missed in her childhood, the happiness and contentment she had failed to taste in her early youth, the gay activity and sprightliness that a harsh mother and an old husband had repressed, and, as it were, crushed within her, had suddenly burst into life in her soul, like the green leaves of the trees, whose germination has been retarded by the snows and frosts of a long and severe winter.

A town-bred lady, familiar with what we call social conventionalities, may find something strange, and even worthy of censure, in what I am about to relate of Pepita. But Pepita, although refined by instinct, was a being in whom every feeling was spontaneous, and in whose nature there was no room for the affected sedateness and circumspection that are customary in the great world. Thus it was that, seeing the obstacles removed that had stood in the way of her happiness, and Don Luis conquered, holding his voluntary promise that he would make her his wife, and believing herself, with justice, to be loved—nay, worshiped—by him whom she too loved and worshiped, she danced and laughed, and gave way to other manifestations of joy that had in them, after all, something childlike and innocent.

But it was necessary that Don Luis should now depart. Pepita took a comb and smoothed his hair lovingly, and kissed him. She then rearranged his necktie.

"Farewell, lord of my life," she said, "dear sovereign of my soul. I will tell your father everything if you fear to do so. He is kind, and he will forgive us."

At last the lovers separated.

When Pepita found herself alone, her restless gaiety disappeared, and her countenance assumed a grave and thoughtful expression.

Two thoughts now presented themselves to her mind, both equally serious; the one possessing a merely mundane interest, the other an interest of a higher nature. The first thought was that her conduct to-night—the delirium of passion once past—might prejudice her in the opinion of Don Luis; but, finding after a severe examination of her conscience, that neither premeditation nor artifice had had any part in her actions, which were the offspring of an irresistible love, and of impulses noble in themselves, she came to the conclusion that Don Luis could not despise her for it, and she therefore made her mind easy on that point.

Nevertheless, although her frank confession that she was unable to comprehend a love that was purely spiritual, and her taking refuge afterward in her chamber—without foreseeing consequences—were both the result of an impulse innocent enough in itself, Pepita did not seek to deny in her own mind that she had sinned against God, and on this point she could find for herself no excuse. She commended herself, with all her heart, therefore, to the Virgin, entreating her forgiveness. She vowed to the image of Our Lady of Solitude, in the convent of the nuns, seven beautiful golden swords of the finest and most elaborate workmanship, to adorn her breast, and determined to go to confess herself on the following day to the vicar, and to submit herself to the harshest penance he should choose to impose upon her, in order to merit the absolution of those sins by means of which she had vanquished the obstinacy of Don Luis, who, but for them, would without a doubt have become a priest.

While Pepita was engaged in these reflections, and while she was aranging with so much discretion the affairs of her soul, Don Luis had descended to the hall below, accompanied by Antoñona.

Before taking his leave, Don Luis, without preface or circumlocution, spoke thus:

"Antoñona, tell me, you who are acquainted with everything, who is the Count of Genazahar, and what has he had to do with your mistress?"

"You begin to be jealous very soon."

"It is not jealousy that makes me ask this; it is simply curiosity."

"So much the better. There is nothing more tiresome than jealousy. Well, I will try to satisfy your curiosity. This same Count has given room enough for talk. He is a dissipated fellow, a gambler, and a man of no principle whatever, but he has more vanity than Don Roderick on the gallows. He made up his mind that my mistress should fall in love with him and marry him, and as she has refused him a thousand times he is mad with rage. This does not prevent him, however, from keeping in his money chest more than a thousand piastres that Don Gumersindo lent him years ago, without any more security than a bit of paper, through the fault and at the entreaty of Pepita, who is better than bread. The fool of a Count thought, no doubt, that Pepita, who was so good to him when a wife that she persuaded her husband to lend him money, would be so much better to him as a widow that she would consent to marry him. He was soon undeceived, however, and then he became furious."

"Good-by, Antoñona," said Don Luis, as he left the house, grave and thoughtful.

The lights of the shops and of the booths in the fair were now extinguished, and every one was going home to bed, with the exception of the owners of the toy-shops and other poor hucksters, who slept beside their wares in the open air.

Under some of the grated windows were still to be seen lovers, wrapped in their cloaks, and chatting with their sweethearts. Almost every one else had disappeared.

Don Luis, once out of sight of Antoñona, gave a loose rein to his thoughts. His resolution was taken, and all his reflections tended to confirm this resolution. The sincerity and ardor of the passion with which he had inspired Pepita, her beauty, the youthful grace of her person, and the fresh exuberance of her soul, presented themselves to his imagination and made him happy.

Notwithstanding this, however, he could not but reflect, with mortified vanity, on the change that had been wrought in himself. What would the dean think? How great would be the horror of the bishop! And, above all, how serious were the grounds for complaint he had given his father! The displeasure of the latter, his anger when he should know of the bond which united his son to Pepita, caused him infinite disquietude.

As for what—before he fell—he had called his fall, it must be confessed that, after he had fallen, it did not seem to him either so very serious or so very reprehensible. His spiritual-mindedness, viewed in the light that had just dawned upon him, he fancied to have had neither reality nor consistency; to have been but the vain and artificial product of his reading, of his boyish arrogance, of his aimless softness in the innocent days of his college life. When he remembered that he had at times thought himself the recipient of supernatural gifts and graces, had heard mystic whisperings, had held spiritual communion with superior beings; when he remembered that he had fancied himself almost beginning to tread the path that leads to spiritual union, through contemplation of the Divine, penetrating into the recesses of the soul, and mounting up to the region of pure intelligence, he smiled to himself, and began to suspect that during the period in question he had not been altogether in his right mind.

It had all been simply the result of his own arrogance. He had neither done penance, nor passed long years in meditation; he did not possess, nor had he ever possessed, sufficient merits for God to favor him with such privileges as these. The greatest proof he could give himself of the truth of this, the greatest certainty he could possess that the supernatural favors he had enjoyed were spurious, mere recollections of the authors he had read, was that not one of them had ever given him the rapture of Pepita's "I love you," or of the soft touch of her hand caressing his dark locks.

Don Luis had recourse to another species of Christian humility, to justify in his eyes what he now no longer called his fall, but his change of purpose. He confessed himself unworthy to be a priest. He reconciled himself to becoming a commonplace married man, a good sort of country gentleman, like any other, taking care of his vines and olives, and bringing up his children—for he now desired to have children—and to being a model husband at the side of his Pepita.

CHAPTER XII

HERE again I think myself under the necessity—responsible as I am for the publication and disclosure of this history—of interpolating various reflections and explanations of my own.

I said at the beginning of the story that I was inclined to think that the narrative part, called *paralipomena,* was composed by the reverend Dean for the purpose of completing the story and supplying incidents not related in the letters; but I had not at that time read the manuscript with attention. Now, on observing the freedom with which certain matters are treated, and the indulgence with which certain frailties are regarded by the author, I am compelled to ask whether the reverend Dean, with the severity of whose morals I am well acquainted, would have spent his time in writing what we have just read.

There are not sufficient grounds, however, for denying positively that the reverend Dean was the author of these *paralipomena.* The question, therefore, may still be left in doubt, as in substance they contain nothing opposed to Catholic doctrine or to Christian morality. On the contrary, if we examine them carefully, we shall see that they contain a lesson to pride and arrogance in the person of Don Luis. This history might easily serve as an appendix to the "Spiritual Disillusions" of Father Arbiol.

As for the opinion entertained by two or three ingenious friends of mine, that the reverend Dean, if he were the author, would have used a different style in his narration, saying "my nephew" in speaking of Don Luis, and interposing, from time to time, moral reflections of his own, I do not think it an argument of any great weight. The reverend Dean proposed to himself to tell what had taken place, without seeking to prove any thesis, and he acted with judgment in narrating things as they were, without analyzing motives or moralizing.

He did not do ill either, in my opinion, in concealing his personality, and in avoiding the use of the word *I,* which is a proof, not only of his humility and modesty, but of his literary taste also; for the epic poets and historians, who should serve us as models, do not say *I,* even when speaking of themselves or when they are the heroes of the events they relate. The Athenian Xenophon, to cite an instance, does not say *I* in his "Anabasis," but speaks of himself, when necessary, in the third person, as if the historian of those exploits were one person and the hero of them another. And there are whole chapters in which no mention at all is made of Xenophon. Only once, a little before the famous battle in which the youthful Cyrus met his death, while this prince was reviewing the Greeks and barbarians who formed his army, and when that of his brother Artaxerxes was already near—having been descried on the broad, treeless plain afar off, first as a little white cloud, then as a dark stain, and, finally, clearly and distinctly, while the neighing of the horses, the creaking of the war-chariots armed with formidable scythes, the snorting of the elephants, and the sound of warlike instruments reach the ears, and the glitter of the brass and gold of the weapons irradiated by the sun strike the eyes of the spectators—only at this moment, I repeat, and not before, does Xenophon appear in his own person. Then he emerges from the ranks to speak with Cyrus, and explains to him the cry that ran from Greek to Greek. It was what in our day would correspond to a watchword, and on that occasion it was *"Jupiter the savior, and victory!"*

The reverend Dean, who was a man of taste and very well versed in the classics, would not be likely to fall into the error of introducing himself into the narrative, and mixing himself up with it, under the pretext of being the uncle or tutor of the hero, and of vexing the reader by coming out at every step, slightly difficult or slippery, with a "Stop there!" or, "What are you about to do?" or, "Take care you do not fall, unhappy boy!" or other warnings of a like sort. Not to open his lips, on the other hand, or manifest disapprobation in any way whatever, he being present at least in spirit, would, in the case of some of the incidents related, have been but little becoming. In view of these facts, the reverend Dean, with the discretion which was characteristic of him, may possibly have composed the *paralipomena* without disclosing his identity to the reader. This much is certain, however: he added notes and comments of an edifying and profitable character, where such and such a passage seemed to require them. But these I have suppressed, for the reason that notes and comments are now out of fashion, and because this book would become unduly voluminous if it were printed with these additions.

I shall insert here, however, in the body of the text, the comment of the reverend Dean on the rapid transformation of Don Luis from spiritual-mindedness to the reverse, as it is curious, and throws much light on the whole matter.

"This change of purpose of my nephew," he says, "does not disappoint me. I foresaw it from the time he wrote me his first letters. I was deceived in regard to Luisito in the beginning. I believed him to have a true religious call, but I soon recognized the fact that his was a vain, poetic spirit. Mysticism was the form his poetic imaginings took, only until a more seductive form presented itself.

"Praised be God, who has willed that Luisito should be undeceived in time! He would have made but a bad priest if Pepita Jiménez had not so opportunely presented herself. His very impatience to attain to perfection at a single bound would have caused me to suspect something if I had not been blinded by the affection of an uncle. What! are the favors of Heaven thus obtained all at once? Is it only necessary to present one's self in order to triumph? A friend of mine, a naval officer, used to relate that, when he was in certain cities of America, being then very young, he sought to gain favor with the ladies with too much precipitation, and that they would say to him in their languid American accent: 'You have only just presented yourself, and you already want to be loved. Do something to deserve it, if you can.' If these ladies answered thus, what answer will not Heaven give to those who hope to gain it without merit, and in the twinkling of an eye?

"Many efforts must be made, much purification is needed, much penance must be done, in order to begin to stand well in the sight of God and to enjoy His favors. Even in those vain and false philosophies that have in them anything of mysticism, no supernatural gift or grace is received without a powerful effort and a costly sacrifice. Iamblichus was not given power to evoke the genii, and cause them to emerge from the fountain of Gadara, without first spending days and nights in study, and mortifying the body with privations and abstinences. Apollonius of Tyana is thought to have mortified himself severely before performing his false miracles. And in our own day the Krausists, who behold God, as they affirm, with corporeal vision, are forced to read and learn beforehand the whole "Analytics" of Sanz del Rio, which is a much harder task and a greater proof of patience and endurance than to flagellate the body until it looks like a ripe fig. My nephew desired, without effort or merit, to be a perfect man, and—see how it has ended!

"The important thing now is that he shall make a good husband, and that, since he is unsuited for great things, he may be fit for smaller ones—for domestic life, and to make Pepita happy, whose own fault, after all, is to have fallen madly in love with him, with all the innocence and violence of an untamed creature."

Thus far the comments of the reverend Dean, written with easy familiarity, as if for himself alone; for the good man was far from suspecting that I would play him the trick of giving them to the public.

CHAPTER XIII

DON LUIS, in the middle of the street, at two o'clock in the morning, was occupied with the thought, as we have said, that his life, which until now, he had dreamed might be worthy of the "Golden Legend," was about to be converted into a sweet and perpetual idyl. He had not been able to resist the lures of earthly passion. He had failed to imitate the example set by so many saints, among others by St. Vincent Ferrer with regard to a certain dissolute lady of Valencia; though, indeed the cases were dissimilar. For if to flee from the diabolical courtezan in question was an act of heroic virtue in St. Vincent, to flee from the self-abandonment, the ingenuousness, and the humility of Pepita would in him have been something as monstrous and cruel as if, when Ruth lay down at the feet of Boaz, saying to him, "I am thy handmaid: spread therefore thy skirt over thine handmaid," Boaz had given her a blow and sent her about her business! Don Luis, then, when Pepita surrendered herself to him, was obliged to follow the example of Boaz, and exclaim: "Daughter, blessed be thou of the Lord; thou hast showed more kindness in the latter end than at the beginning."

Thus did Don Luis justify himself in not following the example of St. Vincent, and other saints no less churlish. As for the ill success of the design he had entertained of imitating St. Edward, he tried to justify and excuse that also. St. Edward married for reasons of state, and without entertaining any affection for Queen Edith; but in his case and in that of Pepita Jiménez there were no reasons of state, but only tender love on both sides.

Don Luis, however, did not deny to himself—and this imparted to his present happiness a slight tinge of melancholy—that he had proved false to his ideal; that he had been vanquished in the conflict. Those who have no ideal, who have never had an ideal, would not distress themselves on this account. Don Luis did distress himself; but he presently came to the conclusion that he would substitute a more humble and easily attained ideal for his former exalted one. And although the recollection of Don Quixote's resolution to turn shepherd, on being vanquished by the Knight of the White Moon, here crossed his mind with ludicrous appositeness, he was in no way daunted by it. He thought, in union with Pepita Jiménez, to renew, in our prosaic and unbelieving time, the golden age, and to repeat the pious example of Philemon and Baucis, creating a model of patriarchal life in these pleasant fields, founding in the place where he was born a home presided over by religion, that should be at once the asylum of the needy, the centre of culture and friendly conviviality, and the clear mirror in which the domestic virtues should be reflected; joining in one, finally, conjugal love and the love of God, in order that God might sanctify and be present in their dwelling, making it the temple in which both should be His ministers, until by the will of Heaven they should be called to a better life.

Two obstacles must first be removed, however, before all this could be realized, and Don Luis began to consider with himself how he might best remove them.

The one was the displeasure, perhaps the anger, of his father, whom he had defrauded of his dearest hopes. The other was of a very different and, in a certain sense, of a much more serious character. Don Luis, while he entertained the purpose of becoming a priest, was right in defending Pepita from the gross insults of the Count of Genazahar by the weapons of argument only, and in taking no vengeance for the scorn and contempt with which those arguments were listened to. But having now determined to lay aside the cassock, and obliged, as he was, to declare immediately that he was betrothed to Pepita and was going to marry her, Don Luis, notwithstanding his peaceable disposition, his dreams of human brotherhood, and his religious belief, all of which remained intact in his soul, and all of which were alike opposed to violent measures, could not succeed in reconciling it with his dignity to refrain from breaking the head of the insolent Count. He knew well that dueling is a barbarous practise, that Pepita had no need of the blood of the Count to wash from her name the stain of calumny, and even that the Count himself had uttered the insults he had uttered, not because he believed them, nor perhaps through an excess of hatred, but through stupidity and want of breeding. Notwithstanding all these reflections, however, Don Luis was conscious that he would never again be able to respect himself, and, as a consequence, would never be able to perform to his taste the part of Philemon, if he did not begin with that of Fierabras, by giving the Count his deserts, asking God, meantime, never to place him in a similar position again.

This matter, then, being decided upon, he resolved to bring it to an end as soon as possible. And as it appeared to him that it would be inexpedient, as well as in bad taste, to arrange the affair through seconds, and thus make the honor of Pepita a subject of common talk, he determined to provoke a quarrel with the Count under some other pretext.

Thinking that the Count, being a stranger in the village and a confirmed gambler, might possibly be still engaged at play in the club-house, notwithstanding the lateness of the hour, Don Luis went straight there.

The club-house was still open, but both in the courtyard and the parlor the lights were nearly all extinguished. In one apartment only was there still a light. Thither Don Luis directed his steps, and on reaching it, he saw through the open door the Count of Genazahar engaged in playing *monte*, in which he acted as banker. Only five other persons were playing; two were strangers like the Count; the others were the captain of cavalry in charge of the remount, Currito, and the doctor. Things could not have been better arranged to suit the purpose of Don Luis. So engrossed were the players in their game that they did not observe him, who, as soon as he saw the Count, left the club-house and went rapidly homeward.

On reaching his house the door was opened for him by a servant. Don Luis inquired for his father, and finding that he was asleep, procured a light and went up to his own room, taking care to make no noise lest he should disturb him. There he took about a hundred and fifty piastres in gold that he had laid by, and put them in his pocket. He then called the servant to open the door for him again, and returned to the club-house.

Arrived there, Don Luis noisily entered the parlor in which the players were, comporting himself with an assumed foppish swagger. The players were struck with amazement at seeing him.

"You here at this hour!" said Currito.

"Where do you come from, little priest?" said the doctor.

"Have you come to preach me another sermon?" cried the Count.

"I have done with sermons," returned Don Luis, calmly. "The bad success of the last one I preached has clearly convinced me that God does not call me to that path in life, and I have chosen another. You, Count, have wrought my conversion. I have thrown aside the cassock. I have come here for amusement; I am in the flower of my youth, and I want to enjoy it."

"Come, I am glad of that," returned the Count; "but take care, my lad, for if the flower be a delicate one, it may wither and drop its leaves before their time."

"I shall take care of that," returned Don Luis. "I see you are playing, and I too feel like trying my luck. Do you know, Count, I think it would be amusing if I could break your bank?"

"You think it would be amusing, eh? You have been dining liberally!"

"I have dined as I pleased."

"The youngster is learning to answer back."

"I learn what it is my pleasure to learn."

"Damnation!" cried the Count; and the storm was about to burst when the captain, interposing, succeeded in reestablishing the peace.

"Come," said the Count when he had recovered his temper, "out with your cash, and try your luck."

Don Luis seated himself at the table, and took out all his gold. At sight of it the Count regained his serenity completely, for it must have exceeded in amount the sum he had in the bank, and he thought he should at once win it of this novice.

"There is no need to cudgel one's brains much in this game," said Don Luis to the Count; "I think I understand it already. I put money on a card, and if the card turns up I win; if not, you win."

"Just so, my young friend; you have a strong intellect."

"And the best of it is that I have not only a strong understanding, but a strong will as well. But though I may have the stubbornness of a donkey, I am not such a donkey as many people in this neighborhood."

"What a witty mood you are in to-night, and how anxious you are to display your wit!"

Don Luis was silent. He played a few deals, and was lucky enough to win almost every time.

The Count began to be annoyed.

"What if the youngster should pluck me?" he said to himself. "Fortune favors the innocent."

While the Count was troubling himself with this reflection, Don Luis, feeling fatigued, and weary now of the part he was playing, determined to end the matter at once.

"The object of all this," he said, "is to see if I can win all your gold, or if you can win mine. Is it not so, Count?"

"Just so."

"Well, then, why should we remain here all night? It is getting late, and according to your advice I ought to retire early, so that the flower of my youth may not wither before its time."

"How is this? Do you want to go away already? Do you want to back out?"

"I have no desire to back out. Quite the contrary. Currito, tell me, in this heap of gold here is there not already more than there is in the bank?"

Currito looked at the gold and answered:

"Without a doubt."

"How shall I explain," asked Don Luis, "that I wish to stake on one card all that I have here, against what there is in the bank?"

"You do that," responded Currito, "by saying, 'I play *banco!*'"

"Well, then I play *banco,*" said Don Luis, addressing himself to the Count; "I play *banco* on this king of spades, whose companion will to a certainty turn up before his opponent, the three, does."

The Count, whose whole cash capital was in the bank, began to be alarmed at the risk he ran; but there was nothing for it but to accept.

It is a common saying that those who are fortunate in love are unfortunate at play, but the reverse of this is often more nearly the truth. He who is fortunate in one thing is apt to be fortunate in everything; it is the same when one is unfortunate.

The Count continued to draw cards, but no *three* turned up. His emotion, notwithstanding his efforts to conceal it, was great. Finally, he came to a card which he knew by certain lines at the top to be the king of hearts, and paused.

"Draw," said the captain.

"It is of no use! The king of hearts! Curses on it! The little priest has plucked me. Take up your money."

The Count threw the cards angrily on the table.

Don Luis took up the money calmly, and with apparent indifference.

After a short silence the Count said:

"My little priest, you must give me my revenge."

"I see no such necessity."

"It seems to me that between gentlemen—"

"According to that rule the game would have no end," said Don Luis, "and it would be better to save one's self the trouble of playing altogether."

"Give me my revenge," replied the Count, without paying any attention to this argument.

"Be it so," returned Don Luis; "I wish to be fair."

The Count took up the cards again, and proceeded to deal.

"Stop a moment," said Don Luis; "let us understand each other. Where is the money for your new bank?"

The Count showed signs of confusion and disturbance.

"I have no money here," he returned, "but it seems to me that my word is more than enough."

Don Luis answered, with grave and measured accent:

"Count, I should be quite willing to trust the word of a gentleman, and allow him to remain in my debt, if it were not that in doing so I should fear to lose your friendship, which I am now in a fair way to gain; but as I heard this morning of the cruelty with which you have treated certain friends of mine to whom you are indebted, I do not wish to run the risk of becoming culpable in your eyes by means of the same fault. How ridiculous to suppose that I should voluntarily incur your enmity by lending you money which you would not repay me, as you have not repaid, except with insults, that which you owe Pepita Jiménez!"

From the fact that this accusation was true, the offense was all the greater. The Count became livid with anger, and, by this time on his feet, ready to come to blows with the collegian.

"You lie, slanderer!" he exclaimed. "I will tear you limb from limb, you—"

This last insult, which reflected on his birth and on the honor of her whose memory was most sacred to him, was never finished; its end never reached the ears of him against whom it was directed. For, with marvelous quickness, dexterity, and force, he reached across the table which was between himself and the Count, and with the light, flexible bamboo cane with which he had armed himself, struck his antagonist on the face, raising on it instantly a livid mark.

There was neither retort, outcry, nor uproar. When the hands come into play, the tongue is apt to be silent. The Count was about to throw himself on Don Luis for the purpose of tearing him to pieces, if it were in his power. But opinion had changed greatly since yesterday morning, and was now on the side of Don Luis. The captain, the doctor, and even Currito, who now showed more courage than he had done on that occasion, all held back the Count, who struggled and fought ferociously to release himself.

"Let me go!" he cried; "let me get at him and kill him!"

"I do not seek to prevent a duel," said the captain; "a duel is inevitable. I only seek to prevent your fighting here like two porters. I should be wanting in self-respect if I consented to be present at such a combat."

"Let weapons be brought!" said the Count; "I do not wish to defer the affair for a single moment. At once—and here!"

"Will you fight with swords?" said the captain.

"Yes," responded Don Luis.

"Swords be it," said the Count.

All this was said in a low voice, so that nothing might be heard in the street. Even the servants of the club-house, who slept on chairs in the kitchen and in the yard, were not awakened by the noise.

Don Luis chose as his seconds the captain and Currito; the Count chose the two strangers. The doctor made ready to practice his art, and showed the emblem of the Red Cross.

It was not yet daylight. It was agreed that the apartment in which they were should be the field of combat, the door being first closed. The captain went to his house for the swords, and returned soon afterward carrying them under the cloak which he had put on for the purpose of concealing them.

We already know that Don Luis had never wielded a weapon in his life. Fortunately, the Count, although he had never studied theology, or entertained the purpose of becoming a priest, was not much more skilled than he in the art of fence.

The only rules laid down for the duel were that, their swords once in hand, each of the combatants should use his weapon as Heaven might best direct him.

The door of the apartment was closed. The tables and chairs were placed in a corner, to leave a free field for the combatants, and the lights were suitably disposed.

Don Luis and the Count divested themselves of their coats and waistcoats, remaining in their shirt-sleeves, and each selected his weapon. The seconds stood on one side. At a signal from the captain the combat began. Between two persons who know neither how to parry a stroke nor how to put themselves on guard, a combat must of necessity be brief; and it was.

The fury of the Count, restrained for some time past, now burst forth and blinded his reason. He was strong, and he had wrists of steel; and with his sword he showered down on Don Luis a storm of strokes without order or sequence. Four times he succeeded in touching Don Luis—each time, fortunately, with the flat of his weapon. He bruised his shoulders, but did not wound him. The young theologian had need of all his strength to keep from falling to the floor, overcome by the force of the blows and the pains of his bruises. A fifth time the Count hit Don Luis, on the left arm, and this time with the edge of his weapon, although aslant. The blood began to flow abundantly. Far from stopping, the Count resumed the attack with renewed fury, in the hope of again wounding his antagonist. He almost placed himself under the weapon of Don Luis. The latter, instead of putting himself in position to parry brought his sword down vigorously on his adversary, and succeeded in wounding the Count in the head. The blood gushed forth, and ran down his forehead and into his eyes. Stunned by the blow, the Count fell heavily to the floor.

The whole combat was a matter of a few seconds. Don Luis had remained tranquil throughout, like a Stoic philosopher who is obliged by the hard law of necessity to take part in a conflict opposed alike to his habits and his ways of thought. But no sooner did he see his antagonist extended on the floor, bathed in blood and looking as though he were dead, than he experienced the most poignant anguish, and feared for a moment that he should faint. He who, until within the last five or six hours, had held unwaveringly to his resolution of being a priest, a missionary, a minister, and a messenger of the Gospel, had committed, or accused himself of having committed, during those few hours, every crime, and of breaking all the commandments of God. There was now no mortal sin by which he was not contaminated. First, his purpose of leading a life of perfect and heroic holiness had been put to flight; then had followed his purpose of leading a life of holiness of a more easy, commonplace sort. The devil seemed to please himself in overthrowing his plans. He reflected that he could now no longer be even a Christian Philemon, for to lay his neighbor's head open with a stroke of a sabre was not a very good beginning of his idyl.

Don Luis, after all the excitement of the day, was now in a condition resembling that of a man who has brain fever. Currito and the captain, one at each side, took hold of him and led him home.

CHAPTER XIV

DON PEDRO DE VARGAS got out of bed in terror when he was told that his son had come home wounded. He ran to see him, examined his bruises and the wound in his arm, and saw that they were none of them attended with danger; but he broke out into threats of vengeance, and would not be pacified until he was made acquainted with the particulars of the affair, and learned that Don Luis had known how to avenge himself in spite of his theology.

The doctor came soon after to examine the wound, and was of opinion that in three or four days' time Don Luis would be able to go out again as if nothing had happened. With the Count, on the other hand, it would be a matter of months. His life, however, was in no danger. He had returned to consciousness, and had asked to be taken to his own home, which was distant only a league from the village in which these events took place. A hired coach had been procured, and he had been conveyed thither, accompanied by his servant and also by the two strangers who had acted as his seconds.

Four days after the affair the doctor's opinion was justified by the result, and Don Luis, although sore from his bruises and with his wound still unhealed, was in a condition to go out, and promised a complete recovery within a short time.

The first duty which Don Luis thought himself obliged to fulfil, as soon as he was off the sick list, was to confess to his father his love for Pepita, and his intention of marrying her.

Don Pedro had not gone out to the country, nor had he occupied himself in any other way than in taking care of his son during his sickness. He was constantly at his side, waiting on him and petting him with tender affection.

On the morning of the 27th of June, after the doctor had gone, Don Pedro being alone with his son, the confession, so difficult for Don Luis to make, took place in the following manner:

"Father," said Don Luis, "I ought not to deceive you any longer. To-day I am going to confess my faults to you, and cast away hypocrisy."

"If it is a confession you are about to make, my boy, it would be better for you to send for the reverend vicar. My standard of morality is an indulgent one, and I shall give you absolution for everything, without my absolution being of much value to you, however. But if you wish to confide to me some weighty secret, as to your best friend, begin by all means; I am ready to listen to you."

"What I am about to confess to you is a very serious fault of which I have been guilty; and I am ashamed to—"

"You have no need to be ashamed before your father; speak frankly."

Here Don Luis growing very red, and with visible confusion, said:

"My secret is, that I am in love with—Pepita Jiménez—and that she—"

Don Pedro interrupted his son with a burst of laughter, and finished the sentence for him:

"And that she is in love with you, and that on the night of St. John's Eve you had a tender meeting with her until two o'clock in the morning, and that, for her sake, you sought a quarrel with the Count of Genazahar, whose head you have broken.

"A pretty secret to confide to me, truly! There isn't a cat or a dog in the village that is not fully acquainted with every detail of the business. The only thing there seemed a possibility of being able to conceal was, that your interview lasted until just two o'clock in the morning; but some gipsy-cake women chanced to see you leave Pepita's house, and did not stop until they had told every living creature in the place of it. Pepita, besides, makes no great effort to conceal the truth, and in this she does well, for that would be only the concealment of Antequera. Since you have been wounded, Pepita comes here twice a day, and sends Antoñona two or three times more to inquire after you; and if they have not come in to see you, it is because I would not consent to their doing so, lest it should excite you."

The confusion and the distress of Don Luis reached their climax when he heard his father thus compendiously tell the whole story.

"How surprised," he said, "how astounded you must have been!"

"No, my boy, I was neither surprised nor astounded. The matter has been known in the village only for four days, and indeed, to tell the truth, your transformation did create some surprise. 'Oh, the sly-boots! the wolf in sheep's clothing! the hypocrite!' every one exclaimed; 'how we have been deceived in him!' The reverend vicar, above all, is quite bewildered. He is still crossing himself at the thought of how you toiled in the vineyard of the Lord on the night of the 23d and the morning of the 24th, and of the strange character of your labors. But there was nothing in these occurrences to surprise me, except your wound. We old people can hear the grass grow. It is not easy for the chickens to deceive the huckster."

"It is true, I sought to deceive you! I have been a hypocrite!"

"Don't be a fool; I do not say this to blame you. I say it in order to give myself an air of perspicacity. But let us speak with frankness. My boasting is, after all, without foundation. I knew, step by step, for more than two months past, the progress of your love affair with Pepita; but I know it because your uncle the dean, to whom you were writing all that passed within your mind, has communicated it to me. Listen to your uncle's letter of accusation, and to the answer I gave him, a very important document, of which I have kept the copy."

Don Pedro took some papers from his pocket, and read aloud his brother's letter:

"My dear Brother:

"It grieves me to the heart to be obliged to give you a piece of bad news; but I trust that God will grant you patience and endurance to enable you to hear it without feeling too much anger or bitterness.

"Luisito has been writing me strange letters for some days past, in which he reveals, in the midst of his mystical exaltation, an inclination, earthly and sinful enough, toward a certain widow, charming, mischievous, and coquettish, who lives in your village. Until now I had deceived myself, believing Luisito's call to be a true one; and I flattered myself with giving to the Church of God a wise, virtuous, and exemplary priest. But his letters have dispelled my illusions. Luisito shows himself, in them, to have more of poetry than of true piety in his nature; and the widow, who must be a limb of Satan, will be able to vanquish him with but a very slight effort. Although I wrote to Luisito admonishing him to flee from temptation, I am already certain that he will fall into it. This ought not to grieve me; for if he is to be false to his vocation, to indulge in gallantries, and to make love, it is better that this evil disposition should reveal itself in time, and that he should not become a priest. I should not, therefore, see any serious objection to Luisito's remaining with you, for the purpose of being tested by the touchstone and analyzed in the crucible of such a love, making the little widow the agent by whose means might be discovered how great is the quantity of the pure gold of his clerical virtues, and how much alloy is mixed with that gold, were it not that we are met by the difficulty that the widow whom we would thus convert into a faithful assayer, is the object of your own addresses, and, it may be, your sweetheart.

"That your son should turn out to be your rival would be too serious a matter. This would be a monstrous scandal, and to avoid it in time I write to you to-day, to the end that, under whatever pretext, you may send or bring Luisito here—the sooner the better."

Don Luis listened in silence, and with his eyes cast down. His father then read him his reply to the dean:

"Dear Brother and Venerable Spiritual Father:

"I return you a thousand thanks for the news you sent me, and for your counsel and advice. Although I flatter myself with not being wanting in shrewdness, I confess my stupidity on this occasion; I was blinded by vanity. Pepita Jiménez, from the time that my son arrived here, manifested so much amiability and affection toward me that I began to indulge in pleasing hopes on my own account. Your letter was necessary to undeceive me. I now understand that in making herself so sociable, in showing me so many attentions, and in dancing attendance on me, as she did, this cunning Pepita had in her mind only the father of the smooth-faced theologian. I shall not attempt to conceal from you that, for the moment, this disappointment mortified and distressed me a little; but when I reflected over it with due consideration, my mortification and my distress were converted into joy.

"Luis is an excellent boy. Since he has been with me I have learned to regard him with much greater affection than formerly. I parted from him, and gave him up to you to educate, because my own life was not very exemplary, and, for this and other reasons, he would have grown up a savage here. You went beyond my hopes and even my desires, and almost made a father of the Church of Luisito. To have a holy son would have flattered my vanity; but I should have been very sorry to remain without an heir to my house and name, who would give me handsome grandchildren, and who after my death would enjoy my wealth, which is my glory, for I acquired it by skill and industry, and not by cunning and trickery. Perhaps the conviction I had that there was no remedy, and that Luis would inevitably go abroad to convert the Chinese, the Indians, or the blacks of the Congo, made me resolve on marrying, so as to provide myself with an heir.

"Naturally enough, I cast my eyes on Pepita Jiménez, who is not, as you imagine, a limb of Satan, but a lovely creature, as innocent as an angel, and ardent in her nature, rather than coquettish. I have so good an opinion of Pepita that, if she were sixteen again, with a domineering mother who tyrannized over her, and if I were eighty, like Don Gumersindo—that is to say, if death were already knocking at the door—I would marry Pepita, that her smile might cheer me on my deathbed, as if my guardian angel had taken human shape in her, and for the purpose of leaving her my position, my fortune, and my name. But Pepita is not sixteen, but twenty; nor is she now in the power of that serpent, her mother; nor am I eighty, but fifty-five. I am at the very worst age, because I begin to feel myself considerably the worse for wear, with something of asthma, a good deal of cough, rheumatic pains, and other chronic ailments; yet devil a bit do I wish to die, notwithstanding! I believe I shall not die for twenty years to come, and, as I am thirty-five years older than Pepita, you may calculate the miserable future that would await her, tied to an old man who would live forever. At the end of a few years of marriage she would be reduced to hating me, notwithstanding her goodness. Doubtless it is because she is good and wise that she has not chosen to accept me for a husband, notwithstanding the perseverance and the obstinacy with which I have proposed to her.

"How much do I not thank her for this now! Even my self-love, wounded by her scorn, is soothed by the reflection that, if she does not love me, at least she loves one of my blood, is captivated by a son of mine. If this fresh and luxuriant ivy, I say to myself, refuses to twine around the old trunk, worm-eaten already, it climbs by it to reach the new sprout it has put forth—a green and flourishing offshoot. May God bless them both, and make their love prosper!

"Far from bringing the boy back to you, I shall keep him here—by force, if it be necessary. I have determined to oppose his entering the priesthood. I dream already of seeing him married. I shall grow young again contemplating the handsome pair joined together by love. And how will it be when they shall have given me a family of grandchildren? Instead of going as a missionary, and bringing back to me from Australia, or Madagascar, or India, neophytes black as soot, with lips the size of your hand, or yellow as deerskin, and with eyes like owls, will it not be better for Luisito to preach the Gospel in his own house, and to give me a series of little catechumens, fair, rosy, with eyes like those of Pepita, who will resemble cherubim without wings? The catechumens he would bring me from those foreign lands I should have to keep at a respectful distance, in order not to be overpowered by their odor; while those I speak of would seem to me like roses of Paradise, and would come to climb up on my knees, and would call me grandpapa, and with their little hands pat the bald spot I am beginning to acquire.

"When I was in all my vigor I had no particular longing for domestic joys: but now that I am approaching old age, if I have not already entered on it, as I have no intention of turning monk, I please myself in thinking that I shall play the part of a patriarch. And do not imagine, either, that I am going to leave it to time to bring this young engagement to a happy close. No! I shall myself set to work to do this.

"Continuing your comparison, since you speak of Pepita as a crucible and Luis as a metal, I shall find, or rather I have found already, a bellows, or blow-pipe, very well adapted to kindle up the fire, so that the metal may melt in it the more quickly. Antoñona has an understanding with me already, and through her I know that Pepita is over head and ears in love.

"We have agreed that I shall continue to seem blind to everything, and to know nothing of what passes. The reverend vicar, who is a simple soul, always in the clouds, helps me as much as Antoñona does, or more, and without knowing it, because he repeats to Pepita everything Luis says to him, and everything Pepita says to Luis; so that this excellent man, with the weight of half a century in each foot, has been converted—oh, miracle of love and of innocence!—into a carrier-dove by which the two lovers send each other their flatteries and endearments, while they are as ignorant as he is of the fact.

"So powerful a combination of natural and artificial methods ought to give an infallible result. You will be made acquainted with this result when I give you notice of the wedding, so that you may come to perform the ceremony, or else send the lovers your blessing and a handsome present."

With these words Don Pedro finished the reading of his letter; and on looking again at Don Luis he saw that he had been listening to him with his eyes full of tears.

Father and son united in a long and close embrace.

Just a month from the date of this interview the wedding of Don Luis de Vargas and Pepita Jiménez took place.

The reverend Dean—fearing the ridicule of his brother at the spiritual-mindedness of Don Luis having thus come to naught, and recognizing also that he would not play a very dignified part in the village, where every one would say he was a poor hand at turning out saints—declined to be present, excusing himself on the ground of being too busy, although he sent his blessing, and a magnificent pair of earrings as a present for Pepita.

The reverend vicar, therefore, had the pleasure of marrying her to Don Luis.

The bride, elegantly attired, was thought lovely by every one, and was looked upon as a good exchange for the hair shirt and the scourge.

That night Don Pedro gave a magnificent ball in the courtyard of his house and the contiguous apartments. Servants and gentlemen, nobles and laborers, ladies and country-girls were present, and mingled together as if it were the ideal golden age—though why called golden I know not. Four skilful, or, if not skilful, at least indefatigable, guitar-players played a fandango; two gipsies, a man and a woman, both famous singers, sang verses of a tender character and appropriate to the occasion; and the schoolmaster read an epithalamium in heroic verse.

There were tarts, fritters, jumbles, gingerbread, sponge-cake, and wine in abundance for the common people. The gentry regaled themselves with refreshments—chocolate, lemonade, honey, and various kinds of aromatic and delicate cordials.

Don Pedro was like a boy—sprightly, gallant, and full of jests. It did not look as if there were much truth in what he had said in his letter to the Dean in regard to his rheumatism and other ailments. He danced the fandango with Pepita, as also with the most attractive among her maids, and with six or seven of the village girls. He gave each of them, on reconducting her, tired out, to her seat, the prescribed embrace, and to the least demure a couple of pinches, though this latter forms no part of the ceremonial. He carried his gallantry to the extreme of dancing with Doña Casilda, who could not refuse him, and who, with her two hundred and fifty pounds of humanity, and the heat of July, perspired at every pore. Finally, Don Pedro stuffed Currito so full, and made him drink so often to the health of the newly married pair, that the muleteer Dientes was obliged to carry him home to sleep off the effect of his excesses, slung like a wine-skin across the back of an ass! The ball lasted until three in the morning; but the young couple discreetly disappeared before eleven, and retired to the house of Pepita.

Although it is the unfailing use and custom of the village to treat every widow or widower who marries again to a terrible *charivari*—that particularly noisy kind of mock serenade—leaving them not a moment's rest from the cow-bells during the first night of marriage, Pepita was such a favorite, Don Pedro was so much respected, and Don Luis was so beloved, that there were no bells on this occasion, nor was there the least attempt made at ringing them—a singular circumstance, which is recorded as such in the annals of the village.

PART III

LETTERS OF MY BROTHER

THE history of Pepita and Luisito should, properly speaking, end here. This epilogue is not necessary to the story, but, as it formed part of the bundle of papers left at his death by the reverend Dean, although we refrain from publishing it entire, we shall at least give samples of it.

No one can entertain the least doubt that Don Luis and Pepita, united by an irresistible love, almost of the same age—she beautiful, he brave and handsome, both intelligent and full of goodness—would enjoy, during a long life, as much peace and happiness as falls to the lot of mortals. And this supposition, which for those who have read the preceding narrative is a logically drawn deduction from it, is converted into a certainty for him who reads the epilogue.

The epilogue gives, besides, some information respecting the secondary personages of the narrative, in whose fate the reader may possibly be interested. It consists of a collection of letters addressed by Don Pedro de Vargas to his brother the Dean, dating from the day of his son's marriage to four years later.

Without prefixing the dates, although following their chronological order, we shall transcribe here a few short extracts from these letters, and thus bring our task to an end:

Luis manifests the most lively gratitude toward Antoñona, without whose services he would not now possess Pepita. But this woman, the accomplice of the sole fault of which either he or Pepita had been guilty in their lives, living as she did on the most familiar footing in the house, and fully acquainted with all that had taken place, could not but be in the way. To get rid of her, then, and at the same time to do her a service, Luis set to work to bring about a reconciliation between her and her husband, whose daily fits of drunkenness she had refused to put up with. The son of Master Cencias gave his promise that he would get *hardly ever* drunk; but he would not venture on an absolute and uncompromising *never*. Confiding in this half-promise, however, Antoñona consented to return to the conjugal roof. Husband and wife being thus reunited, it occurred to Luis that a homeopathic principle of treatment might prove efficacious with the son of Master Cencias in curing him radically of his vice; for having heard it affirmed that confectioners detest sweets, he concluded that, on the same principle, tavern-keepers ought to detest spirits, and he sent Antoñona and her husband to the capital of the province, where at his own cost he set them up in a fine tavern. Both live there together happily; they have succeeded in obtaining many patrons, and will probably become rich. He still gets drunk occasionally; but Antoñona, who is the stronger of the two, is accustomed at such times to give him a good trouncing, to help on his cure.

Currito, anxious to imitate his cousin, whom he admires more and more every day, and seeing and enjoying the domestic felicity of Pepita and Luis, made haste to find a sweetheart, and married the daughter of a rich farmer of the place, healthy, fresh, red as a poppy, and who promises soon to acquire proportions as ample as those of her mother-in-law Casilda.

The Count of Genazahar, after being confined to his bed for five months, is now cured of his wound, and, it is said, is very much improved in manners. He paid Pepita, a short time ago, more than half of his debt to her, and asks for a respite in the payment of the remainder.

We have had a very great grief, although one that we had foreseen for some time past. The father vicar, yielding to the advance of years, has passed to a better life. Pepita remained till the last at his bedside, and closed his eyes with her own beautiful hands. The father vicar died the death of a blessed servant of the Lord. Rather than death, it seemed a happy transit to serener regions. Nevertheless,

Pepita and all of us have mourned him sincerely. He has left behind him only a few piastres and his furniture, for he gave all he had in alms. His death would have made orphans of the poor of the village, if it were not that Pepita still lives.

Every one in the village laments the death of the reverend vicar, and there are many who regard him as a real saint, worthy of religious honors, and who attribute miracles to him. I know not how that may be, but I do know that he was an excellent man, and that he must have gone straight to heaven, where we may hope that he intercedes for us. With all this, his humility, his modesty, and his fear of God, were such that he spoke of his sins in the hour of death as if he had in reality committed many, and he besought our prayers to the Lord and to the Virgin Mary for their forgiveness.

A strong impression has been produced on the mind of Luis by the exemplary life and death of this man. He was simple, it must be confessed, and of limited intelligence, but of upright will, ardent faith, and fervent charity. When Luis compares himself with the vicar, he feels humiliated. This has infused into his soul a certain bitter melancholy; but Pepita, who has a great deal of tact, dissipates it with smiles and caresses.

Everything prospers with us. Luis and I have some wine-vaults, than which there are no better in Spain, if we except those of Xeres. The olive crop of this year has been superb. We can afford to allow ourselves every luxury; and I advise Luis and Pepita to make the tour of Germany, France, and Italy as soon as Pepita is over her trouble, and once more in her usual health. The dear children can afford to spend a few thousand piastres on the expedition, and will bring back some fine books, pieces of furniture, and objects of art, to adorn their dwelling.

We have deferred the baptism for two weeks, in order that it may take place on the first anniversary of the wedding. The child is a marvel of beauty, and is very healthy. I am the godfather, and he has been named after me. I am already dreaming of the time when Periquito shall begin to talk, and amuse us with his prattle.

In order that nothing may be wanting to the prosperity of this tender pair, it turns out now, according to letters received from Havana, that the brother of Pepita, whose evil ways we feared might disgrace the family, is almost—and indeed without an *almost*—about to honor and elevate it by becoming a person of eminence. During all the time in which we heard nothing from him he has been profiting by his opportunities, and fortune has sent him favoring gales. He obtained another employment in the Customhouse; then he trafficked in negroes; then he failed—an occurrence which for certain business men is like a good pruning for trees, making them sprout again with fresh vigor; and now he is so prosperous that he has formed the resolution of entering the highest circles of the aristocracy, under the title of Marquis or Duke. Pepita is frightened and troubled at this unexpected turn of fortune, but I tell her not to be foolish: if her brother is, and must in any case be, a rascal, is it not better that he should at least be a fortunate one?

We might thus go on making extracts did we not fear to weary the reader. We shall end, then, by copying one of the latest letters:

My children have returned from their travels in good health. Periquito is very mischievous and very charming. Luis and Pepita have come back resolved never again to leave the village, though they should live longer than Philemon and Baucis. They are more in love with each other than ever.

They have brought back with them articles of furniture, a great many books, some pictures, and all sorts of other elegant trifles, purchased in the various countries through which they have traveled, and principally in Paris, Rome, Florence, and Vienna.

The affection they entertain for each other, and the tenderness and cordiality with which they treat each other and every one else, have exercised a beneficent influence on manners here; and the elegance and good taste with which they are now completing the furnishing of their house will go far to make superficial culture take root and spread.

The people in Madrid say that in the country we are stupid and uncouth; but they remain where they are, and never take the trouble to come and reform our manners. On the contrary, no sooner does any one make his appearance in the country who knows or is worth anything, or who thinks he knows or is worth anything, than he makes every possible effort to get away from it, and leaves the field and provincial towns behind him. Pepita and Luis pursue the opposite course, and I commend them for it with my whole heart. They are gradually improving and beautifying their surroundings, so as to make of this secluded spot a paradise.

Do not imagine, however, that the inclination of Pepita and Luis for material well-being has cooled in the slightest degree their religious feelings. The piety of both grows deeper every day; and in each new pleasure or satisfaction which they enjoy, or which they can procure for their fellow beings, they see a new benefaction of Heaven, in which they recognize fresh cause for gratitude. More than this, no pleasure or satisfaction would be such, none would be of any worth, or substance, or value in their eyes, were it not for the thought of higher things, and for the firm belief they have in them.

Luis, in the midst of his present happiness, never forgets the overthrow of the ideal he had set up for himself. There are times when his present life seems to him vulgar, selfish, and prosaic, compared with the life of sacrifice, with the spiritual existence to which he believed himself called in the first years of his youth. But Pepita solicitously hastens to dispel his melancholy on such occasions; and then Luis sees and acknowledges that it is possible for man to serve God in every state and condition, and succeeds in reconciling the lively faith and the love of God that fills his soul with this legitimate love of the earthly and perishable. But in the earthly and perishable he beholds the divine principle, as it were, without which, neither in the stars that stud the heavens, nor in the flowers and fruits that beautify the fields, nor in the eyes of Pepita, nor in the innocence and beauty of Periquito, would he behold anything lovely. The greater world, all this magnificent fabric of the universe, he declares, would without its all-seeing God seem to him sublime indeed, but without order, or beauty, or purpose. And as for the world's epitome, as we are accustomed to call man, neither would he love that were it not for God; and this, not because God commands him to love it, but because the dignity of man, and his title to be loved, have their foundation in God Himself, who not only made the soul of man in His own likeness, but ennobled also his body, making it the living temple of the Spirit, holding communion with it by means of the sacrament, and exalting it to the extreme of uniting with it His incarnate Word. In these and other arguments, which I am unable to set forth here, Luis finds consolation.

He reconciles himself to having relinquished his purpose of leading a life devoted to pious meditations, ecstatic contemplation, and apostolic works, and ceases to feel the sort of generous envy with which the father vicar inspired him on the day of his death; but both he and Pepita continue to give thanks, with great Christian devoutness, for benefits they enjoy, comprehending that not to their own merit do they owe these benefits, but only to the goodness of God.

And so my children have in their house a couple of apartments resembling beautiful little Catholic chapels or oratories; but I must confess that these chapels have, too, their trace of paganism—an amorous-pastoral-poetic and Arcadian air which is to be seen only beyond city walls.

The orchard of Pepita is no longer an orchard, but a most enchanting garden, with its araucarias and Indian figs, which grow here in the open air, and its well-arranged though small hothouse, full of rare plants.

The room in which we ate the strawberries on the afternoon on which Pepita and Luis saw and spoke with each other for the second time, has been transformed into a graceful temple, with portico and columns of white marble. Within is a spacious apartment, comfortably furnished, and adorned by two beautiful pictures. One represents Psyche discovering by the light of her lamp Cupid asleep on his couch; the other represents Chloe when the fugitive grasshopper has taken refuge in her bosom, where, believing itself secure, it begins to chirp in its pleasant hiding-place, from which Daphnis is trying, meanwhile, to take it forth.

A very good copy, in Carrara marble, of the Venus de Medici occupies the most prominent place in the apartment, and, as it were, presides over it. On the pedestal are engraved, in letters of gold, this thought of Lucretius:

"Without thee, darkness reigns instead of light,
And nothing lovely is, and nothing ever bright."

A HAPPY BOY

BY

BJÖRNSTJERNE BJÖRNSON

BIOGRAPHICAL NOTE

THE life of Björnstjerne Björnson was so full and active, and involves to such a degree the intellectual and political history of his country in the second half of the nineteenth century, that it is impossible in a short sketch to do more than indicate its main outlines.

He was born, the son of a pastor, in Kvikne, Osterdal, Norway, on December 8, 1832, but his youth was spent mainly in the picturesque district of Romsdal. He was educated in Molde and Christiania, and early began a career as a journalist and dramatic critic. His first book of importance was "Synnöve Solbakken" (1857), and it was followed by "Arne," "A Happy Boy" (1860), and "The Fisher Maiden." These works deal with the Norwegian peasant, portrayed with understanding and sympathy, and, though true to nature, have an idyllic quality which separates them from much of the fiction of rural life that was being written elsewhere in Europe at that time.

Meantime he was also experimenting in drama, and in a series of plays beginning with "Between the Battles" in 1855 and culminating in the trilogy of "Sigurd the Bastard" in 1862, he sought to develop national feeling on another side by reviving the heroic life of the old sagas. After acting as director of the theatre at Bergen for two years, and editing a Christiania newspaper for a short time, Björnson traveled through Europe from 1860 to 1863; and on his return he assumed the directorship of the Christiania theater, where he brought out with great success his "Mary Stuart in Scotland," and a modern comedy, "The Newly Married" (1865). His reputation was still further enhanced by the publication of "Poems and Songs" and the epic cycle "Arnljot Gelline," which placed him in the front rank of Norwegian poets.

Between the ages of thirty-five and forty Björnson's literary activity was suspended, and he threw himself with great vigor into radical political propaganda, becoming the hero of one party and anathema to another. When he returned to literature a great change was evident in his ideas and methods. His next plays, "Bankruptcy" and "The Editor," deal in realistic fashion with modern social problems: the early tendency to the idyllic and romantic has gone. "The King" was, in effect if not in purpose, an attack on the monarchical principle; "Leonarda" (1879), and "A Gauntlet" (1883), dealt with the relations of the sexes in a fashion that roused violent discussion; "The New System" was a keen satire on political and industrial conditions. In the same period he published his study of mystical religion, "Beyond our Powers", which was not acted, however, till 1899.

The violence of Björnson's political activity led to his withdrawing for a time to Germany under threat of prosecution for high treason; and for a time he returned to the writing of novels. Here also he now introduced his theories on such modern subjects as heredity, in "The Heritage of the Kurts" (1884), and "In God's Way" (1889). Of his later work the most important are the stories "Dust", "Mother's Hands," and "Absalom's Hair," and the plays "Geography and Love"—a great theatrical success—"Laboremus," "At Storhove," and "Daglannet" (1904).

In 1903 he was awarded the Nobel Prize for literature; and in spite of the enemies he had created by the vigor with which he championed the causes he espoused, he was recognized not only at home but throughout Europe as one of the great literary figures of his age. He died on April 26, 1910.

It is clear that the varied productions of such a man cannot be represented by any one work. "A Happy Boy", however, though one of his early books and written before he became immersed either in political controversy or modern social problems, is typical of his work in the period when he was recording the simple life of the peasantry among whom he had been born; and by the vividness of its background and the delicate charm of its characterization it has won a wide popularity far beyond the boundaries of Norway.

W. A. N.

CRITICISMS AND INTERPRETATIONS

I

By Hjalmar Hjorth Boyesen

BJÖRNSTJERNE BJÖRNSON is the first Norwegian poet who can in any sense be called national. The national genius, with its limitations as well as its virtues, has found its living embodiment in him. Whenever he opens his mouth it is as if the nation itself were speaking. If he writes a little song, hardly a year elapses before its phrases have passed into the common speech of the people; composers compete for the honor of interpreting it in simple. Norse-sounding melodies, which gradually work their way from the drawing-room to the kitchen, the street, and thence out over the wide fields and highlands of Norway. His tales, romances, and dramas express collectively the supreme result of the nation's experience, so that no one to-day can view Norwegian life or Norwegian history except through their medium. The bitterest opponent of the poet (for like every strong personality he has many enemies) is thus no less his debtor than his warmest admirer. His speech has stamped itself upon the very language and given it a new ring, a deeper resonance. His thought fills the air, and has become the unconscious property of all who have grown to manhood and womanhood since the day when his titanic form first looked up on the horizon of the North. It is not only as their first and greatest poet that the Norsemen love and hate him, but also as a civilizer in the widest sense. But like Kadmus, in Greek myth, he has not only brought with him letters, but also the dragon-teeth of strife, which it is to be hoped will not sprout forth in armed men. . . .

It had been the fashion in Norway since the nation regained its independence to interest one's self in a lofty, condescending way in the life of the peasantry. A few well-meaning persons, like the poet Wergeland, had labored zealously for their enlightenment and the improvement of their economic condition; but, except in the case of such single individuals, no real and vital sympathy and fellow-feeling had ever existed between the upper and the lower strata of Norwegian society. And as long as the fellow-feeling is wanting, this zeal for enlightenment, however laudable its motive, is not apt to produce lasting results. The peasants view with distrust and suspicion whatever comes to them from their social superiors, and the so-called "useful books", which were scattered broadcast over the land, were of a tediously didactic character, and, moreover, hardly adapted to the comprehension of those to whom they were ostensibly addressed. That this peasantry, whom the *bourgeoisie* and the aristocracy of culture had been wont to regard with half-pitying condescension, were the real representatives of the Norse nation; that they had preserved through long years of tyranny and foreign oppression the historic characteristics of their Norse forefathers, while the upper classes had gone in search of strange gods, and bowed their necks to the foreign yoke; that in their veins the old strong saga-life was still throbbing with vigorous pulse-beats—this was the lesson which Björnson undertook to teach his countrymen, and a very fruitful lesson it has proved to be. It has inspired the people with renewed courage, it has turned the national life into fresh channels, and it has revolutionized national politics. . . .

Björnson's style was no less novel than his theme. It may or it may not have been consciously modelled after the saga style, to which, however, it bears an obvious resemblance. In his early childhood, while he lived among the peasants, he became familiar with their mode of thought and speech, and it entered into his being, and became his own natural mode of expression. There is in his daily conversation a certain grim directness, and a laconic weightiness, which give an air of importance and authority even to his simplest utterances. This tendency to compression frequently has the effect of obscurity, not because his thought is obscure, but rather because energetic brevity of expression has fallen into disuse, and even a Norse public, long accustomed to the wordy diffuseness of latter-day bards, have in part lost the faculty to comprehend the genius of their own language. As a Danish critic wittily observed: "Björnson's language is but one step removed from pantomime."—From "Essays on Scandinavian Literature" (1895).

II

By W. D. Howells

He has a great talent, a clear conscience, a beautiful art. He has my love not only because he is a poet of the most exquisite verity, but because he is a lover of men, with a faith in them such as can move mountains of ignorance, and dullness, and greed. He is next to Tolstoy in his willingness to give himself for his kind; if he would rather give himself in fighting than in suffering wrong, I do not know that his self-sacrifice is less in degree.

I confess, however, that I do not think of him as a patriot and a socialist when I read him; he is then purely a poet, whose gift holds me rapt above the world where I have left my troublesome and wearisome self for the time. I do not know of any novels that a young endeavorer in fiction could more profitably read than his for their large and simple method, their trust of the reader's intelligence, their sympathy with life. With him the problems are all soluble by the enlightened and regenerate will; there is no baffling Fate, but a helping God. In Björnson there is nothing of Ibsen's scornful despair, nothing of his anarchistic contempt, but his art is full of the warmth and color of a poetic soul, with no touch of the icy cynicism which freezes you in the other. I have felt the cold fascination of Ibsen, too, and I should be far from denying his mighty mastery, but he has never possessed me with the delight that Björnson has.—From "My Literary Passions" (1895).

A HAPPY BOY

CHAPTER I

HE was called Eyvind, and he cried when he was born. But as soon as he could sit up on his mother's knee he laughed; and when they lighted the candle at evening, he laughed till the place rang again, but cried when he could not get to it.

"This boy will be something out of the common," said his mother.

A bare rock frowned over the house where he was born, but it was not high; fir and birch trees looked down from its brow, and the wild cherry strewed blossoms on the roof. A little goat which belonged to Eyvind roamed about the roof; he had to be kept up there lest he should stray, and Eyvind carried leaves and grass up to him. One fine day the goat hopped over and away up the rock; he went straight ahead and came to a place where he had never been before. Eyvind could not see the goat when he came out after tea, and thought at once of the fox. He got hot all over, looked about, and called: "Goatie-goatie, and goatie-wee!"

"Ba-a-a-a!" said the goat up on the hillside, looking down with his head on one side.

But a little girl was kneeling beside the goat.

"Is he your goat?" she asked.

Eyvind stood with open mouth and eyes, and thrust both hands into the pockets of his little breeches.

"Who are you?" he asked.

"I am Marit, mother's baby, father's mouse, little fairy in the house, grand-daughter of Ole Nordistuen of the hill-farms, four years old in autumn, two days after the first frost-nights, I am!"

"Are you though?" said he, drawing a long breath, for he had not ventured to breathe whilst she was speaking.

"Is he your goat?" asked the girl again.

"Yes," said he, looking up.

"I've taken such a fancy to the goat. Will you not give him to me?"

"No, indeed, I won't."

She lay kicking her legs about and looking down at him, and then she said:

"If I were to give you a butter-cake for the goat, mightn't I have him then?"

Eyvind belonged to poor folks; he had eaten butter-cake only once in his life, that was when grandfather came to see them, and he had never tasted the like before nor since. He looked up at the girl.

"Let me see the cake first," said he. Without waiting to be asked twice, she showed him a large cake which she held in her hand.

"Here it is!" said she, and threw it down.

"Oh, it's all gone to pieces," said the boy, and he carefully gathered up every bit. He couldn't help just tasting the smallest, and it was so good that he had to taste one bit more; and before he knew what he was about he had eaten up the whole cake.

"Now the goat is mine," said the girl.

The boy stopped short with the last bit in his mouth, the girl lay and laughed, the goat with his white breast and dark fleece stood by her, looking down sideways.

"Couldn't you wait a bit?" begged the boy; his heart began to throb within him. Then the girl laughed yet more and started up to her knees.

"No, no, the goat is mine," said she, and flung her arms about its neck; then she loosed a garter and made a halter of it. Eyvind stood and looked on. She rose and began to drag the goat; it would not go with her but stretched its neck down towards Eyvind. "Ba-a-a-a!" it said.

But she caught hold of its fleece with one hand, pulled at the garter with the other, and said prettily:

"Come goatie dear, you shall come indoors and eat out of mother's nice dish and out of my apron," and then she sang:

Come, goat, to your sire,
Come, calf, from the byre;
Come, pussy, that mews
In your snowy-white shoes;
Come, ducklings so yellow,
Come, chickens so small,
Each soft little fellow
That can't run at all;
Come, sweet doves of mine,
With your feathers so fine!
The turf's wet with dew,
But the sun warms it through.
It is early, right early, in summer-time still,
But call on the autumn, and hurry it will.

The boy was left alone. He had played with the goat ever since it was born in the winter, and it had never occurred to him that it could be lost; but now it was done all in a moment, and he was never to see it again.

His mother came singing up from the waterside with some vessels she had been scouring; she saw the boy sitting crying, with his legs under him in the grass, and went to him.

"What are you crying for?"

"Oh, the goat, the goat!"

"Well, where is the goat?" asked his mother looking up on the roof.

"He'll never come back," said the boy.

"Why, what has happened to him?"

He would not confess at once.

"Has the fox taken him?"

"Oh, I wish it were the fox!"

"Are you out of your senses?" said his mother. "What has become of the goat?"

"Oh, oh, oh!—I've been so unlucky—I've sold him for a butter-cake!"

Even as he said the words he realised what it was to sell the goat for a butter-cake; he had not thought of it before. His mother said:

"What do you suppose the little goat thinks of you, since you could go and sell him for a butter-cake?"

The boy himself thought of it, and realised very clearly that he could never be happy again in this world, nor even with God in heaven, he thought afterwards.

He was so heart-broken that he resolved within himself never again to do anything wrong, neither to cut the thread on the distaff, nor to let the ewes out of the fold, nor to go down to the lake alone. He fell asleep there where he lay and dreamt that the goat had gone to heaven.

There sat Our Lord with a long beard, just as He was in the catechism, and the goat stood eating the leaves of a shining tree; but Eyvind sat on the roof alone and could not get up to him.

At that moment something wet poked right into his ear; he started up.

"Ba-a-a-a!" said a voice; and there was the goat come back.

"Oh, you've come back! you've come back."

He jumped up, took hold of his two forelegs and danced with him like a brother; he pulled his beard, and he was just going to take him right in to his mother, when he heard something behind him and saw the girl sitting on the grass just by his side. Now he understood it all, and he let go his hold of the goat.

"Is it you that have come with him?" She sat tearing up grass with her hand and said:

"I wasn't allowed to keep him; grandfather is sitting up there waiting."

As the boy stood looking at her he heard a sharp voice up on the road calling:

"Well!"

Then she remembered what she had to do. She rose and went up to Eyvind, laid one earth-stained hand in his and said:

"Forgive me!"

Then her resolution failed her, and she threw her arms round the goat and wept.

"I think you had better keep the goat," said Eyvind, looking away.

"Be quick now!" said the grandfather up on the slope. And Marit rose and walked up after him with dragging feet.

"You've forgotten your garter!" Eyvind called after her. She turned and looked first at the garter and then at him.

At last she formed a great resolution and said with a thick voice:

"You can keep that."

He went up to her and took her hand. "I thank you," said he.

"Oh that's nothing to thank me for," she answered, heaved a prodigiously deep sigh, and went on her way.

He sat down on the grass again with the goat at his side; but he somehow did not care for it so much as before.

CHAPTER II

THE goat was tethered near the wall of the house, but Eyvind kept looking up the hill-side. His mother came out and sat by him; he wanted to hear tales about what was far away, for the goat was no longer enough for him. So he came to hear how once upon a time everything could talk: the mountain talked to the brook, and the brook to the river, and the river to the sea, and the sea to the sky. Then he wanted to know whether the sky did not talk to anything; and the sky talked to the clouds, and the clouds to the trees, and the trees to the grass, the grass to the flies, the flies to the animals, the animals to the children, the children to the grown-up people; and so it went on until it got round in a circle, and no one knew who had begun. Eyvind looked at the mountain, the trees, the lake, the sky, and had never really seen them before. Just then the cat came out and laid herself on the flags in the sunshine.

"What does the cat say?" asked Eyvind, pointing.

His mother sang:

The evening sun sinks low in the skies
The cat lies lazily blinking her eyes.
"Two little mice,
Some cream—so nice—
Four bits of fish
I stole from a dish;
I got all I desired,
And I'm lazy and tired,"
Says the cat.

Then came the cock with all the hens.

"What does the cock say?" asked Eyvind, clapping his hands.

His mother sang:

Her wings the brood-hen sinks:
Stands on one leg the cock, and thinks:

"The grey gander
Will soar and wander,
But he can never, heigh, heigh!
Be half so clever as I!
In, in, ye hens, and get out of the way!
The sun has a holiday turn to-day."
Says the cock.

Then two little birds sat and sang upon the ridge of the roof.

"What are the birds saying?" asked Eyvind, laughing.

"Dear God, how sweet it is to live
For those who neither toil nor strive,"
Say the birds.

Thus she went through what all the animals said, right down to the ant which crawled through the moss, and the worm that ticked in the bark.

That same summer, his mother began to teach him to read. He had long possessed books and thought a great deal about how it would be when they too began to talk. Now the letters turned into beasts, birds, and everything that existed. Soon they began to group themselves together two and two; *a* stood and rested under a tree called *b*, then *c* came and did the same; but when three or four came together it was as if they were angry with one another; they did not get on well at all. And the more he learned the more he forgot what they were. He remembered *a* the longest because he was fond of it; it was a little black lamb and was friends with all. But soon he forgot even *a;* the book no longer contained fairy tales, but only lessons.

One day his mother came in and said to him:

"To-morrow school begins again, and you are to go with me up to the school-house."

Eyvind had heard that school was a place where many boys played together, and he had no objection. On the contrary, he was much pleased; he had often been at the school-house, but never when school was going on, and he walked quicker than his mother up the hills, for he was eager. They entered the vestibule, and a great hum met them like that of the mill-house at home. He asked his mother what it was.

"It's the children reading," she answered, and he was very glad to hear it, for that was how he had read before he knew his letters. When he went in there were so many children sitting round a table that even at church there were not more. Others sat on their dinner-boxes along the wall; some stood in groups around a blackboard; the schoolmaster, an old grey-haired man, sat on a stool by the fireplace filling his pipe. When Eyvind and his mother entered, they all looked up and the mill-hum stopped, as when the water is turned off. They all looked at the new-comers. Eyvind's mother greeted the schoolmaster, who returned her salutation.

"Here I come with a little boy who wants to learn to read," said his mother.

"What's the young man's name?" asked the schoolmaster, fumbling in his leather pouch for tobacco.

"Eyvind," said his mother. "He knows his letters and he can put them together."

"Ah, indeed!" said the schoolmaster, "come here, little white-head."

Eyvind went to him; the schoolmaster lifted him on his knee and took off his cap.

"What a pretty little boy," said he, and stroked his hair; Eyvind looked up into his eyes and laughed.

"Is it at me you're laughing?" he frowned.

"Yes, of course it is," answered Eyvind, and roared with laughter. Then the schoolmaster laughed too, the mother laughed, the children perceived that they might laugh as well, and so they all laughed together.

And that was how Eyvind entered school.

When he was to take his place they all wanted to make room for him; but he took a good look round first. They whispered and pointed; he turned around to every side with his cap in his hand, and his book under his arm.

"Well, have you made up your mind?" asked the schoolmaster, still working away at his pipe. Just as the boy was turning to the schoolmaster, he saw close beside him, down by the hearth-stone, sitting on a little red box, Marit of the many names; she had hidden her face in her two hands and sat peeping out at him.

"I will sit here," said Eyvind resolutely, and, taking a box, he seated himself by her side.

Now she lifted the arm that was next to him a little and looked at him under her elbow; he instantly covered his face too with both hands and looked at her under his elbow. So they sat behaving in this foolish way until she laughed, then he laughed, the children saw and laughed too: thereupon a terribly loud voice struck in, becoming milder by degrees however:

"Be quiet you young trolls, urchins, imps! be quiet and good, my poppets!"

It was the schoolmaster, who had a way of flying out, but calmed down again before he finished. The school became instantly quiet, until the pepper-mill began to go again and they read aloud each in his book; the trebles struck up in a high key, the deeper voices got sharper and sharper to keep in the ascendant, and now and then one or another gave a great whoop. In all his born days Eyvind had never had such fun.

"Is it always like this, here?" he whispered to Marit.

"Yes, just like this," said she.

By-and-by they had to go to the schoolmaster and read; a little boy was then set to learn with them, and then they were released and allowed to go back and sit quietly again.

"I've got a goat too, now," said Marit.

"Have you?"

"Yes; but he's not so pretty as yours."

"Why have you never come up on the rock again?"

"Grandfather is afraid I shall fall over."

"But it's not very high."

"Grandfather won't let me, all the same."

"Mother knows such a lot of songs," said Eyvind.

"So does grandfather, I can tell you."

"Yes; but he doesn't know the ones mother knows."

"Grandfather knows one about a dance. Do you want to hear it?"

"Yes, very much."

"Well, then, you must come farther over here that the schoolmaster mayn't hear."

He moved along and then she repeated to him a little bit

of a song, four or five times over, so that the boy learned it; and that was the first thing he learned at school.

"Dance," shrieked the fiddle,
And squeaked with its string so
That up jumped the bailiff's
  Son and cried "Ho!"
"Stop!" shouted Ola,
Stuck out his leg, so
It tripped up the bailiff,
  And all the girls laughed.

"Hop," murmured Erik,
And leaped to the roof-tree,
Till all the beams cracked and
  The walls gave a scream.
"Stop!" shouted Elling,
Caught hold of his collar,
And lifted him high—"You're
  As weak as a cat!"

"Hey!" called out Rasmus,
Caught Randi and spun her,
"Hurry and give me
  That kiss, don't you know?"
"No," answered Randi,
And boxed his ears soundly,
And slipped from his arm with
  "Take that for your pains!"

"Up children!" cried the schoolmaster. "As this is our first day you shall go early; but first we must have prayers and a hymn."

At once a great racket sprang up in the school; they jumped on forms, ran about the room, and all talked at once.

"Be quiet you young imps, you young scamps, you young ruffians; be quiet and walk across the room nicely; there's good children!" said the schoolmaster, and they went quietly to their places and calmed down, whereupon the schoolmaster stood up before them and said a short prayer. Then they sang; the schoolmaster led in a strong bass, all the children standing with folded hands and singing with him. Eyvind stood lowest by the door with Marit and looked on; they, too, folded their hands, but they could not sing.

That was his first day at school.

CHAPTER III

EYVIND grew and became an active boy: at school he was amongst the first, and he was capable at his work at home. That was because at home he was fond of his mother and at school he was fond of his master. His father he saw but little, for he was either away fishing or else he was looking after their mill, where half the parish had their grinding done.

The thing which most influenced his mind during these years was the schoolmaster's history, which his mother told him one evening as they sat by the fire. It ran through all his books, it underlay every word the schoolmaster said; he felt it in the air of the schoolroom when all was quiet. It filled him with obedience and respect, and gave him a quicker apprehension, as it were, of all that was taught him. This was the story:

Baard was the schoolmaster's name and he had a brother called Anders. They were very fond of each other; both enlisted, lived in town together, and were together in the war, when they both became corporals and served in the same company. When, after the war, they came home again, everybody thought them two stalwart fellows. Then their father died. He had a good deal of loose property which was difficult to divide evenly, so they said to each other that they would not fall out about it, but would put up the things to auction so that each could buy what he wished and then they would share the proceeds. So said so done. But their father possessed a large gold watch which was widely renowned, for it was the only gold watch people in those parts had ever seen. When this watch was put up many rich people tried for it, until the brothers, too, began to bid; then the others gave way. Now Baard expected Anders to let him get the watch, and Anders expected the same of Baard; each made his bid in turn to prove the other, and they looked across at each other whilst they bid.

When the watch had got up to twenty dollars Baard felt it was not nice of his brother to bid against him, and kept on bidding until it got towards thirty dollars. As Anders still did not give in, it seemed to Baard that Anders neither remembered how good he had been to him, nor yet that he was the eldest. The watch got over thirty dollars, and Anders still kept on. Then Baard ran the watch up to forty dollars in one bid, and no longer looked at his brother. It was very quiet in the auction-room; only the bailiff quietly repeated the figures. Anders thought as he stood there that if Baard could afford to give forty dollars he could too, and if Baard grudged him the watch he would have to take it; so out-bid him. This seemed to Baard the greatest slight that had ever been put upon him; he bid fifty dollars, quite softly. A great many people were standing round, and Anders thought he must not let his brother thus put him to shame in everybody's hearing, so he bid over him. Then Baard laughed: "A hundred dollars and my brotherhood into the bargain," said he; turned, and went out of the room. Some one presently came out to him whilst he was busy saddling the horse he had bought just before.

"The watch is yours," said the man; "Anders gave in."

The moment Baard heard this a sort of remorse fell upon him; he thought of his brother and not of the watch. The saddle was on, but he paused with his hand on the horse's back, uncertain whether he should start. Then a lot of people came out, Anders amongst them; and so soon as he saw his brother standing there by the saddled horse not knowing what was in Baard's mind, he called out to him:

"Much good may the watch do you, Baard! It won't be going on the day when your brother runs after you any more."

"Nor yet on the day when I ride home again," answered Baard, with a white face, as he mounted his horse. The house in which they had lived with their father, neither of them entered again.

Soon after, Anders married and settled as a cottar-tenant, but did not invite Baard to the wedding. Baard was not at church either.

In the first year of Anders' marriage the only cow he possessed was found dead by the north wall of the house, where it was tethered; and nobody could make out what it had died of. Several misfortunes followed, and he went down in the world; but the worst was when in mid-winter his barn was burnt with all that was in it; nobody knew how the fire broke out.

"Somebody that hates me has done this," said Anders, and he wept that night. He became a poor man and lost all heart for work.

Next evening Baard stood in his room, Anders was lying on the bed when he entered, but he jumped up.

"What do you want here?" he asked, but stopped short and stood looking fixedly at his brother. Baard waited a little before he answered:

"I want to help you, Anders; the luck's been against you."

"The luck's been as you wished it to be, Baard. Go, or I mayn't be able to keep my hands off you."

"You are mistaken, Anders; I'm sorry——"

"Go Baard, or God help both you and me!"

Baard drew back a pace or two; with a quivering voice he said:

"If you'll take the watch, you shall have it."

"Go, Baard!" shouted the other, and Baard went.

With Baard things had gone in this wise. So soon as he heard that his brother was in distress his heart melted towards him, but pride kept him back. He felt himself much drawn towards the church, and there he formed good resolutions, but he had not the strength to carry them out. He often set forth and came within sight of the house, but now some one came out of the door, now there was a stranger there, or Anders was out chopping wood; so that there was always something in the way. One Sunday in midwinter, however, he was once more at church and Anders was there too. Baard saw him; he had grown pale and thin, he wore the same clothes as when they were together, but now they were old and ragged. During the sermon he looked up at the pastor, and it seemed to Baard that he was kind and gentle. He remembered their childhood and what a good boy he was. Baard himself took the Sacrament that day, and he made the solemn promise before his God that, come what might, he would be reconciled to his brother. This purpose penetrated his soul just as he drank the wine, and when he rose he intended to go straight over and sit down beside him, but some one was sitting in the way and his brother did not look up. After service there were still difficulties: there were too many people about; his brother's wife was walking by his side and he did not know her. He thought it would be best to go to his house and have a serious talk with him. When evening came he did so. He went right up to the door and listened, but then he heard his own name mentioned. It was the woman who spoke.

"He took the Sacrament to-day," said she. "I daresay he was thinking of you."

"No, he wasn't thinking of me," said Anders. "I know him; he thinks only of himself."

For a long time nothing more was said. Baard perspired as he stood there, although it was a cold evening. The woman inside was busy over a pot that bubbled and hissed on the fire, an infant cried now and then, and Anders rocked the cradle.

Then she said these words:

"I believe you two are always thinking of each other and won't own to it."

"Let us talk of something else," answered Anders. He rose soon after to go to the door. Baard had to hide himself in the woodshed, and Anders came to that very place to fetch an armful of wood. Baard stood in the corner and saw him distinctly; he had taken off his wretched church-clothes and had on the uniform in which he had come home from the war, just like Baard's. The brothers had promised each other never to wear these uniforms, but to leave them as heirlooms in the family. Anders' was now patched and worn out, his strong, well-developed body appeared as if wrapped in a bundle of rags, and just then Baard could hear the gold watch ticking in his own pocket. Anders went to the place where the faggots lay; instead of immediately stooping to load himself, he stopped, leaned back against a pile of wood and looked out at the sky, which was clear and glittering with stars. Then he heaved a sigh and said:

"Well—well—well—my God, my God!" As long as Baard lived he heard those words. He wanted to step forward and greet him, but just then Anders coughed and it sounded so harsh. That was enough to check him. Anders took his armful of wood and brushed by Baard so closely that the twigs scratched his face and made it smart.

He stood motionless on the same spot for quite ten minutes, and might have stood much longer had it not been that after so much strong emotion he was seized with a shivering fit that shook him from head to foot. Then he went out: he acknowledged frankly to himself that he was too cowardly to go in, so he now formed another plan. Out of a cinder-box which stood in the corner he had just left, he took some pieces of coal, found a splinter of resinous wood, went up into the barn, closed the door after him and struck a light. When he had got the wood lighted he looked for the peg upon which Anders hung his lantern when he came out in the early morning to thresh. Baard took off his gold watch and hung it on the peg, then extinguished his splinter and went away. He felt his heart so lightened that he ran over the snow like a young boy.

The next day he heard that the barn had been burned down in the night. Sparks had probably fallen from the splinter which he had lighted that he might see to hang up the watch.

This so overpowered him that all that day he sat like a sick person, took down his psalm-book and sang, so that the people in the house thought there must be something wrong with him. But in the evening he went out; it was bright moonlight. He went to his brother's farm, poked about on the site of the fire—and found, sure enough, a little lump of gold. It was the watch, melted down.

With this in his hand he went in to his brother that evening and besought him to make peace. What came of this attempt has already been related.

A little girl had seen him scraping among the ashes on the site of the fire; some boys, on their way to a dance, had noticed him on the Sunday evening going down towards Anders' farm; the people at home had told how strangely he had behaved on the Monday; and as everyone knew that he and his brother were bitter enemies, the matter was reported to the authorities and an inquiry set on foot. No one could prove anything against him, but suspicion clung to him. Reconciliation with his brother was now more impossible than ever.

Anders had thought of Baard when the barn was burnt, but had said so to no one. When, on the following evening, he saw him in his room, so white and strange-looking, he immediately thought:

"Remorse has got hold of him now, but for such a horrible crime against his brother there can be no forgiveness."

Afterwards he heard how people had seen him go down to the buildings on the evening of the fire, and although nothing was brought to light by the inquiry, he was firmly convinced that Baard was the culprit. They met at the inquiry; Baard in his good clothes, Anders in his rags. As Anders entered, Baard looked over at him with such beseeching eyes that Anders felt the look in his very marrow.

"He wants me to say nothing," thought Anders, and when he was asked whether he believed his brother had done the deed he said loudly and distinctly:

"No."

But Anders took to drink from that day, and soon fell into a bad way. Baard suffered still more, although he did not drink. One would not have known him for the same man.

At last, late one evening, a poor woman came into the little room in which Baard lodged, and asked him to come out a little way with her. He knew it was his brother's wife. Baard at once understood upon what errand she had come; he turned as white as death, put on his things, and went with her without speaking a word. A faint glimmer of light came from Anders' window, and they made for the gleam; for there was no path over the snow. When Baard stood once more in the passage he was met by a strange odour, which turned him sick. They went in. A little child was sitting on the hearth eating coal; its face was black all over, but it looked up, and laughed with white teeth. It was his brother's child. In the bed, with all kinds of clothes over him, lay Anders, wasted, with high, transparent forehead, looking with hollow eyes at his brother. Baard's knees trembled beneath him; he sat down on the foot of the bed and burst into a violent fit of weeping. The sick man looked at him immovably and was silent. At last he told his wife to go out, but Baard motioned her to stay,—and now the two brothers began to talk together. They explained themselves from the day of their bidding for the watch right down to the moment of their present meeting. Baard concluded by taking out the lump of gold which he always carried about him, and each now confessed to the other that in all these years he had not felt happy for a single day. Anders did not say much for he was not able, but Baard sat at his bedside all through his illness.

"Now I am quite well," said Anders one morning when he woke, "now, my dear brother, we will live long together and never part, as in the old days."

But that day he died.

Baard took his wife and child home with him, and from that day forward they wanted for nothing.

What the brothers had said to each other as Baard sat by the bed made its way out through the walls and the night, and became known to every one in the village, and no one was more highly esteemed than Baard. Every one paid respect to him as they would to one who has had great sorrow and found joy again, or as to one who has been long absent. Baard was comforted by the friendliness which surrounded him, and devoted himself to the service of God. He wanted some occupation, he said, and so the old corporal took to teaching school. What he instilled into the children first and last was love; and he practised it himself, so that the little ones were devoted to him as a playfellow and father, all in one.

This, then, was the story of the old schoolmaster, and it took such a hold on Eyvind's mind that it became to him at once a religion and an education. The schoolmaster appeared to him almost a supernatural being, although he sat there so sociably and pretended to scold them. Not to know a lesson for him was impossible, and if he got a smile or a pat on the head after saying it he felt a glow of happiness for a whole day.

It always made the deepest impression on the children when the schoolmaster, before singing, would make a little speech; and at least once every week he used to read them a few verses about brotherly love. When he read the first of these verses there was always a quiver in his voice, although he had read it again and again for twenty or thirty years; it ran thus:

> Love thy neighbour, Christian leal,
> Tread him not with iron heel
> If in dust he lies.
> All things living join to prove
> The creative power of love
> When a pure heart tries.

But when the whole poem was finished and he had paused a moment after it, he would look at them with a twinkle in his eyes:

"Up with you, youngsters, and get you home nicely without any noise—walk nicely so that I may hear nothing but good accounts of you, little people!"

And then, while they were making a very Babel in searching for their books and dinner-boxes, he would cry above the uproar:

"Come back again to-morrow as soon as it's light, or you'll catch it! Come back in good time little girls and boys, then we'll go to work with a will!"

CHAPTER IV

OF Eyvind's further development up to a year before his confirmation there is not much to tell. He read in the morning, worked in the day, and played in the evening.

As he was of an unusually cheerful disposition, it was not long before the young people of the neighbourhood, in their playtime, were glad to be where he was. A long hill ran down to the cove in front of the farm, skirting the rock on the one side and the wood on the other, as already related; every fine evening and every Sunday, all the winter through, this was the chosen toboggan-slope of all the young sledgers of the village.

Eyvind was lord of the slope and owned two sledges "Spanker" and "Galloper;" the latter he lent to larger parties, the former he steered himself with Marit on his lap. At this season, the first thing Eyvind did when he woke was to look out and see whether it was thawing; and if he saw a grey veil lying over the bushes on the other side of the cove, or if he heard the roof dripping, he was as slow over his dressing as if there was nothing to do that day. But if he awoke, especially on Sundays, to crackling cold and clear weather, best clothes and no work, only catechism or church in the forenoon, and then the whole afternoon and evening free, hurrah! then the boy jumped out of bed with one bound, dressed as if the house were on fire, and could scarcely eat any breakfast. The moment it was afternoon and the first boy came on his snow-shoes along the roadside, swinging his staff over his head and shouting so that the hills around the lake rang again, and then one came down the road on his sledge and then another and another—straightway off shot the boy on his "Spanker" down the whole length of the slope, landing amongst the late comers with a long, shrill shout, which was re-echoed from ridge to ridge along the cove, until it died away in the far distance. He would then look round for Marit, but when once she had come, he troubled no more about her.

Then one Christmas came when the boy and the girl were both about sixteen or seventeen and were to be confirmed in the spring. On the fourth day of Christmas week there was a big party at the Upper Hill Farm where Marit lived with her grandparents, who had brought her up. They had promised her this party every year for three years, and at last, these holidays, they had to fulfil their promise. Eyvind was invited.

It was a cloudy evening, not cold; no stars were to be seen; the morrow might bring rain. A drowsy breeze blew over the snow, which was swept clear in patches on the white uplands, while in other places it had formed deep drifts. Along by the roadside where no snow happened to lie there was a margin of slippery ice; it lay blue-black between the snow and the bare ground, and could be seen glimmering here and there as far as the eye could reach. On the mountainsides there had been snow-slips; their tracks were black and bare, while on each side of them the snow lay smooth and white, except where the birch-trees clustered together in dark patches. There was no water to be seen, but half-naked moors and bogs stretched up to riven and lowering mountains.

The farms lay in large clusters in the midst of the level ground; in the dusk of the winter evening they looked like black masses from which light shot forth over the fields, now from one window, now from another; to judge by the lights there was a great deal going on inside. Young people, grown-up and half-grown up, flocked together from various quarters. Very few kept to the road; almost all, at any rate, left it when they drew near the farms, and slipped away, one behind the cowhouse, a pair under the store-house and so forth; while some rushed away behind the barn and howled like foxes, others answered farther off like cats. One stood behind the wash-house and barked like an old angry dog, who had broken his chain, until there was a general chase. The girls came marching along in large bands; they had a few boys, mostly little boys, with them, who skirmished around them to show off. When one of the gangs of girls came near the house and one or other of the big boys caught sight of them, the girls scattered and fled into the passages or down the garden, and had to be dragged out and into the rooms one by one. Some were so extremely bashful that Marit had to be sent for, when she would come out and positively force them in. Sometimes one would come who had not been invited and whose intention it was not to go in, but only to look on, until in the end she would be persuaded just to have one single dance. Those guests whom she really cared for, Marit invited into a little room where the old people sat and smoked and grandmother did the honours; there they were kindly received and treated. Eyvind was not amongst the favoured ones, and he thought that rather strange.

The best player of the village could not come till late, so they had meanwhile to manage with the old one, a cottager called Grey Knut. He knew four dances, two spring-dances, a halling[1] and an old, so-called Napoleon waltz; but he had been obliged gradually to turn the halling into a schottische by taking it in different time; and in the same way a spring-dance had to do duty as a polka-mazurka. He struck up, and the dancing began. Eyvind did not dare to join in at first, for there were too many grown-up people; but the half-grown ones soon banded together, pushed each other forward, drank a little strong ale to hearten them, and then Eyvind also joined in. The room grew very hot, the fun and the ale mounted to their heads.

Marit danced more than any one else that evening, probably because the party was in her grandparents' house, and so it happened that Eyvind often caught her eye, but she always danced with some one else. He wanted to dance with her himself, so he sat out one dance in order to run to her directly it ended, and this he did; but a tall, swarthy fellow with bushy hair pushed in front of him.

"Get away, youngster," cried he and gave Eyvind a shove, so that he nearly fell backwards over Marit. Never had such a thing happened to him, never had any one been other than kind to him, never had he been called "youngster" when he wanted to join in anything. He reddened to the roots of his

[1] The "spring-dance" and "halling" are characteristic peasant dances.

hair, but said nothing, and drew back to where the new musician, just arrived, had taken his seat and was tuning up. There was silence amongst the crowd; they were waiting to hear the first loud note from "the right man." He tuned and tried for a long time, but at length he struck up a spring-dance, the boys shouted and hopped, and pair by pair whirled into the circle. Eyvind looked at Marit dancing with the bushy-haired man, she laughed over the man's shoulder so that her white teeth showed, and Eyvind, for the first time in his life, was aware of a strange, tingling pain in his breast.

He looked at her again and again, and the more he looked the clearer it seemed to him that Marit was quite grown-up.

"But it can't be so," thought he, "for she still goes sledging with us."

Grown-up she was though, and the bushy-haired man drew her down upon his lap after the dance was over; she broke loose from him, but remained sitting at his side.

Eyvind looked at the man. He had on fine blue Sunday clothes, a blue-checked shirt and silk cravat. He had a small face, bold, blue eyes, a laughing, defiant mouth; he was handsome. Eyvind looked again and again, and at last he looked also at himself. He had got new trousers at Christmas, of which he was very proud, but now he saw that they were only grey frieze; his jacket was of the same stuff, but old and soiled, the knitted waistcoat of common yarn, lozenge-pattern, also old and with two bright buttons and one black one. He looked around him and thought that very few were so poorly dressed as he. Marit had on a black bodice of fine stuff, a silver brooch in her neckerchief and a folded silk handkerchief in her hand. On the back of her head she wore a little silk cap which was fastened under her chin with long ribbons. She was red and white; she laughed; the man talked with her and laughed too. Again the music struck up and again they stood up to dance. A comrade came and sat beside him.

"Why aren't you dancing, Eyvind?" said he, gently.

"Oh, no," said Eyvind, "do I look like it?"

"Look like it," said his comrade, but before he could get further Eyvind said:

"Who is that in the blue clothes, dancing with Marit?"

"That's John Hatlen, who's been away so long at the agricultural college; he's going to take the farm now."

At that moment Marit and John sat down.

"Who is that fair-haired boy sitting there beside the fiddler and staring at me?" asked John.

Marit laughed and answered:

"That's the cottar's son, down at the croft."

Of course Eyvind had always known he was a cottar's son, but until now he had never felt it. He had a feeling as though his body had suddenly shrunk and he was shorter than all the others. To keep himself in heart, he had to try to think of everything that had hitherto made him happy and proud, from the sledging-times down to single words that had pleased him. As he thought, too, of his mother and father sitting at home and thinking that he was enjoying himself, he could scarcely help bursting into tears. All around him were laughing and joking, the fiddle boomed right in his ear. There came a moment when something black seemed to rise up before him, but then he remembered the school with all his comrades, and the schoolmaster who patted him on the back, and the minister who had given him a book at his last examination and said he was a clever boy; his father himself had sat and looked on and had smiled at him.

"Be good now, Eyvind," he seemed to hear the schoolmaster saying, and he felt as though he were a little boy again, sitting on his lap. "Good heavens, you know, there's nothing to trouble about; at bottom everybody is good; it only seems as if they were not. We two will be clever fellows, Eyvind, just as clever as John Hatlen; we shall get just as good clothes, and dance with Marit in a bright room among hundreds of people, smiling and talking; then there'll be a bridal pair standing before the minister, and I in the choir smiling across at you, and mother in the house, a big farm, twenty cows, three horses, and Marit good and kind, just as she was at school——"

The dance ended and Eyvind saw Marit before him on a bench, John still by her side with his face close to hers; once more there came a great tingling pain in his breast, and he seemed to be saying to himself:

"It's true, after all, I am suffering." At that moment Marit rose and came straight up to him. She bent down over him.

"You mustn't sit and glower at me like that," said she; "can't you see that people are noticing it? Take a partner and dance now."

He made no answer but looked at her, and in spite of himself his eyes filled with tears. She was just turning away when she noticed this and stopped; she suddenly flushed as red as fire, turned away and went to her seat, but immediately rose again and seated herself in another place. John at once followed her.

Eyvind rose from the bench, went out amongst the people in the yard, seated himself under a pent-house roof, then wondered what he was doing there, got up and then sat down again, for might he not as well sit here as anywhere else? He did not care to go home nor yet to go indoors again; it was all one to him. He was in no state to reflect upon what had happened; he did not want to think about it. Neither did he care to think of the future; there was nothing that had any attraction for him.

"What am I thinking of, after all?" he asked himself half-aloud, and hearing his own voice he thought:

"So you can still speak—can you laugh?"

He tried: yes, he could laugh; and then he went on laughing, loud, still louder; and then it seemed to him a great joke that he should be sitting there laughing all alone, and that made him laugh again. But his friend Hans, who had been sitting by his side indoors, now followed him out.

"Why, what on earth are you laughing at?" he asked, stopping before the pent-house. Then Eyvind left off.

Hans stood there as if waiting to see what would happen next; Eyvind rose, looked cautiously round and then said softly:

"I'll tell you why I always used to be so happy, Hans; it was because I never really cared for anybody. But from the day we care for somebody our happiness is over." And he burst into tears.

"Eyvind!" a voice whispered out in the yard, "Eyvind!" He stopped and listened.

"Eyvind!" repeated the voice once more, a little louder. It must be the person he thought.

"Yes," answered he, also in a whisper, drying his eyes quickly and stepping forward. A girl softly crossed the yard.

"Are you there?" she asked.

"Yes," he answered, and stood still.

"Who is with you?"

"It's Hans." Hans wanted to go.

"No, no!" Eyvind begged of him.

She now came close up to them, but slowly; it was Marit.

"You went away so soon," she said to Eyvind. He did not know what to answer. Thereupon she too became embarrassed; they were all three silent. Hans slipped quietly away and left the two standing there, not looking at each other and not moving. Then she whispered:

"I've been going about all the evening with some Christmas sweeties in my pocket for you, Eyvind, but I couldn't give them to you before."

She fished up some apples, a slice of town-baked cake and a little half-pint bottle, which she held out to him saying they were for him. Eyvind pocketed them.

"Thanks," he said, holding out his hand;[1] hers was warm, and he let it go at once as if he had burnt himself.

"You have danced a great deal this evening."

"Yes, I have," she answered, "but you haven't danced much," she added.

"No, I haven't," answered he.

"Why haven't you?"

"Oh——"

"Eyvind!"

"Yes."

"Why did you sit and look at me like that?"

"Oh——" A pause.

"Marit!"

"Yes."

"Why didn't you like my looking at you?"

"There were such a lot of people there."

"You danced a great deal with John Hatlen this evening."

[1] It is the peasant custom to shake hands in thanking for a gift.

"Oh yes."

"He dances well."

"Do you think so?"

"Don't you think so?"

"Oh yes."

"I don't know how it is, but this evening I can't bear you to dance with him, Marit." He turned away; it had cost him an effort to say this.

"I don't understand you, Eyvind."

"I don't understand it myself: it's so stupid of me. Goodbye, Marit, I'm going now."

He made a step without looking round. Then she said as he moved away:

"You've been seeing things wrongly to-night, Eyvind."

He stopped.

"There's one thing I haven't seen wrongly and that is that you're a grown-up girl."

This was not what she expected him to say, so she was silent; and at that moment she saw the light of a pipe right in front of her. It was her grandfather who had just come round the corner and was passing by. He stopped.

"Oh you're here are you, Marit?"

"Yes."

"Who's that you're talking to?"

"Eyvind."

"Who did you say?"

"Eyvind Pladsen."

"Oh, the cottar's boy at Pladsen: come in at once with me."

CHAPTER V

WHEN Eyvind opened his eyes next morning it was from a long, refreshing sleep and happy dreams. Marit had lain on the rock and thrown down leaves at him; he had caught them and thrown them up again; they went up and down in a thousand colours and figures; the sun shone on them, and the whole rock sparkled. As he awoke he looked round, expecting still to see the picture of his dream; then he recollected the previous day, and immediately the same tingling, bitter pain in his breast began again.

"I suppose I shall never be quit of it," thought he, and he felt unstrung, as if his whole future had slipped away from him.

"You've slept a long time," said his mother, who was sitting beside him spinning. "Up now, and have something to eat; your father is off to the wood already, felling timber."

His mother's voice seemed to help him, he got up with a little more courage. No doubt his mother was thinking of her own dancing-days, for she sat humming to herself as she span, whilst he dressed and ate his breakfast. To hide his face from her he had to rise from table and go to the window. The same weariness and oppression had come over him again, and he had to pull himself together and think of setting to work.

The weather had changed, the air had turned a little colder, so that what yesterday threatened to fall as rain, fell to-day as wet snow. He put on snow-socks, a fur cap, a sailor's jacket and mittens, said good-bye, and went off with his axe on his shoulder.

The snow fell slowly in large, wet flakes; he struggled up the sledging slope, and turning to the left at the top, entered the wood. Never before, winter or summer, had he climbed that hill without remembering something that made him happy, or that he longed for. Now it was a dead, heavy tramp; he slipped in the wet snow; his knees were stiff either from yesterday's dancing or from his general depression. He felt now that it was all over with sledge-running for that year, and that meant for ever. He longed for something else as he went in amongst the tree-trunks where the snow fell silently; a scared ptarmigan shrieked and flapped its wings a few yards ahead of him; otherwise everything stood as though waiting for a word that was never spoken. But what it was that he yearned for he did not distinctly know, only it was not at home, nor yet abroad, it was not merriment nor yet work; it was something high up in the air, soaring like a song. Presently it resolved itself into a definite wish, and that was to be confirmed in the spring, and to take the first place in the confirmation-class. His heart beat fast as he thought of it, and even before he could hear his father's axe in the trembling underwood, this wish had taken a stronger hold of him than anything since he was born.

His father, as usual, did not say much to him; they hewed each by himself and collected the wood into heaps. Now and then they would meet, and on one of these occasions Eyvind remarked gloomily:

"A cottar has a hard time of it."

"Not worse than other people," said his father, spitting in his hands and taking up his axe. When the tree was felled and his father dragged it up into the pile, Eyvind said:

"If you had a farm of your own you wouldn't have to toil like that."

"Oh, then there would be other burdens to bear," and he tugged with all his strength.

The mother came up with their dinner, and they sat down. The mother was cheerful; she sat and hummed, keeping time by tapping one shoe against the other.

"What are you going to be, now you're getting big, Eyvind?" said she suddenly.

"A cottar's son hasn't much choice," he answered.

"The schoolmaster says you must go to the training-college," said she.

"Can you go there for nothing?" asked Eyvind.

"The schoolmaster will pay your fees," said his father, as he ate.

"Would you like to go?" asked his mother.

"I should like to learn, but not to be a schoolmaster."

They were all silent for a moment; she began humming again and looked straight before her. But Eyvind went off and sat down by himself.

"We don't exactly need to borrow from the school-fund," said she when the boy had gone. Her husband looked at her.

"Poor folks like us?"

"I don't like your constantly giving yourself out for a poor man when you're not one."

They both glanced at the boy to see whether he was within hearing. Then the husband looked sharply at his wife.

"You're talking of what you don't understand." She laughed.

"It's like not thanking God that things have gone well with us," said she, becoming serious.

"We can surely thank him without putting silver buttons on our coats," said the father.

"Yes, but not by letting Eyvind go as he did to the dance yesterday."

"Eyvind is a cottar's son."

"That's no reason why he shouldn't be decently dressed, since we can afford it."

"That's right—talk so that he can hear."

"He doesn't hear; but I shouldn't be sorry if he did," said she, looking boldly at her husband who was frowning, and put down his spoon to take up his pipe.

"Such a wretched holding as we have," said he.

"I can't help laughing at you, always talking about the holding. Why do you never say anything about the mills?"

"Oh, you and your mills! I believe you can't bear to hear them going."

"Oh, I love it, thank goodness! I wish they were going night and day."

"They've been standing now since before Christmas."

"People don't have their corn ground in Christmas week."

"They have it ground whenever there's water; but since they got a mill at Nyström, things have been very slack."

"The schoolmaster didn't say so to-day."

"I shall get a closer fellow than the schoolmaster to manage our money."

"Yes, your own wife is the last person he ought to speak to."

Thore did not answer this, he had just got his pipe lighted; he leant up against a bundle of faggots and shifted his gaze, first from his wife, then from his son, until at last he fixed it upon an old crow's nest which hung all askew on a fir-branch a little way off.

Eyvind sat by himself, with the future stretching before him like a long, clear sheet of ice, over which, for the first time, he let his fancy sweep him away from the one shore right to the other. He felt that poverty barred the way on all sides, but for that very reason all his thoughts were bent upon overcoming it. From Marit it had no doubt parted him for ever; he regarded her as almost promised to John Hatlen; but his whole mind was set upon making life a race with him and her. In order not to be elbowed aside again as he was yesterday, he would hold aloof until he had made his way; and that, with God's help, he would make his way, it never entered his head to doubt. He had a dim feeling that his best plan was to stick to his books; to what end they should lead he must find out later.

The snow was fit for sledging in the evening, the children came to the slope, but not Eyvind. He sat by the fire and read, and had not a moment to spare. The children waited for a long time; at last some of them got impatient, came up and put their faces against the window-panes and called in, but he made as though he did not hear. Others came, and evening after evening they hung about outside in great surprise; but he turned his back on them and read, and fought faithfully to grasp the meaning. He afterwards heard that Marit did not come either. He studied with such diligence that even his father could not but think he was overdoing it. He grew very grave; his face, which had been so round and soft, became thinner, sharper, and his eye harder. He seldom sang, and never played; he never seemed to have time enough. When temptation came upon him, it seemed as though some one whispered: "By-and-by, by-and-by!" and always "by-and-by!" For some time the children ran on their snow shoes, and shouted and laughed as before, but as they could not tempt him out to them either by the merry sounds of their sledging or by calling in to him with their faces against the window, they gradually kept away; they found other playgrounds, and soon the slope was deserted.

But the schoolmaster soon noticed that it was not the old Eyvind who learnt his lessons as a matter of course, and played as a matter of necessity. He often talked with him and tried to draw him out; but he could not get at the boy's heart so easily as in the old days. He also talked to his parents, and, having taken counsel with them, he came down one Sunday evening late in the winter and said, when he had sat for some time:

"Come along, Eyvind, let us go out a little; I want to have a talk with you."

Eyvind put on his things and went with him. They happened to take the direction of the Hill Farms, conversing freely on indifferent subjects. When they drew near the farms, the schoolmaster turned off towards one which lay in the middle, and as they advanced they heard shouts and sounds of merriment proceeding from it.

"What's going on here?" asked Eyvind.

"A dance," said the schoolmaster, "shall we not go in?"

"No."

"Won't you join in a dance, my boy?"

"No, not yet."

"Not yet? When, then?"

He did not answer.

"What do you mean by *yet?*"

As the boy still made no answer the schoolmaster said:

"Come now, no nonsense."

"No, I'm not going in!"

He was very determined and agitated besides.

"Strange that your old schoolmaster should have to stand here and entreat you to go to a dance!"

There was a long silence.

"Is there some one in there whom you're afraid to see?"

"How should I know who is there?"

"But there *might* be some one?"

Eyvind was silent.

Then the schoolmaster went close up to him and laid his hand on his shoulder.

"Are you afraid of seeing Marit?"

Eyvind looked to the ground, and his breathing became heavy and short.

"Tell me, Eyvind."

Eyvind was silent.

"I daresay you don't like to own it, since you're not confirmed; but tell me all the same, my dear Eyvind, and you sha'n't repent it."

Eyvind looked up, but could not get out a word, and had to look away again.

"I could see you hadn't been happy lately; does she care more for others than for you?"

As Eyvind did not answer even now, the schoolmaster felt rather hurt and turned from him. They walked homewards.

When they had gone a good way, the schoolmaster stopped to let Eyvind overtake him.

"I suppose you're longing to be confirmed," said he.

"Yes."

"What do you mean to do afterwards?"

"I should like to go to the training-college."

"And be a schoolmaster?"

"No."

"You're above that, eh?"

Eyvind was silent. They again went on a good way.

"When you've been to the training-college, what then?"

"I haven't really thought about that."

"If you had money I suppose you'd like to buy a farm?"

"Yes, but keep the mills."

"Then it would be better for you to go to the School of Agriculture."

"Do they learn as much there as at the training-college?"

"Oh no, but they learn what's going to be of use to them afterwards."

"Can you take honours there, too?"

"Why do you ask?"

"I should like to learn things thoroughly."

"That you can do without taking honours."

They walked on again in silence till they saw Pladsen; a light shone out from the sitting-room, the rock loomed darkly in the winter night, the lake lay below covered with smooth, sparkling ice, the wood, with no snow on it, encircled the still cove; the moon shone out and mirrored the wood in the ice.

"It is beautiful here at Pladsen," said the schoolmaster. Eyvind could sometimes see it with the same eyes as when his mother told fairy-tales, or with the vision he had when he raced down the hill on his sledge: so he saw it now; everything seemed elevated and clear.

"Yes, it is beautiful here," he said, but sighed as he spoke.

"Your father has been contented with the holding; couldn't you be contented here too?"

The happy vision of the place all at once vanished. The schoolmaster stood as though waiting for an answer; receiving none, he shook his head, and they went indoors. He sat there awhile with them, but had very little to say, so that the others became silent too. When he said good-bye, both husband and wife went outside the door with him; they seemed to expect him to say something. Meanwhile they all three stood looking up at the evening sky.

"It seems so unnaturally quiet here," said the mother at length, "since the children have gone elsewhere to play."

"And you have no longer a *child* in the house," said the schoolmaster.

The mother understood what he meant.

"Eyvind is not happy of late," said she.

"Oh no, he who is ambitious is not happy."

He looked with an old man's peace up into God's silent sky.

CHAPTER VI

SIX months later, that is to say in the autumn (the confirmation had been put off till then), the candidates for confirmation sat in the servants' hall of the minister's house waiting to be called in for examination, and amongst them Eyvind of Pladsen and Marit of the Hill Farms. Marit had just come down from the minister's room where she had received a beautiful book and much commendation. She laughed and chatted with her girl-friends on all sides, and looked round amongst the boys. Marit was now a full-grown girl, light and free in all her movements, and the boys as well as the girls knew that the finest bachelor of the village, John Hatlen, was paying court to her; she might well be happy as she sat there. By the door stood some girls and boys who had not passed; they were crying whilst Marit and her friends laughed. Amongst them was a little boy in his father's boots and his mother's Sunday kerchief.

"Oh God, oh God!" he sobbed, "I daren't go home again."

This seized those who had not yet been up, with the force of fellow-feeling; there was a general silence. Anxiety clouded their eyes and gripped them by the throat; they could not see distinctly, and neither could they swallow, though they constantly wanted to. One sat and went over all he knew, and though he had discovered some hours before that he knew everything, he now found out with equal certainty that he knew nothing—could not even read. A second went over his whole list of sins, from as far back as he could remember, till now, and came to the conclusion that it would not be in the least wonderful if Our Lord did not let him pass. A third sat and watched everything in the room: if the clock, which was on the point of striking, did not begin until he had counted twenty, he would pass; if the person he heard coming into the passage was the stable-boy, Lars, he would pass; if the big raindrop that was creeping down the window came right to the frame, he would pass. The last and decisive proof was to be whether he could get his right foot twisted round his left, and this he found quite impossible. A fourth was sure that if he was questioned on Joseph in history and on baptism in doctrine, or on Saul, or on the Decalogue, or on Jesus or—he was still going over it all when his turn came. A fifth had set his heart on the Sermon on the Mount; he had dreamt of the sermon, he was sure he would be questioned on the sermon; he went over the sermon to himself, he had to slip out to read the sermon over again—then his turn came, and he was examined on the major and minor prophets. A sixth thought of the minister, what a kind man he was, and how well he knew his father and mother; and of the schoolmaster, who had such a gentle face; and of God, who was so very gracious and had helped many before, both Jacob and Joseph; and then he thought how his mother and sisters were at home praying for him, and that was sure to help. The seventh sat and knocked down all the castles in the air he had built. First he had determined to become a king, then a general or a minister—that stage had long been past: but until he had entered this room he had still thought of going to sea and becoming a captain, perhaps a pirate, and amassing enormous wealth: then he gave up the idea of riches, then the idea of becoming a pirate, then of becoming a captain, then of becoming a mate; he stopped at common sailor or at highest boatswain—it was even possible that he would not go to sea at all, but set to work on his father's farm. The eighth was a little more confident, yet not quite sure of passing; for not even the cleverest could be *quite* sure. He thought of the clothes he had got to be confirmed in, and what they would be used for if he didn't pass. But if he passed he was to go to town and get splendid Sunday clothes, and come home again and dance at Christmas, to the envy of all the boys and the admiration of all the girls. The ninth reckoned otherwise; he opened a little account with God in which he placed upon the one side as Debit: 'He will allow me to pass,' and on the other side as Credit: 'I will never tell any more lies, nor gossip, will always go to church, let the girls alone, and break myself of swearing.' But the tenth thought that as Ole Hansen had passed last year, it would be worse than injustice if he did not pass this year, for he had always been above him at school, and besides, his parents were not respectable. At his side sat the eleventh, nursing the most bloodthirsty plans for revenge in case he did not pass—he was going either to set fire to the school, or leave the neighbourhood and come back as a fulminating judge to call the minister and the whole school-commission to account, and then magnanimously let mercy stand for justice. As a beginning he would go into service with the minister of the next parish, and there be first in the examination next year, and answer so that the whole church should wonder and admire. But the twelfth sat by himself underneath the clock, with both hands in his pockets, and looked sorrowfully at the rest. No one knew what a burden he bore and what anxiety was racking him. But at home there was one who knew it—for he was betrothed. A big, long-legged spider crept over the floor and came near his foot: he used always to tread upon the ugly insects, but to-day he lifted his foot tenderly and let it pass in peace. His voice was as mild as a collect; his eyes kept on repeating that all men were good; his hand moved humbly from his pocket to his hair, in order to smooth it down. If he could only wriggle by hook or by crook through this terrible needle's eye, he would soon swell out again on the other side, chew tobacco and make his engagement public. On a low stool, with his legs bent underneath him, sat the restless thirteenth; his small sparkling eyes made the round of the room three times in a second: and inside the strong, rough head the thoughts of all the other twelve were tossing about in wild confusion, from the brightest hope to the darkest despair, from the humblest resolves to the most annihilating plans of vengeance; and meanwhile he had eaten up all the loose skin from his right thumb and was now busy with his nails, of which he scattered great fragments on the floor.

Eyvind sat over by the window; he had been up and answered everything he was asked, but the minister had said nothing nor the schoolmaster either. He had been thinking for more than six months what both would say when they came to know how he had worked, and he now felt disappointed, and hurt withal. There sat Marit who, for far less labour and knowledge, had received both encouragement and reward. It was precisely for the sake of shining in her eyes that he had toiled, and now she laughingly enjoyed all that he had worked for with so much self-renunciation. Her laughter and joking burnt into his soul, the freedom with which she carried herself hurt him. He had sedulously avoided speaking to her since that evening; "I won't for years yet," he thought; but the sight of her sitting there, so gay and at her ease, crushed him to the earth, and all his proud projects drooped like leaves in the rain.

Little by little, however, he tried to shake off the depression. The thing was to know whether he was Number One to-day, and for this he waited. The schoolmaster generally remained a little while in the minister's room to arrange the young folks in order, and then came down to announce the result; not the final order, indeed, but that which the minister and himself had provisionally agreed upon. Conversation in the room became livelier by degrees, as more and more were examined and passed. But now it became easy to distinguish the ambitious from the contented ones; the latter, so soon as they could get company on the way, went off to tell their parents of their good luck, or else waited for others who had not yet been examined; the former, on the contrary, became quieter and quieter, straining their eyes towards the door.

At length all had been examined, the last had come down, and the schoolmaster was now consulting with the minister. Eyvind looked at Marit; she seemed quite indifferent, but remained sitting, whether on her own or on some one else's account, he did not know. How lovely Marit had grown! He had never seen such a dazzlingly soft complexion; her nose turned up a little, her mouth was smiling. Her eyes were half-closed when she did not just happen to be looking at you, but that gave her glance an unexpected brilliance when it came—and, as if to explain that she meant nothing by it, she would half smile at the same time. Her hair was rather dark than fair, but it curled in little ringlets and came far forward at the sides—so that together with her half-closed eyes it gave her face an effect of mystery which it seemed one could never quite fathom. It was impossible to tell exactly at whom she was looking when she sat by herself or among others, or what she was really thinking of when she turned and talked to any one—for she seemed immediately to take back what she gave.

"No doubt John Hatlen is lurking under all this," thought Eyvind; but still he kept on looking at her.

Now the schoolmaster came. They all started from their seats and crowded round him.

"What's my number?"

"And mine?"

"And mine, mine?"

"Hush you overgrown children, no noise here; be quiet boys, and you shall hear."

He looked slowly round.

"You are Number Two," said he to a boy with blue eyes who was looking beseechingly at him, and the boy danced out of the ring.

"You are Number Three," and he gave a little slap to a red-haired, active little fellow who stood pulling his coat.

"You are Number Five, you Number Eight," and so on. He caught sight of Marit.

"You are Number One of the girls." She flushed crimson all over her face and neck, but tried to smile.

"You, Number Twelve, have been lazy, you rascal, and a great vagabond; you Number Eleven couldn't expect anything better, my boy; you, Number Thirteen, must study hard and come to the repetition class, else you'll come off badly."

Eyvind could bear it no longer; it was true Number One had not been mentioned, but he was standing the whole time where the schoolmaster could see him.

"Master!"—he did not hear. "Master!" He had to repeat it three times before he was heard. At last the schoolmaster looked at him.

"Number Nine or Ten, I don't exactly remember which," said he, and turned to the others.

"Who is Number One then?" asked Hans, who was Eyvind's great friend.

"Not you, curly pate!" said the schoolmaster, hitting him over the knuckles with a roll of paper.

"Who is it then?" asked several. "Who is it—yes, who is it?"

"The one who has the number will be told of it," answered the schoolmaster, severely; he would have no more questions. "Go home nicely now, children, thank your God and gladden your parents! Thank your old schoolmaster too; you would have been badly enough off without him!"

They thanked him and laughed, they dispersed rejoicing, for at this moment when they were to go home to their parents they were all happy. But one there was who could not immediately find his books and who, when he did find them, sat down as if to con them all over again.

The schoolmaster went up to him.

"Well, Eyvind, aren't you going with the others?"

He did not answer.

"What are you looking up in your books?"

"I want to see what I have answered wrong to-day."

"I don't think you answered anything wrong."

Then Eyvind looked at him, the tears in his eyes; he looked fixedly at him whilst one tear after another ran down, but he said not a word. The schoolmaster sat down in front of him.

"Are you not glad now that you've passed?"

His mouth quivered but he did not answer.

"Your father and mother will be very much pleased," said the schoolmaster looking at him.

Eyvind struggled a long time to get a word out, at last he asked him, speaking low and in broken phrases:

"Is it—because I—am a cottar's son—that I am Number Nine or Ten?"

"No doubt it is," answered the schoolmaster.

"Then it's no good for me to work," said he in a dead voice, crushed under the wreck of his dreams. Suddenly he raised his head, lifted his right hand, struck the table with all his might, flung himself on his face and burst into an agony of weeping.

The schoolmaster let him lie and have his cry right out. It lasted a long time, but the schoolmaster waited until the weeping became more like that of a child. Then he took the boy's head between his hands, lifted it up and looked into the tear-stained face.

"Do you think it is God who has been with you now?" said he, putting his arm tenderly round his shoulders.

Eyvind was still sobbing, but not so violently; the tears flowed more slowly, but he did not dare to look at his questioner, nor yet to answer.

"This, Eyvind, has been your just reward. You have not studied for the love of heaven and your parents; you have studied for vanity's sake."

It was all silent in the room in the intervals of the schoolmaster's speaking. Eyvind felt his gaze resting on him and he was melted and humbled by it.

"With such anger in your heart you could not have presented yourself to make a covenant with your God; could you, Eyvind?"

"No," he stammered as well as he could.

"And if you stood there in vainglorious joy because you were Number One, would you not be bringing sin to the altar?"

"Yes," whispered he, with trembling lips.

"You still love me, Eyvind?"

"Yes;" and he looked up for the first time.

"Then I will tell you that it was I who got you placed lower; for I love you so much, Eyvind!"

The other looked at him, blinked several times, and the tears rained down thickly.

"You don't bear me a grudge for it?"

"No." He looked up fully and clearly although he was nearly choked.

"My dear child! I will take care of you as long as I live."

The schoolmaster waited for him until he had pulled himself together and arranged his books, and then said he would go home with him. They walked slowly homewards; at first Eyvind was still silent and struggling with himself, but gradually he got into a better frame of mind. He felt quite sure that what had happened was for the best, and before they reached home his conviction had become so strong that he thanked God and told the schoolmaster.

"Ah, now we can think about doing something in life," said the schoolmaster, "and not run after nothings and numbers. What do you say to the seminary?"

"Yes, I would like to go there."

"You mean the Agricultural College?"

"Yes."

"That's certainly the best; it offers better prospects than schoolmastering."

"But how shall I get there? I want so much to go, but I've no money."

"Be industrious and good and we shall find means."

Eyvind was quite overcome with gratitude. He had that sparkle of the eye, that lightness of breath, that infinite fire of love which comes over one when one feels the unexpected goodness of a human creature. The whole future presents itself for a moment like wandering in the fresh mountain air; one seems to be wafted forward without effort.

When they got home, both parents were in the room where they had been sitting in silent expectation, although it was working-time and they were busy. The schoolmaster went in first, Eyvind followed; both were smiling.

"Well?" said the father, laying down a hymn book in which he had just been reading "A Communicant's Prayer." The mother stood by the fireplace and dared not speak: she laughed, but her hands were unsteady; she evidently expected good news, but would not betray herself.

"I thought I'd just come with him, for I knew how glad you would be to hear that he answered every question, and that the minister said when Eyvind had gone that he has never had a better-prepared candidate."

"Oh, did he really!" said his mother, much moved.

"That was good," said his father, clearing his throat undecidedly.

After a long silence the mother asked softly:

"What Number will he get?"

"Number Nine or Ten," said the schoolmaster, calmly.

The mother looked at the father, and he looked first at her and then at Eyvind.

"A cottar's son can expect no more," said he.

Eyvind looked back at him; he felt as if the tears would rise to his throat again, but he controlled himself by hastily calling to mind things dear to him, one after another, until the impulse subsided.

"I had better go now," said the schoolmaster, nodding and turning away. Both parents went out with him as usual to the doorstep; here the schoolmaster cut a quid of tobacco and said smiling:

"He will be Number One all the same; but had better not hear it until the day comes."

"No, no," said his father, nodding.

"No, no," said his mother, nodding too; then she took the schoolmaster's hand: "You must let us thank you for all you have done for him," said she.

"Yes, we thank you," said the father, and the schoolmaster went away; but they stood a long time looking after him.

CHAPTER VII

THE schoolmaster had gone on the right track when he advised the minister to put Eyvind's fitness to the test. During the three weeks which elapsed before the confirmation he was with the boy every day. It is one thing for a young and tender soul to receive an impression, and another thing to retain it steadfastly. Many dark hours fell upon the boy before he learnt to take the measure of his future by better standards than those of vanity and display. Every now and then, in the very midst of his work, his pleasure in it would slip away from him. "To what end?" he would think, "what shall I gain?" and then a moment afterwards he would remember the schoolmaster's words and his kindness; but he needed this human stand-by to help him up again every time he fell away from the sense of his higher duty.

During those days preparations were going on at Pladsen not only for the confirmation, but also for Eyvind's departure to the Agricultural College, which was to take place the day after. The tailor and shoemaker were in the house, his mother was baking in the kitchen, his father was making a chest for him. There was a great deal of talk about how much he would cost them in two years; about his not being able to come home the first Christmas, perhaps not even the second; about the love he must feel for his parents who were willing to make such an effort for their child's sake. Eyvind sat there like one who had put out to sea on his own account but had capsized and was now taken up by kindly people.

Such a feeling conduces to humility, and with that comes much besides. As the great day drew near, he ventured to call himself prepared and to look forward with trustful devotion. Every time the image of Marit tried to mingle in his thoughts he put it resolutely aside, but felt pain in doing so. He tried to practise doing this, but never grew stronger;

on the contrary, it was the pain that grew. He was tired, therefore, the last evening when, after a long self-examination, he prayed that Our Lord might not put him to this test.

The schoolmaster came in as the evening wore on. They gathered in the sitting-room after they had all washed and tidied themselves, according to custom the evening before one is to go to communion. The mother was agitated, the father silent; parting lay beyond to-morrow's ceremony, and it was uncertain when they would all sit together again. The schoolmaster took out the psalm-books, they had prayers and sang, and afterwards he said a little prayer just as the words occurred to him.

These four persons sat together until the evening grew very late and thought turned inwards upon itself; then they parted with the best wishes for the coming day and the compact it was to seal. Eyvind had to own as he lay down that never had he gone to bed so happy; and by that, as he now interpreted it, he meant: "Never have I lain down so submissive to God's will and so happy in it." Marit's face at once came to haunt him again; and the last thing he was conscious of was lying there saying to himself: "Not quite happy, not quite," and then answering: "Yes I am, quite," and then again: "Not quite."—"Yes, quite."—"No, not quite."

When he awoke, he immediately remembered the day, said his prayers and felt himself strong, as one does in the morning.

Since the summer, he had slept by himself in the loft; he now got up and put on his handsome new clothes carefully, for he had never had the like before. There was, in particular, a short jacket which he had to touch a great many times before he got used to it. He got a little mirror when he had put on his collar, and for the fourth time put on his coat. As he now saw his own delighted face, set in extraordinarily fair hair, smiling out at him from the glass, it struck him that this, again, was doubtless vanity. "Well, but people must be well-dressed and clean," answered he, while he drew back from the mirror as though it were a sin to look in it. "Certainly, but not quite so happy about it." "No, but Our Lord must surely be pleased that one should like to look nice." "That may be, but He would like it better if you did so without being so much taken up about it." "That's true, but you see it's because everything is so new." "Yes, but then by degrees you must leave it off." He found himself carrying on such self-examining dialogues in his own mind, now on one subject, now on another, in order that no sin should fall upon the day and stain it, but he knew, too, that more than that was needed.

When he came down, his parents were sitting full-dressed, waiting breakfast for him. He went and shook hands with them and thanked them for the clothes.

"May you have health to wear them."[1]

They seated themselves at table, said a silent grace, and ate. The mother cleared the table and brought in the provision-box in preparation for church. The father put on his coat, the mother pinned her kerchief, they took their hymn-books, locked up the house and set off. When they got upon the upper road they found it thronged with church-going folk, driving and walking, with confirmation candidates amongst them, and in more than one group white-haired grandparents, determined to make this one last appearance.

It was an autumn day without sunshine—such as portends a change of weather. Clouds gathered and parted again, sometimes a great assemblage would break up into twenty smaller ones which rushed away bearing orders for a storm; but down on the earth it was as yet still, the leaves hung lifeless, not even quivering, the air was rather close; the people carried cloaks but did not use them. An unusually large crowd had assembled round the high-lying church, but the young people who were to be confirmed went straight in to be settled in their places before service began. Then it was that the schoolmaster, in blue clothes, tail-coat and knee-breeches, high boots, stiff collar, and his pipe sticking out of his tail-pocket, came down the church, nodded and smiled, slapped one on the shoulder, spoke a few words to another, reminding him to answer loud and clear, and so made his way over to the poor-box, where Eyvind stood answering all his friend Hans's questions with reference to his journey.

"Good morning, Eyvind; how fine we are to-day,"—he took him by the coat-collar as if he wanted to speak to him.

[1] A customary phrase.

"Listen; I think all's well with you. I've just been speaking to the minister: you are to take your place, go up to Number One, and answer distinctly!"

Eyvind looked up at him astonished; the schoolmaster nodded, the boy moved a few steps, stopped, a few more steps and stopped again. "Yes, it's really so, he has spoken for me to the minister;" and the boy went up quickly.

"You're Number One after all, then?" someone whispered to him.

"Yes," answered Eyvind, softly, but he still was not quite sure whether he dared take his place.

The marshalling was completed, the minister arrived, the bell rang, and the people came streaming in. Then Eyvind saw Marit of the Hill Farms standing just opposite him. She looked at him, too, but both were so impressed by the sacredness of the place that they dared not greet each other. He saw only that she was dazzlingly beautiful and was bareheaded; more than that he did not see. Eyvind who, for more than six months, had been nursing such great designs of standing opposite her, now that it had come to the point forgot both her and the place—forgot that he had ever thought of them.

When it was all over, kinsfolk and friends came to offer their congratulations; then his comrades came to bid him good-bye, as they had heard that he was to go away next day; and then came a lot of little ones with whom he had sledged on the hills and whom he had helped at school, and some even shed a tear or two at leave-taking. Last came the schoolmaster and shook hands silently with him and his parents and made a sign to go,—he would come with them. They four were together again, and this evening was to be the last. On the way there were many more who bade him good-bye and wished him luck, but they did not speak amongst themselves until they were sitting indoors at home.

The schoolmaster tried to keep up their courage; it was evident that now it had come to the point, they were all three dreading the long two years' separation, seeing that hitherto they had not been parted for a single day; but none of them would own it. As the hours went on, the more heart-sick did

Eyvind become; he had to go out at last to calm himself a little.

It was dusk now and there was a strange soughing in the wind; he stood on the doorstep and looked up. Then, from the edge of the rock he heard his own name softly called; it was no delusion, for it was twice repeated. He looked up and made out that a girl was sitting crouched amongst the trees and looking down.

"Who's that?" he asked.

"I hear you are going away," said she, softly, "so I had to come to you and say good-bye, as you would not come to me."

"Why, is that you, Marit? I will come up to you."

"No don't do that, I have waited such a long time and that would make me have to wait still longer. Nobody knows where I am, and I must hurry home again."

"It was kind of you to come," said he.

"I couldn't bear that you should go away like that, Eyvind; we have known each other since we were children."

"Yes, we have."

"And now we haven't spoken to each other for six months."

"No, we haven't."

"And we parted so strangely the last time."

"Yes—I must really come up to you."

"No, no, don't do that! But tell me; you're not angry with me, are you?"

"How can you think so, dear?"

"Good-bye then, Eyvind, and thank you for all our life together!"

"No, Marit——!"

"Yes, I must go now, they will miss me."

"Marit, Marit!"

"No, I daren't stop away any longer, Eyvind; good-bye!"

"Good-bye!'

After that he moved as if in a dream, and answered at random when they spoke to him. They put it down to his going away and thought it only natural; and indeed that was what was in his mind when the schoolmaster took leave at night, and put something into his hand which he afterwards found to be a five-dollar note.

But later on, when he went to bed, it was not of his going away he was thinking, but of the words which had come down from the edge of the rock and of those which had gone up again. As a child she had not been allowed to come to the edge because her grandfather was afraid she might fall over. Perhaps she would one day come over all the same!

CHAPTER VIII

"My dear Parents,

"We have got a great deal more work to do now, but now I have nearly made up to the others so that it is not so hard upon me. And there is much that I shall alter on the farm when I come home, for things are very bad there, and the only wonder is that it has held together at all. But I shall get it all into shape again, for I have now learned a great deal. I am longing to get to some place where I can put in practice what I know, so I must seek a good position when my course is finished. Here they all say that John Hatlen is not so clever as they think at home; but he has a farm of his own, and it's his own affair whether he knows much or little. Many who have gone through our course earn large salaries; that is because ours is the best agricultural college in the country. Some say that one in the next county is better, but that is not at all true. Here they teach us two things: the first is called theory, and the second practice, and it is good to have them both, and the one is no good without the other, but still the last is the best. And the first word means to know the cause and reason for a piece of work, but the other means to be able to do the work, for instance as it might be with a bog. Many know what ought to be done with a bog, but do it wrongly all the same, for they haven't the power. Many have the power and don't know the reasons for things, and they may go wrong too, for there are many kinds of bogs. But we at the Agricultural College learn both things. The principal is so clever that no one can come near him. At the last Agricultural Congress he managed two questions whilst the other masters of agriculture had only one each; and when they took time to think things out, they were always as he said. But at the former Congress, when he was not present, they only talked nonsense. It is on account of the principal's cleverness that he has got the lieutenant who teaches land-surveying; for the other schools have no lieutenant. But he is so clever that they say he was the very best in the school for lieutenants.

"The schoolmaster asks whether I go to church. Yes, certainly I go to church, for now the minister has got an assistant, and he preaches so that all the people in church are frightened, and that is a pleasure to hear. He is of the new religion that they have in Christiania, and people think he is too severe, but it does them good all the same.

"At present we are learning a good deal of history which we have not studied before, and it is strange to see all that has gone on in the world, and especially in our country. For we have always won except when we have lost, and that was when we were much fewer than the other people. Now we have freedom, and no other people have so much of that as we, except America; but there they are not happy. And we should love our freedom above everything.

"Now I will close for this time, for I have written a long letter. I daresay the school-master will read the letter, and when he answers it for you, let him tell me some news of the neighbours, for that he never does.

"Accept best greetings from

"Your affectionate son,

"E. Thoresen."

"My dear Parents,

"I must tell you that there has been an examination here, and I have come out remarkably well in many things, and very well in writing and surveying, but only pretty well in composition in the mother tongue. The principal says that is because I have not read enough, and he has presented me with some books by Ole Vig which are splendid, for I understand everything in them. The principal is very kind to me, he tells us so many things. Everything in this country is on a very small scale compared with what they have in foreign countries; we understand almost nothing, but learn everything from the Scotch and Swiss, and from the Dutch we learn gardening. Many travel to these countries; in Sweden, too, they are much cleverer than we, and the principal himself has been there. I shall soon have been here a year, and it seems to me that I have learned a great deal; but when I hear of all that the pupils know who go out after examination, and think that even they know nothing in comparison with foreigners, I get quite discouraged. And then the soil is so poor here in Norway compared with what it is abroad; nothing we can do with it pays. Besides, people have no energy. And even if they had, and if the land were much better, they have no capital to work with. It is wonderful that things go as well as they do.

"I am now in the highest class, and it will be a year before I have done with it. But most of my comrades have gone, and I am longing for home. I seem somehow to stand alone, although of course I do not really; but it is so strange when one has been away a long time. I thought at one time that I should become so clever here, but there seems little enough chance of that.

"What shall I do when I come away from here? First, of course, I shall come home. Afterwards I suppose I must look out for something to do, but it must not be far away.

"Good-bye, dear parents. Greet those who ask after me, and tell them that I am well, but that I am longing to be home again.

"Your affectionate son,

"EYVIND THORESEN PLADSEN."

"DEAR SCHOOLMASTER,

"This is to ask you whether you will forward the enclosed letter and say nothing about it to anybody. And if you will not, then you must burn it.

"EYVIND THORESEN PLADSEN."

"TO THE HIGHLY-HONOURED MARIT KNUT'S-DAUGHTER NORDISTUEN AT THE UPPER HILL FARMS.

"You will be much surprised to receive a letter from me, but you need not be, for I only want to ask how you are getting on in every respect. You must let me know as soon as possible. As for myself, I have to tell you that I shall have finished my course here in a year.

"Most respectfully,

"EYVIND PLADSEN."

"To Bachelor Eyvind Pladsen, at the Agricultural College.

"I have duly received your letter from the schoolmaster, and I will answer since you ask me to. But I am afraid, because you are so learned, and I have a letter-writer, but there is nothing in it that will do. So I must try, and you must take the will for the deed, but you mustn't show it, or you are not the person I take you for. And you are not to keep it either, for then it might easily fall into some one's hands, but you are to burn it, you must promise me that. There are such a lot of things I should like to write about, but I don't think I dare. We have had a good harvest, potatoes are a high price, and we have plenty of them here at the Hill Farms. But the bear has been terrible amongst the cattle this summer; at Ole Nedregaard's he killed two head, and at our cottar's he knocked one about so that it had to be killed. I am weaving a large web of cloth; it is like that Scotch stuff, and it is difficult. And now I will tell you that I am still at home, and that others would fain have it otherwise. Now I have no more to write about this time and so good-bye.

"Marit Knut's-daughter.

"P.S.—Be sure you burn this letter."

"To Agricultural-Student Eyvind Pladsen.

"I have told you, Eyvind, that whoso walks with God, he has a portion in the good heritage. But now you shall hear my counsel, and that is: not to take the world with yearning and tribulation, but to trust to God and never let your heart consume you, for then you have another God besides Him. Next, I must tell you that your father and mother are well, but I have a bad hip; for now the war makes itself felt again, and all that one has been through. What youth sows age reaps, and that both in soul and body; which latter now smarts and aches, and tempts one to continual complaining. But age must not complain, for wounds instruct us and aches preach patience, so that a man may have strength for the last journey. To-day I have taken up my pen for many reasons, and first and foremost on Marit's account, who has become a God-fearing girl, but is as light-footed as a reindeer and unsettled in her purposes. She would like to hold to one, but her nature will not let her. But I have often seen that with such weak hearts our Lord is lenient and long-suffering, and never lets them be tempted beyond their strength, so that they are broken in pieces; for they are very fragile. I duly gave her the letter, and she hid it from all save her own heart. And if God gives this matter His countenance, I have nothing against it; for she is a delight to the eye of youth, as can plainly be seen, and she has plenty of earthly goods, and heavenly goods as well, for all her instability. For the fear of God in her mind is like water in a shallow pond: it is there when it rains, but when the sun shines it is gone.

"My eyes will bear no more now; they see well enough out in the open, but ache and water over small things. In conclusion, I would say to you, Eyvind, in all your aspirations and labours take your God with you; for it is written, Better is an handful with quietness than both the hands full with travail and vexation of spirit.

"Your old schoolmaster,

"BAARD ANDERSEN OPDAL."

"TO THE HIGHLY-HONOURED MARIT KNUT'S-DAUGHTER, OF THE HILL FARMS.

"Thank you for your letter, which I have read and burnt as you told me. You write about many things, but not a word of what I wanted you to write about. I dare not write about anything certain either, untill I get to know something of how it is with you in *every way*. The schoolmaster's letter says nothing that you can take hold of; but he praises you, and then he says that you are unstable. You were that before. I don't know what I am to believe, and therefore you must write, for I shall not be happy until you write. At present what I most like to remember is that you came on the rock that last evening, and what you then said to me. I will say no more this time, and so good-bye.

"Most respectfully,

"EYVIND PLADSEN."

"TO THE BACHELOR EYVIND THORESEN PLADSEN.

"The schoolmaster has given me another letter from you, and I have now read it. But I don't understand it at all; I suppose that is because I am not learned. You want to know how I am in every way; and I am quite well and strong, and have nothing whatever the matter with me. I eat well, especially when I get milk-food, and I sleep at night, and sometimes in the day, too. I have danced a great deal this winter, for there have been lots of parties and great goings-on. I go to church when there is not too much snow, but it has been deep this winter. Now I hope you know everything, and if you don't then I know nothing for it but that you must write to me again.

"MARIT KNUT'S-DAUGHTER."

"TO THE HIGHLY-HONOURED MARIT KNUT'S-DAUGHTER.

"I have received your letter, but you seem to want me to be just as wise as I was before. I dare not write anything of what I want to write about, for I do not know you. But perhaps you don't know me, either.

"You must not believe that I am any longer the soft cheese out of which you pressed water when I sat and watched you dance. I have lain upon many a shelf to dry since that time. Nor yet am I like those long-haired dogs that for the slightest thing let their ears droop, and slip away from people, as I used to do; I take my chance now.

"Your letter was playful enough; but it was playful just where it ought not to have been; for you understand me well; and you could guess that I did not ask for fun, but because of late I can think of nothing but what I asked about. I waited in deep anxiety, and then came nothing but trifling and laughter.

"Good-bye Marit Nordistuen; I shall not look too much at you, as I did at that dance. I hope you may both eat and sleep well, and finish your new web of cloth, and especially that you may shovel away the snow that lies before the church door.

"Most respectfully,

"EYVIND THORESEN PLADSEN."

TO EYVIND THORESEN, STUDENT OF AGRICULTURE
AGRICULTURAL COLLEGE.

"In spite of my old age, and weak eyes, and the pain in my right hip, I must yield to the urgency of youth; for it finds a use for us old folks when it has stuck fast. It coaxes and weeps until it has its way, and then it is off again directly, and will not listen to another word.

"Now it is Marit. She comes with many sweet words to get me to write as follows, for she dares not write alone. I have read your letter; she thought she had John Hatlen or some other fool to deal with, and not one whom schoolmaster Baard had brought up, but now she finds she's mistaken. Yet you have been too hard upon her, for there are some girls who joke in order not to cry, and both mean the same thing. But I like to see you take serious things seriously, else you cannot laugh at nonsense.

"As to the fact of your caring for each other, that is plain enough from many things. As to her, I have often had my doubts, for she is as hard to grasp as the wind; but now I know that she has stood out against John Hatlen, and has thereby made her grandfather very angry. She was happy when your offer came, and when she joked it was not with any evil intention, but from joy. She has borne much, and she has done so in order to wait for him upon whom her heart is set. And now you will not take her, but throw her aside as a naughty child.

"This was what I had to tell you. And I will add this advice, that you should come to an understanding with her, for you will probably have plenty to contend with in any case. I am an old man who has seen three generations; I know folly and its courses.

"I am to greet you from your father and mother, they are longing for you. But I would not mention this before for fear of making you unhappy. You do not know your father; for he is like the tree that gives no sign before it is hewn down. But if you once get a little nearer him, then you will learn to know him, and you will marvel as in a rich place. He has been oppressed and silent in worldly matters, but your mother has eased his mind from worldly anxiety, and now it grows clearer towards the evening of his day.

"My eyes are getting dim now, and my hand is weary. Therefore I commit you to Him whose eye ever watches, and whose hand never tires.

"BAARD ANDERSON OPDAL."

"To Eyvind Pladsen.

"You seem to be angry with me, and that hurts me very much. For I didn't mean it like that, I meant it well. I remember that I have often treated you ill, and therefore I will now write to you, but you must not show it to anybody. At one time I had everything my own way, and then I was not good; but now nobody cares for me any more, and now I am unhappy. John Hatlen has made up a song in mockery of me, and all the boys sing it, and I dare not go to any dances. Both the old people know about it, and they scold me. But I am sitting alone, and writing, and you mustn't show it.

"You have learnt much, and can advise me, but you are now far away. I have often been down to your parents' house, and I have talked with your mother, and we have become good friends; but I did not dare to say anything because you wrote so strangely. The schoolmaster only makes fun of me, and he knows nothing about the song, for no one in the parish would dare to sing such a thing before him. Now I am alone, and have no one to talk with. I remember when we were children, and you were so good to me, and always used to let me sit in your sledge. I wish I were a child again.

"I dare not ask you to answer me any more; because I dare not. But if you would answer me, just once more, I would never forget it, Eyvind. Marit.

"Dear, burn this letter; I scarcely know whether I dare send it."

"Dear Marit,

"Thanks for your letter; you wrote it in a good hour. Now I will tell you, Marit, that I love you so that I can hardly stay here any longer, and if only you love me too, then John's songs and other evil words shall be only leaves that the tree bears too many of. Since I got your letter I am like a new creature; double strength has come to me, and I fear no one in the wide world. When I had sent my last letter, I repented it so much that it nearly made me ill. And now you shall hear what that led to. The principal took me aside and asked what was the matter with me; he thought I was studying too much. Then he told me that, when my year was up, I might stay for another and pay nothing; I might help him with one thing and another, and he would teach me more. I thought then that work was the only thing left to me and I thanked him much: and even now I don't regret it although I am longing for you, for the longer I am here the better right shall I have to ask for you one day. Now that I am so happy, I work for three, and never will I be behind in anything! You shall have a book I am reading, for there is a great deal about love in it. At night I read it when the others are asleep, and then I read your letter over again too. Have you thought of when we shall meet? I think of it so often, and you must try thinking of it too, and see how delightful it is. I am glad that I managed to write so much, although it was so hard; for now I can tell you all I want to and smile over it in my heart.

"I will give you many books to read so that you may see how many crosses they have had who truly loved each other, and how they have rather died of grief than give each other up. And so shall we do also, and do it with great joy. It may be nearly two years before we see each other, and yet longer before we get each other, but with every day that goes it is one day less; this is what we must think whilst we work.

"In my next letter I will tell you so many things, but to-night I have no more paper and the others are asleep. So I will go to bed and think of you and go on thinking of you until I fall asleep.

"Your friend,

"EYVIND PLADSEN."

CHAPTER IX

ONE midsummer Saturday Thore Pladsen rowed across the lake to fetch his son, who was to arrive that afternoon from the Agricultural College where he had now completed his course. His mother had had women in to help her for several days beforehand, and everything was clean and scoured. Eyvind's room had long been in readiness, a stove had been put in and there he was to live. To-day the mother had strewn fresh sprigs on the floor, put out clean linen for use and arranged the bed, looking out now and then to see if any boat were coming across the lake. Downstairs there was a great table spread, and always some finishing touch to be given, or flies to be chased away; and in the best room there was always something that needed dusting. No boat yet; she leant against the window frame and looked out. Then she heard a step close beside her on the road and she turned her head; it was the schoolmaster coming slowly down, leaning on a stick, for his hip was troublesome. His shrewd eyes looked calmly around; he stopped and rested on his stick and nodded to her.

"Not come yet?"

"No, I expect them every minute."

"Good weather for the hay."

"But hot walking for old people."

The schoolmaster looked smilingly at her.

"Have young people been out to-day?"

"Yes, they have, but they've gone again."

"Of course, yes; they're to meet this evening somewhere I suppose."

"Yes, no doubt; Thore says they sha'n't meet in his house until they have the old people's consent."

"Right, right!"

Presently the mother cried:

"There they come, I really believe!"

The schoolmaster looked far over the lake.

"Yes, that's they!" She left the window and he entered the house. When he had rested a little and had something to drink, they went down to the lake whilst the boat scudded swiftly towards them, for both father and son were rowing. The rowers had thrown off their coats, and the water foamed under the oars so that the boat was quickly abreast of them. Eyvind turned his head and looked up, and catching sight of those two at the landing-place, rested on his oars and called out:

"Good-day, mother; good-day, schoolmaster."

"What a grown-up voice he has got," said the mother, her face shining. "Oh, look, look, he's just as fair as ever!" she added.

The schoolmaster fended off the boat, the father shipped his oars; Eyvind sprang past him ashore, and gave his hand first to his mother and then to the schoolmaster. He laughed and laughed again, and, quite against the peasants' custom, related at once in a stream of words all about his examinations, his journey, the principal's certificate and kind offers. He asked about the year's crops, and all acquaintances, save one. The father set about unloading the boat, but, wanting to hear also, thought this could stand over, and went with the others. So they turned homewards, Eyvind laughing and pouring forth his news, the mother laughing too, for she did not know what to say. The schoolmaster limped slowly along beside them, and looked shrewdly at him; his father walked modestly a little farther off. And so they reached home. He was delighted with all he saw; first that the house had been painted, then that the mill had been added to, then that the leaden windows had been taken out of the downstairs room. and white glass put in instead of green, and the window-frames enlarged. When he went indoors everything was strangely smaller than he remembered it, but so cheerful. The clock clucked like a fat hen; the cut-away chairbacks seemed almost as if they could speak; he knew every cup upon the table; the fireplace smiled a whitewashed welcome; branches were stuck all along the walls, and gave off fragrance; juniper sprigs were strewn on the floor in token of holiday. They sat down to eat, but there was not much eaten, for they talked without intermission. Each one now examined him more at leisure, noticed differences and likenesses, and observed what was entirely new about him, even to the blue Sunday clothes he was wearing. Once, when he had told a long story about one of his fine comrades and had at last finished, there was a little pause, and his father said:

"I can scarcely understand a word of what you say, boy; you talk so frightfully fast."

They all burst out laughing, Eyvind as much as any of them. He knew quite well that it was true, but it was impossible for him to speak more slowly. All the new things he had seen and learnt in his long absence had so seized upon his imagination and intelligence, and so shaken him out of the rut of custom, that powers which had long lain dormant had, so to speak, started out of their sleep, and his head was incessantly working. And they noted, too, that he had a trick of repeating a word or two here and there without any reason, repeating it over and over again from sheer hurry; it seemed as though he tripped over himself. Sometimes it was comical, and then he laughed, and it was forgotten. The father and the schoolmaster sat and watched whether his thoughtfulness had worn away, but it did not appear so. He remembered everything; he it was who reminded them that the boat must be unloaded. He unpacked his things immediately and hung them up, showed them his books, his watch, and all his new possessions, and they were well taken care of, his mother said. He was extremely delighted with his little room; he wanted to remain at home to begin with, he said, to help with the haymaking, and to study. Where he would go afterwards he did not know, but it was all the same to him. He had acquired a rapidity and strength of thought which was refreshing, and a vivacity in expressing his feelings which was so good to those who, the whole year round, had been studiously repressing theirs. It made the schoolmaster ten years younger.

"Well, we've got *so far* with him," said he beaming, as he rose to go.

When the mother came in after the usual parting word on the doorstep, she called Eyvind into the best room.

"Some one will be expecting you at nine o'clock," whispered she.

"Where?"

"Up on the rock."

Eyvind looked at the clock; it was getting on for nine. He would not wait indoors, but went out, climbed up the rock, stopped, and looked down. The roof of the house lay close underneath; the bushes on the roof had grown larger; all the young trees round where he stood had grown, too, and he knew every one. He looked down over the road which skirted the rock, with the wood on the other side. The road lay grey and solemn, but the wood was clothed in all sorts of foliage; the trees were tall and straight. In the little bay lay a vessel with flapping sails; she was laden with planks, and waiting for a wind. He looked across the water which had borne him forth and back. It lay still and shining. A few sea-birds were hovering over, but without cries, for it was late. His father came out of the mill, stopped at the doorsteps, looked out like his son, then went down to the water to see after the boat for the night. His mother came out from a side door leading from the kitchen. She looked up towards the rock as she crossed the yard with food for the fowls, and again looked up, humming to herself. He sat down to wait. The brushwood grew thick so that he could not see far in, but he listened for the slightest sound. For a long time he heard nothing but birds, which flew up and disappeared, and now a squirrel jumping from one tree into another. But at last, a long way off, there comes a crackling sound; it stops a moment, then crackles again. He rises; his heart beats, and the blood rushes to his head. Something comes breaking through the bushes close at hand. But it is a large shaggy dog that comes and looks up at him, stands still on three legs, and does not move. It is the dog from Upper Hill Farm; and close behind him there is a crackling again. The dog turns his head and wags his tail. And here is Marit.

A bush had caught her dress; she turned to disengage herself, and so she stood when he first saw her. She was bareheaded and had her hair rolled up according to the everyday fashion of girls; she had on a stout, checked bodice without sleeves, nothing on her neck but the turned down linen collar; she had stolen away from working in the field, and had not dared to make herself fine. Now she looked up sideways and smiled; her white teeth and half-closed eyes shone; she stood thus a moment disentangling herself, then she came on, and got redder and redder at every step. He went to meet her, and took her hand in both his; she looked down, and so they stood.

"Thanks for all your letters," was the first thing he said, and when she looked up a little at that, and laughed, he felt that she was the most roguish fairy he could possibly have met in a wood; but he was embarrassed, and she no less.

"How tall you have grown!" said she, but she meant something quite different. She looked at him more and more, and laughed more and more, and so did he; but they said nothing. The dog had seated himself on the edge of the rock, and was looking down at the house; Thore noticed the dog's head from the water below, and could not for the life of him imagine what it was that showed up on the rock.

But the two had let go each other's hands, and began by degrees to talk. And when he had once begun, Eyvind soon talked so fast that she could not but laugh at him.

"Yes, you know, that's when I am happy, really happy you know; and when it was all right between us two, it was just as if a lock had burst open inside me, burst open you know."

She laughed. Presently she said:

"I know all the letters you sent me almost by heart."

"So do I yours! But you always wrote such short ones."

"Because you always wanted them long."

"And when I wanted you to write more about anything, you always chopped round and away from it."

"I look best when you see my back," said the witch.

"But, by-the-bye, you never told me how you got rid of John Hatlen."

"I laughed."

"What?"

"Laughed; don't you know what it is to laugh?"

"Oh yes, I can laugh!"

"Let me see!"

"What an idea! I must have something to laugh at."

"I don't need that when I'm happy."

"Are you happy now, Marit?"

"Am I laughing now?"

"Yes, that you are!" He took both her hands and struck them together—clap, clap!—whilst he looked at her.

At this moment the dog began to growl, then all his hair bristled up, then he began to bark at something right below; he got angrier and angrier until at last he was beside himself with rage. Marit started back alarmed, but Eyvind stepped forward and looked down. It was at his father that the dog was barking; he was standing right under the rock with both hands in his pockets, looking up at the dog.

"Are you up there too? What mad dog is that you've got up there?"

"It's a dog from the Hill Farms," answered Eyvind, somewhat abashed.

"How the devil did he get up there?"

But the mother, hearing the horrible noise, had looked out at the kitchen window, and understood the situation; so she laughed and said:

"That dog comes here every day, so there's nothing to be surprised at."

"It's a ferocious dog."

"He'll be better if he's patted," said Eyvind, and he patted him; the dog left off barking but continued to growl. The father went unsuspectingly away, and the two were saved from discovery.

"That was one time," said Marit as they met again.

"Do you mean it'll be worse another time?"

"I know some one who will keep a sharp eye on us."

"Your grandfather?"

"Exactly."

"But he can't do us any harm."

"Not a bit."

"You promise me that?"

"Yes, I promise you that, Eyvind."

"How lovely you are, Marit!"

"That's what the fox said to the crow, and got the cheese."

"I want the cheese too, I promise you!"

"But you won't get it."

"I shall take it."

She turned her head, and he did not take it.

"I'll tell you something, Eyvind," she looked up sideways.

"Well?"

"How ill-mannered you've grown!"

"You'll give me the cheese all the same."

"No, I won't;" she turned away again. "I must go now, Eyvind."

"I am coming with you."

"But not beyond the wood; grandfather would see you."

"No, not beyond the wood. Why, how you're running, dear."

"We can't walk side by side here."

"But this isn't being together."

"Catch me, then!"

She ran, he ran after her, and her dress was soon caught so that he overtook her.

"Have I taken you now for always, Marit?" He had his arm round her waist.

"I think so," she said softly, and laughed, but flushed red, and was instantly serious again. Well, now's the time, thought he, and he tried to kiss her, but she ducked her head down under his arm, laughed and ran away. But she stopped at the last trees.

"When shall we meet again?" she whispered.

"To-morrow, to-morrow!" he whispered back.

"Yes, to-morrow!"

"Good-bye," and she ran off.

"Marit!"

She stopped.

"Wasn't it strange that we met first upon the rock?"

"Yes, wasn't it?" and she ran on again.

He looked long after her; the dog ran on in front, barking up at her, and she after, hushing him.

He turned round, took off his cap and tossed it in the air, caught it and tossed it up again.

"Now, I really believe I am beginning to be happy," said the boy; and he sang as he went homewards.

CHAPTER X

ONE afternoon later in the summer, as the mother and a maid were raking up the hay, and the father and Eyvind were carrying it home, a little barefooted, bareheaded boy came hopping down the hill and across the field to Eyvind, to whom he handed a note.

"You run well!" said Eyvind.

"I am paid for it," answered the boy. No answer was required, he said, so he made his way back again over the rock; for there was some one on the road, he explained, whom he did not want to meet. Eyvind opened the note with some trouble, for it was first folded in a strip—then folded again, then sealed and tied up.

Its contents were:

"He is on his way; but it is slow work. Run into the wood and hide yourself.

"You Know Who."

"No, I'll be hanged if I hide," thought Eyvind, looking defiantly up the hill. It was not long before an old man came in sight at the top of the hill; he rested, walked a little way, then rested again; both Thore and his wife stopped to look at him. Thore presently smiled; his wife, on the contrary, changed colour.

"Do you know him?"

"Yes, one couldn't easily mistake him."

The father and son resumed their hay-carrying, but the latter managed it so that they were always one behind the other. The old man on the hill drew slowly nearer, like a heavy sou-wester. He was very tall and rather stout; his legs were weak, and he walked foot by foot leaning heavily on a staff. He soon came so near that they could see him distinctly; he stopped, took off his cap and wiped his head with his handkerchief. He was bald right to the crown of his head; had a round, puckered face, small, glistening, blinking eyes and bushy eyebrows; he had not lost a single tooth. When he spoke it was in a sharp, barking voice which hopped as if over gravel and stones; but every now and then it would dwell with great satisfaction upon the letter "r," rolling it out, as it seemed, for yards, and at the same time jumping from one key to another. In his younger days he had been well known as a cheerful but hot-tempered man; in his old age, contrarieties of many sorts had made him passionate and suspicious.

Thore and his son had crossed and recrossed the meadow several times before Ole came up with them; they both knew quite well that he came for no good, therefore it seemed all the funnier that he could not get at them. They had both to appear quite serious and to speak very softly; but when this went on and on indefinitely the situation became irresistibly comic. A mere shred of a phrase that comes in aptly is enough, under such circumstances, to set people off; especially if there happens to be some danger in laughing. When at last the old man was only a few yards away, but seemed unable to get nearer, Eyvind said drily and softly:

"What a heavy load he must be carrying!" and it needed no more.

"You're surely out of your senses," whispered the father, although he was himself laughing.

"H'm, h'm!" coughed Ole, on the hillside.

"He's tuning up!" whispered Thore.

Eyvind fell on his knees before the haycock, buried his head in it and laughed. His father also bent down.

"Let's get into the barn," whispered he, taking an armful of hay and marching away with it; Eyvind took up a small bundle and ran after him, bent double with laughter, and threw himself down in a convulsion as soon as he got into the barn. The father was a serious man, but if anybody set him off laughing he began with a gurgling, then came longer but broken trills until they flowed together in one roar, after which came wave upon wave with an ever-increasing back-draught. Now he was fairly set off; while the son lay on the floor, the father stood over him, and they both went into peals of laughter. They were subject every now and then to such hysterical fits; but "this one came at the wrong time," said the father. At last they did not know what would come of it, for the old man must by this time have got to the farm.

"I am not going out," said the father, "I have no business with him."

"Well, then, I sha'n't go either," answered Eyvind.

"H'm, h'm!" was heard just outside the barn-wall. The father shook his finger at the boy.

"Will you get out with you?"

"Yes, if you go first."

"No, off with you!"

"You go first!" And they brushed each other down and went solemnly forth. When they had crossed the bridge[1] they saw Ole standing facing the kitchen door as if considering; he was holding his cap in the hand with which he held his staff, wiping the sweat off his bald head with his handkerchief, and at the same time ruffling up the bristles behind his ears and on his neck, so that they stuck out like spikes. Eyvind kept behind his father, who had therefore to bear the first brunt; and to get it over he said with stupendous solemnity:

"This is a long way for a man of your years to come."

Ole turned round, looked keenly at him, and put his cap on straight before he answered: "Yes, you're right there!"

"You must be tired; won't you come in?"

"Oh, I can rest where I am; my errand is not a long one."

Some one was peeping from the kitchen door; between her and Thore stood old Ole with the peak of his cap over his eyes; for the cap was too large now that his hair was gone. He had thus to throw his head very far back in order to see clearly; he held his staff pressed against his side when he was not gesticulating, and his one gesture was to throw his arm half out from him and hold it motionless as though guarding his dignity.

"Is that your son standing behind you?" he began, in a resolute voice.

"They say so."

"He is called Eyvind, isn't he?"

"Yes, they call him Eyvind."

1 An inclined place for driving hay-carts up into the barn.

"He has been at one of these farming-schools down south?"

"Yes, I don't say he hasn't."

"Well, my girl, my granddaughter Marit, she has gone mad lately."

"I am sorry to hear it."

"She won't marry."

"Really?"

"She won't have anything to do with any of the farmers' sons who offer themselves."

"Indeed!"

"And it's his fault, his—that's standing there."

"Indeed!"

"They say he's turned her head: yes, that fellow, your son Eyvind."

"The devil he has!"

"Look here, I don't like people running off with horses when I turn them out to pasture, and I don't like people running off with my daughters either, when I let them go to a dance; I don't like it at all."

"No, of course not."

"I can't go after them; I am old, I can't look after them."

"No—no, no—no!"

"I like things kept in order, you know—the chopping-block to stand there and the axe to lie there, and the knife there; and here they're to sweep and here they're to throw out the rubbish, not at the door, but over in the corner, precisely there and nowhere else. So, when I say to her: not him, but him! then him it must be and not him!"

"No doubt."

"But it isn't so. For three years she has said no, and for three years things have been amiss between us. This is bad; and it's he that's to blame for it all; and I tell him before you, his father, that it's no use, he must put a stop to it."

"Well, well."

Ole looked a moment at Thore, then he said, "You answer shortly."

"I've nothing more to say."

Here Eyvind could not help laughing, although he was in no laughing mood. But with cheerful people fear ever borders on laughter, and now he felt an impulse to laugh.

"What are you laughing at?" asked Ole, shortly and sharply.

"I——?"

"Are you laughing at me?"

"God forbid!" but his own answer made him want to laugh more.

Ole saw this and became furious. Both Thore and Eyvind tried to patch it up by putting on serious faces and inviting him to go indoors; but the accumulated wrath of three years was seeking an outlet, and was not to be stopped.

"You mustn't think you're going to make a fool of me," he began; "I am here to do my duty; I am looking to my grandchild's happiness as I understand it, and the laughter of a young puppy is not going to hinder me. One doesn't bring up girls to dump them down on the first cottar's holding that offers, and one doesn't manage a farm for forty years to hand over everything to the first fellow that makes a fool of a girl. My daughter went and moped and carried on till she got herself married to a vagabond, and he drank them both to ruin, and I had to take the child and pay the piper; but curse me if my granddaughter is to go the same road! As sure as I am Ole Nordistuen of the Hill Farms, I tell you the minister shall sooner call the banns for the fairy folk up on the Nordal forest than he shall speak such names from the pulpit as Marit's and yours, you jackanapes! Are you to go and scare proper suitors away from the farm, forsooth? Just you show your face there, my man, and you'll travel down the hill again in a way you won't relish. You giggling imp, you! Do you suppose I don't know what you're thinking of, you and she? You're thinking that old Ole Nordistuen will soon turn up his toes in the churchyard, and then you'll trip away to the altar together! No, I've lived sixty-six years now, and I'll show you, boy, that I'll live till you're both mighty sick of it! And, what's more, you can hang about the house till all's blue and you won't see so much as the sole of her foot, for I'll send her out of the district; I'll send her where she'll be safe, so that you can flutter around like a laughing joy and marry the rain and the north wind. And now I've nothing more to say to you; but you, his father, you know my mind, and if you wish him well you'll make him bend the river in the way it's got to run; I warn it off *my* ground."

He turned away with short, quick steps, lifting his right foot a little more strongly than the left, and muttering to himself.

Complete seriousness had fallen upon those he left behind; a foreboding of evil had mingled itself with their joking and laughter, and a blank pause followed as after a shock of terror. The mother, who had heard all from the kitchen door, looked anxiously at Eyvind with tears in her eyes; but she would not make things harder for him by saying a single word.

They all went indoors in silence, and the father, seating himself by the window, looked after Ole with a very serious countenance. Eyvind watched intently his slightest change of expression; for did not the future of the young people almost depend upon his first words? If Thore added his refusal to that of Ole, they could scarcely hope to get over it. His thoughts ran apprehensively from obstacle to obstacle; for a moment he saw only poverty, opposition, misunderstanding and wounded self-respect, and every resource he could think of seemed destined to fail him. His uneasiness was increased by his mother's standing there with her hand on the latch of the kitchen door, uncertain whether she had courage to stay in and await the upshot, and by her at last losing heart and slipping out. Eyvind looked steadily at his father, who, it seemed, was never going to look round; nor did the son venture to speak, for he understood that the thing must be fully thought out. But presently his soul had run its course of anxiety and regained its firmness. "After all," he thought within himself as he looked at his father's knitted brow, "God alone can part us." And just at this moment something happened. Thore heaved a long sigh, rose, looked into the room and met his son's gaze. He stopped and looked long at him.

"I should be best pleased if you gave her up, for one ought not to beg or bully oneself forward in the world. But if you won't give her up, tell me when you've made up your mind, and perhaps I may be able to help you."

He went to his work and his son went with him.

By the evening Eyvind had his plan complete: he would try for the post of District Inspector of Agriculture, and would beg the Principal of the College and the Schoolmaster to help him. "Then, if she holds out, with God's help I will win her through my work."

He waited in vain for Marit that evening, but as he waited he sang his favorite song:

Lift thy head, brave lad, for token
That, if past-time hopes be broken,
New ones sparkle in an eye,
That takes light from God on high.

Lift thy head, and gaze around thee,
Something new hath sought and found thee;
Something that with myriad voice
Bids the heart in thee rejoice.

Lift thy head; for harps are ringing,
Footsteps dancing, voices singing,
And the vault of heaven so blue,
Is thine own soul beaming through.

Lift thy head, and sing unchidden!
Spring disdains the winds frost-ridden;
When the sap is rich and clear
Burgeoning shoots will greet the year.

Lift thy head, baptized for ever
In the flood of hope's bright river,
That across the gleaming world
Like a rainbow is unfurled.

CHAPTER XI

IT was the middle of the dinner-hour. The people were sleeping at the big Hill Farm; the hay lay tossed about the meadows just as they had left it, and the rakes were stuck in the ground. Down by the barn-bridge stood the hay-sledges, the harness was heaped on one side, and the horses were tethered a little way off. Except the horses, and a few hens which had strayed into the field, there was not a living creature to be seen on the whole plain.

In the mountain above the farms there was a gap, through which the road passed to the Hill Farm sæters, on the great, grassy mountain meadows. On this day a man stood in the gap, and looked down over the plain, as if he were expecting somebody. Behind him lay a little mountain lake, from which flowed the beck that formed the ravine. Around this lake, on both sides, cattle-paths led up towards the sæters, which he could see in the far distance. There was a shouting and barking away beyond him, bells tinkled along the hillsides, for the cows were hurrying to seek the water, while the dogs and herd-boys tried to collect them, but in vain.

The cows came tearing along with the most wonderful antics, made leaps where the ground was rough, and ran, with short and fierce bellowings and their tails in the air, right down into the water, where they remained standing. Their bells chimed over the surface of the lake every time they moved their heads. The dogs drank a little, but remained on dry land. The herd-boys followed, and seated themselves on the warm, smooth rock. Here they took out their provisions, exchanged with each other, bragged about their dogs, their oxen, and their people at home. They presently undressed, and jumped into the water beside the cows. The dogs would not come into the water, but poked lazily about with drooping heads, hot eyes, and tongues hanging out on one side. On the surrounding leas no bird was to be seen; no sound was heard but the youngster's chatter and the tinkling of the bells. The heather was withered and burnt up. The sun shone bakingly on the expanses of the rock, so that everything was suffocatingly hot.

It was Eyvind who sat up here in the midday sun, and waited. He sat in his shirt-sleeves close by the beck that flowed out of the lake. No one was as yet to be seen on the Hill Farm plain, and he was beginning to be a little afraid, when suddenly a large dog came heavily out of a door at Nordistuen, and after it a girl with white sleeves. She ran over the grassy hillocks towards the mountain. He wanted very much to shout to her, but he dared not. He watched the house attentively to see whether any one should chance to come out and notice her; but she was sheltered from view. He, too, lost sight of her, and rose several times in his impatience to watch for her coming.

At last she came, working her way up along the bed of the stream, the dog, a little in front, sniffing the air, she holding by the bushes, and with ever-wearier pace. Eyvind ran down; the dog growled and was hushed, and directly Marit saw him she sat down on a large stone, her face all flushed, wearied and overcome by the heat. He swung himself up on the stone beside her.

"Thank you for coming!"

"What heat, and what a road! Have you been waiting long?"

"No. Since they watch us in the evening we must use the dinner-hour. But I think that henceforward we oughtn't to be so secret and take so much trouble: that's just what I wanted to talk to you about."

"Not secret?"

"I know things please you best when there's a touch of mystery about them; but to show courage pleases you too. I have a lot to say to you to-day, and you must listen."

"Is it true that you are trying for the post of District Inspector?"

"Yes; and I shall get it too. I have a double object in that: first, to make a position for myself, and after that, and more especially, to accomplish something that your grandfather can see and appreciate. It's a lucky thing that most of the owners of the Hill Farms are young people who want improvements and are seeking help; they have money, too. So I shall begin there. I will look after everything, from their cowhouses to their irrigation-channels. I shall give lectures and keep things going. I shall, so to speak, besiege the old man with good work."

"That's bravely spoken. Go on, Eyvind."

"Well, the rest concerns us two. You mustn't go away——"

"But if he orders me to?"

"Nor keep anything secret about yourself and me."

"But if he persecutes me?"

"We shall produce more effect and make our position better by letting everything be open. We should make a point of being so much under people's eyes that they can't help talking of how we love each other; they will wish us well all the more. You must not go away. When people are apart there is always a danger of gossip coming between them. For the first year we should not believe anything, but in the second year we might gradually begin to believe a little. We two will meet once a week, and laugh away all the mischief they will try to make between us. We shall be able to meet at dances, and foot it so that it rings again, whilst our backbiters sit around and look on. We shall meet at the church, and greet each other in the sight of all those who wish us a hundred miles apart. If any one makes up a song about us, we will lay our heads together, and try to make up one in answer; we're sure to manage it if we help each other. No one can hurt us if we hold together, and let people see that we do. Unhappy lovers are always either timid people or weak people, or unhealthy people, or calculating people who wait for a certain opportunity; or crafty people who at last burn their fingers with their own cunning, or ease-loving people who don't care enough about each other to forget differences of wealth and station. They go and hide themselves, and send letters, and tremble at a word; and this terror, this perpetual unrest and pricking in the blood they come at last to take for love; they are unhappy and melt away like sugar. Pooh! If they really loved each other they would not be afraid, they would laugh; in every smile and every work, people should see the church-door looming ahead. I've read about it in books, and I've seen it too: it's a poor sort of love that goes the back way. It must begin in secrecy because it begins in timidity, but it must live in openness because it lives in joy. It is like the changing of the leaves: those that are to grow cannot hide themselves, and you see how all the dry leaves hanging to the trees fall off the moment the sprouting begins. He to whom love comes lets drop whatever old, dead rubbish he may have clung to; when the sap starts and throbs, do you think no one is to notice it? Ha, girl, they'll be happy at seeing us happy! Two lovers who hold out against the world do people a positive service, for they give them a poem which their children learn by heart to shame the unbelieving parents. I have read of so many such cases, and some of them live, too, in the mouths of the people hereabouts; and it's precisely the children of those who once caused all the trouble that now tell the stories, and are moved by them. Yes, Marit, we two will shake hands upon it—like that, yes—and promise each other to hold together, and you'll see all will come right. Hurrah!" He wanted to put his arm round her neck but she turned her head, and slipped down from the stone.

He remained sitting, and she came back, and with her arms upon his knee she stood and talked to him, looking up in his face.

"Tell me now, Eyvind, if he's determined to send me away, what then?"

"Then you must say no, straight out."

"Is that possible, dear?"

"He can't very well carry you out, and put you in the carriage."

"If he doesn't exactly do that, he can compel me in many other ways."

"I don't think so. Of course you owe him obedience so long as it's no sin; but you owe it to him also to let him understand how hard it is for you to be obedient in this matter. I think he'll come to his senses when he sees that; at present he thinks, like most people, that it's only child's play. Show him it is something more."

"He isn't easy to manage, I can tell you. He keeps me like a tethered goat."

"But you slip your tether many times a day."

"No. I don't."

"Yes; every time you secretly think of me you slip it."

"Yes, that way. But are you so sure that I think so often of you?"

"You wouldn't be here else."

"My dear, didn't you send me a message to come?"

"But you came because your thoughts drove you."

"Say rather because the weather was so beautiful."

"You said just now that it was too hot."

"To go *up* hill, yes; but *down* again!"

"Then why did you come up?"

"So as to run down again."

"Why haven't you run down already?"

"Because I had to rest."

"And talk with me of love."

"There was no reason why I shouldn't give you the pleasure of listening to you."

"Whilst the birds were singing"—"and the folk slept sound"—"and the bells were ringing"—"in the woods around."

Here they both saw Marit's grandfather come stumping out into the yard and go to the bell-rope to ring the people up. The people dragged themselves out of the barns, sheds and rooms, went sleepily to the horses and rakes, dispersed over the fields, and in a few minutes all was life and work once more.

The grandfather, left alone, went from one house into another and at last up on the highest barn-bridge to look out. A little boy came running to him, he had probably called him. The boy, as they foresaw, set off in the direction of Pladsen, the grandfather meanwhile searching round the farm; and as he often looked upwards he seemed at least to have some suspicion that the black speck up on the Big Stone must be Marit and Eyvind. A second time Marit's big dog must needs make mischief. He saw a strange horse drive into the Hill Farm, and fancying himself on active service as watch-dog, he began to bark with all his might. They tried to hush him, but he had got angry and would not leave off, the grandfather meanwhile standing below and staring straight up into the air. But matters grew worse and worse, for all the herd-boys' dogs were astonished to hear the strange voice and ran to the spot. When they saw that it was a great wolf-like giant, all the straight-haired, Finnish dogs set upon him. Marit was so frightened that she ran away without any leave-taking; Eyvind rushed into the thick of the fray and kicked and belaboured, but they only shifted their battle-ground and then met again with horrible howls. He dashed after them again, and so it went on until they waltzed themselves down to the edge of the beck. Then he ran at them, and the consequence was that they all rolled down into the water just at a place where it was nice and deep. This parted them at last and they slunk away ashamed; and so ended the battle. Eyvind went through the wood till he struck the by-road; but Marit met her grandfather up at the farm fence; and for this she had her dog to thank.

"Where have you come from?"

"From the wood."

"What were you doing there?"

"Gathering berries."

"That's not true."

"No; it isn't true."

"What were you doing then?"

"I was talking to some one."

"Was it to that Pladsen boy?"

"Yes."

"Look here now, Marit, to-morrow you go away."

"No."

"I tell you, Marit, you have just got to make up your mind to it—you *shall* go away."

"You can't lift me into the carriage."

"No? can't I?"

"No, because you won't."

"Won't I? Now look here, Marit, just for the fun of the thing, just for fun I tell you, I'll thrash that beggar-boy of yours within an inch of his life."

"No, you wouldn't dare to."

"Wouldn't dare to? Do you say I wouldn't dare to? Who would do anything to me? Who, eh?"

"The schoolmaster."

"The schoo—school—schoolmaster? Do you suppose he bothers himself about him?"

"Yes; it was he who kept him at the Agricultural College."

"The schoolmaster?"

'The schoolmaster."

"Look here Marit, I won't have these goings-on; you shall go out of the place. You bring me nothing but trouble and grief; it was the same with your mother before you, nothing but trouble and grief. I am an old man; I want to see you well provided for; I won't be the laughing-stock of the district when I am dead and gone, on your account. I'm only thinking of your own good; you ought to thank me for that, Marit: It will soon be all over with me, and then you'll be left alone. What would have become of your mother if I hadn't been there to help her? Be sensible now, Marit, and attend to what I say. I'm thinking only of your own good."

"No, you're not."

"Indeed? What am I thinking of, then?"

"You want simply to have your own way, that's what you want; and you never trouble about what *I* want."

"So you're to have a will of your own, are you, madam? Of course you understand what's best for you, you fool! I'll give you a taste of my stick; that's what I'll do, for all you're so big and bouncing. Look here now, Marit, let me talk sense to you. You're not such a fool at bottom, but you've got a bee in your bonnet. You must listen to me. I am an old man, and I know what's what. I want you to see reason. I'm not so well off as people think; a pennyless ne'er-do-well would soon run through the little I have; your father made a big hole in it, he did. Let us take care of ourselves in this world; there's nothing else for it. It's all very well for the schoolmaster to talk, he has money of his own; so has the minister; they can afford to preach, they can. But we, who must toil for our living, with us it's another matter. I am old, I know a great deal, I have seen many things. Love, you know, love's all very well to talk about, yes, but it's worth mighty little; it's good enough for ministers and the like; peasants must take things in another way. First food, you see, then God's Word, and then a little writing and reckoning, and then a little love if it happens so; but curse me if it's any use to begin with love and end with food. What do you answer to that, Marit?"

"I don't know."

"You don't know what you ought to answer?"

"Yes, I know that."

"Well, then?"

"Shall I say it?"

"Yes, say it, of course."

"My whole heart is in this love."

He stood a moment dismayed, then remembered a hundred similar conversations with a similar issue, shook his head, turned his back on her and walked away.

He descended upon the labourers, abused the girls, thrashed the big dog, and nearly frightened the life out of a little hen which had strayed into the field, albeit to her he said nothing.

That night when she went up to bed Marit was so happy that she opened the windows, leant on the window-sill, looked out and sang. She had got hold of a delicate little love-song and she sang it:

Art thou fond of me?
I'll be fond of thee
All the years of life we live together.
Summer may slip away,
The grassy fields decay,
But memory holds the sports of sweet spring weather.

What you said last year.
Aye murmurs in my ear,
Like a caged bird fluttering in my bosom:
Sits and shakes its wings,
Twitters there and sings,
Waiting till the sunshine wakes the blossom.

Litli-litli-lo!
Hearest thou me so,
Boy behind the sheltering hedge of birches?
The woods will flicker past,
The dusk is falling fast,
Canst find the way for which my blind foot searches?

I shut my window wide,
What do you want beside?
The sounds come back through evening's tender gloaming;
With laughing, beckoning notes,
Their music towards me floats.
What wilt thou? Ah, how sweet a night for roaming.

CHAPTER XII

SOME years have passed since the last scene.

It is late autumn; the schoolmaster comes up to Nordistuen, opens the outer door, finds no one at home; opens another, finds no one at home; goes on and on to the innermost room of the long building, and there sits Ole Nordistuen alone by the bed, looking at his hands.

They exchange greetings; the schoolmaster takes a stool and seats himself opposite Ole.

"You sent for me," he says.

"Yes, I did."

The schoolmaster takes a fresh quid, looks around the room, takes up a book which is lying on the bench and turns over the leaves.

"What was it you wanted to say to me?"

"I am just thinking about it."

The schoolmaster is very leisurely in his movements, takes out his spectacles to read the title of the book, polishes them, and puts them on.

"You're getting old now, Ole."

"Yes, it was about that I wanted to speak to you. I am going downhill; I shall soon be bedridden."

"Then you must see to it that you lie easy, Ole." He shuts the book and sits looking at the binding.

"That's a good book that you have in your hands."

"It's not bad; have you often got beyond the cover, Ole?"

"Yes, just lately, I've——"

The schoolmaster lays down the book and puts by his spectacles.

"Things are not just as you would wish with you now, Ole?"

"They haven't been for as far back as I can remember."

"Oh, for a long time it was the same with me. I fell out with a good friend, and waited for *him* to come to *me*, and all that time I was unhappy. Then I contrived to go to *him* and then it was all right."

Ole looks up and is silent.

The schoolmaster: "How is the farm getting on, Ole?"

"It's going downhill, like myself."

"Who is to take it when you are gone?"

"That's just what I don't know; and that's what's worrying me."

"Your neighbours are getting on well, Ole."

"Yes, they have that Inspector of Agriculture to help them."

The schoolmaster, turning indifferently towards the window: "You ought to have help too, Ole. You can't get about much, and you're not up in the new methods."

Ole: "There's no one that would be willing to help me."

"Have you *asked* any one?"

Ole is silent.

The schoolmaster: "I was like that, too, with our Lord for a long time. 'Thou art not kind to me,' I said to him. 'Have you asked me to be?' he replied. No, I had not; so then I prayed to him and since then all has been well with me."

Ole is silent, and the schoolmaster too is silent now.

At last Ole says:

"I have a grandchild; she knows what would make me happy before I go, but she doesn't do it."

The schoolmaster smiles.

"Perhaps it would not make her happy?"

Ole is silent.

The schoolmaster: "There are many things that are worrying you, but so far as I can make out they are all in the end connected with the farm."

Ole says quietly: "It has passed from father to son through many generations and it's good land. All the labour of my fathers, man after man, lies in the soil; but now it does not bear. And when they drive me away I don't know who is to drive in. There is no one of the family."

"Your granddaughter will keep up the family."

"But he who takes her, how will he take the farm? That's what I want to know before I lie down. There's no time to be lost, Baard, either for me or for the farm."

They are both silent; then the schoolmaster says: "Shall we go out a bit and have a look at the farm in this fine weather?"

"Yes, let us; I have workpeople upon the slopes, they are gathering in the leaves; but they don't work except just when I have my eye on them."

He shambles about to get his big cap and his stick, and says meanwhile: "They don't seem to like working for me; I don't understand it."

When they had got out and were turning the corner of the house he stopped.

"Here, do you see? No order: the wood scattered all about; the axe not stuck into the chopping-block;" he stooped with difficulty, lifted it and struck it firmly in. "There you see a trap that has fallen down, but no one has picked it up." He did it himself. "And here, the storehouse. Do you think the steps have been taken away?" He moved them aside. Then he stopped, looked at the schoolmaster and said: "And that's how things go every day."

As they went upwards they heard a merry song from the uplands.

"Come now, they're singing at their work," said the schoolmaster.

"That's little Knut Ostistuen who is singing; he's gathering leaves for his father. My people are working over there; you may be sure they're not singing."

"That song doesn't belong to these parts, does it?"

"No, so I can hear."

"Eyvind Pladsen has been over at Ostistuen a great deal; perhaps it's one of the songs he brought into the parish; there's plenty of singing where he is."

To this there was no answer. The field they were crossing was not in good order; it had been neglected. The schoomaster remarked upon it and Ole stopped.

"I haven't the strength to do more," said he, almost with tears. "Strange workpeople with no one to look after them come too expensive. But I can tell you it's hard to go over fields in this state."

As the talk now fell upon the size of the farm and what parts stood most in need of cultivation, they decided to go up on the slopes and look over the whole of it. When at last they had reached a high spot where they had a good view, the old man was moved.

"I am very loth to go and leave it like this. We have worked down there, I and my fathers, but it doesn't show much sign of it."

A song burst forth right over their heads with the peculiar piercingness of a boy's voice when he sings with all his might. They were not far from the tree in whose top little Knut Ostistuen sat pulling leaves for his father, and they had to listen to the boy:

When you tread the mountain-path
  With a scrip to tarry,
Put no more within its fold
  Than you well can carry.
Never drag the valley's cares,
  Up steep precipices;
Hurl them in a joyous song,
  Down the wild abysses.

Birds shall greet you from the bough
  The hamlet sounds grow shyer,
The air becomes more pure and sweet
  Ever as you climb higher.
Fill your happy breast, and sing,
  And as your old life closes,
From every bush dear childlike thoughts
  Will nod with cheeks like roses.

If you pause, and listen well,
  With ear attuned to wonder,
The mighty song of solitude
  Will fill the void like thunder;
Even a rivulet's hurrying course,
  Even a stone down stealing,
Will bring neglected duty by
  As with an organ's pealing.

Quake, but plead, thou timorous soul,
  Amidst thy memories shield thee;
Go on and up, the better part
  The topmost peak shall yield thee.
There, as of yore, with Jesus Christ,
  Elias walks, and Moses:
In such a blest ecstatic sight
  Thy toilsome journey closes.

Ole had sat down and hidden his face in his hands.

"I will talk to you here," said the schoolmaster, and sat down beside him.

. . . .

Down at Pladsen Eyvind had just come home from a longish journey; the post-chaise was still at the door, whilst the horse rested. Although Eyvind was now making a good income as District Inspector, he still lived in his little room down at Pladsen, and gave a helping hand between whiles. Pladsen was under cultivation from one end to the other, but it was so small that Eyvind called the whole of it Mother's Doll Farm; for it was she who specially looked after the farming.

He had just changed his clothes; his father had come in all white and floury from the mill, and had also changed. They were talking of going for a little walk before supper, when the mother came in quite pale.

"Here are strange visitors coming. Just look!"

Both men went to the window, and it was Eyvind who first exclaimed: "That's the schoolmaster, and—why, I declare, yes, it's really he!"

"Yes, it's old Ole Nordistuen," said Thore turning from the window so as not to be seen, for the two were already coming up to the house.

As he left the window Eyvind caught the schoolmaster's eye. Baard smiled, and looked back at old Ole, who was plodding along the road with his stick, taking his usual short steps, and always lifting one leg a little higher than the other. The schoolmaster was heard to say outside:

"He has just come home."

And Ole said twice: "Well, well!"

They stood a long time silent in the passage. The mother had crept over to the corner where the milk-shelf was; Eyvind was in his favourite position, with his back against the large table and his face towards the door; his father sat beside him. At last there was a knock, and in walked the schoolmaster and took off his hat; then Ole, and took off his cap; after which he turned to close the door. He was slow in turning, and was obviously embarrassed. Thore rose, and asked them to come in and sit down. They seated themselves side by side on the bench by the window. Thore sat down again.

And the wooing went on as follows:

The schoolmaster: "We've got fine weather this autumn after all."

Thore: "It has settled now at last."

"It will be settled for some time, too, since the wind has gone over to that quarter."

"Have you finished harvesting up yonder?"

"No; Ole Nordistuen here, whom I daresay you know, would be glad of your help, Eyvind, if it's not inconvenient."

Eyvind: "If it is desired I will do what I can."

"You see it's not mere momentary help he means. He thinks the farm is not getting on very well, and he thinks that it's method and supervision that's wanting."

Eyvind: "I'm so much from home."

The schoolmaster looks at Ole. Feeling that he must now put in his oar, Ole clears his throat a time or two, and begins quickly and shortly:

"The idea was—it is—yes—the idea is that you should, in a manner of speaking—that you should make your home up there with us—be there when you aren't out."

"Many thanks for the offer, but I prefer to live where I live now."

Ole looks at the schoolmaster, who says: "You see Ole's a little confused to-day. The thing is that he came here once before, and the remembrance of that puts his words out of order."

Ole, quickly: "That's it, yes. I behaved like an old fool. I tugged against the girl so long that our life went to splinters. But let bygones be bygones; the wind breaks down the grain, but not the breeze; rain-driblets do not loosen big stones; snow in May does not lie long; it is not the thunder that strikes people dead."

They all four laughed. The schoolmaster says: "Ole means that you must not think of it any more; nor you either, Thore."

Ole looks at them, and does not know whether he dares begin again. Then Thore says: "Briars scratch with many teeth but don't make deep wounds. There are certainly no thorns left sticking in me."

Ole: "I didn't know the boy then. Now I see that what he sows grows; autumn answers to spring; he has money in his finger-ends, and I should like to get hold of him."

Eyvind looks at his father, then at his mother; she looks from them at the schoolmaster, and then they all look at him.

"Ole means that he has a large farm——"

Ole interrupts: "A large farm, but ill managed. I can do no more. I am old, and my legs won't run my head's errands. But it would be worth any one's while to put his shoulder to the wheel up there."

"The largest farm, by far, in the district," the schoolmaster put in.

"The largest farm in the district, that's just the difficulty; shoes that are too big fall off; it's well to have a good gun, but you must be able to lift it." Turning quickly to Eyvind: "You could give us a hand, couldn't you?"

"You want me to be manager?"

"Exactly, yes; you would have the farm."

"I should *have* the farm?"

"Exactly, yes; then you would manage it."

"But——"

"Don't you want to?"

"Of course I do."

"Well, well, then that's settled, as the hen said when she flew across the lake."

"But——"

Ole looks in surprise at the schoolmaster.

"Eyvind wants to know if he's to have Marit too?"

Ole quickly: "Marit into the bargain, Marit into the bargain!"

Then Eyvind burst out laughing, and jumped up from his seat, the other three laughing with him. Eyvind rubbed his hands and went up and down repeating incessantly:

"Marit into the bargain, Marit into the bargain!"

Thore laughed with a deep chuckle, and the mother up in the corner kept her eyes fixed on her son until they filled with tears.

Ole, very anxiously: "What do you think of the farm?"

"Splendid land!"

"Splendid land, isn't it?"

"Capital pasturage!"

"Capital pasturage! It'll do, won't it?"

"It shall be the best farm in the country."

"The best farm in the country! Do you think so? Do you mean it?"

"As sure as I stand here!"

"Now isn't that just what I said?"

They both talked equally fast, and fitted in with each other like a pair of cog-wheels.

"But money, you see, money? I have no money.

"It goes slowly without money, but still it goes."

"It goes! yes, of course it goes. But if we *had* money it would go quicker, wouldn't it?"

"Ever so much quicker."

"Ever so much? If only we had money! Well, well; one can chew even if one hasn't all one's teeth; though you only drive oxen you get in at last."

The mother was making signs to Thore, who looked at her sideways, quickly and often, as he sat rocking his body and stroking his knees with his hands; the schoolmaster blinked at him. Thore had his mouth open, cleared his throat a little and tried to speak; but Ole and Eyvind answered each other so incessantly, and laughed and made such a noise, that no one could get a word in edgewise.

"Please be quiet a bit; Thore has something he wants to say," the schoolmaster puts in; they stop and look at Thore. He begins at last quite softly:

"It's been like this: here at Pladsen we have had a mill; latterly it has been so that we have had two. These mills have always brought in a trifle in the course of the year, but neither my father nor I ever used any of the money, except that time when Eyvind was away. The schoolmaster has invested it for me, and he says it has thriven well where it is; but now it will be best for you, Eyvind, to have it for Nordistuen."

The mother stood over in the corner, and made herself quite small whilst with sparkling joy she gazed at Thore, who was very serious and looked almost stupid; Ole Nordistuen sat opposite him with his mouth agape. Eyvind was the first to recover from his astonishment and exclaiming: "Doesn't luck follow me!" he went across the room to his father, and slapped him on the shoulder so that it rang again. "Father!" said he, rubbed his hands and continued to pace the room.

"How much money might there be?" asked Ole at last, but softly, of the schoolmaster.

"It's not so little."

"A few hundreds?"

"A little more."

"A little more?—a little more, Eyvind! God bless me, what a farm we shall make of it!" He rose and laughed heartily.

"I must come up with you to Marit," says Eyvind; "we can take the post-chaise that is standing outside, we shall get there quicker."

"Yes, quick, quick! Do you, too, want to have everything quick?"

"Yes, quick as quick can be!"

"Quick as quick can be! Exactly like me when I was young, exactly!"

"Here's your hat and stick; now I'm going to show you the door!"

"You show me the door, ha, ha! but you're coming too, aren't you? you're coming? And you others too; we must sit together this evening, so long as there's a spark in the stove; come along!"

They promised, Eyvind helped him into the chaise and they drove off up to Nordistuen. Up there the big dog was not the only one to be astonished when Ole Nordistuen drove into the yard with Eyvind Pladsen. Whilst Eyvind helped him out of the chaise and servants and hired folk stood gaping at them, Marit came out into the passage to see why the dog kept on barking so, but she stopped as if spell-bound, flushed all red and ran in again. Old Ole, however, shouted so loud for her when he came into the house, that she had to come forward again.

"Go and tidy yourself, girl: here is he who is to have the farm!"

"Is that true?' said she, in a ringing voice, without knowing what she said.

"Yes, it is true," answered Eyvind and claps his hands; whereupon she swings round on her toes, throws what she is holding in her hands far from her, and runs out—but Eyvind runs after her.

Shortly after, the schoolmaster, Thore and his wife arrived; the old man had candles on the table which was covered with a white cloth; wine and ale were produced, and he himself went round continually, lifting his legs higher even than usual, but always lifting the right foot higher than the left.

. . . .

Before this little tale ends it may be stated that five weeks later Eyvind and Marit were married in the parish church. The schoolmaster himself led the singing that day as his assistant was ill. His voice was cracked now, for he was old; but Eyvind thought it did one good to hear him. And when he had given his hand to Marit and led her up to the altar, the schoolmaster nodded to him from the choir just as Eyvind had seen him do when he was sorrowfully watching that dance; he nodded back, whilst tears rose to his eyes.

Those tears at the dance were the prelude to these; and between them lay his faith and his work.

Here ends the story of a Happy Boy.

SKIPPER WORSE

BY

ALEXANDER L. KIELLAND

BIOGRAPHICAL NOTE

ALEXANDER KIELLAND was born in Stavanger, Norway, on February 18, 1849, of a wealthy family of shipowners. After studying law at the University of Christiania he bought a brick and tile factory at Malk, near his native town, and for some years it appeared as if he were to follow the family tradition and become merely a substantial citizen of provincial importance. But about 1878 he began to publish some short stories in the Christiania "Dagblad," and in 1879 and 1880 there appeared two volumes of "Novelettes." These were marked by a light satirical touch and a sympathy with liberal ideas, and were written in a style which may well have owed some of its clarity to the study of French models, made during the author's visits to Paris. His first regular novel was "Garman and Worse," a picture of the same small-town society which we find in the novel here printed. "Laboring People" followed in 1881, when Kielland sold out his business and became purely a man of letters. "Skipper Worse" was his third novel, and among the more important of his other works are "Poison," "Fortuna," "Snow," "St. John's Eve," "Jacob," and a number of dramas and comedies. He died at Bergen, on April 6, 1906.

Kielland's method is realistic, and a number of his works are written with a fairly distinct "purpose." As this purpose often involves sharp criticism of conventions and beliefs dear to the comfortable classes, Kielland roused no small amount of opposition and disapproval. But as it grows more possible to see his work in perspective, it becames more evident that his clear-sightedness and honesty of purpose as well as his mastery of style will give him an honored place among Norwegian writers.

"Skipper Worse" is not only thoroughly typical of Kielland's work, but, so far as there can be said to be general agreement, it is regarded as his masterpiece. Like so many of his books, it gives a picture of the well-to-do merchants, skippers, and fisher-folk of the west coast of Norway, the special subject being the workings of the Haugian pietistic movement. Although this particular movement was specifically Norwegian, it is sufficiently typical of a kind of revival familiar in many countries to make this study of it interesting to foreign readers. Kielland's handling of the Haugians is remarkable for its fairness and restraint. The sincerity of the best representatives of the sect is abundantly exhibited, as well as the limitations of the weaker brethren; but this balanced treatment does not prevent the author from showing with great force and poignancy the deplorable crushing of the innocent human affections by unintelligent fanaticism.

The portraiture of individuals is as successful as that of the society in which they move. Worse himself is rendered with a rare mingling of humor and pathos; Hans Nilsen is a striking example of the religious enthusiast, drawn with feeling and subtlety; and Madame Torvestad, though belonging to a familiar type, is well individualized.

It requires a high degree of art to take a provincial group, in special local circumstances, and to present these in such a way as not only to interest the outsider, but to convince him of the truth of the presentation by showing the characters as acting from motives valid for human nature in general. This is what Kielland does, displaying in the doing of it, an uncommon delicacy of perception and accuracy of perspective. He is one of the writers who have done most to make Scandinavia count in the modern world.

W. A. N.

CRITICISMS AND INTERPRETATIONS

I

By H. H. Boyesen

KIELLAND'S third novel, "Skipper Worse," marked a distinct step in his development. It was less of a social satire and more of a social study. It was not merely a series of brilliant, exquisitely finished scenes, loosely strung together on a slender thread of narrative, but was a concise and well-constructed story, full of admirable portraits. The theme is akin to that of Daudet's "L'Évangéliste"; but Kielland, as it appears to me, has in this instance outdone his French confrère, as regards insight into the peculiar character and poetry of the pietistic movement. He has dealt with it as a psychological and not primarily as a pathological phenomenon. A comparison with Daudet suggests itself constantly in reading Kielland. Their methods of workmanship and their attitude toward life have many points in common. The charm of style, the delicacy of touch, and felicity of phrase, are in both cases preeminent. Daudet has, however, the advantage (or, as he himself asserts, the disadvantage) of working in a flexible and highly finished language, which bears the impress of the labors of a hundred masters; while Kielland has to produce his effects of style in a poorer and less pliable language, which often pants and groans in its efforts to render a subtle thought. To have polished this tongue and sharpened its capacity for refined and incisive utterance, is one—and not the least—of his merits.

Though he has by nature no more sympathy with the pietistic movement than Daudet, Kielland yet manages to get psychologically closer to his problem. His pietists are more humanly interesting than those of Daudet, and the little drama which they set in motion is more genuinely pathetic. Two superb figures—the lay preacher Hans Nilsen and Skipper Worse—surpass all that the author had hitherto produced in depth of conception and brilliancy of execution. The marriage of that delightful, profane old sea-dog, Jacob Worse, with the pious Sara Torvestad, and the attempts of his mother-in-law to convert him, are described not with the merely superficial drollery to which the subject invites, but with a sweet and delicate humor which trembles on the verge of pathos.—From "Essays on Scandinavian Literature" (1895).

II

By William H. Carpenter

ALEXANDER KIELLAND is the least Norwegian of all the Norwegian writers, not only among his contemporaries, like Björnson and Jonas Lie, but among the newer men of the subsequent generation, like Gabriel Finne, Knut Hamsun, and Vilhelm Krag, whose names we Americans have hardly yet learned to know. I mean this, however, less in regard to his matter than to his manner. Although several of his short stories are French in their setting and others are Danish, the greater part of his work and all of the important novels and plays act and have their being in Norway. Kielland's attitude towards his material, on the other hand, is new to Norwegian literature. For the first time in his pages, among both his forbears and his contemporaries, we meet with the point of view of a man of the world. Björnson and Jonas Lie have always a sort of homely provincialism, inherent and characteristic, that is part and parcel of their literary personality, whose absence would be felt under the circumstances as a lack of necessary vigour. Kielland, on the contrary, as inherently, has throughout unmistakably an air of *savoir vivre,* in the long run much surer in its appeal to us outside of Norway because of its more general intelligibility. Björnson and Jonas Lie in this way have secured places in literature in no small part because of their characteristic Norwegianism; Kielland to some little extent has secured his place because of the want of it. Ibsen is here left out of the discussion. He is quite *sui generis,* and apart from the mere choice of environment, for his work could belong anywhere. . . .

Kielland's novels are one and all novels of tendency. With his first short stories as a criterion, and a knowledge of his own personal antecedents and the almost necessary predilections that he might be supposed to possess, his career as a novelist could not have been foreseen. His early stories betray no great seriousness of purpose, and his personal environment removed him as far as possible from liberalism in ethics and religion, from socialistic proclivities even remotely democratic, and a ready susceptibility to the whole spirit of the age. Yet these are just the characteristics of his later books. They are strong, liberal, and modern; so much so that many of them have evoked a loud spirit of protest in Norway, where leaven of this sort is still striven against in many quarters.—From "Alexander Kielland," in "The Bookman" (1896).

SKIPPER WORSE

CHAPTER I

"HERE, Lauritz, you young scamp, go aloft and clear the dogvane."

Skipper Worse was standing on his quarter-deck, a fresh north wind was blowing in the fjord, and the old brig was gliding along quietly under easy sail.

A chopping sea, caused by the ebbing tide, was breaking outside the cape which marked the entrance to Sandsgaard Bay.

As the *Hope of the Family* rounded the point, she seemed to feel that she was safe at home. Captain Worse winked at the helmsman, and declared that the old thing knew well enough where she was now that they were round.

The *Hope of the Family* was not quite like other ships. It might be that some looked smarter and lighter; indeed, it was not entirely beyond the range of possibility—though, as for Jacob Worse, he had never yet seen such a one—that, amongst the new-fangled English craft, one or two might be found that could sail just the least trifle better.

No further admission, however, would he make. Anything stronger, more seaworthy, or more complete than the *Hope* did not, and never would, float upon the sea. The sun shone brightly upon the buildings at Sandsgaard, on the garden and the wharf, and over all the pleasant bay, where the summer ripples chased each other to the land, hurrying on with the news that Jacob Worse had entered the fjord.

Zacharias, the man at the wharf, had, however, already announced the fact.

"Are you so sure about it?" asked Consul Garman sharply.

"We've made her out with the telescope, Herr Consul, and I'm as sure it's the *Hope* as that I am a living sinner. She is steering right in for Sandsgaard Bay."

Morten W. Garman rose up from his armchair. He was a tall, ponderous man, with crisp white hair and a heavy underlip.

As he took his hat and stick, his hand trembled a little, for the *Hope* had been away a very long time at sea. In the outer office the book-keeper was standing by the little outlook window; taking the telescope from his hand, the Consul spied out over the fjord, and then closing the glass, said: "All right; Jacob Worse is a man one can depend upon."

It was the first time that a ship from those parts had sailed to Rio de Janeiro, and the perilous voyage had been due entirely to Jacob Worse's enterprise.

He had, however, been away so long that the Consul had given up the *Hope,* as he had given up so many other ships of late years.

Although he was now relieved of all anxiety on account of the ship and his trusty Captain Worse, his footstep was heavy, and resounded sadly as he left the office and strode through the entrance hall, whence a broad staircase led up to the next story.

Much more, indeed, than merely a profitable voyage would be required in order to console the embarrassed merchant, for his home at Sandsgaard was empty and desolate. Youth and social pleasures had fled, and little remained but bygone memories of gay friends and brilliant ladies; a faint odour of the past lingering in out-of-the-way corners, and causing his heart to beat again.

Ever since the death of his wife in the past summer, all the reception-rooms had been closed. Both his sons were abroad, Christian Frederik in London, and Richard in Stockholm; and Consul Garman, who had always been accustomed to gay company, found that living alone with the sisters of his deceased wife—two elderly spinsters who quarrelled over the management of his domestic affairs—was not very exhilarating.

As Jacob Worse, standing on the deck of his good ship, gazed at the stir along the wharves and round about the bay, his heart swelled with pride.

All the boats in the place came rowing out towards the brig. The relatives of his men, the mothers and the sweethearts, waved handkerchiefs and wept for joy. Many of them had, indeed, long since given up the *Hope* as lost.

No relations came out to welcome Skipper Worse. He was a widower, and his only son was away at a commercial school in Lübeck. What he looked forward to was talking about Rio with the other captains at his club, but the chief pleasure in store for him was the yarns he would spin with Skipper Randulf.

What would Randulf's much-boasted voyage to Taganrog be, compared with Rio? Would not he—Worse—just lay it on thickly?

In his younger days Jacob Worse had been a little wild, and was now a jovial middle-aged man, about fifty years of age.

His body was thickset and short, his face that of a seaman—square, ruddy, frank, and pleasant. If any one could have counted the hairs upon his head, the result would have been surprising, for they were as close as on an otter's skin, and growing in a peculiar manner. They looked as if a whirlwind had first attacked the crown of his head from behind, twisting up a spiral tuft in the centre, and laying the remainder flat, pointing forwards, along the sides. It seemed as if his hair had remained fixed and unmoved ever since. About his ears there were rows of small curls, like the ripple-marks on sand after a breeze of wind.

When Jacob Worse saw the "ladies' boat"[1] waiting, ready manned, alongside the quay, he rubbed his hands with delight, for this preparation betokened a singular distinction; and when he saw the Consul step into this boat, he skipped round the deck in boyish glee. It was, in fact, unusual for the Consul to come on board to welcome the arrival of a ship. Generally some one was sent from the office, if neither of the sons was at home; for both Christian Frederik, and especially Richard, liked to board the ships far out of the fjord, that they might have a sail homewards and drink marsala in the cabin.

When the brig came to anchor, the ladies' boat was still a little way off; Skipper Worse, however, could no longer restrain himself. Laying hold of a shroud, he swung him-

[1] In the larger mercantile houses of Norway, at the seaports, a "Fruens Baad," or ladies' boat, is kept for the especial use of the lady of the house.

self on the top rail and waving his hat, cried out, in a voice that rang out all over Sandsgaard, "We come late, Herr Consul, but we come safely."

Consul Garman smiled as he returned the salute, at the same time quietly removing the rings from the fingers of his right hand; for he dreaded the grip of Jacob Worse on his return from a voyage.

The delighted captain stood on deck, hat in hand, in a respectful attitude, whilst the Consul, with stiff and cautious steps, ascended the accommodation ladder.

"Welcome, Jacob Worse."

"Many thanks, Herr Consul."

The Consul surrendered his hand to be duly squeezed.

The crew stood round in a respectful circle to receive the friendly salute of the owner; they were already cleaned up and in their shore-going clothes, for so many friends and relations had boarded the brig as she was standing in, that there was no necessity for them to lend a hand in mooring the brig.

The manly, sunburnt faces bore a somewhat strange aspect here in the cool early summer time, and one or two wore a red shirt, or a blue Scotch bonnet brought from that wonderful Rio.

Their beaming faces showed what heroes they considered themselves, and they longed to get on shore to recount their adventures.

"Here's a young scamp," said Captain Worse, "who went out a cabin boy, but now we have given him the rating of an apprentice. The Consul must know that we had two deaths at Rio—the devil's own climate.—Come, Lauritz, step forward and show yourself."

A lad of about seventeen was at last shoved forward, awkward and blushing; much soaping had made his chubby red face shine like an apple.

"What is his name?" said the Consul.

"Lauritz Seehus," answered the lad.

"Lauritz Boldemand Seehus," added the captain, giving the name in full.

The men tittered at this, for they were in the habit of calling him "Bollemand," or "The Baker."

"We always give special attention to Captain Worse's recommendations, and if the young man will but follow the example of such a worthy officer"—here the Consul made a low bow to the captain—"the firm will advance him according to his merits. Moreover, when we come to pay off, the crew will receive a bonus, in consideration of the long and perilous voyage. The firm offers its best thanks to all for good and faithful service."

The Consul bowed to them all, and went below with the captain.

The men were much pleased, both on account of the bonus, and because it was unusual for shipowners thus to come on board and speak to common folk. It was not the habit of Consul Garman to trouble himself much about the persons in his employ. Not that he was a hard master—on the contrary, he always returned a salute with courtesy, and had a word or two for everybody; but his manner was so extremely distant and lofty, that the least demonstration of friendliness on his part was a condescension accepted with gratitude and wonder.

Half an hour later, when he entered his boat again to go on shore, the men cheered him. Standing up, he raised his hat to them; he was, in fact, much moved, and was anxious to get home, and to be alone in his office.

The Consul took the ship's papers and a bag of gold on shore with him, for the venture had been a prosperous one. The firm "C. F. Garman" had not done so good a business for a long time. So far it was satisfactory, but it was not enough; for in spite of all Morten Garman's efforts during the years that had elapsed since his father's death, he had never succeeded in bringing life and vigour to the large and widely extended business.

The firm had suffered so much during the period of war, and from a reduction in the currency, that it was paralyzed for many years, and at one time indeed seemed past recovery.

The fact was that from the first its means were locked up in landed property to an extent which was out of all proportion to its diminished available capital. Besides this, there were debts which pressed heavily upon it.

Time brought no improvement; Morten W. Garman, who was an exceptionally able man of business, was compelled to put forth all his energy and diligence to maintain the ancient reputation of his firm.

So long as he remained young, the concern struggled on; but now that he was advanced in years, his wife dead, and his home desolate, it pained him to think that he might leave the business which had been his joy and pride, and which he had hoped to make so great and so enduring, bereft of its vitality and in a feeble and disorganized condition.

The household expenditure at Sandsgaard had always been considerable, for his attractive and vivacious wife had been fond of parties, masquerades, and entertainments, and her tastes had been fully shared by her husband.

The freer mode of life which came in with the century, as well as his position as the eldest son of a large mercantile family, had encouraged somewhat extravagant views of life, and in the town his ostentation had given rise to not a little derision and offence. Of this, however, nothing reached his ears.

Owing to his foreign education, and to his frequent journeys abroad, he brought back a peculiar atmosphere which pervaded his whole life, his views, and his opinions—which latter were, indeed, very different from those prevailing in the frugal little town, which at this period found itself in a state of fermentation, owing on the one hand to commercial progress, and on the other to a strong religious movement.

As yet, however, the old-fashioned mode of entertainment prevailed at Sandsgaard, where the civil and military personages of the grander sort kept up their ancient traditions at festivals where they ate well and drank deeply. Freedom and courtesy were so well balanced in this society, that little restraint was put upon conversation. A *risqué* word, the stray touch of a too daring hand or foot, or a whisper behind a fan, which was in truth a furtive kiss, with a hundred other trifling liberties, were permitted. Frivolity enveloped the company as with a silken veil, and yet everything moved as politely and as sedately as a minuet.

In this sort of life Consul Garman carried himself as easily and as adroitly as a fish in its native element.

When he sat in his office on the mornings of his great dinner parties, his pen flew over the paper, and on such occasions he indited his ablest letters.

His thoughts were so clear, and his mind so prompt and unembarrassed, that everything was arranged and ordered with the utmost precision.

In the same despatch in which he bespoke a cargo of coffee, he would not forget twelve packets of sealing-wax and two hampers of Dutch tobacco pipes for his store. He would descend without difficulty from instructions to a captain who had lost his ship, to the most minute details respecting certain stove pipes which he had seen in London, and which he wished to introduce into the town hospital.

But when the post had been despatched, and the hour of three—the usual hour for dinner parties—approached, and when the Consul had shaved himself carefully, and had applied himself to sundry pots and flasks of pomades and essences, he stepped up the broad staircase, dressed in a long-skirted blue coat with bright buttons, a closely fitting waistcoat, and a frilled shirt with a diamond breast-pin, his comely iron-grey hair slightly powdered and curled. Perhaps, too, he would be humming some French ditty of questionable propriety, thinking of the gallantries of his youth; and as he stepped daintily forward with his shapely legs, he would sometimes indulge in a hope that knee breeches would again come into fashion.

In spite of his gallantries, however, Consul Garman had been an exemplary husband, according to the standard of the times; and when his wife died he really grieved for her, placing sundry tablets with affectionate inscriptions in those parts of the garden which were her special favourites.

After her death he gave up society, so that this item of expenditure diminished perceptibly. Two other items, however, showed a tendency to increase—the expenses connected with his sons, especially Richard.

His affections were now bestowed upon these sons. Richard was at once his pride and his weakness; a handsome exterior and easy temperament were a reflection of his own youth; and when Richard took his best horse and saddle, as well as his riding whip, which no one else was allowed to touch, he stole from window to window, as long as his son was in sight, pleased to observe his bearing and his seat on horseback.

With his eldest son, Christian Frederik, the Consul was, however, more strict.

He would write to Richard somewhat after the following fashion, when his extravagance became serious:

"I can well understand that the *carrière* which you, with the sanction of your parents, have adopted, involves you in sundry expenses, which, although apparently unnecessary, may on a closer scrutiny be found, to a certain extent, warranted by circumstances. On the other hand, however, I would have you to consider whether you could not, at a perceptibly less cost, attain the same results as regards your future in the diplomatic profession.

"Especially would I exhort you to keep regular accounts. Not so much that I desire to limit your expenditure, as that, according to my own experience, such accounts are an aid to self-control."

But accounts, and especially regular ones, were not to Richard's liking. Sometimes, indeed, he pretended to render them; but the letter soon drifted into jests and amusing stories, which diverted his father, and made him forget all about the money.

Christian Frederik, however, had sent regular monthly extracts from his account book ever since he had been at the Institute in Christiania, and these extracts were scrutinized by his father with unfailing rigour.

If there was any error in the address, not to mention any mistake in the posting up, or if any item appeared which seemed unusual or excessive, the son received a sharp admonition, warning him that inaccuracy or extravagance were absolutely unpardonable in a man of business.

This kept Christian Frederik in constant dread of his father, and sometimes he felt much hurt; but he would have been consoled had he known with what satisfaction the Consul examined these well-kept accounts, and with what care they were filed and laid aside in a certain drawer.

Christian Frederik, however, was the only person whom the Consul admitted to his confidence, and in the copious letters which he wrote to him at least once a month, he kept him informed upon business matters. Latterly, too, he had sometimes asked him his opinion upon one thing or another. The Consul was much interested, and to some degree disturbed, by the development of the town during the last two years. Moneyed strangers, who bought and cured herrings on their own account, shipping them off by thousands of barrels in the spring season, began to appear.

Large fortunes were made by the Haugians and others, who interlarded their business letters with Scripture phrases, and who had not the least idea of book-keeping.

The town was alive with stir and business, mixed up with religion, to the unceasing astonishment of the old merchant. Money, too, was abundant among these new folks.

At this period the anxieties of the Consul were revived, but he kept them to himself. On no account should Christian Frederik know what difficulties he often had to encounter.

The *Hope* lay safely moored, with her ensign at the peak, and flying the distinguished flag of the firm. Whilst the crew went on shore, a constant stream of visitors came on board, both from Sandsgaard and from the town.

The captain's white gig having been manned, he seated himself in the stern sheets, a large flag trailing in the water behind him. Lauritz Seehus, creeping in behind him, took the yoke lines, so that everything should be done man-of-war fashion. The six men pulled with a long stroke, their oars dipping along the surface of the sea as they feathered them.

It was in this style that Captain Worse had always looked forward to making his appearance on his return, and as he neared the quay he became highly elated.

It would never have suited him to be landed at Sandsgaard and to go on foot thence to the town, although it was the shortest and quickest way. It was one of his fancies to look upon Sandsgaard as an island, and, however bad the weather, he always went by boat to and from the town.

He could see that a flag was displayed at his own warehouse by the market quay—for he owned a straggling old building which occupied one side of the market, and ended in a large five-storied structure projecting into the sea. Jacob Worse was, in fact, a rich man, partly from his own savings during many years as a captain, and partly from successful speculations of his own.

But when he was at home for the winter season, he busied himself with the fishery from the moment it began, buying, selling, and curing on his own account. The firm "C. F. Garman" did not trouble itself with the herring fishery; it traded directly and by commission in salt and grain, in addition to its banking and discounting business.

Captain Worse had in the course of years become a comparatively wealthy man, and when, as on this occasion, he had been away for a long time, he was anxious to learn how the persons in his employ had conducted themselves in his absence.

But his chief desire was to meet Captain Randulf; and every time he thought of it he slapped his leg and laughed aloud.

As it was summer, there were but few vessels in the harbour; most of these, however, hoisted their colours when they saw Jacob Worse's boat approaching. His acquaintances hailed him from wharf and warehouse on each side of the bay, and he saluted in return, beaming with pride and pleasure.

"Where are you going to lodge, Lauritz?" said he, as they approached the wharf, for Lauritz Seehus's home was away at Flekkefjord.

"I think I shall stay with Madame Torvestad, where I always used to lodge," said the lad.

"Oh, bother!" said Skipper Worse; "now that you are grown up you cannot stay with that old bundle of tracts."

Observing, however, a certain expression on the countenances of his men, he remembered himself, and added, "Ah, you scamp, it is for the girls' sake that you wish to go to Madame Torvestad's. Mind what you are about; remember that I command that ship too."

This was his joke, for Madame Torvestad rented a portion of the back of his house.

When Skipper Worse reached the market quay he met with a sad disappointment. Captain Randulf was away in the Baltic with a cargo of herrings.

CHAPTER II

"SARAH, are you going to the meeting this afternoon?" said Madame Torvestad to her eldest daughter.

"Yes, mother."

"Captain Worse has returned; I shall step across and welcome him home. The poor man is probably still in his sins. Only think, Sarah, if it should be granted to one of us to recover this wanderer from the fold!"

Madame Torvestad looked hard at her daughter as she said this, but Sarah, who stood at the kitchen dresser washing up the dinner plates, did not raise her eyes, which were dark and large, with long eyelashes, and heavy black eyebrows.

"You can just inquire among the friends if any would like to drop in and talk over the subjects discussed at this meeting, that we may strengthen and encourage one another."

"Yes, mother."

Madame Torvestad went into the sitting-room, which was rather dark, being at the back part of the building. For the rest, it was well and solidly furnished, very clean and orderly, but withal a little formal. She was the widow of an elder among the Brethren, and after her husband's death no other person had been forthcoming to supply his place. The number of the genuine Herrnhutters was neither large nor increasing, for the prevailing religious movement was rather in the direction of Haugianism.

There was, however, so much conformity of doctrine, and such a similarity in outward conduct, that the ordinary public could hardly see a shade of difference between the Herrnhutters and the Haugians; and, in truth, there was a gradual amalgamation of the two sects.

Originally there was no small difference between the Brethren and the followers of Hauge. Hauge sought and found his earliest and most devoted disciples among the peasants. The Brethren, on the other hand, consisted chiefly of well-to-do townspeople, who, under their German leaders, and by their frequent visits to Christiansfeldt and other stations of the Herrnhutters, had attained a higher degree both of intellectual and social culture.

But at a later period, when Hans Nilsen Hauge's revivals had overrun the land, and had emerged from innumerable troubles; especially, too, when Hauge's long imprisonment and subsequent death became known, as well as the disgraceful persecution which blameless and God-fearing people had undergone at the hands of the authorities—the movement gained adherents among those who had hitherto looked with contempt and aversion upon the peasant fanatics and visionaries.

All this contributed to an amalgamation of the two sects; Hauge's followers were, moreover, always inclined to tolerance and brotherly love when they met with living Christian faith. The Herrnhutters, on their part, were neither strong nor numerous enough to maintain a completely independent position, even had they desired it.

It was for such reasons that Madame Torvestad sent her daughter to the new Haugian meeting-house; and in the same way the converts of both persuasions came to her own small meetings. She retained certain words and phrases which reminded those who frequented them of her long residence in Gnadau, and she was also in the habit of reading aloud to her guests certain small tracts which she herself had partly translated from the German.

Madame Torvestad passed from the parlour to the workroom, where the servant girl sat weaving steadily and skilfully. Distaffs and reels of yarn lay about, and on the table by the window materials for dressmaking; for this was a house where devotion was mixed up with constant and useful work.

"Where is Henrietta?" asked Madame Torvestad.

"She went out to learn why the vessels in port have hoisted their colours," said the girl.

"Ah, Martha, how the hearts of the young are drawn to worldly follies!"

In the mean time, Sarah continued her work, humming a psalm tune. This week it was her turn to manage the kitchen; she took it turn about with the girl, for Henrietta was as yet too young.

Sarah was twenty-six years of age. Although a laborious and regular life had made her strong and robust, she was very pale, for she seldom went out of doors, and never farther than the church or meeting. Her comely face contrasted pleasantly with the full chin, which bore a trace of the commanding expression of her mother. She wore her hair quite smooth, with plaits coiled round the back of her head.

The charm of Sarah's face and figure was not such as is apparent one year and vanishes the next; on the contrary, there was something about her soft rounded features, pale clear complexion, and steadfast eyes resulting in a calm, attractive beauty which promised to be lasting.

Standing at the dresser amid the clatter of plates and cups, humming her psalm tune, she did not hear the footsteps of a man ascending the kitchen stairs; but when the door opened, she turned round, then blushed a little, and cast her eyes down upon the ground.

The man in the doorway, who was tall and broad-shouldered, also cast his eyes down, and said: "Look here, Sarah, I bring you 'Life in Death,' the book we were speaking of. I hope you will like it."

"Thanks, Hans Nilsen," answered Sarah, without looking up from her work. She could not take the book in her hands because they were wet, so he laid it on the bench by her side and went away.

She listened to his step as he went up the stairs to the attic, for Hans Nilsen Fennefos was one of Madame Torvestad's lodgers. Sarah dried her hands hastily, and took up the book, dipping into it here and there with evident interest and pleasure.

It was written by Hauge himself, of whom Fennefos often spoke, but for whom her mother did not seem to care much; at all events she possessed none of his works.

Sarah had, however, something else to do than to read; so she laid the precious little volume, which Fennefos had bound with his own hands, upon the window seat by her side, and renewed her work and her hymn, a little more vigorously than before.

Sometimes she leant forward, and as she turned her head on one side, gazing up at the narrow streak of blue sky which was visible between the roofs, her dark eyes shone with a guileless, rapturous light, as if they were piercing the vault of heaven itself.

Soon, however, another footstep became audible on the stairs below, and this time Sarah heard it distinctly. It was Henrietta—there could be no mistake about that. Two or three careless hasty steps, then a stumble, and then much clatter, then more steps; just as young girls blunder up a staircase when they first wear long gowns.

Henrietta, who entered heated, radiant, and out of breath, with her hair in a tangle, exclaimed; "Oh, Sarah, you *should* have seen it! Do you know who has come back?"

"Hush, hush! Henrietta," said Sarah, chiding her; "only think if our mother were to see you such a figure."

Upon this Henrietta began to smooth her unruly hair; but, unable to restrain herself, she whispered with portentous eagerness: "I was in the market, right down by the quay —don't tell it to mother—and Skipper Worse came rowing —Skipper Worse has arrived from Rio, you know—came rowing in with a six-oared boat and a flag, and behind him sat Lauritz. I did not recognize him till he jumped on shore; he has grown so tall"—raising her hand up. "He saw me; indeed, I think he is following me here."

"Oh, Henrietta!" said Sarah, somewhat severely, knitting her eyebrows.

But the graceless Henrietta stuck her tongue out and stole into the passage, whence she hoped to reach the workroom unobserved. Sarah's look grew anxious; she could not comprehend her unruly sister. She herself had never been like this. Such a worldly disposition must needs be subdued.

Nevertheless, she sometimes felt touched when Henrietta boiled over with youthful animation, and almost felt a wish to share her high spirits.

There was the old Adam in her, which ought to be suppressed and overcome; but yet—but yet——

Presently she was again disturbed by the appearance of a round, sunburnt, smiling face at the kitchen door. But the smile vanished as Lauritz, looking sheepish and awkward, walked in. He had evidently expected to see some one else.

"Welcome home, Lauritz," said Sarah, in a friendly voice.

"Thank you," said Lauritz, in his deepest tones, as he stood rubbing his hands together in the doorway.

"Do you wish to see my mother?"

"Yes; I want to know if I can lodge here."

"My mother is in the sitting-room."

Lauritz Seehus was almost like a younger brother to Sarah, for he had boarded at Madame Torvestad's ever since his school days. His own home at Flekkefjord was not a happy one; his father drank, and there was a swarm of small children.

In a few moments Lauritz reappeared, crestfallen and wretched.

"What, Lauritz," said Sarah, "are you going away so soon?"

"Yes," said he, hurrying out, "I could not manage it."

As he descended the old well-known kitchen stairs, he thought himself the most unfortunate creature in the world; in fact, he wept—for the first time since his boyhood.

During the whole of the voyage he had dreamt of securing his old attic room again, of being constantly near Henrietta, and of presenting her with all the wonderful things he had brought back in his sea chest. He had dreamt of stealing out with her in a boat, or of gliding with her on a hand sledge on the moonlight winter evenings when Madame Torvestad was at meeting.

All these glorious plans had been carefully cherished and pondered over a hundred times, and pictured down to the smallest detail, as he paced the deck in the long and lonely night watches.

Now, however, it seemed as if there was no more hope or pleasure for him, either in this world or the next.

Sarah seemed to take pity on him. Her mother came out and said:

"You saw Lauritz, Sarah?"

"Yes, mother."

"Did you speak to him?"

"No; I merely gave him a welcome."

"Do you think that he is changed?"

Sarah hardly knew what to answer, but her mother added with severity: "Say no, my child; repentant sinners have a very different appearance."

In her heart Sarah could not but allow that her mother was in the right, especially when it occurred to her that Lauritz and Henrietta were no longer children, and that sinful affections might take the place of the old companionship.

Since she had entered the room she had also come to the conclusion that it was her duty to confide her misgivings to her mother. Now, however, she was spared this, and she was satisfied that it would be better for the young people that they should be separated.

But then, again, she remembered how miserable he looked, as he crept out of the kitchen, and she thought how disappointed Henrietta would be; for had he not always lodged there?

No doubt it would be for the good of both that temptation should be removed—but nevertheless—

By five o'clock Jacob Worse had returned home from the club; he could stand it no longer. Everything had gone wrong, and nothing had happened as he wished, from the time that he had set his foot on shore.

At the club he had met two Finn captains, whose ships were detained in the harbour, quite young fellows, who had lately arrived from America.

One of them, a mere puppy, with a beard of English cut and a gold chain, had been at Rio—and twice!

Oh! Randulf, Randulf, why were you away in the Baltic?

It happened to Skipper Worse as it happens to all easy temperaments. The slightest pleasure would put him in good humour, and help him over the greatest difficulties; but if, on the other hand, he encountered any trifling annoyance, everything seemed to go wrong, misfortune seemed to accumulate upon his head, and he thought that no one was ever so persecuted and maltreated by fate as himself—but for one day only. A night's rest generally restored his equanimity.

This was just one of his unlucky days from the moment when he heard of Randulf's absence. Nothing had satisfied him, either at the club, at the office, or at his warehouse; although there was absolutely nothing to complain of in the management of his affairs during his absence.

The people in his employ had, in fact, deserved much more praise than he had vouchsafed to them.

Grumbling and dispirited, he traversed the well-kept rooms. The sun was low in the north-west, and in the sunset glow he could distinguish the *Hope's* top-gallant yards over the point of land that separated the harbour from Sandsgaard Bay.

Nothing, however, could cheer him up. Moreover, after a while he bethought him how old Harbour-master Snell had led him aside into a corner at the club, and had whispered, as he laid his finger to his long red nose; "Pop—pop—Jacob, it was about time that you brought the old one some cash; they say—pop—pop—that he is in want of it just now."

"What in the world did he mean?" thought Skipper Worse, as he recalled the conversation. "Does the old swindler think to persuade me that C. F. Garman is in want of cash?"

"What do you want, Lauritz!" cried he suddenly, seeing the lad at the door.

"Nothing, captain," said Lauritz, meekly, going out again.

But Worse following him, caught him in the passage, and pulled him back into the room.

That Lauritz did not want anything was true; but when in his sorrow and despondency he saw the captain, who had always been so good to him, passing the window to and fro, he ventured to approach him on the chance of meeting with some comfort.

Worse gripped him by the neck and looked at him.

"H'm! so there's another who has found little satisfaction in coming home. Come, let us have a drop of something together, my son, and you shall then tell me what is the matter."

Skipper Worse opened a door in the corner cupboard, produced two round Dutch glasses, and poured out some cherry brandy for Lauritz and some old Jamaica rum for himself.

"Now, then," said Worse, when they had emptied their glasses, "let's hear all about your troubles."

But instead of beginning his story, Lauritz suddenly replaced his glass on the shelf, seized the captain's, put it away also, slammed to the cupboard, and seated himself on a wooden chair near the door.

Worse thought the lad was going out of his senses; but before his wrath had time to break out, there was a knock at the door, and Madame Torvestad entered.

Lauritz had seen her pass the window, and respect for her was so thoroughly ingrained in him, that her appearance drove everything else out of his head.

Anything rather than that she should see they were drinking. Even Worse himself would not have wished Madame Torvestad to find him hob-nobbing with the young man, and comprehending the position of affairs, he winked amiably at Lauritz, as he conducted Madame Torvestad to a seat upon the sofa.

She wore a black silk cloak, a dark grey hat with a wide brim, and a broad satin ribbon under her chin.

Her dress and bearing gave the impression of solid well-being, and steadfast purpose.

The somewhat full double chin, and the carriage of her head, gave her a masterful look. In this she differed from others of her sect, who strove to convey the idea of humility both outwardly and inwardly. Moreover, it had become the fashion among the Haugians of the west country to speak in a soft, lisping tone.

Madame Torvestad never allowed herself to forget that she was the widow of an elder among the Brethren, and it was her ambition to constitute both herself and her house a centre of the religious movement. She therefore thought much of her own small meetings, which were half-religious, half-social. For the same reason she took in lodgers, although as far as money was concerned there was no need to do so.

Lauritz had not been admitted upon these grounds; she took him at the earnest request of friends in Flekkefjord. Generally, her lodgers were spiritually minded young men, often wandering lay-preachers, who came and went, remaining a few days among the Brethren in order to exhort and edify one another.

By such means as these, Madame Torvestad had succeeded in making her house a place of rendezvous for the Brethren in the town, and herself one of its most influential matrons, one whom the elders often consulted.

She was always a little less austere with Skipper Worse than with others, either because she had been his tenant for so many years, or that she considered such behaviour more likely to win him over, or perhaps, for some other reason.

At all events, it was strange how seldom she brought Scripture phrases into her conversation with him. She tolerated, indeed she sometimes even smiled at the gallant captain's pleasantries, when they were of a harmless sort.

After she had spoken a few words of welcome, and chatted with him on sundry matters which had occurred during his absence, she concluded by asking whether, as he was alone, he would come to supper at her house. It would greatly please her daughters.

"Anybody else coming?" inquired Worse, suspiciously.

"Possibly two or three of the Brethren might drop in on their way back from meeting."

"Thank you, indeed," muttered the skipper, with some signs of irritation; "but you know that I am not fit for such company, madame."

"Do not say so, Captain Worse; let us rather hope that you may be fitted for company where the word of God is heard." This she said with much cordiality, at the same time watching him closely.

Skipper Worse was a little embarrassed, and paced round the room. It was not easy to give an answer; he could not abide her meetings, but he was at a loss for a decent excuse.

At this moment Lauritz rose from his chair, and made as if he would take his departure.

"No, no, Lauritz!" cried the captain; "you can't leave yet. We must have a word or two together. Where are you bound?"

"I must go to the town and seek lodgings for the night," answered Lauritz, gloomily, but still a little emboldened by the cherry brandy he had drunk.

"What! aren't you going to lodge at Madame Torvestad's? Can't he, madame?"

"No," she replied drily. "You know that those who lodge with me are chiefly religious persons. I do not take in sailors."

"Yes; but your house has hitherto been like a home to Lauritz. It is hard for the poor lad on his return to find himself turned out into the street."

Worse now understood the young man's troubles, and, in his good nature, would willingly endeavour to help him. But Madame Torvestad made no response; she gathered up the folds of her cloak and prepared to depart.

"Well, good-bye, Captain Worse," said she; "I am heartily glad to welcome you home again. In half an hour or so I expect Sarah and a few friends from the meeting. Do you feel no inclination to join them, and to offer thanks to Him who has protected you in the tempest, and has brought you home unhurt over the stormy sea?"

"Yes, yes—of course, madame; you see—but—" and Jacob Worse stood and fidgeted about.

"Come now, you will not refuse," said she, holding out her hand, and looking at him with an expression of kindness.

But Worse still held back, and said, half in jest: "I am sorry to seem so obstinate; but I think that you too, Madame Torvestad, are also a little obstinate in your refusal to give house room to this poor lad. Come, let us make a bargain. I will attend your meeting if you will allow Lauritz to lodge with you. Will you say 'done,' Madame Torvestad?"

"I would willingly do more than that, Captain Worse, if it would tend to satisfy you," said she, offering him her hand.

Then, turning to Lauritz, she added, in her usual tone: "Mind, I do this for the captain's sake. I trust that you will so conduct yourself that I may not have to repent of it. You can have your old room; it is quite ready for you."

Saying this, she left the room.

But the captain and Lauritz paid another visit to the cupboard. This exhilarated Worse, and when he saw with what unbounded glee Lauritz rushed off towards the wharf, in order to bring up his sea chest, containing all his treasures, he forgot for a moment how dearly he had paid for his young friend's little loft in the attic.

CHAPTER III

HANS NILSEN FENNEFOS came of a family that had long since become followers of Hauge, on the occasion of one of his visitations to their neighbourhood. From his earliest childhood he had heard of the beloved teacher; his mother used to sing the hymns he had written, and Fennefos himself was named after him.

There was, therefore, much that might seem likely to make him a disciple; but the boy had a headstrong and passionate disposition, and up to his twentieth year his wild and thoughtless life was a source of grief to his mother.

One night, however, it happened that he came home late from a dance, and as he crept up to his bedroom, he heard his mother singing, as she laid awake:

"Commit thou all thy goings,
  Thy sorrows all confide,
To Him who rules the heavens,
  The ever-faithful Guide.
For He who stills the tempest,
  And calms the rolling sea,
Will lead thy footsteps safely,
  And smooth a way for thee."

It was a hymn lately introduced into the neighbourhood, and one which his mother, as he knew, prized greatly; but hitherto he had never taken any special notice of it.

At the sound of his mother's voice, the recollections of the dance and the fumes of drink vanished, and, as he listened, the words took a marvellous hold of him.

He wandered all night in fear and sorrow round his father's house, and it was not until the rising of the sun that he was enabled to find any peace.

It was the first time that he had been absent a whole night. As he entered the room, his mother rose up from her seat, and was about to rebuke him; but when she saw his altered look and bearing, she only said gently: "My son, the Lord has visited you this night."

From that time forward Hans Nilsen went no more to dances. After many years of tribulation and inward struggles, he at last gained confidence, and spoke with his friends and others of the one thing needful. He appeared also at the meetings, and it was the general opinion that so captivating a speaker had not been heard among them for many a day.

But the elders, mindful of Hauge's injunctions, would not permit him to go forth among the Brethren round about the country until he was thoroughly grounded in doctrine, and until a change of life had manifested itself in him.

He was more than twenty-five when he was first sent out; and after five or six years of almost uninterrupted wanderings from place to place, partly by invitation, and partly as he was led by the Spirit, he had become a well-known and highly valued lay-preacher over all the west country and northward, even beyond Trondhjem.

The times had long since gone by when a clergyman, accompanied by a bailiff or a drunken lieutenant, could break up the meetings, revile the lay-preacher, spit in his face, and cause him to be driven out of the parish.

But if the lay-preachers were less exposed to outward violence than in the old days of persecution, there were dangers of another sort, which in many ways made their position difficult.

The clergy had not changed their minds; but as they could no longer imprison or publicly revile "these enthusiasts, deceivers, and hypocrites," they preferred to scheme against and vilify them in private.

A new ordeal of patience and long-suffering was thus imposed upon the Brethren, especially upon their leaders and preachers; for as their numbers increased, it could not but happen that some disciples would fall into open sin, or be discovered to be hypocrites and impostors.

On such occasions the clergy were on the alert; active and energetic, both in public and in private, they gave currency to disparaging stories about the Haugians, men who despised the house of God, and worshipped Him in their own dismal meetings, where all sorts of profanities were said to be carried on.

From the official class this spirit of suspicion, and often of hatred, spread itself among educated people, to the injury of these peaceable and thoroughly worthy folks.

From such sources the current literature also proceeded to picture the ignorant lay-preachers, and to draw comparisons with the regular deans and pastors, the men of light and peace. The writers of the day, as a rule, knew but little about the lay-preachers, and relied on these descriptions; the clergyman they were well acquainted with.

Most people knew him from holiday visits to the parsonage, which stood out as bright spots in the memories of their younger days—the journey thither in summer by moonlight through the woods, and in winter over the crisp white snow, with accompaniment of tinkling sledge-bells.

It was thus that they knew their pastor, genial, friendly, and earnest. What a capital talker he was at the social board, and how ready to join in harmless merriment! How pleasant, too, was the great roomy parsonage, full of youthful mirth, tempered by the gentle gravity of their reverend host!

He was the central point of attraction for all, not only for the cares of wives and daughters, but in all the joys and sports of youth. "Father's" presence was looked upon as necessary to complete enjoyment.

His meerschaum pipe was kept filled for him, and when it went out, the children rushed to light it again with paper spills. When the wife, with a practised hand, enveloped him in his furs and wraps as he drove off to his other church the day after Christmas, all gathered round him, in an affectionate circle.

Nor could any one forget the quiet Saturday afternoons when all left the house in order not to disturb the pastor, who was preparing his sermon in the study, the smoke of his pipe stealing out of the keyhole like a blue serpent. Nor could they forget the Sunday mornings when his reverence took his dose of egg-flip before church, in order to clear his voice.

But this genial pastor could be quite another man when he sat alone among his peasants, discussing school or parish affairs; for language such as one would hardly expect from a man of light and peace might then be heard inside his study.

Sometimes it happened that, if on such occasions the young people gathered in the hall to seek their coats and cloaks for some outing, a frieze-clad peasant would come tumbling out of the study, and a momentary glimpse of a red face and a violently agitated dressing-gown would be obtained through the open door.

Then the wife or one of the daughters would say: "Poor father! that is one of those horrid Haugians, who give him so much trouble in the parish."

This feeling against the sectaries did not die out, even after the movement had become respected and honoured by the university.

The new teachers and clergy who were indebted to Hauge and his movement, not only for greater sincerity in doctrine and in its application, but who had even adopted the humble exterior and meek tones which prevailed from the time that Haugianism began to wane, seemed suddenly to forget that the Christian life, on the feeble remains of which they took their stand, was something that the people, after a long struggle, had gradually acquired of themselves.

Like their imperious predecessors, they coolly began to assume that they alone were the people's pastors and guides, and that any one who would so much as touch a hair of their heads, who would deprive them of one iota of their power and authority, destroyed—yes, destroyed the people's respect for all that was sacred, and disturbed with a presumptuous hand the ancient, beautiful, and patriarchal relations between the flocks and their beloved pastors.

But when Fennefos first began his wanderings, he encountered clergy of the old school who lay in wait for every word and deed, causing all the injury and annoyance in their power, both to him and to his friends.

The utmost circumspection became necessary, and the young preacher had to bear up against much strife and opposition. His undaunted spirit was, however, in proportion to his vast bodily strength.

Old people declared that he reminded them of Hauge in his earlier days, before he had been enfeebled by persecution.

For this reason the letters from the elders at home, which preceded Fennefos's visits to the Brethren at a distance, always urged that the young man should be exhorted to submit to those in authority, in order to avoid strife and offence.

He gradually learnt to control himself, and, in many instances, even succeeded in preventing disputes between the clergy and their flocks.

This had always been Hauge's desire, and Fennefos, like all the rest of the Brethren, conformed to it.

In this way, like many other lay-preachers, he so prepared the minds of the people that a pastor could almost everywhere, and without any exertions on his own part, find a little nucleus of Christian folk prepared to attach themselves to any teachers who would not merely, like the former clergy, give them stones for bread.

Sometimes, however, he found it difficult to control himself. In his earlier days at home, at Fennefos, he had learnt from the older people all the circumstance of Hauge's life. He knew the names not only of all the bailiffs and magistrates, but especially of the clergy, who had scoffed at, persecuted, and almost worried to death, the beloved teacher.

And now, as he journeyed through the land, he encountered the same names. Both bench and pulpit were filled not only in spirit, but in the body, by the actual successors of the odious persecutors of the past generation.

This often made his young blood boil again; and when, at the meetings, plain and free speech prevailed, he observed the same glow among his companions. Still they rebuked and restrained one another; for the powers that be are ordained of God.

When he journeyed in West Norway, Fennefos always stayed awhile with Madame Torvestad. The town was a central point in the widely ramified religious movement, and gradually her house became more of a home to him than his native place, Fennefos.

Here, too, he received letters and communications from the Brethren round about the country, when anything went wrong with them, or when they particularly wished him to preach to them.

He was in the habit of visiting or writing to them; and here the elders sent to him, if they happened to have a trustworthy envoy.

It was not, however, the Brethren or Madame Torvestad that attached him so much to the place; in fact, he was more at home among the peasantry.

He had, indeed, great objections to Madame Torvestad. Upon some points she was too lax; and she was full of German mysticism, which he could not endure. Above all, she was too imperious and ambitious, both among the disciples and in her own house.

What really attracted him was Sarah; not that he was actually in love with her, of this he was confident. But she was so penetrated by the spirit of the movement, and so well versed in the Bible and in religious books, that he knew of no one with whom it was more delightful to converse.

Sarah stood very high in the estimation of the Brethren, and it was a real pleasure to the older people to hear her at the meetings. It was, however, but seldom that she spoke, and she had not much that was original to say; but she knew so many hymns, texts, and passages of good books by heart, and, above all, she was so familiar with the Scriptures, that among all the Brethren her equal was hardly to be found.

On the table, in Madam Torvestad's sitting-room, there was a fixed desk, and upon it an open Bible; this was Sarah's place, and by her side Madame Torvestad had this day placed a comfortable chair for Skipper Worse.

Several women had arrived, who seated themselves round the room, laid their hands on their laps, and sighed. Near the stove a couple of young girls packed themselves by the side of Henrietta, on a bench that was too short for them; and a small boy, with a sallow face, whose parents dragged him from meeting to meeting, seated himself on the extreme end of a bench by the door.

By-and-by the men began to arrive in succession. There were the brothers Endre and Nicolai Egeland, who had the largest store in the town; Sivert Jespersen, who in a few years had made a fortune out of herrings; and four or five of the most eminent followers of Hauge, either artisans or shopmen.

Madame Torvestad shook hands with them all, and found seats for them, not a very easy task after a while, although the room was spacious and the chairs abundant.

Hans Fennefos entered, saluted Sarah, and at the same time inquired for whom the armchair was placed by her side.

"Skipper Worse is coming this evening," said Sarah, without looking up.

Hans Nilsen was surprised, and a little disquieted, although he hardly knew why. Madame Torvestad, who received him graciously, did not take her usual seat, but moved about in a restless manner, until at last Jacob Worse arrived.

As he opened the door, an involuntary desire to escape seized him. He had come from his own airy room, bright with the twilight afterglow. Here it was dark and stuffy. Two tallow candles in brass candlesticks threw some light on the table and the reading-desk, but out in the room nothing was visible, save a row of faces along the wall.

Escape, however, was out of the question; for Madame Torvestad, with a friendly gesture, took him by the hand and led him in. Moreover, every one knew him, and all the men came forward to shake his hand, and to welcome him home again.

His presence at the meeting gave general satisfaction; for Jacob Worse was an important man in the town, and hitherto he had rather belonged to those who opposed and derided the Haugians.

They nodded and smiled at Madame Torvestad, who greatly enjoyed her triumph.

Sivert Jespersen was especially pleased—he and Worse were acquaintances of old, up at the northern fishery; and Sivert Gesvint, as he was nick-named, was, when outside the meeting-house, a lively and enterprising man. Whilst, on the one hand, his tongue was always ready with texts and hymns, he was no less ready at a pinch to give any one a helping hand, or to "carry on" recklessly if it was a question of sailing out first to the fishing grounds.

Skipper Worse growled a little and rubbed his head, when Sivert Gesvint pressed his hand and welcomed him with effusion. There was an old affair between them about a consignment of salt, respecting which Skipper Worse declared that Sivert had cheated him; indeed, he had told him as much, to his face, many times, when they had met at the fishing. Sivert Gesvint, however, used only to smile, and pat him on the shoulder.

Madame Torvestad now led Worse to the armchair. He felt extremely ill at ease, and inwardly cursed both Madame Torvestad and Lauritz, which latter sat on a low stool behind two stout females, where he could catch a glimpse of Henrietta.

Sarah bashfully welcomed Skipper Worse, who patted her on the head; he had known her ever since she was a small child.

When they were all seated, and order was restored, Madame Torvestad said: "Now little Erik Pontoppidan, what was the subject discussed at the meeting?"

"Sanctification," said the pale boy near the door, in a prompt but mechanical manner.

"What hymn did they sing, Henrietta," said her mother; "you remember of course?"

Henrietta had indeed been at the meeting, but being quite absorbed by the sad news that Lauritz could not lodge with them, she had derived but scanty benefit from it. When she returned home and learnt that after all he had received permission, she was so delighted that now her mother's question came upon her like a bucket of cold water.

She turned very red, and felt as if her senses were leaving her.

Madame Torvestad looked severely at her for a while, and then turned to Erik Pontoppidan, who gave the first line of the hymn, without hesitation, the moment he caught her eye.

People nodded and smiled approvingly at the boy. His mother, a stout, pale woman, and his father, Endre Egeland, were proud of him. Erik Pontoppidan himself, however, took it very composedly.

Except Lauritz, no one looked at Henrietta, who felt very much ashamed, and crept behind her two friends. Madame Torvestad now struck up a hymn, in which all the company joined. To Jacob Worse's ear, all these voices in the low room, the subdued tones of the women, and the rough bass of the men, sounded weird and unpleasing.

They sang so very slowly that it seemed as if the hymn would never finish, especially as Sivert Jespersen, in a manner peculiar to him, threw in certain shakes and quavers at the end of each verse.

One of the elders had delivered an address at the meeting, and, as she did not happen to be present, Madame Torvestad inquired whether any one could tell her something of what he had said. She turned towards Fennefos, as did several others; but he sat unmoved, with his lips firmly closed, and looking as if he would not utter a word that evening.

"According to my poor opinion," said Sivert Jespersen, "the old man spoke well and simply; it was on the work of the Spirit, as little Erik remembered so well. He took for his subject Luther's words on the article, which says: 'I believe that of my own strength and wisdom I can neither believe in Christ nor come to Him;' and he showed clearly, at least in my opinion, both from Scripture and from our daily experience, our miserable shortcomings in the spiritual as well as in the temporal life, so long as we put our trust only 'in the arm of flesh and in our own feeble judgment.'"

At this point Nicolai Egeland, who was not very highly gifted in a spiritual sense, exclaimed: "Lord, I believe; help thou mine unbelief!"

He knew, in fact, no more than five or six texts, and these he brought in as they occurred to him, often quite inappropriately; but the Brethren knew his sincerity, and were lenient with him. He was not one of those servants to whom many talents had been entrusted.

One of the women sighed, and said: "Yes, that is true, indeed, Sivert Jespersen; we should not trust to our own wisdom in spiritual things."

Madame Torvestad now took up the conversation, as she sat turning over the leaves of sundry small books, which lay on the table by her side, just opposite to where Sarah was seated.

Some of these were tracts, and some, books of hymns; and as she met with any passage that struck her, she wove it into her conversation in such a manner that it seemed to be half her own utterance and half a quotation.

"A Christian should always bear in mind," she began, "that much that is high and mysterious can never in this life be comprehended by feeble man. We should, therefore, never attempt to fathom it, but should resign ourselves to the might and truth of God, who has brought us into contact with it. Yes, directly our own wisdom begins to dwell upon the possibility of that which is revealed to us, we may be sure that temptation and Satan are at hand—the old wily serpent who deceived Eve; and we should instantly invoke the protection of the Almighty against death and hell itself. To this end may grace be vouchsafed to all of us."

"Amen," said Nicolai Egeland.

"But," asked Sivert Jespersen, turning to the younger people, "how should we receive this grace?"

"It is the work of the Holy Spirit," said a voice by the door.

"Very properly answered, little Erik. And what do you mean by the Spirit's work?"

"Sanctification."

"And of how many parts does sanctification consist? can you give me an answer to that also?"

"New birth, justification, and regeneration."

Everybody was pleased with the quickness of the boy, who sat without moving a muscle of his face, his mouth open, and generally prepared to give answers much as an instrument responds to its keys.

At this point Nicolai Egeland became ambitious, and thrust himself into the conversation, quoting the longest text he knew—"By man sin came into the world:" but Madame Torvestad interrupted him quietly:

"Very wonderful is the state of the regenerate man; he is the slave neither of sin nor of worldly affections, not even indeed of innocent things. When I say that he is not a slave, I do not assert that in a moment of weakness he may not be overtaken by sin, but that he will not continue in it. If surprised by the flesh or the devil, he may fall into sin; but he will rise up and lay his troubles before God, and seek forgiveness. So long as he is thus established again in faith, and enjoys peace with God, he remains superior to sin, and continues to walk in the Spirit."

Sarah watched Fennefos, for she was certain that he would not approve of the book her mother was reading from. He made no signs, however; and in the feeble glimmer she could see only the vigorous, clear cut profile, somewhat turned upwards, as if gazing at the ceiling.

When it became manifest that he would not speak that evening, the conversation dragged on without animation for about another quarter of an hour.

All this time Sarah sat by the Bible, and, in the course of the conversation, looked out a text here and there, sometimes on her own account, and sometimes when one of the company sought to have his memory refreshed. She readily found all that was required, and in many cases was able to repeat the passage at once by heart.

Skipper Worse could not understand what they were talking about, and he became very weary. The only thing that kept him awake was Sarah's shapely fingers moving deftly among the pages of the sacred book.

But at last, as he was on the point of dropping asleep, Madame Torvestad proposed that they should conclude with a hymn.

Sarah took a hymn-book, and held it up for the captain, and the singing began.

As Worse was sitting half asleep, watching Sarah's fingers, she suddenly turned her great dark eyes upon him, and said:

"Sing with us."

In a moment Skipper Worse was wide awake, and began to hum, as she moved her fingers along the lines. He had never been very good at such singing, and when he came to sacred words he felt ashamed to pronounce them with his sinful lips.

But he was awake, and, more than this, he began to be at his ease. Now and then he looked up at Sarah's well-turned shoulders, her white neck, and the throat which swelled so gracefully as she sang.

They sat so close to each other, as she bent towards him with the hymn-book, that Skipper Worse was conscious of something pleasant in her company, the first homelike feeling he had experienced that day.

There was another person also who enjoyed himself thoroughly, although he did not give a very close attention to the meeting, and this was Lauritz Seehus in his corner.

He was so elated after his first disappointment, that he did not find the meeting as wearisome as usual—he could see Henrietta.

Moreover, the sacred words and the singing made so great an impression on one who had long been absent from such things that he was much affected, and thanked the Almighty, who had sent him a brief but bitter trial, that he might the better learn how all things worked together for his good.

As soon as the hymn was finished, the daughters of the house brought in tea and bread and butter. After a grace from Endre Egeland, they all ate well, and drank much tea; and at nine o'clock the party broke up.

When Worse returned to his own rooms, and saw Madame Torvestad's guests crossing the market-place as they left her house, he hardly knew whether to be amused or angry at having been compelled to spend his first evening on shore among such people.

There among them he observed Endre Egeland, whose moral reputation was none of the best, and Sivert Jespersen, who had overreached him so confoundedly in the matter of the salt.

"If Randulf should hear of all this!"

Nevertheless, he could not help remembering how pleasant it had been by the side of Sarah, and he felt how dull and lonely were his own spacious rooms.

CHAPTER IV

THE following evenings, Skipper Worse visited the club again, and enjoyed himself amazingly. It was only on the first evening, when he met with the two young captains from America, that things had been so contrary.

By-and-by, as his old friends rallied round him, he spun many a yarn about Rio. He also sang a couple of English songs with a Spanish refrain, which he had learnt from a very nice young lady whom he had met with, swinging in a grass hammock slung between two palm trees.

These two songs rather took at the club, where there was singing almost every evening; and when the company had mastered the Spanish refrain, their chorus made the spoons rattle again in the steaming tumblers of toddy.

There was Harbour-master Snell, the Exciseman Aarestrup, and the Custom-house Officer Preuss, the chief of the fire brigade, and several captains and shipowners.

Of course, it was soon noised about the town that Skipper Worse had been at the Haugian meeting, and he had to submit to a good deal of rallying in consequence.

He preferred to join in the laugh, for there was nothing to gain by losing his temper, and at last the reprobate even gave an imitation of Endre Egeland's grace.

Moreover, he was not entirely displeased to find it the prevalent opinion in the club that Jacob Worse was a sly old dog, who had visited the sectaries for a certain young woman's sake.

Madame Torvestad had not molested him of late. When they met, she merely invited him to look in whenever it was agreeable to him; and when he did not respond to these invitations, she manifested no annoyance.

When he got all his things on shore, he sent Lauritz to Sarah, with a box covered with shells. This was the greatest treasure which he had brought from Rio.

Madame Torvestad, on Sarah's behalf, thanked the captain for the handsome present he had made, remarking at the same time, in a somewhat admonitory tone, that such fine things were calculated to arouse worldly thoughts and vanity in the young.

In the course of the summer he became reconciled to the absence of Randulf. The interval of tranquillity at home was not irksome to him; his business prospered, and his voyage to Rio procured him a certain amount of consideration among his fellowtownsmen.

He did not hear often from his son in Lübeck; but the bills he had to pay for him showed that he was alive, and apparently enjoying life pretty freely.

Their mutual relations had never been of a very intimate description, partly because the father had been so much away from home, and partly because the son had been much spoilt and indulged by the mother, who was an affected, sentimental sort of person, full of romantic notions, and whose thoughts ran only on knights and damsels, combats, moonlight, long tresses, trapdoors, and winding staircases.

Once upon a time she had fascinated Worse when he was a mate, during a certain boating excursion by moonlight. Such a fine lady, with such large bright eyes, and such long auburn hair, he had never seen, either in the Baltic or the Mediterranean.

She had consented to become his for life or death on that occasion, when, after the company had taken coffee on a little island, he bore her in his arms, and waded out to the boat with her, instead of waiting until it could be brought to the shore.

It reminded her a little of Romarino, who, encircling Miranda's slender waist with his strong right arm, swung himself into the saddle with his gentle burden, and rode out through the castle gates upon his snorting steed.

It proved, however, a most unfortunate expedition for both of them. He was as little like a knight-errant as she was to a sea captain's wife. When she had devoured all the romances in the lending library, she lapsed into a sickly dreaminess, from which she aroused herself only to lament and bewail her fate; and it was this which drove Jacob Worse to sail on long voyages.

On one occasion, when he was expected home from Lisbon, a child was born to him, and his wife hastened to have it christened "Romarino."

This went to Worse's heart. He could take no pleasure in the pale little creature in its cradle, on account of its name, which seemed to separate the child from him, and to remove it to the fantastic world of the mother. In fact, to hear Skipper Worse utter the word Romarino was one of the most ludicrous things imaginable.

When the feeble, querulous mother died, Romarino was fifteen years of age. He was then sent to Copenhagen to live in a family which received him at the request of Consul Garman. It was out of the question that he should remain in the great lonely house, his father being away so much at sea.

At the present time he was about twenty, and just before Jacob Worse had sailed on his long voyage to Rio, Romarino had paid a visit to his home.

He was a pale little creature, with light hair. He wore an olive green coat, yellow waistcoat, and light grey trousers, strapped over his boots. His extravagantly tall fluffy hat was so perched on the top of his head that it was a wonder it did not fall off more frequently.

In this costume he created a great sensation in the little fishing town, strutting about flourishing a thin cane, and surveying everybody and everything with disdain.

Moreover, he could not speak Norwegian properly.

His father's feelings were divided between admiration and embarrassment; but the admiration received a serious blow when Thomas Randulf swore that Romarino used pomatum on his pocket-handkerchief.

However, Worse still thought a good deal of his son, although he could have wished that there was more of his own sailor spirit in him.

He often thought that if he could have resigned the *Hope* to a son, such a one as Lauritz Seehus that son ought to have been.

Romarino Worse was, however, what he seemed to be, an idler who spent his father's money; while in his heart he despised the simple captain, as he had long since been taught to do by his mother.

When Skipper Worse had settled himself down to his life in the town, he often wondered what was the matter at Sandsgaard. It was not at all as it used to be; what in the world ailed the place?

Madame Garman's death had, of course, made a great difference, but would hardly suffice to explain the dullness and constraint which prevailed there.

At last he began to feel uneasy. It was not only that Harbour-master Snell had, on the occasion of the first evening, hinted at the pecuniary difficulties of C. F. Garman, but the same story reached him from all sides. At first he ridiculed it; but little by little it began to make some impression on him.

Several times when he had gone in his boat to Sandsgaard, he had determined to speak to the Consul.

Heavens! if the firm of C. F. Garman really was in want of money, Jacob Worse had plenty at hand, and could procure more. But he never could muster up courage enough to put the question.

It was the established custom at Sandsgaard, that whenever Worse's boat was seen entering the bay, Zacharias, the man at the wharf, was ordered to take a large cod out of the fish-tank; for this was Jacob Worse's favourite dish.

The Consul's two sisters-in-law, the spinsters Mette and Birgitte, were always delighted when he came, although they were prodigiously angry with him when he teased them, as he always did.

After paying his respects to the ladies, Jacob Worse always made for the office, which, with its door usually open, was close to the sitting-room. Here he conned the almanac, and when he found that it was the day of Saint Crispin or Saint Hieronymus, or some such other saint, he used to rub his hands saying:

"Is it, indeed? I remember him when I was in Italy—one of the grandest of the lot. Yes, we must certainly have some toddy this evening."

Consul Garman would smile, and the old book-keeper, Adam Kruse, seated behind his desk, would prick up his ears.

He was always invited to take a glass when the captain was there.

Worse, who was free of the house, would then take the keys of the office cupboard, and bring out certain old-fashioned square Dutch flasks.

In the evening, he played cards, with the spinsters, the Consul looking on and laughing heartily, whilst the captain played so unfairly, and so befooled the good ladies, that their very capstrings quivered with rage.

At other times, the Consul and Worse would talk politics, and discuss the Hamburg "Nachrichten," whilst the old book-keeper, with his tumbler and his long clay pipe, sat in silence in his humble corner behind the big clock.

In the old sitting-room, which looked out upon the harbour, two tallow candles were placed every evening on the table near the sofa, where the Consul was wont to sit; and when there were guests, two more were placed on the toddy-table by the stove.

Above the white panelling, which was carried up as high as the tops of the straight-backed chairs, the walls were covered with canvas, painted green. The grey window-blinds which had lately come from Copenhagen, were decorated with representations of Christiansborg, Kronborg, and Frederiksborg. A tall wayfarer under a tree in the foreground gazed across the water at the castle, while three ladies with long shawls, and bonnets like the hoods of carriages, walked towards the right. In the corner by the stove stood a winder for yarn, which the two sisters used when they were not running after one another, looking after the household work.

After his wife's death, the Consul had never succeeded in dividing this duty satisfactorily between them. When Birgitte had inspected the table linen and silver, and had looked over the washing, etc., she felt an uncontrollable desire to see that too much butter was not used in the kitchen; and when Mette, during her week, had controlled the household expenses and the cooking, she could not sleep until she had counted over the spoons and napkins.

This led to no little confusion in domestic matters, and to serious bickering between the sisters, of which, however, only distant echoes reached the Consul.

There was but one subject on which they were in accord, and that was the canary bird. In the course of years they had possessed many, and every time the cat took one they protested that never again would they expose themselves to such a calamity.

But, according to Captain Worse's calculation, the period of court mourning for the canary bird lasted precisely three weeks, after which a new one was installed. They were always hens; for the sisters objected to males of every description; moreover, they objected to the singing.

Their present canary was quite the most delightful little creature they had ever possessed. In addition to all its other perfections, there was one which embarrassed them—it could lay an egg.

But the crafty little thing would not provide a nest, but laid its eggs in such places that they were soon destroyed.

This greatly distressed Birgitte and Mette, who devised many plans to induce the bird to act more circumspectly.

They placed cotton and fine wool all about the room, and even endeavoured to construct small nests of wool and horsehair. But the incorrigible little creature seemed to take an especial delight in eluding them, and in laying eggs in out-of-the-way places.

This grieved the sisters, and in moments of irritation they went so far as to blame one another.

One evening at the club, the harbour-master inquired maliciously: "Is old Adam gone to Bergen?"

"Yes; he went last week," answered Worse.

"What in the world does he go there for?"

"Business, of course. C. F. Garman has many transactions in Bergen."

'Borrow money, perhaps?"

"Come, harbour-master, we have had enough of this!" exclaimed Jacob Worse.

But the other, taking no notice of him, went on.

"No knowing; bad times for all. Spoke to Captain Andersen, *Freya,* just come from Bergen. Old Adam wanted two thousand dollars, they say, if he could only get them; but he could not, not a rap. No; those Bergensers are not to be taken in."

This was too bad. Worse went home. It was in everybody's mouth that things were going ill with the firm C. F. Garman, and if its credit was impaired, it was high time for him, Jacob Worse, to come to the rescue.

Next morning he presented himself at the office, and entering, shut the door towards the sitting-room, as well as that to the inner office. He desired to have a few words quite alone with the Consul.

His manner was so very strange that morning—a mixture of hesitation and craftiness—that it made the Consul lean back in his armchair, and inquire if anything had happened to him.

"No, nothing whatever, nothing," answered Worse as he stood and shifted uneasily from one leg to another; "it was only something I wished to ask the Consul."

"We are always ready to meet all the reasonable wishes of our old friends, as far as it lies in our power. Sit down, Captain Worse."

"Well, it was just this. I was thinking of going to the fishing this winter on my own account, and—so—so—"

"I opine that Captain Worse knows that when he has been at home in the winter season we have never raised any objection to his trading on his own account at the herring fishery, nor do we now."

"Yes, thank you; I am quite aware of it; many thanks, but that was not it. H'm! A deal of money will be wanted, Herr Consul."

At these words a somewhat rigid expression stole over the Consul's face; but Worse mustered up his courage, and fired off his big gun.

"Will the Consul lend me two thousand dollars on my note of hand?"

Morten Garman gave a start in his armchair. "What! does Jacob Worse also want to borrow money?"

"Yes. You see, Herr Consul, everybody wants money for the autumn fishing, and I particularly wish to cope on equal terms with Sivert Jespersen and the others up there."

"Yes, that is just how it is," exclaimed the Consul; "that is how it is nowadays! One wishes to outstrip the other, and so they borrow and speculate; but when the day of reckoning comes, then comes the pinch."

"As for that, Herr Consul, the firm must be aware that Jacob Worse is good for two thousand dollars, and a little more besides."

"No doubt, no doubt," answered the Consul. "But now we have demands upon us for money from all sides, there seems no end to them; it is really more than we can do these bad times."

Jacob Worse was beginning to be pleased with the success of his little comedy, and now proceeded farther with it.

"It is very sad," said he, "that I should have to turn elsewhere. People will say that I have quarrelled with the firm, or, perhaps, they will believe some of the lies concerning C. F. Garman which are going about."

"What do you mean? What do they say about the firm?" asked the Consul, quickly.

"Ah! well, for example, it was reported in the club yesterday that a certain person had gone to Bergen in order to borrow money for certain people."

Consul Garman turned his face away and looked out into the garden, where the first yellow leaves of autumn were beginning to fall.

Never before had he seen danger so imminent; his easy disposition and his pride had never permitted him to realize that the firm C. F. Garman, the old Sandsgaard house, was hanging by a thread, and that it was possible for it to collapse in a vulgar insolvency.

"Yes," he muttered, "it was a mistake, sending Kruse to Bergen; but—" And then all of a sudden, as if weary of bearing his burden alone, he turned full round upon Worse, and said: "Things are not so prosperous with C. F. Garman as you suppose, Jacob."

He called him Jacob, as in the old days when Jacob Worse was a sailor lad, and he, Morten Garman, a schoolboy.

The cunning Skipper Worse had now reached the decisive point. He tore open his coat, produced a bundle of banknotes from his breast pocket, threw them on the table in front of the Consul, and said: "Five thousand dollars to begin with, Herr Consul, and twice as much more if necessary, when I have had time to scrape it together."

His face beamed with pleasure, and he laughed with an internal chuckling sound; his joy, however, was suddenly damped when the Consul pushed the notes from him, and inquired in his iciest manner:

"What does all this mean? What do you wish me to do with this money?"

"Use it, borrow it, keep it as long as you will, Herr Consul."

"Oh! that is what I am to understand, is it? You have allowed yourself a little diversion at our expense; very fine, indeed, Herr Captain Worse. Things are not come to such a pass with the firm that it must borrow of its own people."

The crafty captain sat for a moment quite dumbfounded; but he could bear it no longer. His spirit was up, and bringing his fist down with a thump, he exclaimed: "Morten, you are a little too bad with your confounded airs! If the firm wants money, is it unreasonable to borrow it of me, I who have gained every farthing I possess in the service of your father and you?"

"But don't you understand," said the Consul, who was getting rather excited; "cannot you see how our credit would suffer, if it were known that one of our own captains had helped the firm out of difficulties?"

"Stuff and nonsense with your credit; cash beats credit any day. My money is as good as yours, Morten Garman; and if you won't have it, you are not the man I take you for."

Jacob Worse was now beside himself with eagerness, and, without either of them noticing it, the ceremonious style was dropped, and they talked in familiar language.

"Come, come, Jacob, don't let us quarrel," said the Consul, pulling up his neckcloth. It was the first time that any one had thus got the better of him.

He looked at the money, and then gazed out upon the garden. A long pause ensued.

Skipper Worse had got up and stood with his back to the table, examining a map on the wall. The old clock in the sitting-room ticked terribly slowly.

At last Consul Garman got up, and approaching him, said: "Listen, Jacob Worse. I will take your money if you will enter into partnership with me."

"What! what do you say? Partnership? Are you mad, Herr Consul?"

"Listen to me. You invest your capital—that is to say, as much of it as you please—in the business, and to that extent you become a partner in the firm of Garman and Worse. The rest we can arrange at leisure."

"No, no, Herr Consul; I never intended this. Change the name of the firm indeed! It is out of the question, and you don't mean it, either."

"Yes, I do mean it. It is the only way in which the affair can be arranged. Let us sit down and examine the matter calmly. It is absolutely intolerable to me to borrow money of you; but, on the other hand, there is no reason, as far as my own feelings are concerned, or as regards the external relations of the firm, why we, at a busy and, shall I say, a critical moment, should not admit into the house, a man who for many years has worked with us, or why we should not, as a consequence of the agreement, add his name to ours, so that for the future the business should be carried on under the name of 'Garman and Worse.' "

"Yes; but—but—all the rest is practicable; but the name—your father's name!"

"Possibly my father would not have done it, but I will have it so. This arrangement is—h'm—the saving of the firm; I am bound to acknowledge it, and I therefore urge you to agree to my proposal."

"But my good Herr Consul," resumed Worse, who had suddenly come down again to his former position, and could not reconcile himself to the notion of entering into partnership with Morten W. Garman, the Consul himself.

The other, however, held firmly to his purpose; and as he made a request, there was nothing for it but to accept the offer.

They remained in conversation a long time, discussing future arrangements. The Consul said plainly that he did not expect Jacob Worse to mix himself up with the business, an idea which made him laugh outright, as it would never occur to him to interfere.

As he rowed back to the town, it seemed to him that he was quite a different Jacob Worse to the one who had rowed from it. Certain ambitious views of his new dignity began to assert themselves, and he sat repeating: "Garman and Worse," wondering what sort of impression it would make on Randulf.

Nevertheless, he was not entirely happy; it was too much —it had come upon him too suddenly—and he did not care to talk about it.

Consul Garman, however, made no secret of the change in the firm, and the next day the news was announced in the two local papers, each about the size of an ordinary cabbage leaf.

It is easy to conceive what a welcome opportunity this event afforded for festive meetings, and for extra libations and singing at the club.

Jacob Worse was fêted at the club, speeches were made in his honour, and, as the drinking went on, was chaffed unmercifully. Envy is always very witty, and his elevation became by no means a source of unmixed pleasure to him.

And from Randulf, that old rascal who had written from Riga that he was on the point of sailing, came tidings that he had been in collision with a Rostock trader, and that he had put back to Bolderaa, where he must discharge and repair. It only required that he should be frozen up there for the winter to make the disappointment complete.

When Romarino heard of the arrangements that had been made, he wrote to his father, as if acknowledging him for the first time in his life.

Worse, however, was hurt when addressed in the following terms: "For a mere sailor, I must admit that on this occasion you have managed pretty well for yourself."

Madame Torvestad redoubled her attentions; and when the autumn came, with its rain and bad weather, Jacob Worse found it pleasant enough to drink tea with madame and her daughters, when there was no meeting.

They bantered him so terribly at the club.

CHAPTER V

LATE in the autumn, when the sun set in lurid clouds full of storm and rain, the little town was shrouded in a darkness which was only relieved by a small lantern, which glimmered on the wall at the door of the town hall.

Otherwise it was dark, pitch dark, in the narrow, crooked streets, and down by the wharves, where one might fall headlong into the sea if tipsy, or a stranger.

In the small shops train-oil lamps or tallow candles were burning, in the larger ones suspended "moderator" lamps were beginning to be used.

A faint light was thus thrown upon the puddles, and those who were well acquainted with the street could pick their way dryshod.

Most people, however, wore long boots, and came tramping along, so that they could be heard splashing through the mud.

Here and there a small lantern might be observed swinging along, at one moment lowered carefully in order to seek a path in the worst places, at others casting its inquisitive light in the faces of the passers-by, or against the sides of the low wooden buildings.

Ladies with cap baskets, from which knitting needles were sticking out, might be seen going to evening parties; or servant maids carrying lanterns, and followed by little girls with thin white legs and big goloshes on their feet, on their way to the dancing-school.

After seven o'clock there was scarcely any light in the shops, and the streets seemed deserted. Now and then a ray of light was cast upon the mud and puddles when the door of a tavern, where sailors and topers quarrelled and rioted, was thrown open.

About this time the night watch would sally out of the town hall, in order to take up its beat. It was composed generally of old seamen or ship carpenters, who were past their work, men with hoarse, thick voices, bent with age and hard of hearing.

They crept along very slowly, clad in long, thick, frieze coats, bearing lanterns in their left hands, and thumping along the pavement with their ponderous staves.

At certain appointed corners they cried out the hour and the state of the weather, each in his own peculiar fashion, so that he could be understood in his own beat, but nowhere else in the whole world.

When those who had been at parties came home at the usual respectable hour of about ten o'clock, the lanterns reappeared in the streets. When they fell in with a watchman, they wished him good night, the young people asking the hour in order to tease him, the older ones inquiring seriously about the direction of the wind.

After that the town became dark and silent. A drunken man would reel from one side to the other until he fell down a cellar trap-door, into the gutter, or into the sea. If by chance he stumbled upon the watch, he soon found himself in the lock-up.

But it was not so easy to stumble upon the watch; for they had their secret sleeping-corners, from which they only issued in case of emergency, when they thought the time was come for crying out something, or when the shuffling sound of leather boots was heard approaching.

This was the watch which went the rounds, the fire watch of the town consisting of four or five ancient watchmen, who had no voices left.

They wore their coat collars turned up, and their fur caps drawn down, so that they could hardly notice a fire until it singed their very beards. Nevertheless the town reposed in perfect security.

Perchance, however, some one would wake up and begin to think of the quantity of rye which lay in the warehouses, or there came a series of visions, clear and definite, such as appear to us in the darkness of the night; first, an ember somewhere smouldering, spreading, and then setting fire to the walls, seizing and enveloping the house, and consuming the rye, salt, barrels, the store, and everything.

Then a shuffling noise of stiff leather boots and staves along the pavement, all coming nearer every moment, and then passing out of hearing.

Ah! the fire-watch going the rounds. All right, one can sleep now in peace and comfort.

Or perhaps a child would wake up in a troubled dream, and would lay and listen, terrified by hideous imaginations of thieves and robbers climbing in at the kitchen window to kill father and mother with long knives. But outside the watchman cries: "Two o'clock, and a still night."

Ah! the watch; yes, of course, that was the watch; so no thieves or robbers can come in at the kitchen window. All bad people must stay at home, or the watch will take them to the lock-up. Yes, it was not bad people, only good and kind folks and watchmen.

So it sleeps on again in peace and dreams no more.

But when they *did* come, those three terrible cannon shots which announced a fire, shaking and even bursting in the windows, unbounded terror prevailed. High above the dark streets the hazy sky was glowing like a sea of fire.

The drummer, Long Jorgen, beat furiously with the thicker ends of his drumsticks; men with hoarse voices, and boys with shrill notes like those of sea-gulls, rushed through the streets shouting: "Fire! fire!"

Outside the engine-house, people carrying lanterns were assembling, swearing, and shouting for the keys.

They hang behind the fire inspector's bed.

Off, then, to the fire inspector's.

In the pitchy darkness, the messenger encounters him, and running full tilt against him, knocks the bunch of keys into the mud. Whilst search is made for them with three lanterns, some sailors break open the doors, and the engine is run out with a dismal rumbling sound.

Old women in their nightcaps run into the streets, with a washhand basin or a flatiron. In the houses all flock to the parents' bed-chamber. The smaller children sit up in bed and cry, whilst the elder girls, half dressed, their hair hanging down their backs, and white and trembling with fear, strive to comfort them.

But the mother sets to work to make coffee—hot coffee is good for everything, and under all circumstances.

From time to time the father returns home to report how things are going on.

Long since the boys have dressed themselves and disappeared. It is a holiday to them, a festival of terror. The red sky overhead, the darkness of the night, the flames which now and then pierce the canopy of smoke, the men rushing about and shouting—all this fills them with an excitement equal to ten romances.

Determined to attempt something prodigious, to distinguish themselves by something manly beyond conception, they rush into houses where there is neither fire nor danger, and fasten upon the most immovable and impossible objects.

The fire inspector stands by the engines and takes command; two rows of men and lads pass the water forwards, and return the empty buckets. At the seaside, or down by some well, the younger sailors take it in turn to fill the buckets, until they are wet through and their arms benumbed.

Officers of the Citizen Corps, in their blue tail coats with white facings, run here and there, and with their long swords are in the way both of themselves and of every one else.

But the sailors plunge into the very fire itself; entering the houses, they strive to rescue the contents until the roofs fall in. They climb up on the neighbouring houses with wet sails, and pull down sheds and boardings.

Thomas Randulf and Jacob Worse were known from their boyhood as the most daring on such occasions.

They were always the first on the spot, carrying out the aged and the invalids, and afterwards taking the hottest and most dangerous posts. In fact, they were the real commanders, although the fire inspector had yellow and crimson feathers in his three-cornered hat.

At such time the merchants were in greater anxiety than the rest of the population. Insurance was not usual; indeed, some of the sectaries looked upon it as sinful. Others said that their insurance was in the hands of the Almighty.

But when the wind set in their direction, and the wooden houses blazed up, one after the other, the wisest and the best of them lost their heads, and ran about throwing sacks of corn and flour into the sea, labouring to destroy, whilst they forgot to save the cash in the office close at hand.

Through the flame and smoke, through the uproar and the shouting, is heard the booming of the great cathedral bell. Two or three slow peals, then a long pause, and then more quickly intermittent single peals, a dismal, hope-dispelling sound.

It is not an alarm bell rousing people to come to the rescue, it is rather the church's prayer for mercy, a despairing appeal to God to stop the raging flames.

But the winter nights could also show a different life in the dark little town. It might be Christmas time, or just after New Year's Day, when the northwest wind was bringing snow-storms every half hour, the stars shining brightly between whiles.

Suddenly a boat would appear in the inner fjord, another and yet another, then a small smack, followed again by a couple more boats, each steering for its own destination in the harbour, and groping its way to the ring-bolts under the warehouses and along the quays.

A man would jump on shore and run at full speed up into the town, his huge sea-boots leaving marks as of elephants' feet on the newly fallen snow. The watchman would hold up his lantern and survey the wayfarer, whose boots, trousers, and even his sou-wester, shine with countless starlike, silvery specks.

The watchman smiles, and, as he is a knowing old fellow, cries out, when he reaches the corner by Skipper Worse's house, "Wind north-west! The herring is on the coast!"

More boats and smacks arrive; the rattling of anchors and chain cables is heard in all directions. Men knock at the walls of the warehouses, and people sally forth with lanterns, doors are thrown open, and the light falls on the men yonder in a boat, and on the heaps of fat, glittering spring herrings.

Up in the town the merchant's house resounds as the man with the sea-boots picks up a stone and hammers at the wall. He strikes boldly, knowing that he brings welcome news.

All arouse themselves, thinking at first that it is a fire; but the master of the house springing up, throws the window open.

"Ivar Östebö sends his compliments. He has bought four hundred barrels on your account."

"Do you know the price?"

"Three marks eighteen shillings. We are lying off the northern warehouse with eighty barrels; the rest is close behind."

"How is the wind?"

"North-westerly, with snow-storms."

"Run off to Lars up on the hill, and bid him rouse up the women; he knows what to do."

Upon this the window shuts down again, and the man in the sea-boots hurries on, knocking against other men also running in the dark.

The merchant begins to put on his working clothes, which are always at hand. His wife calls to him to put on two of his thickest woollen coats, which he does; for he well knows what it is like in the warehouse, with the wind at north-west with snow-storms.

The wind increases in gusts, and the snow is whirled about.

Boats and smacks arrive in such numbers before the north-west wind, that the harbour is full of noise and shouting, the plashing of the waves, the sound of furling sail, and the clanking of chain cables as they rattle through the hawse-holes.

In the upper stories of the warehouses lights appear. Oil lamps are placed in all directions, and people begin to arrive —men, old women, and girls.

The magazine of salt is opened, the cooper rummages among the barrels, and the men in the boats grow impatient; they cry out that they are going to begin, and the first herrings are shot upon the floor. The whole town to its farthest corner is now on the alert; lights shine in the small windows, and innumerable coffee-pots are set by the fires. Bustle and hilarity prevail; the herring has arrived, the herring that all have been expecting, and from which all hope to get something.

The girls and women who have to clean the fish put on their working dresses amidst noise and laughter, although the cold makes their teeth chatter. Over everything they fold thick handkerchiefs, as a protection to the head so that only the eyes and nose are visible; for if the brine of the fish touches the hair, it causes a sore.

When they are ready they hasten in a crowd to the warehouse, where they have entered into a contract beforehand. At once they join the party to which they belong, and take their places in the midst of the herring, which come higher than their wooden shoes, amidst barrels and bowls of brine.

The unfortunate tallow candles placed on sticks in the heap of fish are always in danger of being upset, or of being put out by being snuffed with wet fingers.

They are soon supplied with short, sharp knives, and they proceed to clean the herrings with great rapidity.

The snow is presently covered with huge footmarks, and the new layer brought by each passing shower is soon trampled into mud.

Only up in the town and in the wider streets round about the school is there enough for the boys to carry on their snow-balling, when at last the morning arrives.

When the pale and sallow youngsters at the top of the school come toiling along, with their dull burdens of Greek and Latin books, their thoughts running upon a bygone literature, and their brains crammed with grammar, half consisting of rules and half of exceptions to those rules; and when they meet a troop of girls on their way homewards, after having worked among the herrings half the night, it may happen that the noisy girls will put their heads together and laugh at them.

They have drawn down their handkerchiefs, so that their mouths are now free. Chattering and laughing, they march up the middle of the street, warm and rosy-cheeked after their labours, besprinkled with fish scales up to the eyes.

Many of them are about the same age as the learned young gentlemen, but they feel so much their superiors, that they laugh at the half-admiring, half-contemptuous looks which they provoke.

The students feel this a little, but they find a solace in quoting *"Plebs plebis,"* or *"Semper mutabile,"* or some such other classic witticism.

They know that the herrings have come during the night, and they see the harbour swarming with vessels, and the town astir with business.

But what of that? Was it for them to think of vile lucre? Their world lay far above the common herd; they are on the road to Parnassus and despise the grovelling souls—the mob—who toil and drudge, stooping over their work like the beasts that perish, uncheered by a single ray from the sacred altar of the muses.

This contempt for the masses they cherish until they have to descend from Parnassus and enter the public service. Then they learn to discourse eloquently on the benefits of commerce, whilst in reality they are completely indifferent to it.

Scarcely any of the official classes, except the clergy, to whom on such occasions offerings flowed more liberally, rejoiced in a good fishing season. When the herring was abundant, and money was plentiful in the country, so that everybody was able to clear off incumbrances and to lay by something, the lawyers complained of bad times.

But when, on the other hand, the people were badly off, when the fishing or the harvest failed, when a tightness of money stopped supplies, so that bankruptcies, distress warrants, and forced sales by auction, with heavy law charges were frequent, then it was that the lawyers throve.

With the exception of the official class, and of the few families that lived upon pensions or dividends, there was a feeling of joy over all the town when the herrings arrived. All were interested in a prosperous fishing, which should bring the fulfilment of long-cherished hopes, or relief from embarrassments.

First and foremost everything relating to the sea—and this comprised the whole town—was in a state of activity, from the fishermen themselves to the dealers in salt and the speculators. All moved in a sort of delirium so long as the fishing lasted.

Not only skippers, but even young mates, were entrusted with vessels, and the most daring feats were performed in order to arrive first at the fishing-ground, and to secure a full cargo.

Men misled one another with false information, occasionally came to blows, and drank deeply when time and opportunity offered.

In the club, the evenings were noisy; all the rooms were full, and people even sat on the edge of the billiard-tables, which was contrary to rules.

Every new-comer was expected to bring tidings of the fishing, of the prices, and of how many shoals were surrounded by the nets, also, if there were any news from the north.

These were the only available sources of information, and business was regulated accordingly. Sometimes they were correct, sometimes altogether wrong.

Sometimes the fishing was best after it had been declared that the herrings had spawned and gone out to sea. Sometimes, again, there was no fishing, even when enormous shoals were reported; and people were left with dearly purchased salt and empty barrels.

At the club after the dinner hour, and when business was considered over for the day, there was a good deal of drinking and singing.

There was almost always some young skipper who, stepping forward, would, in the deepest and gruffest tones at his command, ask permission to treat the company to a glass. They know that he has made more than a hundred dollars on one cargo, so he can afford to be free with his money.

When the punch-bowl is placed before the seniors of the party, Harbour-master Snell and the master pilot, a song in praise of the herring is struck up; they empty their glasses after the fashion of their forefathers, and sing in honour of "Gamle Norge," of the shipping trade, and of the constitution.

Late into the night the windows rattled again with the chorus, and the longer they sat the louder they sang, beating time on the table with the thick tumblers.

But there were others in the town who never drank, nor set their feet in the club, and yet whose interest and welfare lay in the fishing. These were the Haugians, the holy ones, as scoffers called them.

Besides Sivert Jespersen and the brothers Egeland, who carried on a large salting business in addition to their store, many other Haugians speculated in herrings. Generally they had been peasant boys, who had come to the town to take service with some of the elders, and had thus learnt the Haugian frugality, exactness, and diligence. As soon as they could start some little business on their own account, they advanced rapidly.

At the fishing, where the life was very wild, they took their part, although they were much ridiculed, because they sang hymns instead of drinking and using bad language.

Gradually people began to see that these good folks were not to be despised. There was nothing whatever against them; they were neither rioters nor spendthrifts; their boats were always ready, and their gear in good order, and although they neither swore nor drank, they would sail a boat with the most daring.

While they bore themselves peaceably and quietly they were ever ready to assert their rights, and people thought twice before they meddled with them.

Sivert Jespersen, too, had been a peasant lad who had worked himself up from nothing. He now owned two large warehouses in the town and several salting-houses in the north. Moreover, he had several shares in sundry vessels.

He no longer went to the fishing himself, as he was over sixty, much bent, and very rheumatic, like most of those who had frequented the winter fishing in their youth.

But when the herring came in, he strolled up to the warehouse in his old-fashioned coat and fur cap, and on such occasions he was radiant with good humour. The whole building is full of people, herrings, salt, and barrels; noise and shouting, the sound of coopering and of hoisting and lowering by ropes.

The floors and steps are wet and slippery with brine and with the blood of herrings dripping down from one floor to another. Fish scales cover the walls, and everywhere there is a smell as if one were in the belly of a whale.

Amidst all this, Sivert Gesvint moves about with a tallow candle in his hand, up and down and round about the whole house, humming a psalm tune as he goes.

There is some disturbance among the fish-girls; they are either quarrelling or playing some practical joke, but so roughly that two barrels packed with herrings are upset, and the contents scattered on the floor and into the salt tubs, making a sad mess.

"Come, come," says Sivert Jespersen, approaching them, his voice mild and soft as usual; "you must treat the gifts of God with care, so that they may not be injured or wasted. Is it not so, dear children?"

He looks from one to the other with his cold grey eye and fixed smile, while the girls silently busy themselves in gathering up and repacking the fish.

It was always considered much more disagreeable to be called "dear children" by Sivert Jespersen than to be called "young devils" by any one else.

Although in their quiet way they throve, and seemed to conduct their affairs with much prudence and discretion, the business affairs of these Haugians rested upon anything but a solid foundation. Two years of failure in the fishing, or a disastrous fire in their uninsured property, and many apparently large fortunes would melt away almost to nothing.

They felt this themselves sometimes, when the herring were late in coming, or when, in the spring time, they found the till empty and the barrels of herrings unsold, and when everything depended upon the rise or fall of prices in Russia or Prussia.

At such times their hands trembled when the post, which only came once a week, arrived. They spent sleepless nights, and it was especially at such times that they would sing hymns.

When they assembled at daily meetings, they read, they prayed, they sang; and as they sat and looked at one another, each knowing how much his neighbour had at stake, knowing, too, how peaceful and guileless they were, and how God had hitherto protected them, they were satisfied that He would not now abandon them—"if not for my sake," some speaker would say, "yet for the sake of others." Then they felt strengthened in prayer, and smiling affectionately at each other, would depart to their homes, greatly comforted.

They were not disappointed; for year after year they throve, and their capital increased. Those who had salted one thousand barrels one year would take three thousand the next. They were on the look-out at all points; they pressed forward at all hazards; and while they seemed so quiet with their psalm-singing and gentle mode of speech, they were, in truth, energetic, even desperate, speculators.

This was thoroughly displeasing to Hans Nilsen Fennefos, not that it was against Hauge's rule that the Brethren should enter into trade, on the contrary.

But this was not the old style of industry, with its reasonable desire for moderate profits. The money came too easily, and in too great abundance. Fennefos observed also that luxury was beginning to creep in among the Brethren; there were even dinner parties, where the eating was excessive.

The fact was that these frugal people were so unaccustomed to joints and puddings, that when they found they could afford them, they took a half-childish pleasure in ordering dinners like those supplied to the great houses.

Fennefos reasoned with and rebuked them; but although they listened, smiled, and thanked him, no change resulted.

Moreover, in the public life of the town, these quiet men, who had become rich unnoticed, began to assert themselves, and it was found that, for many reasons, they had to be considered. Their gentle manners and humble address ceased to provoke ridicule.

By degrees, as the Haugians advanced in worldly affairs, and lost in spiritual life, a superficial piety, proceeding from them and from their movement, crept into society, both in town and country—a sort of perfunctory formalism, which seemed to prosper.

Such was the condition of the place at that time—an old town of new ideas, narrow, crooked, unenlightened, and yet religious; at the same time fresh and bright, looking down upon the blue sea with its gallant ships and hardy seamen.

It should be seen on a summer day, in bright sunshine and a clear northerly wind, when the gulls fly out over the fjord and backwards and forwards along the front of the white-painted warehouses of the harbour, where they are unloading salt, and the wind bears the sound of the sailors' chorus, "Amalia Maria, from Lisbon we come," as the salt rustles along the broad wooden trough down into the lighters alongside, with a never-to-be-forgotten merry sound; the whole town smelling somewhat of herrings, but chiefly of the sea, the fresh North Sea.

Those who had been long away from home, and who had travelled the whole world round, declared that such an air is to be met with nowhere else.

CHAPTER VI

SARAH and Henrietta sat in the workroom winding yarn. Henrietta talked in a whisper. Their mother sat writing letters in the parlour, the door of which was open. She was a little hard of hearing.

". . . And, then, you must know—yes, is it not strange what people will do? for they stole a rope. Just fancy!"

"Who, Henrietta?"

"Why, Lauritz and the others."

"Stole, did you say?"

"Are you out of your senses?" said Henrietta, scandalized at the suggestion. "Do you suppose that Lauritz steals? No; they only took a rubbishing piece of old rope not worth sixpence, which was hanging behind the door of Skipper Worse's storehouse. The rich Skipper Worse, as if such a thing were worth notice!"

"But, Henrietta, you know that it does not depend upon its value. Every one who steals——"

"Is a thief; yes, I know!" exclaimed Henrietta. "But now you must know what they did with the rope; Lauritz told me yesterday afternoon, when I was in the kitchen getting tea ready."

"Whilst there was a meeting here!" said Sarah, in a tone of remonstrance.

Henrietta nodded assent. "On no account must you tell our mother. Lauritz is so funny, I can't help laughing at him. Just imagine! they stretched a rope across the street when it got dark, and two of them held each end. When any one came whom they disliked, they tightened it, and tripped him up. After a time the Commissioner came—you know, the one who is so cross and red-faced—and he tumbled head over heels, and broke his arm."

"I think you must be out of your senses, Henrietta. Surely you do not think it was right to do such a thing?"

"Yes, quite right. You know what a horrid man he is; all the boys in the town hate him, and so do I. At the sessions he sits swearing and scolding incessantly, and when he is at his worst—just think!—he lays about him with his whip. Bah! it serves him right; I wish he had broken both arms, the brute!"

Sarah was thoroughly shocked. At this moment her mother seemed as if she were about to rise from her chair, and the sisters resumed their work diligently.

Sarah sat thinking that this affair of Henrietta's was very wrong, and she doubted whether it was not her duty to tell her mother. Madame Torvestad was strangely lenient towards her younger daughter; she had once said, "As for Henrietta, I am under no apprehension; she is easily influenced, and will in due time improve. It was very different with you, Sarah; for you had a stubborn disposition, which required early discipline. I am thankful to say that neither I nor your excellent father spared the rod, and a blessing has followed it, in that you have become what you are."

This she said with unusual effusion; generally the relations between the mother and daughter were a trifle stiff. They could talk to one another both on worldly and spiritual matters, but there was no real familiarity between them.

Sarah had been brought up under the strongest sense of the duty of children to their parents, and she regarded her mother with veneration. She would sooner have cut off her hand than oppose her, but she could not cast herself on her neck as she often wished to do.

When Henrietta, in the exuberance of her spirits, kissed and embraced her, she experienced a wonderful pleasure, but she would tear herself away, knowing that her mother did not like such demonstrations.

When they had worked on for a short time in silence, Henrietta whispered again:

"He was drunk on Saturday."

"Who?"

"Lauritz."

"Oh! how do you know it?"

"He told me himself."

"But has he no feeling of shame?"

"Well, it was not so bad as all that; he was not downright drunk, you know, only a little 'tight,' as they say."

It was evident that Henrietta was rather proud of him.

Before Sarah could regain her composure after this last shock, her mother called to her.

"Sarah, come here and help me! Where is it that our Lord speaks of the vine?"

"The fifteenth chapter of St. John."

"Read it to me."

Sarah began, and as she was reading, her mother, although apparently absorbed in her letter and in listening, was watching her closely.

Madame Torvestad was in the habit of writing many letters, which were held in much estimation by the Brethren around. They were read out at the meetings, and afterwards carefully preserved, for lending to those who required good counsel. Her letters were indeed kindly and full of affection.

When Sarah read the twelfth verse, "This is my commandment, That ye love one another, as I have loved you," her mother stopped her.

"Yes, that was the verse I was thinking of." She looked down on her letter almost as if she was thinking over what she had written. Sarah was conscious that what her mother said was also directed at her.

"Brotherly love is the first fruits of the true Vine, and that is the love to which the apostle alludes. But, dear brethren, consider how and why you love another, whether because he is a child of God, or whether for earthly reasons, and, mark well, whether when you find that he loves God, he becomes so dear to you that all his other qualities are forgotten."

Sarah blushed a deep red, and bent over her Bible. She was about to read the thirteenth verse, when her mother said: "Thanks, Sarah; you need not read any more, it was only that these reflections on brotherly love made me wish to refresh my memory from Holy Writ."

She proceeded in the same tone, half to Sarah and half to herself: "See, the tempter has again prepared his snares; be watchful, and pray for guidance, that you fall not into them. Sinful affection lies in wait behind brotherly love.

just as the serpent concealed itself among the pleasant fruits of the tree of knowledge. See, then, that you love in the spirit, and not in the flesh. If you love in the spirit, and if you meet with one who seeks the same God, you should love that seeker; and should he be only——" here her words became very impressive—"should he be only a distant seeker, yes, even a wanderer, who but dimly catches a glimpse of the light, and who follows it but feebly, and be his appearance, conversation, and natural mind ever so doubtful, you should love him for the sake of Him who first loved you.

"Thanks, my child, for your assistance. Now go back to your work, and pray that it may be given to you to know what brotherly love is, and that you may not go astray."

When Sarah reached the door, her mother added: "It surprises me that when you and Henrietta are alone together you do not sing a hymn. In my younger days we used always to do so. It lightens labour, and drives away evil thoughts."

Soon afterwards the sisters, in low, clear tones, sang a hymn, which they knew to be a favourite with their mother.

When Henrietta was unable to remember the words, she hummed the tune; while Sarah, who was very pale, sang on with downcast but flashing eyes.

Neither of the girls had observed that Hans Nilsen Fennefos had come up the steps, and was standing outside on the landing.

He stopped and listened to the singing; it reminded him of that night long since, when he heard his mother singing. He was much affected, Sarah's soft voice seemed like his mother's, and his eyes filled with tears.

When he reached his own little room, he sat for some time, distracted by conflicting thoughts. How he wished that at that moment his mother were at his side to counsel him! She, however, had died two years since, and those who stood by her death-bed declared that she had sung herself into heaven.

Hans Nilsen had come from a meeting of the elders. He himself was one of their number, not by reason of his years, but because of his faith, his uprightness, and his experience, conjoined with true wisdom.

A letter had reached him from his native place, complaining that a certain lukewarmness was beginning to manifest itself among the Brethren thereabouts.

It begged imploringly that some man or woman might be sent, who would be able to rekindle the dying flame before it was utterly quenched.

They would prefer Hans Nilsen, but, at the same time, would be grateful for any one whom the elders might send to them.

When this letter was read out, the oldest man among them, a veteran who had known and laboured with Hauge, said: "Now, my dear Hans Nilsen, what is your opinion? Does the spirit call upon you to respond to the appeal of our brethren, or do you know of any other person more fitted for the work?"

"I think that Hans Nilsen seems very well content to be where he is," said Sivert Jespersen, without raising his eyes from the pages of the sermon-book which he was turning over.

Nothing more was spoken; but they were so well acquainted with one another, understood so well the least hint or the slightest inflection of voice, that the pause which followed was as suggestive and as interesting to them as a discussion.

At last Fennefos stood up, and said: "I will search myself, and pray for guidance; to-morrow, or perhaps this evening at the meeting, I may, God willing, give you my answer."

He sat down, purposing in all sincerity to examine himself, and to seek guidance.

He had already observed here and there something of the disapprobation which had manifested itself in Sivert Jespersen's remark. The majority, no doubt, would gladly retain him; but there were some to whom his presence was oppressive.

From such quarters came whispers that Madame Torvestad's house might be dangerous to a lay-preacher, and might tempt him to weakness.

As soon as Hans Nilsen observed this, he had at once thought of Sarah. He had searched his own heart with the utmost rigour, but he could not be certain that the pleasure he experienced in her company was not the beginning of a sinful affection, or, if not so, whether it were what it ought to be, a heartfelt friendship and a true feeling of devotion for a woman who was purer and better than all others.

In the mean time, he was unable to arrive at any decision, and he began to be pained and disturbed in mind. At last, one day, he went straight to Madame Torvestad, asking if she would advise him to marry, and, if so, whether she could recommend any Christian-minded woman as his helpmate.

Madame Torvestad was not taken by surprise; it was a common custom among the Haugians, and especially the Herrnhutters, to follow the guidance of the elders in such matters. Malicious persons in the town even declared that the lamented Torvestad had got his wife in a lottery at Christiansfeldt.

It seemed so natural for Madame Torvestad to think of her own daughters, and first and foremost of Sarah, that Hans Nilsen's question seemed almost as good as a proposal for her.

She answered evasively; she did not believe that so well-known and so highly valued a preacher could be permitted to give up his journeyings throughout the country. He must be aware, she said, that when a man is married it is not easy for him to absent himself from home. Nor could she at that moment think of any woman who would suit him.

Hans Nilsen was surprised and disappointed. He could not see why Madame Torvestad should not give her daughter to him, and it never occurred to him that she might harbour other designs. He did not for a moment think of opposing or attempting to overcome her determination; on the contrary, he strove to convince himself that she was in the right, and with some effort he succeeded.

A week had passed since the conversation with Madame Torvestad, and during this time Hans Nilsen had examined himself closely. He came to the conclusion that if he had been drawn to Sarah by any earthly feeling, the disappointment must needs have caused him grievous pain.

That he did not feel some grievous pain, he was not prepared to say. He would have been exceedingly happy if all had gone as he wished; but now that he was near Sarah, and felt no unusual desire either to approach her or to fly from temptation, he was satisfied that his thoughts were pure, and he began to feel more at peace with himself, although somewhat depressed.

But that letter which had arrived to-day, and the evident suspicion which had lurked behind Sivert Jespersen's words, and his own feelings when he listened to Sarah's singing! All his doubts broke out afresh, and as he sat on his small hard sofa, when the evening shades began to fall, tumultuous feelings arose, and thoughts hitherto strange to him arose in his mind, accusing and answering each other.

Why did he not depart and obey the call, journeying from cottage to cottage throughout the dark winter? Why did he not hasten to the poor anxious souls scattered about the country, struggling in their loneliness with doubts and temptations? Why did he not long, as formerly, to combat with the powers of hell?

Was it not, after all, as Sivert Jespersen had said? Was he not living too much at ease where he was; and was it not Sarah—Sarah alone that made him so contented and so happy in everything around him?

He felt that one of the evil moods which sometimes visited him, especially when he was younger, was near. He wrung his hands, and prayed that the spirit might guide him, and that all might be made clear to him. He writhed as if in pain, and his breathing became short and laboured.

Thoughts, evil thoughts, which were not his own, stormed around him, and instead of earnest self-examination, he was only able to recall the doubts and scoffings which he had encountered. Confused phantasms crowded his brain; and when he strove to come to a decision, to find solid ground somewhere, everything vanished, he lay powerless, bound hand and foot, and Satan's self appeared deriding him.

Then, crying aloud: "Get thee behind me, Satan!" he threw himself, crushed and exhausted, upon the sofa, burying his face in his hands.

But as he closed his eyes, small rays of light blazed under his eyelids, glimmered, vanished, and then returned, until it seemed to him that suddenly—in the darkness—he could read in his closed eyes the word "Go."

He sprang up, and looking around in the dimly lighted room, repeated "Go! go!" His brain became clearer, his peace of mind returned, his prayer had been heard. The spirit had guided him, and had dispelled the darkness. He knelt down and gave thanks.

He threw off his coat and waistcoat, opened the window, and let the rain fall on his face; he could now see his way clearly. Here he was in danger; he must go, and the sooner the better. Now once more, God be thanked, he longed to struggle with the powers of hell.

He lighted his candle, and shaved himself with an unshaken hand. He was calm, a little exhausted, but wonderfully happy and contented. Afterwards he washed and dressed himself anew.

His forehead was not very high, but broad and open; his hair dark and wiry, for which reason he kept it cut short. His nose was large and aquiline, his mouth from his lips thin, and his chin well formed and powerful.

As his lips were beardless, his teeth were plainly visible, close-set, well-formed peasant teeth; and there were many persons who liked to fix their eyes on his mouth when he spoke or sang at the meetings. It was a mouth red and white, fresh and clear, which never touched tobacco or spirits.

Cleanliness was especially the characteristic of the man, not only in his clothes and linen, but in his face, with its regular features and closely shaved chin. From his eyes, which were grey and bright, a pure, earnest light shone, and there were those who did not care to face them.

He had nothing of that inquisitive, offensive gaze with which many of the Brethren seemed to bore into a sinner, as if they were piercing downwards into a deep abyss of secret vice and wickedness. The look of Hans Nilsen, on the contrary, gave the impression of expecting to meet with the same purity as that from whence it came.

Perhaps it was for this reason that so many looked to one side when they stood in front of him.

Nearly all the Haugians in the town were at the meeting, for it was a Saturday. There was a movement of satisfaction among them when Fennefos went to Endre Egeland, who stood by the little desk, about to read out a sermon, and asked permission to say a word.

All roused themselves, in order to enjoy the words of the popular preacher; it was long since they had heard him, for of late he had not been much inclined to speak in public.

But their joy was not unmixed when Hans Nilsen began:

"Beloved brothers and sisters, I stand here in order to bid you farewell."

Still they were pleased to hear him, the elders nodding their heads approvingly, and smiling at one another.

It was the old sound, the well-known weighty words as of Hauge's own time, before much and many things had weakened and corrupted the pure wine.

Hans Nilsen differed in manner from those who generally conducted the meetings. His voice was not forced, nor his head bowed down, and a smile never rested on his features. Tall and grand, he stood among them with few and simple gestures; and as he turned his head, the light of his clear, grey eyes lit up the distant corners of the room.

First, he exhorted them earnestly, and as one in authority; then he thanked them warmly for their kind and faithful brotherly feeling, turning himself as he said it, in such a way that all noticed it, towards Sivert Jespersen; and, again, he especially thanked those who had held out a helping hand when he was almost stumbling and going astray.

Lastly, he offered up a prayer, which was long remembered among them. It was one of those moments when his words were winged, and his whole being glowed with love and fire.

They afterwards flocked round him, in order to press his hand, or to get just one word from him; for no one knew how long he would be absent. When a lay-preacher so valued as Fennefos began such a journey, he might be led from district to district round the whole country; for all were desirous to hear him, and there would be many who would urge him to come to them, when it was known that he was on his travels.

There was, therefore, sorrow and tears among them; for Fennefos was, in truth, one of the strongest supports of the community. With respect to many others, Endre Egeland or Sivert Jespersen, for example, there was some drawback; at least, people had always something to say against them, and they were environed by slander and ridicule.

But on Hans Nilsen, not the smallest stain had ever appeared. The new clergyman in the town, who seemed to have some sympathy with the Haugians, spoke of him with the utmost respect; and of this the Brethren were not a little proud, for it did not happen every day that a lay-preacher was praised by a regular pastor.

Hans Nilsen was to depart in two days, as soon as the elders had prepared his credentials, as well as the books and tracts which he was to distribute.

It was the end of October, and he proposed to journey along the coast, from farm to farm, as far as Christiansand, gathering the Brethren together as opportunity offered.

From Christiansand he intended to travel over Soetersdal, and at Christmas he expected to reach his native place.

CHAPTER VII

MADAME TORVESTAD was really in earnest when she declared how much she valued Hans Nilsen's presence in her house, and that she grieved at his departure.

That his removal at this juncture was extremely convenient was a fact that, on the other hand, she carefully concealed.

She was scheming to the utmost to secure Skipper Worse for her daughter.

Her motives were very complicated. She would talk of her interest in the poor erring soul that could only be saved by such means. Those, however, who knew her best, knew well that her strongest passion was a constantly increasing desire for power and influence.

From her point of view Jacob Worse was well worth capturing, especially since he had entered into partnership with Garman. Not only would such an alliance strengthen the Brethren outwardly, but—what was more important in her eyes—it would greatly enhance her own position if this new and wealthy brother should be added to them by her efforts.

That she would succeed in making a brother of Jacob Worse, Madame Torvestad never for a moment doubted. She had some experience of the world, and she had known many elderly men who had married even younger women. She would work upon him through her daughter, and her influence would extend itself from her humble apartments over the whole house.

The Brethren would be grateful to her, and the cause of religion would be furthered.

Sarah foresaw all that was coming; after those words about the vine, she was in no doubt as to what was in store for her.

When Hans Nilsen left, he presented her with his greatest treasure, an autograph letter from Hauge to his mother.

The paper was old and worn, and the ink had faded. Fennefos, who was a skilful bookbinder, had himself made a handsome case, in which to keep it, and had printed her name and a text on the cover.

The womenfolk talked about this. It seemed strange that Hans Nilsen should part with such a treasure.

Those who made any allusion to the affair in Madame Torvestad's presence, met with such an icy reception that they were not encouraged to pursue the subject.

Sarah was in a distracted state, pleased with the gift and with the kind words he had spoken to her when he left, but otherwise she was wretched, hopelessly wretched. At night when she lay in bed, she wept, and prayed for strength to control herself.

One night her mother entered her bed-chamber; it was dark, and Sarah, who was bathed in tears, heard nothing until she spoke. "You can see now that I was right, my child. Thank the Lord that your eyes were opened in time to the danger."

She said this in such an imperious and reproachful tone that Sarah started up in her bed, and continued to sit up for some time without weeping, whilst harsh and bitter thoughts took possession of her.

It was the old Adam! but she could not struggle against it. She allowed the evil thoughts to take their course—wherever they would, over all the faults she had detected among the Brethren or suspected in her own mother; over Skipper Worse, with his oaths and his flavour of stale tobacco-smoke, until he seemed quite unbearable—away, far away into forbidden regions, where there was sunshine and joy, where she was alone with a tall, strong man.

She threw herself back on the bed, dreaming and drowsy. When she awoke in the morning, a mountain of misery seemed to weigh upon her.

At first, Jacob Worse was unaware of the happiness in store for him. Many hints from Madame Torvestad were necessary before it dawned upon him that the fair Sarah, whom he had seen grow up from childhood, might be the wife for him.

But when he was awake to it, the sentiment which both blinds and invigorates old men took possession of him.

There was a successful fishing that year, and Jacob Worse was indefatigable and in high spirits. Thoughts of the snug room at Madame Torvestad's, his comfortable place by the side of Sarah, the soft white hands which brought him his tea—in which, as a great favour, Madame Torvestad permitted a few drops of rum—all tended to make him happy; and even when he was most actively engaged among the herrings, a quiet almost dreamy smile, which few observed and none understood, would steal over his weather-beaten face.

Never before had he been so enterprising or so successful. This year he salted on account of the firm and for himself, and bought a quantity of herrings. Brisk and cheerful, he brought life and gaiety with him wherever he went, and all agreed that Jacob Worse was a fine old fellow.

It was not safe, however, to call him old to his face. "Old, forsooth!" he would say, pushing his glass from him, when any one was so ill-advised as to propose the health of "Old Worse."

Whenever during the fishing season he could find an opportunity for going into the town with a cargo of herrings, he would hasten to finish his work at the warehouse, and to wash himself.

He scrubbed himself with soap, and changed from top to toe. At the same time, he was not quite certain that a little of the flavour of the herring might not cling to him, and so—if Randulf should but hear of it!—he sprinkled himself with scent, which Lauritz in all secrecy had purchased for him.

Dressed, shaved, washed, and combed, with his grizzled hair sticking up stiffly from above his ears—in such guise Captain Worse, of the firm of Garman and Worse, sallied forth across the yard to woo.

On these occasions there was something almost chivalrous about him, which became him well, and would have become him even better had he been paying his attentions to the mother instead of to the daughter.

But to marry a serious, elderly widow was something which had never occurred to the gay captain, and of this Madame Torvestad had long been conscious.

Now that she had got him on the track, and had observed the youthful ardour with which he followed it, madame changed her tactics, began to hold back, would not understand his hints, and, when they became obvious, raised innumerable objections.

Sarah should be purchased dearly. First, there was the great difference of age; she must say it was greater than she had any idea of; she never could have believed that Captain Worse was so much over fifty.

That, however, was of comparatively little consequence. The most important point was his religious state, his habit of swearing, his worldly mindedness, manifested in his devotion to all things pertaining to this life.

Worse admitted that he was not one of the best of men, but, at the same time, he protested that he was very far from being the worst; moreover, he might improve.

He would indeed have to improve, if it came to a question of marrying Sarah. He would have to change many of his ways.

Worse promised everything; he felt certain that he could submit to any number, even of the longest meetings, if he could but have Sarah by his side, and could take her home with him afterwards.

The affair, however, made no progress. Worse hardly knew whether it moved backwards or forwards. In the meantime he was completely infatuated, and trotted about after Sarah like an old turkey cock.

What Sarah's own feelings might be was not much discussed by her mother and her admirer. Madame Torvestad "knew her daughter;" and Jacob Worse, the elderly gallant, fancied that when Sarah blushed, was constrained when she was alone with him, and refused his presents, it was only girlish prudishness, of which he had seen instances, both in the Baltic and in the Mediterranean.

Although Consul Garman seemed to keep up such slight intercourse with the town, he had his feelers out, and all that happened there, both small and great, was pretty well known at Sandsgaard. The two sisters, Birgitte and Mette, especially interested themselves in everything without exception.

It came, therefore, to the Consul's ears that Jacob Worse was courting, and it both displeased and made him anxious.

That his partner should enter upon any new matrimonial alliance was very distasteful to him, as it would tend to complicate matters; and his especial fear was that these good people—he knew the family well—would be the ruin of his excellent captain.

Consul Garman almost hated the sectaries, although he knew but little about them. It revolted him to think that religion, which was given to man for enlightenment and instruction in virtue and rational conduct, should be so misused by ignorant fanatics and enthusiasts as to pervert and distract the lower classes, who were rather in need of sound and practical guidance.

He therefore sent a boat for Captain Worse, as soon as he learnt from his sisters-in-law that he was likely to marry Madame Torvestad's daughter.

When Worse arrived, the Consul began to talk with much eagerness about a certain vessel which was for sale at Bremen. They got hold of the register, looked into dimensions, discussed age and value, and finally came to the conclusion that it might prove fit for the business of the firm.

The one became infected with the eagerness of the other. It was not often that the Consul plunged so deeply into a novel scheme; but before Worse knew what he was about, it was proposed that he should leave either to-morrow or the day after, in a Bremen schooner, which lay in the roads waiting for a fair wind, in order to purchase the vessel, if it answered the description given, and if there were no other reason to the contrary.

Having done this, he was to navigate it to Sandsgaard, or, if an opportunity offered, he should take a good cargo on board and sail—no matter where.

Full of zeal and energy, Worse departed, in order to make his preparations for the voyage. When he found himself again in the boat it occurred to him, all of a sudden, that he would be separated from Sarah. The good ship lost its interest, and the affair assumed a doubtful aspect. His zeal cooled, and he conjured up a thousand difficulties as they rowed across the bay.

Consul Garman, however, rubbed his hands; he had taken matters in time. He sat down and proceeded to make calculations about this Bremen ship, wondering whether the venture would prove successful.

In the afternoon, Madame Torvestad observed that Worse's servant-girls were very busy in the yard, brushing his clothes and preparing his kit.

"Is the captain going away, Martha?" she inquired, in a friendly tone, speaking from the verandah, which ran round the portion of the building which she occupied.

"Yes," answered Martha, rather sulkily. Madame Torvestad was no favourite with the servants.

"Ah, indeed! and do you know whither?"

"No; but it is going to be a long voyage, longer even than the last, I believe."

Martha had a suspicion that this would annoy Madame Torvestad, and she was right. Madame was in a state of the utmost consternation, still she maintained her composure, returning to her apartments, and standing for some time, in order to consider what she should do.

"Sarah, put the kettle on. Captain Worse is going away. Martha says so, but I think she must be mistaken. What is your opinion?"

"Mine, Mother!"

Madame Torvestad would have said more, but the expression of Sarah's face was so peculiar that she desisted. "Sarah is prudent," she thought to herself. "It is not necessary."

Upon this she smoothed her hair, took her cloak, and left the room. She went out the back way, and so round to the front door; she did not care to pass through the yard, where Martha was.

Jacob Worse was in an irritable condition; he was talking with the head man at the warehouse, who managed for him during his absence. His own private business in the town was not affected by his admission into the firm.

Sandsgaard, with all its various branches of business, remained as before, entirely under the control of the Consul. The partnership, in fact, confined itself to certain departments in which Jacob Worse's capital was actually employed, especially to those pertaining to their business as shipowners.

When Jacob Worse saw Madame Torvestad, he dismissed the warehouseman, and saluted her in an excited manner.

"I come to wish you a prosperous and happy voyage, Captain Worse."

"Thanks—h'm—many thanks, madame. I would otherwise—"

"Will it be a long voyage?"

"It is impossible to say. He wishes me to—"

"Who did you say?"

"The Consul—Consul Garman; he is sending me to Bremen to purchase a ship."

"Sending!" said Madame Torvestad, with an incredulous smile. "I did not know that one partner could 'send' another."

"Partner! oh yes! You see, he is Consul Garman, and I am Skipper Worse; and it will never be otherwise. Moreover, when it comes to purchasing a ship, it is just the job for me."

"You surprise me, and it distresses me that you do not tell me the real reason of your departure. I think we might have expected it of you."

He stared at her with his mouth open.

"You must know this, Captain Worse," she continued, "that I am satisfied you would not undertake this voyage unless you wished to get out of your engagement with us altogether."

She was about to proceed in this somewhat menacing manner, but the captain sprang up, excited, and red in the face.

"No, Madame Torvestad! I tell you what it is—you do me a confounded injustice. Pardon me, I should not have sworn, but I cannot help it. From the very first I have worried and schemed until I was black in the face, in order to escape this voyage; and then you come and tell me that I am behaving with deceit and devilry. I think everybody is mad to-day."

He stamped round the room, clawing at his hair; but Madame Torvestad eyed him with satisfaction—a weight had been removed from her heart.

A certain nervousness and uneasiness which had oppressed her when she entered vanished at once, and she resumed her usual imperious manner, as a mother should who has to deal with a wavering suitor.

"After all we have talked of lately, I must say I was much surprised on hearing of this sudden voyage."

"Do you suppose that I have not thought of this? I assure you, Madame Torvestad, that when I think that I am about to leave without so much as a definite promise, it almost drives me mad. The devil may take the Bremen ship, if I can find an excuse or some way out of it."

"Ah, twenty years ago, Jacob Worse would have found some way out in such a case, I am sure."

This was to attack him on his weakest side. That any one should consider him too old, touched him to the quick; and he proceeded to give Madame Torvestad so warm a description of his feelings, that she was constrained to stop him in all haste.

"Good, good, Captain Worse! Yes, yes; I don't doubt it!" she kept on exclaiming. "But more than earthly love is necessary, however real it may be. The man to whom I could with confidence entrust my child, my Sarah, must also be joined to her in the love of God; and, you know, I have often told you that your life as a seaman is full of temptations, and little likely to bring forth good fruits."

"Ah, yes, madame, the flesh is weak in many respects," answered Captain Worse, who fancied he was quoting Scripture.

"Yes, that it is, Captain Worse—some of us more, some less; but just for that reason we should avoid a life which especially leads us to temptation. Fancy, if I had given you my daughter, and you had suddenly left her like this soon after the marriage!"

"No, madame; there would have been nothing of the sort, you may take your oath of that."

"If I were now—I merely put the case before you—if I were now to give my consent, do you believe that the

Consul—that your partner would permit you to put off the voyage?"

"Of course, of course; that is understood." He was becoming excited at the prospect before him.

"Could I depend upon you?"

"Yes, by—"

"Stop; don't swear! I can believe you better without it. Sit down again, and listen to what I have to say.

"I have thought much of all this of late; a voice within me seems to say that an alliance with my daughter would be for the good of your soul. Yes, after much anxiety and deliberation, I had thought of fixing the wedding for next Sunday—"

"I beg your par— What do you say?" cried Worse, jumping up from his chair. "Ah, madame, you are a devil of a woman!"

"But now, when I find that a sudden order to go to sea can tear you away from your family, and expose you to danger and to temptations, which can easily—we know how easily—choke the good seed, I cannot think of entrusting my child, my beloved Sarah, to you."

"But, Madame Torvestad, I won't go! I will tell the Consul that he must get some other person. I swear to you I won't go!"

"Not this time, perhaps; but the next time that your partner wants—"

"Never! If I get Sarah, I promise—"

He stopped, and, as he looked out of the window, he caught sight of the *Hope's* top-gallant yards away out in Sandsgaard Bay.

Madame Torvestad, smiling somewhat sourly, proceeded. "Do not promise that which you cannot perform and do not allow any consideration for our feelings to prevent your drawing back. No doubt Sarah would be prepared, but as yet she knows nothing with certainty. I have merely talked of the affair with some friends, and I had thought of celebrating the wedding very quietly, as is the custom with us; just the pastor and a couple of the Brethren. Your house is ready, and you would simply bring her to it."

"I promise you that I will give up the sea from the day that I marry your daughter," said Jacob Worse, giving her his hand.

He was beginning to think of bringing Sarah to his house, and having her there always, by his side.

But madame said: "It is a perplexing affair. I have heard of many sailors who were unable to give up the sea, although advanced in years, and possessed of worldly goods, as well as of wife and children. It is difficult to understand it. I should have thought that, on the contrary, a sailor would be grateful for a haven of rest after a stormy life."

"You are quite right, madame. It is just so; I see it now. Give me your daughter, and you will see how I shall improve in every way, just as you wish."

They shook hands, and Worse proposed that they should at once go across to Sarah. But when they reached the yard, where Martha received orders to put the clothes back into the house, he began to hesitate.

"What do you think she will say to it?" he inquired, in a low voice.

"Sarah will be faithful and affectionate to the man whom her mother, prayerfully, has chosen for her," said Madame Torvestad, in such a positive tone that he was much comforted.

Sarah heard them approaching. She had long expected them; and when they came, there was no trace of the tears she had been shedding. Pale as usual, and with downcast eyes, she entered the room, whither her mother called her.

"Sarah, here is a man who seeks you as his wife. I have promised on your behalf that you will be a good and faithful helpmate to him before God and man. Am I not right my child? You will comply with your mother's wish, and so obey the mandate of God."

"Yes, Mother."

"Take each other's hands, then. In God's name, Amen."

Jacob Worse was much affected. He tried to say a few words about being a father to her, but when he reached the middle of the sentence, it struck him that it was not appropriate. When he essayed to utter something more suitable, there was no sense in it.

He therefore squeezed the hand of Madame Torvestad somewhat severely; and then, taking that of his betrothed more tenderly, was pleased to find how soft and delicate it was.

He comported himself very awkwardly all the evening; but he was so thoroughly happy, that he never noticed the expression of Sarah's pale face.

When he returned to his own house, he paced up and down in ecstasy. It was Tuesday—only four days to Sunday. He must put his house to rights; it was not half smart enough.

When he had left, madame sent Henrietta to bed; Sarah would have gone also, but her mother detained her.

"You should thank God for all His loving-kindness, Sarah."

"Yes, Mother."

"Will you not also thank me?"

Sarah stood silent and unmoved.

Her mother felt as if she had been pierced through. "Sarah!" she said, sharply.

But when Sarah looked up, there was a something in her steadfast eyes which made her mother recoil; she said no more, except to bid her "Good night," and upon this her daughter left.

Madame Torvestad fell into a reverie. The memories of her own youth rose up before her, and they were not very pleasant. She, too, had been given to a man whom she did not know; he, too, was older than she was, but he had known how to deal with her in the right way. She remembered the tears she had shed at the first, and how in time all went well with her. She had been saved from worldly vanities, and from these she would now protect her daughter.

But in that look of Sarah's there was something which made her shrink, and which stung her deeply. She, who was generally so confident about herself and all that she did, felt a painful misgiving.

All these newly revived memories, and a vague feeling that she did not fully comprehend this impassive daughter, made her slumbers uneasy, and troubled her with evil dreams.

Henrietta, who heard Sarah sobbing, crept into her bed, and strove to comfort her.

CHAPTER VIII

THE first shadow which fell on Skipper Worse's happiness was the meeting with Consul Garman, when he went to report his betrothal to him.

"Good morning, Worse," said the Consul. "The Bremen captain has just been here; he will take you with the greatest pleasure, and as he is quite ready to go to sea, it might be as well if you drove out to Smörvigen to-day. Our carriage shall meet you in the town, and you will thus be ready to sail directly the wind is fair.

"Yes; thanks, Herr Consul; but—I'm——"

"Is there anything the matter?"

"Yes, unfortunately there is something the matter."

"Anything gone wrong?"

"No; rather gone right," said Worse, simpering. It seemed as if he was a little emboldened. "I am going to be married."

"Good Heavens!" exclaimed the Consul, forgetting himself. "H'm! going to marry. I never expected this. With whom, if I may venture to inquire?"

"With Madame Torvestad's daughter; the Consul knows that she lives in a portion of my house."

"Yes; but I did not know—I should hardly have thought that Madame Torvestad had a daughter of a suitable age."

"She is rather young—rather younger than I am," answered Worse, who was growing red in the face, "but otherwise a very sedate and serious girl."

"Her family belongs to the Brethren. Does Captain Worse propose to join the Haugians?"

"No, indeed," answered the other; and he would have smiled, but that the Consul's manner did not give him any encouragement.

"Well, that is your own affair, my dear Jacob Worse," said the Consul, rising up in order to give him his hand. "Accept my congratulations, and I hope you may never repent of the step you are taking. When is the wedding to take place?"

"On Sunday!"

"Well, that is rather sharp work. I trust you may never have to repent of it."

When he left, the Consul thought for a moment of running after him, and of enlightening him thoroughly about the Haugians and all their hypocrisies—from his point of view. But on consideration he desisted.

Morten W. Garman was a prudent man, who never wasted words. He had seen enough of Jacob Worse in their brief conversation, and he was well versed in the various symptoms of persons who were enamoured.

Jacob Worse did not regain his equanimity until he got back to his own rooms, where there was a detestable turmoil of charwomen and all sorts of workpeople.

But he went about happy and contented, now and then visiting the back building, in order to get a glimpse of his Sarah. It was not much that he was able to see of her; for there, also, every one was busy with needles and thread and with marking-ink, and she sat bending over her work.

In this way he spent his time, restless from very happiness. He was quite unconscious of the fact that his friends ridiculed him, predicting all sorts of misfortunes. He also forgot the uncomfortable interview with the Consul.

As for the ship at Bremen, which had interested them both so much, not another word, strangely enough, was ever again spoken about it.

On Sunday, they were married in Madame Torvestad's parlour, only a few intimate friends being present. In the afternoon, Sarah removed with Jacob Worse to his house.

At last Skipper Randulf returned, and Worse hastened to greet him. They plunged at once into conversation, narrating their mutual adventures; still it was not so pleasant as it might have been. The subject of Rio had grown rather out of date, and there was a certain constraint between them, until Randulf broke out: "Now, you old heathen! I hear you have married one of the eleven thousand wise virgins."

"Yes, my boy; she is one of the right sort," said Worse, winking at him.

"Well, take care that she does not make a fool of you, as Sivert Gesvint and the others did."

"Thank you for nothing; Jacob Worse knows what women are before to-day."

"Ah! do you know, Jacob, I sometimes think you were not very fortunate in your first wife."

"Don't talk about her, she was half mad. Mind you, Sarah is very different." And then he began a long story about all her perfections, sometimes sinking his voice to a whisper, although they were quite alone in Randulf's parlour.

Thomas Randulf, however, smiled incredulously, which secretly annoyed Worse; and the more earnest he became in describing his wife's merits and his own happiness, the more suspiciously did Randulf's long nose draw down towards the upturned corners of his mouth, until at last Worse, becoming bored with him, was about to leave.

"Oh, no! Come, just take a glass; there is no such hurry, Jacob."

"Yes, I must go; it is half-past eleven, and we dine at twelve."

"A-ha, it's beginning already!" cried Randulf, triumphantly. "You are tied to your wife's apron-strings. I suppose you don't dare take another glass for fear she may notice it. Ha, ha! you have done for yourself, Jacob, while I was away."

The result of this was that Worse remained until half-past twelve, and came home rather red in the face and with watery eyes.

His wife had waited dinner. She looked very grave, graver than usual; and when he essayed to tell her in a light airy way that Randulf was come, she added, to his great annoyance: "Yes, I can see that he has."

It was worse, however, when, without saying a word, she removed the decanter from the table. He was always accustomed to a dram at dinner.

However, he made no objection. Randulf's strong marsala had begun to work upon him, and he did not feel so confident of his powers of speech as to venture upon a remonstrance. They dined, therefore, in silence, and afterwards he laid himself down as usual on the sofa for a siesta.

Generally he took only a short nap, but on this occasion he did not wake up till five o'clock, when he was much surprised to find himself enveloped in a grey wrapper, and on a chair by his side a basin of gruel.

He lay still, and tried to collect his thoughts. His head throbbed, and his memory was neither clear nor perfect. He remembered that two boys had laughed at him when he jumped lightly over the doorstep outside the Brothers Egeland's store, and that he had felt much inclined to complain of them to the police. He had also a vision of a decanter which moved away, and vanished in a cupboard.

He was about to get up; but at this moment Sarah entered the room. "No, no; you are ill. You must keep quiet."

"Oh, nonsense, Sarah! there is nothing the matter with me. It was just—"

"I will go and fetch mother," she said, moving towards the door.

"No, no! What do we want with her? I would rather remain lying here, as you insist upon it."

He laid himself down again, and she reached him the gruel, which proved a great relief to his parched and fevered throat. He thanked her, and would have taken her hand but that he was unable to seize it.

She stood behind him, looking at his grey head, and it was well for him that he could not see her eyes.

Jacob Worse spent the rest of the day upon the sofa, and, after the lassitude caused by his morning excess, felt all the better for it. The next day he was all right again; but he did not dare ask for the decanter; it was gone, and it never reappeared.

From his son Romarino, Worse received a very disagreeable letter. This young gentleman pointed out to him the folly of taking a young wife at his advanced age, and, without the least compunction, bewailed the pecuniary loss which it might entail on him, Romarino.

Worse was very angry, and handed the letter to Sarah, who read it, whilst he walked up and down the room, fuming.

"Yes, you cannot expect it otherwise," said Sarah. "The young man was never taught anything better, either by you or by his mother. As you sow, so will you reap. Shall I answer the letter?"

"Yes; I should be very grateful to you, if you would, Sarah," said Jacob Worse. It was a great relief to him.

It was surprising to see how readily Sarah assumed her position, and how completely she changed everything, and put the house in order. It was, in fact, necessary; for there was much waste and mismanagement, as was natural where the head of the house was a man, who was, moreover, often absent from home.

During the first weeks after the marriage, Sarah took no interest in anything. When her half-developed youth, her dawning wishes and hopes were suddenly and unmercifully crushed, a thick cloud seemed to descend upon her, obscuring her life, and leaving no prospect of escape, except by a welcome death.

But one day a new feeling was awakened in her. Returning home from shopping in the town, she found her mother making a clearance in her rooms, placing chairs along the walls, and laying her small books about upon the tables.

As Sarah entered, her mother said, and in a voice not quite so resolute as was her wont: "I think we will hold the meeting here in your rooms; they are larger and lighter than mine."

"Have you asked my husband?"

"My husband!" It was the first time, and there was such a stiffness and determination about these two words, that the widow unconsciously drew herself back.

Sarah quietly collected her mother's small books in a heap, which she placed on a seat by the door, put a couple of chairs back into their proper places, and, without looking up, said: "I cannot have a meeting in my house without having consulted my husband."

"You are quite right, dear Sarah," said Madame Torvestad, in an affectionate tone, but with quivering lips; "and

I ought to have thought of it. I hope you will come over to us in the evening."

"If my husband will."

Upon this her mother left, taking her books with her. Sarah pressed her hands upon her bosom; for, quietly as the affair had passed off, both felt that there had been a struggle, and that the daughter had remained the victor. She stood for some time looking at the solid mahogany furniture, the curtains, mirrors, and the key-cupboard, the key of which she carried in her pocket. She opened it, and looked at the numerous keys which hung inside.

It was true that her husband, in the first fulness of his happiness, had said: "See, all this is yours, and you can do what you will with it; if there be any thing wanting, and you desire to have it, only speak the word, and it shall be yours at once."

She had never given much heed to these words. Of what good was it all to her? Could anything recompense her for her marred life?

It was the sight of her mother busying herself in her room that roused her, and henceforth she became alive to her position.

Before long the system of joint purchasing for the two households, which Madame Torvestad had at first managed, was brought to an end. Sarah undertook to manage her own affairs. Gently, but inexorably, the mother's rule was restricted to her own apartments.

Sarah was intelligent and well trained; she inherited all her mother's aptitude for rule and order. Hitherto she had never had an opportunity of manifesting it at home, her mother being always over her, and she had toiled like a servant girl, faithful and upright, yet with no other interest for the things under her charge than that they should not be injured.

Now, however, she had her own household, was her own mistress, and had, moreover, ampler means at her command than her mother had.

The rich Madame Worse, as people began to term her in the shops, was, in fact, a very different person, and much more important than the widow Torvestad. It was a consciousness of this that first gave Sarah a new interest in life, and tended to thaw some of that frigidity which had begun to settle upon her. When the first and the worst period was over, she buried her hopes and her youth as well as she could, giving herself up to prayer and study, whilst, at the same time, the management of her household affairs prevented her from sinking into melancholy.

This change was much to the advantage of Jacob Worse. The icy coldness with which she had treated him from the first had been occasionally apparent to him in the midst of his happiness; but now her behaviour was different—never indeed affectionate, scarcely even friendly, but she reconciled herself to him, made his home comfortable, and interested herself in his business affairs.

Jacob Worse explained them to her, and was never weary of expressing his surprise that women could show so much intelligence. It was not long before she was able to give him good advice, and it ended by his consulting her about everything.

In this way the year passed on, and the winter began. Sarah was as regular as formerly at the meetings, and, when at her mother's, she often sat in her old place by the Bible. Her comeliness increased, and her manner became more self-possessed, her dress also was improved; not that it was too conspicuous, for the most austere of the Haugians would not have been able to find fault with it; but the womenfolk, who understood such things, noticed that her linen was of the finest that could be procured, that the woollen stuffs she used were almost as costly as silk, and that when she wore a white collar round her neck, it was of real lace, worth a couple of dollars an ell.

The men, too, noticed something unusual about the young wife, and would say to their spouses: "Look at Sarah; you should dress like her; you should manage the house as she does." The mother also received her meed of praise for having brought up her daughter so well.

Skipper Worse did not always attend the meetings. Whenever he manifested a preference for the club, or for a visit to Randulf, Sarah raised no objection.

But, in truth, he preferred his own house, and throughout the winter, when the candles were lit early, he sat at the table with his work. Jacob Worse was very neat-handed, and in his youth had learnt something of ship-building. He now applied himself to the construction of a model, an ell and a half long, which he intended to rig and equip after the pattern of the *Hope of the Family* down to the smallest detail.

Sarah read aloud to him, knitting the while. It was Scriver, Johan Arndt, Luther, or some such other. Worse did not listen very attentively; but her voice was pleasant to him; and she looked so well when the light fell on her clear forehead and dark smooth hair.

At the club, they were far too facetious; even Randulf rallied him in a disagreeable manner. I do not know how it was, but Randulf's return had proved a disappointment; he was always making remarks about the marriage, he himself being a widower with grown-up children. His eldest son was a captain, and lived in the same town.

Another thing, too, annoyed him. Randulf was always speculating upon what sort of a fishing they might expect that year; and Worse remembered his promise to Madame Torvestad.

One day, however, Sarah let fall a few words, showing that she was prepared for his departure as usual.

"But I should tell you," said Worse, "that before I married, I promised your mother that I would never——"

"I know it. Mother told me all about it; but as she exacted the promise on my account, so I now release you from it. You are free to go if you wish."

Sarah had said as much to her mother when they talked the matter over. It was either because she had no objection to be rid of her husband for a time, or because in that respect also she wished to show herself independent of her mother.

At least this was the way in which the latter interpreted it, and it made her reflect more and more.

Worse now became very eager to talk of all that he would do at the fishing. Randulf thought to himself, "He has got leave."

The fishing that year was bad; the fish were unevenly dispersed, and much on the move. The weather, also, was stormy and bad. Things did not go well with Skipper Worse, his former luck deserted him, and, as some thought his former daring. It was the universal opinion that Worse was growing old.

"Ah!" said Randulf, at the club, "when so old a man gets so young a wife, it is all up with him"; and saying this he made a movement, as if wringing a clout and casting it from him.

Jacob Worse returned from the fishing with rheumatism, and took to the chimney corner. It was best for him to remain at home; and in the spring, when the *Hope* was going on a long voyage, he himself proposed that one of the other captains in the employ of the firm should take command of her.

Lauritz Seehus was promoted to be mate; in the winter he had been up to Bergen, and had passed in navigation. Before he went, he obtained a promise for life or death from Henrietta.

Neither did Worse go to sea the next spring. He complained of rheumatism and of pains in his stomach. The doctor could not make out what it was, but fancied there was something wrong with his liver.

In the mean time, he became more than ever infatuated about his wife. When his infirmities began with rheumatism and bad digestion, she nursed him as if she had been his daughter. Her tenderness made him doubly grateful and happy. Besides this, all the singing and reading which went on around him produced, in the course of time and without his observing it, a considerable effect upon him.

Jacob Worse had always thought of the Almighty as he might of Consul Garman, as an exacting master, who was, however, forgiving and placable, if one only kept clear of deceit and downright wickedness.

But now he learnt something very different. It was of no avail that he had been an excellent seaman, that he had never deceived a fellow countryman—Germans and Swedes he did not take into reckoning—and that he was upright and just in his dealings. Much, much more than this was required of him.

Often when they talked and read of the obstacles to conversion, and of the perils of the hour of temptation, he thought to himself: "Can this, can all this be true?"

He had little trust in Sivert Gesvint, and he did not rely much on the spiritual strivings of Endre Egeland, for he knew the other side of him too well.

But Sarah, Sarah who in all respects was perfection itself, said, literally said, that every day he must combat the old Adam and strive against Satan.

This began to trouble him, and he inquired if she perceived much of the old Adam in him?

She did, indeed; and he learnt to know more of himself than was agreeable. First, he learnt that he swore. He could now see that that was wrong. He endeavoured to overcome the habit, but it was too thoroughly ingrained in him; still he fancied that he improved even in this respect. So much, however, of the old Adam, even of Satan's self, remained in him, that he was ill at ease.

Sarah wished him to join in prayer and singing; but it was out of his power. He had not yet made such spiritual progress as was necessary, she said.

No, unfortunately, he had not; he wished he had. It would be the better for him.

When he observed how Sivert Jespersen handled sacred things at the meetings, when he listened to his fawning unctuous voice, and at the same time remembered how infamously he had cheated him in the affair of the salt, the desire for spiritual things evaporated, and Jacob Worse betook himself to his club.

The following day he was always treated as an invalid, and, in spite of all that he could say, whether in jest or earnest, he had to submit to gruel and the grey wrapper for a day, his wife sitting and knitting by his side.

At last he came to believe that he was ill whenever she said he was.

The letter which Sarah had written to her stepson had produced a good effect, and when Romarino, shortly after, came home, in order to set up in business on his own account, the relations between him and his young stepmother were perfectly amicable.

Romarino paid a little court to her in his frivolous way; but she did not observe it, or, at all events, took no notice of it. However, it brought a little of the spirit of youthfulness into the house.

Though Jacob Worse never took any step without consulting Sarah, it always seemed as if it was the old man who was difficult, whilst the two younger people agreed well enough.

But when Romarino set up for himself, and married a young lady, of whom all that was known was that she was gay and worldly minded, the mutual relations became more distant. The young and old Worses had no common interests, and seldom saw one another.

When Romarino bought a house and lived in grand style, old Worse shook his head.

It was some time before Madame Torvestad realized that she had completely misunderstood her daughter, but gradually she became conscious that there was no remedy. Ever since that look which she had noticed on the evening of the betrothal, Sarah had shaken off her authority, and had asserted herself as an equal.

Indeed, Madame Torvestad was soon nothing more than Madame Worse's mother.

She was wise enough to conceal her disappointment, and she promised herself that it should not recur in the case of Henrietta, who should have a husband more amenable to control, while she, Henrietta, should be under stricter rule than before. As a beginning, the poor child should learn to sit in Sarah's place by the Bible, when Sarah was not there.

For the last two years but scanty tidings had been received of Hans Nilsen Fennefos. He was said to be travelling in the north, farther north than he had ever been before, away up in the most benighted parts of Finmarken, as some declared.

Occasionally news of him reached the elders, but they did not communicate it at the meetings. Any one inquiring about Fennefos was recommended to mind his own business, or was told that the Lord's ways are inscrutable.

The fact was, that what the Brethren round about had to report about Hans Nilsen was anything but satisfactory.

He who formerly had moved from place to place as a messenger of love and peace, now left confusion and terror behind him. It was said that he passed through the country like a hurricane, his speech was as of fire, many became crazy after hearing him, and one young girl was reported to have destroyed herself in consequence.

The clergy began to notice him in their reports. His former reputation for gentleness and moderation was injured; and scoffers cried triumphantly: "See, even he also!"

There was much consternation among the Friends when these tidings arrived, and it gradually became evident how much the elders had endeavoured to withhold from them.

Many wrote and urged Fennefos to come southwards again; they thought that when he met his old friends, his equanimity would be restored. But he did not come, and the country was full of reports about the infatuated preacher, who wandered singing from hut to hut through the snow, leading a band of haggard men and women with dishevelled hair, who wept and tore their clothes.

The elders then begged Madame Torvestad to write to him, and the next day she delivered to them a sealed letter. This was contrary to rules, but the circumstances were unusual, and no objection was raised. In the autumn the letter was despatched, and in the spring it was reported that Hans Nilsen was wending his way southwards.

It was Sarah, however, who had written the letter. It was done at her mother's request.

CHAPTER IX

FOR several years the fortunes of Garman and Worse prospered. Jacob Worse's money ran like a stream of fresh blood in the business, spreading itself through the limbs and invigorating the whole body, and the firm soon recovered its own renown, both at home and abroad.

The Consul's brow grew calm and unclouded, and his step was vigorous and youthful, as he mounted the great staircase to superintend the foreign workmen, who had come from Copenhagen to decorate the reception-rooms upstairs.

Christian Frederik was expected home in the spring; his education abroad was completed, and he had spent the last winter in Paris.

The Consul was delighted to have his son at home again, especially now that he could show him how prosperous the firm was and how the business flourished.

There was only one thing which troubled him, namely, Worse.

The Consul, in his heart, cursed the Haugians more than ever. It had happened as he feared—they had spoiled Skipper Worse as far as he was concerned.

His sisters-in-law, Birgitte and Mette, were of the same opinion. It was true that, after his marriage, Worse often visited Sandsgaard, and tried to show that he had not altered. But it was of no use; he could no longer adapt himself to the tone which prevailed there, and it was painfully apparent on both sides that the good old times had departed for ever.

On one occasion only had Sarah been to Sandsgaard, when the Consul gave a grand dinner in honour of the newly married pair. With downcast eyes she sat by his side in the brilliant dining-room, surrounded by grand ladies and gentlemen, whom she knew by sight in the streets or at church.

Jests, laughter, and mirth, the like of which she had never before encountered, reigned around, although the guests imagined that they put some restraint upon themselves that day, in deference to the well-known strictness of the young wife.

Jacob Worse, on the other hand, who was accustomed to it, and who was at his ease with them all, was well pleased, and nodded to her. She, however, scarcely raised her eyes during the whole of the dinner, and when they reached home, she announced to Worse that she felt as if they had visited the very purlieus of hell itself.

"Oh, Sarah! how can you say such things! they are all really good, kind people."

"No;" she said, sharply. "I suppose you know what a butt they made of you?" This was the impression made upon her when the judge, or some one else, had begged the honour of drinking a glass of wine with the old captain and the young bridegroom.

She never went there again; from the first she was acute enough to perceive that she could never get a footing in such society. Moreover, these gay, light-hearted people, who laughed loudly and drank the perilous wine, seemed almost fiendish to one who, from her childhood, had been accustomed only to grave and serious conversation.

Consul Garman constantly upbraided his sisters-in-law for not having given him earlier information of Worse's relations with the Haugians, for he fancied he could have cured him had he taken him in hand before the evil had gained the mastery.

In the mean time, Worse appeared to be content, which was very well so long as it lasted.

His loss was felt at Sandsgaard; and when he abandoned the sea and relinquished the *Hope* to others, the Consul gave him up as lost and useless.

The Consul was now more lonely than ever; absorbed in melancholy, he often paced up and down in the broad gravel paths by the pavilion in the garden.

It stood by a pond, round which grew a dense border of rushes. Formerly this pond must have been larger, for the Consul remembered that in his childhood there had been water on both sides of the building, and a bridge which could be drawn up. He had a dim recollection of ladies in a blue and white boat, and a tall man in a red silken jacket, who stood in the bow with an oar. Now, however, the pond was so small that a boat would have looked ridiculous. The Consul often wondered how it could have so diminished in size. It must, he thought, be the rushes which encroached upon it; and although he continually told the gardener to keep his eye upon them, it was of no use.

The garden had been originally laid out in the French fashion, with broad rectangular paths, high thick hedges, alleys, and borders of box.

There was a circular open space, where four paths met; seats were placed around it, and in the centre stood a sun-dial.

In the outer part of the garden, especially towards the north-west, a thick border of trees encircled it, as with a frame. They were common native trees, placed there to protect the fine French garden and the exotic plants and flowers from the cold sea wind.

The pavilion by the pond lay to the west of the mansion, and although only a few paces distant; it was looked upon in old times as a sort of Trianon. Here they assembled to drink coffee, or to listen to music. The Company, filing along by the most ingenious roundabout paths over the bridge and about the pond, embarked in the boat, and were ferried across with three strokes of the oar, amidst innumerable compliments and witticisms.

Morten Garman remembered all this from his youth. He himself had endeavoured, but with only partial success, to keep up the old customs and manners.

People were changed, the pond was filling up, and even his father's stately garden seemed likely to become a wilderness.

On both sides of the gravel path leading to the pavilion there was a hedge, so thickly grown that, to the great disgust of the gardener, young ladies used to seat themselves on its top. At regular intervals the box bushes were clipped into pyramidal shapes, and it was here that the Consul delighted to pace up and down. Here, too, remained all that was left of the ancient grandeur.

The garden beyond was beginning to be somewhat irregular. The trees that had been planted to give shelter, now that their trunks were thick and their roots strong, spread on their own account; and as they could not face the north-west wind, their boughs stretched inwards upon the garden, over the rectangular paths and the winding dolls' hedges of clipped box.

It was not the gardener's fault that the plantation had so spread that it was now more of a park than a garden, and it would have been impossible to restore the former French model, except by cutting down the trees and planting anew.

When the Consul walked here in the calm summer evenings, he could, through the towering trees, catch a glimpse of the bright afterglow, which shed its light upon Sandsgaard Bay and westward over the sea, whose glassy surface heaved in long undulations.

He remembered the glorious view of the sea that in his youth could be obtained from the roof of the pavilion; it was, however, no longer visible, for it was with the garden as with the town, both growing and overgrowing, so that neither the one nor the other resembled its former self.

At the back of the pavilion there was a secret door in the panelling, the key of which the Consul always carried in his pocket. Many a light recollection of the gallantries of his youth rose up before him, when at rare intervals he now opened this small back door, from which a narrow spiral stair led to a chamber above, so narrow that it was now difficult for him to ascend it; but in his younger days—good Heavens!—how lightly he flew up and down it!

"Le nez, c'est la mémoire," he said, as he inhaled the odour of old mahogany, and paced up and down in the small remnant of the garden of his youth, stepping daintily with his well-shaped legs and dreaming of the period of low shoes and silk stockings.

In the road outside stood a wayfarer, gazing upon the fjord. It was the well-known lay-preacher, Hans Nilsen Fennefos. Tall, gaunt, with bright searching eyes, he stood absorbed in thought, and leant against the post of the gate leading from the garden.

On his back he bore a large wallet, in which he carried his books and tracts. He was dusty and weary, with a long day's tramp in the sun.

For three years he had not visited these parts, and much had happened in the mean time. When, at a distance, he had learnt that Sarah had married Skipper Worse, he felt as if he had received a stab, and he suffered bodily pain, which almost overcame him. He immediately realized that this woman had enthralled his affections, and that his love to the Brethren, nay, to the Almighty Himself, was as nothing in comparison.

He was terrified, and cast himself on the ground in an agony of remorse and prayer. It seemed to him as if no punishment or penance could atone for such deception and for so great a crime.

Bitter feelings towards others also took possession of him, and with fiery zeal he began to preach repentance, rebuking sinners in language far more severe than was customary.

For three years he had maintained this vehement crusade against sin, both in himself and in others, and during this period he succeeded in shaking off the sinful affection. It now became evident to him that both he and the Brethren had hitherto manifested insufficient austerity in life and doctrine.

He had, therefore, responded to the call, and had journeyed southwards. His feelings when he read Sarah's letter were those of pity for her, and for all the Brethren in that part, who were wandering blindly in their sins and self-righteousness. But on his way south, travelling through friendly districts, among people who had known him of old and who received him with kindness, it could not but happen that his asperity should be mitigated; and as he passed through Sandsgaard, he stopped, overcome by memories which the sight of the familiar bay and of the church towers of the neighbouring town had revived.

Hans Nilsen searched his heart anew, but found nothing which should not be there. Sarah was as a sister or a brother to him; she was another man's wife, and he hoped that she might be happy.

Before he went on he happened to look over the hedge, and, amidst the trees, he discovered Consul Garman, pacing up and down.

Fennefos recognized him, and his feelings were roused again by the sight of the old man, so unconcerned in his sins, surrounded by riches, and absorbed in worldly contemplation, whilst he was drawing near the depths of hell with open eyes.

He seized his staff and went on. They should soon feel in the town that Hans Nilsen Fennefos had come back.

In the mean time, the last gleam of the twilight faded away, and the sky paled along the horizon, the spreading boughs of the beech trees swayed to and fro in the cold wind, and Consul Garman re-entered his house.

The garden lay in repose, the tree tops waved overhead, and, in the struggle for life, either forced themselves upwards or perished, stunted by the shade and drip of their companions.

Above and below branches stretched out, ever encroaching on the narrow space around the pavilion, where the pond was growing smaller year by year.

CHAPTER X

A LONG table was spread in the low, old-fashioned room of Sivert Jespersen. Although the table-cloth and the napkins were of fine damask, the knives were of a common sort, and the forks of steel. Here and there, at long intervals, stood a bottle of Medoc; besides this there was nothing but water, salt, and bread upon the table.

The host, however, was afraid that even this might appear too sumptuous. In ordinary life an oil-cloth covered his dining-table, and he was in the habit of taking potatoes out of the dish with his fingers, and peeling them with his pocket-knife. The dinner party to-day was to celebrate Hans Nilsen's return. No one could tell how strict he might not have become.

The elders had arranged that, at first, Fennefos should be invited to meet a limited circle of the most confidential and trustworthy of the community, in order to ascertain his present state of mind.

It was not worth while to let him speak at the meetings just yet. In fact, they were all afraid of him, and all felt a little conscience stricken.

Fennefos had been three or four days in the town, but nobody had seen much of him. He stayed a good deal at home, conversing with Madame Torvestad; he had also visited Worse's portion of the building across the yard.

When he and Sarah met for the first time, they were alone, and when she fixed her dark eyes upon him, there was a tremor in his voice. However, he soon overcame it, and talked calmly and earnestly, without looking much at her.

Sarah said scarcely anything, she was only listening to his voice. Skipper Worse entered, and gave a hearty welcome to Hans Nilsen, who was startled when he observed how old he had grown of late, for his mouth had fallen in and his face was sallow.

As they talked of the party which was to be given at Sivert Jespersen's next day, Worse walked up and down, rubbing his hair. It was evident that there was something on his mind.

"H'm, h'm," he repeated at intervals during the conversation. "It's the 24th of June to-morrow—yes that it is. Yes, it's St. John's Eve."

"Has St. John's Eve any particular interest for Captain Worse?" inquired Fennefos, who was anxious to be civil to Sarah's husband.

"Any interest? I should rather think it had, Hans Nilsen. Yes, for many years. It is Randulf's birthday, you see; and ever since we were boys—— Well, it is not worth mentioning; those times have gone by."

"Probably, then, you would prefer being with Skipper Randulf to-morrow to going to Sivert Jespersen's?"

"I am ashamed to confess it, but I really would rather."

"No one, I think, will mind it if you do not go to Sivert Jespersen's," said Sarah, glancing at Hans Nilsen.

She was not sorry to be rid of her husband for a day.

Jacob Worse was as pleased as a child at this unexpected turn of events, and hurried off to Randulf, to tell him he had got leave to come.

Sarah and Fennefos remained together, and there was a little pause.

"Is your husband unwell?"

"Yes. I fancy he has some internal malady."

"You allude to his body. I am thinking of his soul. Is he still in his sins?"

"Yes, Hans Nilsen, I fear he is. The Word has no power over him."

"Have you tried to help him, Sarah?"

"Yes, indeed, but without much success."

"Perhaps you have not tried in the right way. He has been a strong man, and strong measures may be required to subdue him."

She would have discussed this further with him, but at this point they were interrupted by Madame Torvestad, who came to fetch Fennefos. They had an engagement to visit an orphanage for girls, which had been established by the Haugians.

Sarah accompanied them, not entirely to her mother's satisfaction. Latterly she had been thrust so much into the shade by her daughter, that she was doing all in her power to keep Fennefos to herself.

In the mean time, she pretended to be pleased, and all three went off together. Sarah felt a particular satisfaction in the company of Fennefos, although he devoted himself entirely to her mother, who talked to him in a low voice about the people they met on their way.

When they returned, Hans Nilsen bade Madame Torvestad farewell outside the house and followed Sarah to her own home.

They conversed for some time, Sarah telling him much about the Brethren, and informing him of what had occurred during his absence.

As she soon observed that he took a more severe and a darker view of everything, she herself also was led to give a worse aspect to what had occurred. She spoke of the great lukewarmness that prevailed amongst them, of the sordid desire for worldly gain, and of the sinful servility with which they sought the approval of men.

She told him also how they allowed themselves to be flattered and cajoled by the younger clergy, who sought to intrude themselves into their charitable undertakings and their missions to the heathen.

Fennefos listened to her, and thanked her when she had finished.

"But you, Sarah, how is it with you?"

"Thanks, Hans Nilsen," said Sarah, looking up at him; "of myself I can do nothing, but the Lord has been my strength, and I may venture to say that all is well with me."

He turned away quickly, and bid her farewell.

The dinner at Sivert Jespersen's the following day was silent, for all were in a state of suspense. The attention of all was fixed on Hans Nilsen, who sat by the side of Sarah, grave and taciturn, as had been his wont ever since his return.

Before the soup, a grace was read by an old man with blue hands—he was a dyer. Afterwards they sang a hymn. There should have been salmon after the soup; but, at the last moment, the host was troubled by certain compunctions, and, to the cook's intense disgust, forbade its being placed on the table.

There was, therefore, only roast mutton, of which a good deal was eaten. The cook had ventured to serve a salad with it, a dish which few of them had ever seen before.

One of the seniors said, jestingly: "What next! shall we eat grass like King Nebuchadnezzar?"

They laughed a little at this, and Madame Torvestad, taking advantage of the occasion, told them that in her younger days in Gnadau, she got little else to eat than such "grass" and other vegetables.

After this, the conversation was directed to the various institutions of the Brethren, to their leading men, and to the teachers and preachers of the olden time, men who in the last century had awakened a new life among the Christians in Germany.

Hans Nilsen either remained silent, or merely spoke a few words in a low voice to Sarah. But the others were anxious to talk on these subjects, which interested them all, and on which they were well informed.

Madame Torvestad was especially interested; in such subjects she was thoroughly at home, and she let no opportunity escape her of relating what she knew of the men who were so famous in her younger days.

"Yes, truly," said Sivert Jespersen, "many a blessed word remains to us from Johan Arndt, Spener, and Francke; also among the Herrnhutters of later times there have been many godly men."

"We might learn something from them, and they from us," said the old dyer.

"The other day, I read in a little book of mine of a vision that appeared to a pious follower of Francke. Shortly afterwards, this man learnt that Francke had died at the very moment when he had seen the vision." As she said this, Madame Torvestad took from her pocket one of her everlasting small books. Sivert Jespersen begged her to read the account of the apparition, if that happened to be the book of which she spoke.

It was the book; she had, in fact, brought it because she and the elders had agreed that by soothing and gentle words they should endeavour to bring back their dear friend and brother, Hans Nilsen, to a more settled frame of mind.

The guests prepared themselves to listen. Most of them had finished, but some of the men took a little more, and ate whilst she read. They began to be more at ease, and viewed Fennefos with less apprehension.

Madame Torvestad read well, without pronouncing the foreign words so incorrectly as some of the others, who were not so well educated.

"'At last it happened that Elias'—that is Francke—'was taken away. This was in 1727. I, a dweller in darkness, caught a glimpse of him in the abode of the blest. I heard the great Prince of Peace, who was surrounded by an innumerable multitude of the saved, say to them, "Ye blessed of my Father, ye love me, and I you, we rejoice together, and we have now a fresh occasion for our joy. In this our new Jerusalem, we shall rejoice to-morrow; for a great soul is just about to leave its earthly tenement, and will receive its crown." The whole host of heaven cried rapturously, "Amen, amen."

"'But who, who shall this new and honoured saint be? My attention was now directed to three who were among the worthiest, adorned with crowns, and in the silken garb of archangels. Who is this, and this, and this, asked my heart. Straightway I recognized them. Luther, Arndt, and Spener.

"' "Brothers," said Spener, "do you think that I can guess who the king means by this glorified friend that the day will reveal to us? It must be Francke who will be crowned, for he has conquered in the strife."

"'So spake the beloved Philip Jacob, and the Lord, who was near him, said, "Thou art in the right."

"'The whole heaven resounded with joyful acclaim; and so the day that Francke's soul had longed for arrived. A multitude of ministering spirits, ready and anxious to obey their Lord's behest, were directed to bring the soul of Francke. The chariot of Israel and the horsemen thereof sallied forth to fetch him.'"

Most of the company manifested their approval by smiles and gestures, but a few looked thoughtful, and Sivert Jespersen regretted that he had not come to a definite understanding beforehand with Madame Torvestad.

She was a woman of intelligence, who could usually be trusted to handle the most difficult subjects; in this case, however, she had shown her weakest side, and Sivert Jespersen knew only too well how much Fennefos disliked such extravagant rhapsodies.

In the mean time, however, Fennefos remained silent, and seemed to be absorbed in thought.

Amongst the others a tranquil geniality began to prevail. The sour Medoc was sparingly drunk, mixed with sugar and water; some drank home-brewed small beer, the majority only water.

As the affectionate and brotherly feelings which united them and took possession of many, they smiled and patted one another on the shoulder or cheek. By degrees they forgot their dread of Hans Nilsen, and felt glad to see him, although he remained silent.

No one could tell, they thought, to what the Lord might not have subjected him; and when his troubled spirit was more tranquil, they hoped that his former frankness might be restored.

Suddenly his voice was heard, and a deathlike stillness ensued.

"Beloved brothers and sisters—"

They knew the voice, and one and all thought: "Now it is coming!"

At first he spoke calmly and almost sadly of the first love. He reminded them how Hauge himself became conscious that in his later years the first love did not burn in him as in the earlier days of grace. He then drew a picture of the tribulations of the Brethren in the evil days gone by. He praised and thanked God that strength had been given to their forefathers, so that the light had not been extinguished, but now shone brightly throughout the land.

Next, he spoke of the temptations of the Brethren in the better times that followed, and all bowed their heads, thinking: "Now it is coming!"

It came, indeed, and like a hurricane. Blow after blow, his words fell upon them, now here, now there, on every point of weakness. Every allusion was understood, and none dared to look at the others. They had no time to wonder how he came to know so much, for he held their minds completely enthralled.

"What is there," cried he, "what is there of the first love among you? Think you, would he recognize his friends, if he were to walk the earth again in the flesh, he who aroused your fathers, and whom many of the elders among you have seen face to face?

"Think you that the Saviour will acknowledge you in the day of judgment?

"Woe, woe! The spirit has departed from you, and you have received an evil spirit, full of worldly cares, of pride and luxury; and, by reason of your misdeeds, the name of God has become a derision among the heathen.

"Have you forgotten the ancient enemy, or do you blindly imagine that the old serpent slumbers? Woe to you; for it is you who slumber, and your awakening will be like that of the rich man's in hell fire!"

Many of the women began to weep; the men sat and cowered as each blow fell.

But when he had finished, Sivert Jespersen, with a cringing smile, said: "I think now we had better sing a hymn."

At the third verse the cook entered with the dessert. The host made the most frightful grimaces, and shook his head; for he was leading the singing, and had to mind his trebles and basses.

The cook understood the case well enough. She had submitted to giving up the salmon, but the devil himself should not cheat her out of her dessert. Her character would be utterly ruined in all the best families were it to transpire that, at a dinner of twenty-two persons, she had served only soup and a roast—no fish; no dessert!

Never would she stand such a thing! Red in the face, with smothered indignation, she brought in an enormous dish of rich pastry, which she placed right in front of Sivert Jespersen.

It caused an exceedingly painful impression, and the host almost lost his voice as he began the fourth verse. Nobody ventured to touch the dessert, and, after the hymn, the old dyer read a grace after meat.

When the coffee came, there was an oppressive silence; for some were seriously affected and distressed, others glanced uneasily at the elders. The women began to collect their cloaks, in order to proceed to the meeting-house, where there was to be a Bible-reading, Fennefos and some of the men accompanying them. But in the little office behind Sivert Jespersen's store, five or six of the elders were assembled. They lit their long clay pipes, and for some time sat smoking in silence. No one liked to begin the conversation.

"Does any one know the price of salt up at Bergen?" inquired Endre Egeland, who was always inclined to pass over anything unpleasant.

Apparently, however, no one knew anything about the price of salt. It was clear that something else had to be discussed.

"Yes; we all deserve it," sighed Sivert Jespersen. "I suppose that we have all been benefited."

"Yes, indeed," said another, "there is, in truth, much to correct and much to censure, both in you and me."

"You see the mote in your brother's eye, but not the beam in your own," said Nicolai Egeland, appropriately.

"It is not always that the advice and conversation of womenfolk softens a man," said the old dyer quietly.

There was a pause, until all, even Nicolai Egeland, had taken in what was said. At last one of them remarked, "We shall require much help up on our farm this year, for the Lord has blessed both tillage and pasture."

It was a farm near the town, which was owned in common by several of the Haugians.

"What we most require is some one who can take a part in the work, and who, at the same time, knows how to meet the servants and labourers in worship during the hours of rest," said Sivert Jespersen.

Again a long pause. One looked at his neighbour, and he again into the corner, where the old dyer sat, until at last many eyes were turned in his direction.

It was not easy to see the old man as he sat blinking in the dense tobacco smoke, but, after a while, he nodded several times, saying: "Well, as it seems to be your wish, I will try to mention it to him." Upon this the others, who evidently felt relieved, began to talk eagerly about the price of salt.

CHAPTER XI

THE little white house of Skipper Randulf stood on an elevation, looking over the bay and the fjord.

The two friends, who had dined, and dined well, were now enjoying their after-dinner nap, the host in his usual place on the sofa, the guest in a large armchair.

The window stood open, there was a warm sun, and the town lay still in the quiet summer afternoon. The flies buzzed in and out, and the window curtains moved gently in the breeze.

Large drops of perspiration stood on Jacob Worse's nose, as he lay back in his chair, with his mouth open, snoring frightfully.

Randulf snored also, but not quite so loudly. Over his eyes was spread a yellow silk handkerchief, which his old housekeeper always tied round his head, for without it he could not get his nap.

On the slope in front of the house, some boys, who were playing, noticed the strange noise made by the two sleepers, and collected, laughing and skylarking, under the window.

Suddenly Randulf's housekeeper fell upon them with a broom, and the boys scampered away, amidst shouts and laughter. Worse half opened his eyes for a moment, and then laid his head back again on the other side.

All was still again, until the snoring recommenced. The sound of oars, and the cries of sea-gulls out on the fjord, could be heard in the distance. The housekeeper stood sentry with the broom, and the worthy captains slept on for another half-hour.

At last, Randulf moved, lifted the handkerchief from his eyes, and yawned.

Upon this, Worse—half awake—said, with an assumption of superiority; "Well, you *have* slept! I began to think you would never wake up."

"Wake!" said Randulf, scornfully, "why, I could not get a wink of sleep for your snoring."

"I never snore," said Worse decisively; "besides, I have been awake all the time you were sleeping."

"Sleeping! I tell you I never slept."

"Come, I am the best judge of that, I who sat here and—

"And snored; yes, that you did, and like a hero."

They wrangled on for a few moments, until they were both thoroughly awake.

Upon this they lit their pipes, and put on their coats—at Randulf's they always sat in their shirt sleeves, which was a treat to Worse. At home it was never allowed.

Afterwards the two old skippers sauntered about the wharves, peeped into the warehouses and the rope-walk, discussed the vessels in the harbour, and, with highly disparaging comments, examined a ship which was building by the wharf.

At every point they fell in with acquaintances, with whom they gossiped. Randulf was in excellent spirits, and Worse also roused himself, although he was not as he had been in old days.

Such a tour as this through the town was something new and unusual to him, for of late he had never been much beyond his own warehouse.

There was something strange about him, which he himself was unable to comprehend; but from the moment when he gave up the *Hope* to others, he had nearly lost all interest in his old calling.

Indeed, it was almost painful to him now to see a vessel in the fjord under full sail; formerly such a sight was the finest he knew.

To-day, however, Randulf had quite thawed him; he became lively, and even swore twice without being aware of it. This greatly comforted his friend.

Like Consul Garman, Randulf grieved that Jacob Worse had, as he termed it, stranded himself.

He teased him no longer; it would be of no use. At the club, over a tumbler of warm toddy, Randulf would confide to his friends how sad it was to see so splendid a seaman as Jacob Worse spoilt by a pack of women.

He used to wind up his lamentations with "that confounded tub of a ship from Rostock," alluding to the Rostock trader, with which he had been in collision at Bolderaa.

It was his firm belief that if he, Randulf, had been at home, they should never have trapped Jacob Worse.

At seven o'clock they turned back to Randulf's little house, in high spirits, and ravenously hungry.

When they had again eaten—and Worse had not had such an appetite for many a day—they took their steaming tumblers of toddy to the open window, and the blue smoke of their pipes came puffing out like cannon shots, first from the one and then from the other, like two frigates saluting.

After they had smoked on awhile in silence, Worse said: "The sea can be very fine on such a summer evening. Your health."

"The sea is always fine, Jacob. Your health."

"Well, as long as one is young."

"Young! why, you are not more than three years my senior; and that Thomas Randulf has no idea of sneaking to the shore for the next ten years, you may be certain."

"It is otherwise with me. There is something wrong in my inside, you must know."

"Oh, nonsense!" said Randulf. "I don't know much about liver and lungs, and all the trash they say we have in our insides, but what I do know is, that a seafaring man is never well on shore, just as a landsman is as sick as a cat when he comes on board. That is a fact, and it is not to be gainsaid."

Jacob Worse had nothing to say in answer to this speech, he only grumbled, and rubbed his hands across his stomach,

"Have you tried Riga balsam?" inquired Randulf.

"Are you out of your senses? It is my inside that is bad."

"Don't you suppose that Riga balsam is good for the inside, too? If you only get the right sort, it is good for everything, inboard and outboard. I ought to know that. However, it is not your stomach that is wrong," added Randulf, profoundly, "it is rather your heart. It is these women who play the mischief with you, when they get you in tow; I have noticed it both in the Mediterranean and the Baltic.

This last affair, however, has been the worst. These pious ones, you see——"

"Mind what you say about Sarah. She has been a real blessing to me. What should I, an ailing old man, have been without her?"

"You would not have become an old man but for her," Randulf blurted out. But at this Worse looked so ferocious, that his friend took a long sip, and followed it by a fit of coughing.

"No, no," said Worse, when he, too, had refreshed himself. "She has been a good wife to me, both as regards body and soul. I have learnt much from her of which I was ignorant before."

"Yes, that's true, Jacob. You have learnt to sit behind the stove like an old crone, and to dangle at the apronstrings of the women. You have been dragged to meeting as tamely as a Spanish monk's mule; that is what you have learnt."

"Gently, Thomas," said Worse, nodding significantly. "You are proving the truth of my words. Such as you are, I was; but now I have learnt to feel differently, as you will, too, when the time comes. You will then understand what sinners we are."

"Sinners! Oh yes! But I am not so bad as many others, nor are you, Jacob. I have known you, known you well, for forty years, and a better man by land or sea is not to be found in all Norway. Now, you know it," he said, bringing his fist down on the window-ledge.

Worse was not entirely impervious to this flattery, but he muttered, as he shook the ashes of his pipe into the stove; "Yes, but much more than this is required, very much more."

"Listen to me seriously, Jacob Worse. You know Sivert Jespersen, also called Gesvint?"

"Yes, I should think I did."

"Perhaps you remember a certain two hundred barrels of salt which you bought of him?"

"Yes. I shan't forget them in a hurry."

"Answer me one thing, just one little thing; did he, or did he not, cheat you?"

"Horribly!" answered Worse, without hesitation.

"Now, then, answer me another thing. Which do you

suppose the Almighty likes best, an honest seaman who holds his tongue and looks after his ship, or a hypocrite who cheats his fellow-creatures, and then sings hymns? Hey! Which do you think He prefers?"

"Neither you nor I can say, Randulf. Judgment is of the Lord, who searches the hearts and reins."

"Reins!" cried Randulf, scornfully. "Sivert Jespersen's reins—a pretty thing to search. The Lord is not one to be cheated."

Jacob Worse smiled. Theology was now put aside, and they mixed a fresh tumbler.

"But there is one thing you cannot get over, Jacob. It was a sin and shame that you gave up the sea so early. Everybody who inquires about you says so."

"Does any one inquire about me?"

"Inquire about you! why, they talk about you from Copenhagen to Kronstadt. Do you remember the stout damsel at the 'Drei Norweger' in Pillau?"

"Was that where we danced?"

"No; that was at Königsberg. Good gracious!" said Randulf, compassionately, "have you forgotten it already? No; the stout individual at Pillau wept salt tears when she heard you were married. *'Ach du lieber,'* said she. *'Was soll now the arme Minchen machen when the lustige Jacob Worse has gegiftet sich.'*"

"Did she really say that?" cried Worse, touched. "However, it is not correct as you repeat it. I wonder, Thomas, you never learnt to speak German."

"I tell you what: I can get on well enough. I soon find out when they are trying to cheat me; then they come smirking and smiling with *'Guten Abis.'* But when they say *'Das gloobis,'* look out for yourself, for then they are most deceitful."

"Just let them try me. I know how to manage them," said Worse, boastingly. "Old Bencke in Dantzic learnt the truth of that. At first they cheated me in herrings, as they always do."

"Always," said Randulf, assentingly.

"In rye, too."

"Don't talk about it."

"But at last they introduced some new devilry into the bills of lading."

"What was that?"

"How in the world could I tell! I saw it was something new and out of the regular course, and so I would not sign it."

"No, of course not."

"The clerk, who was some sort of a Dane, stood ready with the pen, and tried to persuade me that it meant nothing, that it was for the benefit of the ship, and so on; all of which one could see was a lie.

"So it ended by my swearing that I would only have the bills of lading to which I was accustomed, and that rather than sign, the brig and the rye should remain in Dantzic Roads until they both rotted."

"Of course," said Randulf.

"But whilst we stood and disputed about this, old Bencke himself came out into the office, and the Dane explained the case to him. The old man became dreadfully angry, you may guess, and began to scold and curse in German. I, too, got angry, and so I turned round and said to him, in German, you understand—I spoke just like this to him: *'Bin Bencke bös, bin Worse also bös.'* When he saw that I knew German, he did not say another word, but merely, turning round on his heel, bundled out of the room. Some one got another bill of lading, and that person was me."

"That was clever, Jacob," cried Randulf. It was a long time since he had heard that story.

They drank a tumbler in memory of old times, and for a while meditated in silence.

They were both very red in the face, and Worse looked quite fresh and well. The sallowness of his complexion was gone, but the short locks of hair about his ears were as white as froth.

At last Jacob Worse said:

"When I look at such a table as that by the sofa, I cannot understand how it could be broken. You remember that night in Königsberg?"

"Yes; but you see, Jacob, we danced right against the table at full swing."

"Yes, you are right; it was at full swing," said Worse, smiling.

"But, good Heavens! how we ran away afterwards!" said Randulf, shaking with laughter.

"And how pitch dark it was before we found the boat! I wonder what that table cost?"

"You may well ask, Jacob. I have never been in the house since."

"Nor have I."

They now fell to talking of the wild doings of their mad youth, telling their stories only half way, or by allusions; for did they not both know them all by heart?

"What do you say to just another drop, Jacob?"

"Well, it must be a little one."

The host was of opinion that they might take just enough for a nightcap, and so went after the hot water.

It was now past ten o'clock, and as Worse had permission to stay till eleven, his conscience was perfectly clear. As he warmed up under the influence of Randulf's old Jamaica rum, he forgot both his internal malady and his anxieties for his soul.

At the third tumbler, Randulf proposed that they should talk English, which they proceeded to do with much gravity, but after their own fashion.

The last rays of the sun from behind the cloud banks, caused by the north wind, made the faces of the two friends look redder than ever, as they sat at the open window and talked their English.

The fjord below lay as smooth as a mirror, the outermost headlands and islands seeming to stand out of the water. Nearer the town, on the larger islands, and here and there to the eastward up in the mountains, the young people had lit St. John's Day bonfires, whose smoke went straight up, while the flames were paled by the twilight of the summer evening.

Boats full of boys and girls moved about. A sailor, who had brought an accordion with him, was playing; "While the North Sea roars," and other popular airs. A procession of boats followed him, and at times some of the people joined in with their voices.

Most, however, were silent, listening to the music, and gazing over the fjord out towards that "roaring North Sea," which woke up memories of hope and sorrow, of longings, uncertainty, love, and bereavement.

The Haugians had long since left their meeting-house. Some of Sivert Jespersen's guests had returned to sup at his house, others went straight home. Sarah and Fennefos met in the passage; both were conscious that there was some slight mistrust of them among the others. It was natural, therefore, that they should meet and keep together; indeed, when they reached the market-place, they turned off to the left, instead of going home, and strolled along the road leading to Sandsgaard.

Neither of them had an eye for the beauties of nature; they had always been taught that temptations lurk in everything which surrounds the Christian here below.

Sarah had not seen much; but Fennefos himself, who had journeyed throughout the land in all directions, had no higher conception of the beauty of nature than that a beautiful country was one that was fertile, and that an ugly one was one which was full of fields, lakes, and precipices, and devoid of rich pastures.

Nevertheless, the calm, pleasant summer evening was not without its effect upon them. They had again discussed the chief defects of their community, and how desirable it was that some one should take them seriously in hand.

But now the conversation flagged. They stopped and gazed over the fjord, where the fires were being lighted up. Boats rowed about, and song and music reached their ears. Sarah unconsciously heaved a deep sigh, and turned to go back to the town.

Hans Nilsen was about to say something about the sinfulness of the children of this world, but was unable to frame words. He abandoned the attempt, and, before he knew what he was doing, asked her if she was pleased with the letter he had given her when they last separated.

"Oh yes, Hans Nilsen!" she said, turning her face towards him, her colour heightened. She said no more, and he, too, became quite confused.

They turned towards the town. At the street door Sarah

asked him if he would not come in for a moment. He followed unconsciously, and, when they entered the room, sat down on a chair.

He was glad to rest, he said, for he was weary. The evening rays lit half the room, but the back part was already dark. Sarah went out into the kitchen to see if the door was shut. The servants had gone upstairs, and the house was still and deserted, for it was nearly ten o'clock.

She brought some water and raspberry syrup, and Hans Nilsen, contrary to his custom, took a long draught. He was both tired and thirsty, he said.

Sarah sat at the other end of the sofa, and neither of them spoke. After a minute or two, the silence grew oppressive, and they began to converse again, but soon again lapsed into silence.

"What were you going to say?" inquired Hans Nilsen.

"I—I only asked if you would have some more syrup and water," said she, with some embarrassment.

"No, thank you. I ought to be going."

He got up and walked across the room. His hat lay on the table; but Fennefos moved, as if he hardly knew where he was, towards the window, and looked out on the pale evening sky.

Sarah got up also, and went to the cupboard, which was between the windows, where she began to busy herself with one thing or another.

Observing that she was behind him, he turned round and went back to his seat.

"It has been fine, warm weather to-day," he said; but his voice was thick and strange, and, in spite of what he had drunk, his throat was dry.

Sarah answered somewhat unintelligibly, took up the tumbler he had used, and placed it on the sideboard, her hand shaking so that the glass clinked as she put it down.

Hans Nilsen got up again, moving about as if he were in a stupor, and at last stood opposite her, as if he were about to speak.

She turned her face towards him, and the light fell upon it.

His lips moved, but no sound issued forth, until at last he said: "You are very pale."

"What do you say?" she whispered. His voice was so indistinct that she could not understand him.

He essayed once more to speak, and then, suddenly taking her in his arms, kissed her.

She made no attempt to release herself; but he relaxed his hold, crying; "Lord, help us; what are we doing!"

When the door closed behind him, she hastened across the room, and listened. She heard him stumbling along the passage, heard the house door shut, and heard him pass by the window with a hurried step.

She turned towards the light, her hands were pressed against her heart, the corners of her mouth quivered as with a bitter smile, and young and vigorous though she was, she sank down upon the floor, sobbing.

When Jacob Worse, cheerful and rather "fresh," came groping his way home an hour later, he found his wife reading the Bible, with two candles on the table, and the curtains drawn.

"Good evening," said he, pleasantly. "Is the little wife still sitting up? Is it not bed-time, little Sarah?"

She continued to read, without looking up. Worse laid his hat down, faltering a little as he crossed the floor.

"We have had a very jolly day, Sarah."

"All three?"

"Three!" exclaimed Worse, stopping short; "why, there was only Randulf and I."

"You lie; there were three," said Sarah, calmly.

Jacob Worse was now seized with the unlucky idea that she was joking with him.

He approached her, smiling, and with boozy eyes, in order to put his arm round her neck.

"Hey! so you know more about it than I do. Where did you go to school that you are so wise? Who was the third? Hey!"

"The devil," answered Sarah, lifting her eyes suddenly. "The loathsome fiend was sitting between you."

Jacob Worse started back.

"You may be sure that it is he who has had the pleasantest day. He rejoiced when he heard your oaths, the foul words, and all the corruption of your hearts. Did you not see his crooked claws when he set the bowl before you, that you might wallow in the debasing drink? Did you not hear him laugh, when you sat befouling yourselves in the mire of your sin, ripening for the pains of hell?"

Worse involuntarily began to rub his stomach. He felt the old complaint there again.

"Oh, Sarah, don't say that!" he cried. But she continued fixing her large cold eyes upon him the while, in such a way that he held up his hand to shade himself from her gaze.

"How long, old man, will you trifle with the Lord? Have you no fear of the doom of the impenitent, or have you heard and learnt nothing of the terrors of the outer darkness?"

Worse crept, terrified, towards his room. Half drunk as he was, he could not make it all out; he only heard the fearful words, and knew that two flashing eyes were pursuing him.

Twice he piteously begged her to desist, but each time he got a new scare, until at last, crushed and wretched, he slunk away to his room, and crept into bed.

CHAPTER XII

EVERY night when she retired to rest, Henrietta repeated the promise she had given to Lauritz when he left.

"I promise and swear to love you faithfully in life or death, and never to marry any other."

But every morning when she rose, she sighed and wept; for the way seemed dark before her, and she dreaded each day as it came.

On her twentieth birthday, her mother told her plainly that she must soon marry. Lauritz was away on a long voyage, he would be absent for two years, and even if he came back, she knew only too well that her mother would never consent to their union. Henrietta fluctuated between the downright promise and black hoplessness; at one moment much cast down, at another, cheering herself with the thought of her brave Lauritz, of how much he loved her, and how absolutely he confided in her.

Her figure was not so full as her sister's, but was rather slight and thin. Her bright vivacious countenance looked as if she was always on the alert.

She confided in Sarah, who spoke to her, and urged her to obedience.

But Henrietta was too sharp-sighted not to have observed how it fared with Sarah in her married life, and, moreover, there was not any especial force in Sarah's exhortation when she counselled obedience.

For some time after Sivert Jespersen's party, Hans Nilsen was not to be seen; he did not appear at meal times, and he never spent the night in the house.

Madame Torvestad should not have thought much of this, as it had occurred before. Fennefos had many friends in the neighbourhood, whom he occasionally visited. What really troubled her was, that the old dyer had been several times to inquire after Hans Nilsen, and was unwilling to tell her the reason.

Madame Torvestad had now almost got over her disappointment about Sarah. When she found that her daughter had got the better of her, she was wise enough to be contented with the lustre reflected upon her by the good and prosperous marriage.

Although Henrietta by no means filled Sarah's place at the Bible desk, madame's small meetings continued to be attended, and she retained the esteem of the elders.

But latterly a change was going on which alarmed her. She became aware that what she had read at the dinner about Francke's journey to heaven, had produced a very doubtful impression.

Moreover, she discovered that the elders had met in council about Fennefos, without asking her to be present. The old dyer was evidently the bearer of a secret message to him.

Madame Torvestad considered the matter carefully, and made up her mind. When Hans Nilsen at last appeared, after a five days' absence, she met him on the steps, and led him into her room.

"When you were last in town, Hans Nilsen," she began, without any preface, "you asked me if I thought you ought to marry. I did not think it expedient at that time, but I now think differently."

He moved in his chair, and she now observed for the first time that there was something strange in his aspect.

He sat in a stooping position, half turned away from the light. The clear grey eyes, which generally looked so frankly on those with whom he talked, were cast down, and when he lifted them they were slowly turned to one side. Moreover, he was pale, but blushed at times, passing his hand over his face as if he would conceal it.

Her surprise was such that she forgot to proceed, and merely repeated; "I am now of opinion that the time has come."

Fennefos, on his part, thought she knew all as well as he did, and that every one would detect his misconduct by his outward appearance. And now, when she persisted in repeating that it was time for him to marry, he felt so overwhelmed with shame, that he hardly knew which way to look.

Madame Torvestad did not comprehend what she saw, but

she discovered that by some means or other Fennefos had received a shock; perhaps it might make him the more easy to manage.

"You also asked me at that time, Hans Nilsen, if I knew of any Christian young woman who would suit you. I believe that I have now found one—my daughter."

He looked so wildly at her for a moment, that she was almost frightened. "Are you unwell, Hans Nilsen?" she said.

"No; I am only weary."

Madame Torvestad's suspicions were now aroused. "If it be that you have suffered worldly love to deceive your heart, pray to God, Hans Nilsen, to protect you, and to aid you in the strife with Satan. You should be able to withstand him, and to avoid such vile snares. Henrietta is indeed young, but with you I am satisfied that she would be in safe hands, and I hope and believe that she would be a blessing to you."

Fennefos had so far recovered himself that he was able to thank her. "In truth," said he, "he had not been thinking of marrying now. It was a serious matter."

"It is not good to be alone, least of all for men;" said Madame Torvestad, with emphasis. "You know that well enough, Hans Nilsen; and you remember what Paul says."

"Yes, yes," he said, interrupting her hastily. "If you think I ought to marry, I will pray that it may be for the best."

"I will speak to Henrietta," said Madame Torvestad.

"Thanks; but I would rather—"

"Well, then—I have confidence in you. She is yonder in the workroom."

"Now, at once? I thought that perhaps—"

"There is no reason for delay," said Madame Torvestad, as she opened the door, and, calling out the servant girl, led Fennefos in.

He suffered her to lead him as if he were a dog. "There could be no doubt," he thought, "that Madame Torvestad knew all"; and this feeling of shame, combined with his weariness, left him helpless in her hands. For four days he had wandered along the coast quite alone, shunning acquaintances, and living entirely with strangers. All this time, in fear and sorrow, he had striven to repent; but he returned uncomforted, unsettled, with a vague intention of packing up and going far away.

When he found himself face to face with Henrietta, who looked uneasily at him, he knew not what to say. But she, who of late had got sufficient intimation of what was intended, took courage and said, in a low voice; "Hans, I am betrothed. I have given my promise to Lauritz Seehus, for life or death," she added, fixing her eyes on him.

Hans Nilsen looked at the girl who so openly confessed her love, for life or death; in her innocence so greatly his superior.

"Listen, dear Hans," said Henrietta, laying her hand confidentially on his shoulder. "You have always been kind to me, and you are so good yourself. You will not take me in this way, I am sure; but you will protect me from my mother?"

"I certainly would not wish to make you unhappy, Henrietta; but you ought not to oppose your mother."

"But I will not, I cannot, marry any one but him whom I love."

"Listen, child," he now said quietly, looking sadly at her. It was not the first time that heart-stricken women had sought counsel of Hans Nilsen, and this day he was more than ever in a mood to sympathize with such. There is no suffering more bitter than that of our wounded affections in our youth, but there is strength and healing given to those who seek peace, if they bear their lot in obedience to the will of God, and to those who are placed over them. "You say you cannot marry one whom you do not love; but consider how often the heart deceives itself in youth and—"

"Yes; just look at Sarah, for example," said Henrietta, interrupting him. "Of what avail are all her riches and piety? I know that she is the most miserable woman on earth."

Hans Nilsen turned away; he was again completely disarmed.

Henrietta moved towards the window, and, gazing up at the sky, which was visible over the yard, struck one hand resolutely upon the other, and said, half aloud: "Besides, I have sworn it."

Hans Nilsen went back to Madame Torvestad, and merely said that he and Henrietta could not come to any agreement.

She wished to learn more from him; but he could bear it no longer, and left the room without answering her.

Upstairs, however, he did not find the rest he so much needed, for in his room the old dyer sat waiting for him.

"I have been anxious to see you, Hans Nilsen, and have sought you many times. There is a great desire among us to speak with you, and to meet you in confidential intercourse, but at present it seems to us that you are entirely taken up in this house with the conversation and society of the women."

Fennefos was so tired, that he was half asleep as he listened to the old man. He comprehended that they wished him to leave Madame Torvestad's, and this he himself was anxious to do.

"There are a number of people up at our farm," continued the dyer, "and more will soon come when the harvest begins. Many of us think it would be well if we could find a reliable man who could work and who could preach during the hours of rest. Sivert Jespersen and the others have much to occupy them in the town, and so we thought we would ask Hans Nilsen to move up there."

"Willingly will I do it, if it be thought desirable."

"We were thinking that perhaps you could go to-morrow."

Fennefos was rather taken by surprise, but, for the sake of peace, consented, and as soon as the dyer left, threw himself on the bed, and fell asleep.

Madame Torvestad stood for a moment, thoughtful as usual, when Hans Nilsen had departed; then, opening the door of the workroom, she said with a certain air of solemnity; "Henrietta, go to bed."

"Yes, mother," said Henrietta, who after the conversation with Fennefos, had fallen into the deepest despondency.

Trembling, she approached her mother to say "Good night," although the sun was still high in the heavens.

"I will not say 'Good night' to you, and you shall have no supper, either," said her mother, shutting the door.

This was the mode of applying correction in Gnadau, and Madame Torvestad remembered well how it would bend even the most refractory.

When Jacob Worse woke in the morning after the memorable birthday at Randulf's, he felt extremely unwell. His head was heavy and beating violently, and he felt the pain in his stomach.

His wife had long been up; and when Worse was really awakened, it was by two of the warehouse people, who came in and began to remove her bed.

"What are you about?" he inquired, petulantly.

"We are taking madame's bed into the other room."

"Nonsense!"

"Hush, hush!" said the old foreman. "The captain must not excite himself. You are ill, captain, and I was to tell you from madame that you must not talk."

Worse muttered something, and with sleepy eyes watched the departure of the bed.

When his wife soon afterwards entered the room, he said: "I shall be all right to-morrow, Sarah; it is only the first day that is so confoundedly bad. Bah! I will never touch toddy again. It's beastly, that's what it is."

"You are more ill than you suppose, both in body and soul, and I think you should seek healing for both, especially for your soul, before it be too late."

"Yes, dear, you know I will; but you must help me. Come sit by me, and read to me a little."

"Not to-day," she answered.

He lay in bed all that day, suffering much. The next day his head, at least, was clear, but the pains in his stomach troubled him, and he found it best to remain lying down.

From time to time Sarah visited his room, and he begged her piteously to come and sit by him; for when he was alone, he was troubled by many evil and dismal thoughts.

She seated herself by the window, with some small books —like her mother, she had also taken to small books.

"I suppose you will repent, and seek forgiveness for your sins, Worse; or will you persist in putting it off?"

"No, no, dear. You know how gladly I would repent. But you must help me, Sarah; for I know not what to do."

"Well, I will begin by reading to you from an excellent book on nine important points, which should arouse us to a feeling of our sinfulness, and lead us to repentance and amendment. Listen to me, not only with your ears, but with your stubborn heart, and may a blessing accompany the words."

Upon this she read slowly and impressively: "'The mercy of God first leads us to repentance; as the Apostle says (Rom. ii. 4), "The goodness of God leadeth thee to repentance."

"'Secondly, the Word of God clearly points to contrition. As the prophets of old were sent, even so preachers and other means of grace are now sent to us, daily sounding forth His Word as with a trumpet, and arousing us to repentance.

"'We should take heed to the judgments which, ever since the beginning of the world, have fallen upon hardened sinners; for example, floods, tempests, thunder and lightning in the heavens above, and destructive earthquakes from underneath our feet.'"

"Lisbon," muttered Worse. He had a picture of the great earthquake over the sofa in the sitting-room.

"'The fourth is the vast multitude of our sins which we committed when we lived in wantonness, drink, gluttony, and godlessness.

"'The fifth is the shortness of life, calling us to repentance; for our life passes quickly away, and we spend our years as a tale that is told.

"'The sixth is the small number of the saved; for strait is the gate, and narrow is the way, and few there be that enter therein.

"'For the seventh, death threatens us, and is a terror to the flesh. Its anticipation is bitter to all who are sunk in worldly pleasures.'"

Worse turned uneasily in his bed, as if he would interrupt her; but she continued—

"'We should, therefore, think of the day of judgment, which "will come as a thief in the night; in the which the heavens shall pass away with a great noise, and the elements shall melt with fervent heat, the earth also and the works that are therein shall be burned up."

"'But the ninth and last is the pains of hell, which are insupportable.

" 'Scripture gives a terrible description of the state of the condemned in everlasting flames, "where their worm dieth not, and the fire is not quenched." ' "

"Don't you think you could find something else to read, Sarah?" said Worse, anxiously.

" 'The days of hell will never end,' " she continued. " 'When as many years have passed and gone as there are beings in the world and stars in the firmament, when as many thousand years have passed as there are grains of sand in the bottom of the sea, there will yet be a million times as many more to come.

" 'Those who do not take this to heart will hereafter suffer for it. All drunkards and scoffers, as well as those who make their belly their god, those who are slaves to their passions, and all unbelievers, will then be revealed before the judgment-throne.

" 'The devil will stand on one side to accuse them, and their own consciences on the other to condemn them, and down below the gates of hell will stand open to swallow them.' "

"Sarah, Sarah! read no more!" cried Worse.

But she continued to read, and the words cut like a knife. The wrath of God, the flames of hell, and the never-ending sufferings of the damned were depicted in clear and terrible language.

"Sarah! for God's sake, stop!" shrieked Worse, sitting upright. The perspiration flowed down his cheeks, and he trembled so that the bed shook.

She fixed a stern eye upon him, and said, "I wonder if you have yet placed yourself in the hands of the living God?"

"Sarah, Sarah! What shall I do?"

"Pray," she answered, and left the room.

He lay and writhed with pain and fear, and when he heard her in the next room, called to her, begging her to have pity on him.

At last she came in again.

"Sarah, why are you so harsh with me? You were never so before."

"I never before dealt with you in the right way."

"Do you suppose that *this* is the right way?"

"I hope so."

"Well, you know best; but you must help me, Sarah. Do not leave me now!" And he clutched her hand with the grasp of a drowning man.

Some days after he was allowed to get up, and he followed her about the house; for he was uneasy when she left the room.

At times he sat in a corner with a good book in his hands not so much for the purpose of reading as for a protection against the assaults of Satan.

The fact was, that he now for the first time began to fancy that Satan was everywhere in pursuit of him.

When Sarah had succeeded in frightening him away from her, she became a little less severe, and it was only when he became troublesome that she talked or read in such a manner as almost to drive him out of his senses.

She herself went about in the deepest gloom all this time. She could neither pray nor sing, and at the meetings she heard, but gave no heed.

The one second she had been in Hans Nilsen's arms had suddenly revealed to her the deceit which had been practiced upon her. Her youth, her warm, unbounded affection for this man, had been repressed and crushed by religious exhortations, hymns, texts, and formalities.

But after all, they were only words which she now cast aside with contempt. Faith and hope had left her; and as to love, she knew that she loved one man only, and loved him to desperation.

Whilst Fennefos was away, she was in a state of fever. When he returned, he left her mother's house and moved up to the Haugian farm.

It was near the town, and Sarah, who rarely went beyond the neighbouring streets, now began to take long walks into the outskirts.

She would stand behind a boulder or a hedge, and would watch him while he laboured in the field. When she could not discover him, she would seat herself on a rock and gaze in all directions, or she would pick a flower and examine it, as if it were something new and rare. She watched him at the meetings; but he never spoke to her, nor did he ever turn his eyes in the direction where she was sitting.

No one observed anything peculiar about her; but as regarded Fennefos, the friends thought that a great change had come over him. The highly wrought austerity of manner with which he had begun had now left him; indeed, there was something almost humble in his demeanour.

CHAPTER XIII

THE farm, which was owned in common by a number of the leading Haugians, was of a considerable size. In addition to the farm, they also carried on various industries.

Those, therefore, who had to superintend the business were fully occupied, and Fennefos undertook the duty with a zeal and vigour unusual even for him.

On the other hand, during the first weeks of his stay, he was unable to lead the devotions among the labourers, who, after the custom of the Haugians, assembled for meals and for family worship in a great room, where they all ate in common at a long table.

Hans Nilsen confined his energies to the manual work of the farm, and at the meetings he was silent and oppressed. But after a couple of months had passed in this way, he began to lift up his head again.

In the hard bodily labour, and in all the responsibility which rested upon him as superintendent, his strong, sound nature recovered its equilibrium.

Although he continually deplored his one moment of weakness, and although he condemned himself, he yet began to understand that such might happen even to the best; and as this occurrence had revealed to him his own frailty, and had sorely shaken his self-confidence, so it also brought with it doubts as to whether he was right in expecting so much from mortal man as had been his wont.

He bethought him of the poor anxious inquirers whom he had left up in the North, and it seemed to him a sin to impose such heavy burdens on them. Then he thought of the well-to-do, easy Haugians, and it seemed a sin to remain among them. Sometimes, again, in his hopelessness he thought that it was as bad for him to be in the one place as in the other, and he longed for something entirely different.

Having got thus far, it became necessary to consider his

future life. Stay here, he could not. He was not uneasy on his own account, although after this he could not be sure of himself. For her sake, however, it was imperative that he should depart.

Separated they must be, that was clear; this he repeated to himself, but still he continued to stay on. Here there was work which would last over the harvest; and besides, whither in the world should he go?

When he left that place, there would be no spot in the wide world that could hold out any attraction to him, which could offer either home or friends. He would rather see no one, and live alone.

His heart was deeply wounded, and he often thought of Henrietta. He, too, was bound for life and death by an affection into which no evil thoughts should intrude. As for Sarah, he would pray for her.

In the meantime the elders regarded Hans Nilsen with concern. The address in Sivert Jespersen's house had done much harm; an impression went abroad that the Haugians were divided among themselves, and that Fennefos had separated from them.

There was a want of confidence among the Brethren themselves; those who had not been present wished to know what he had said, while those who had, gave evasive answers. There was much inquisitiveness and a great desire both among friends and foes to learn if there was really anything against so respected and well-known a man as Hans Nilsen.

Besides, since the meeting a change had taken place in his appearance. Something must have happened. Everybody had his own opinion, and the elders met to consult.

"I think," said Sivert Jespersen, looking round, "we are all agreed upon this, that there must be women at the bottom of the affair."

"I have heard it mentioned," said Endre Egeland, "that he has been very much in the company of Henrietta, Madame Torvestad's daughter."

"With Henrietta!" said Sivert Jespersen, in a somewhat incredulous tone.

The astonishment which this announcement produced led to a short pause.

"No, no," said the old dyer at last; "it is impossible to believe such a scandal."

"At any rate," said Sivert Jespersen, mildly, "we ought to consider how best to help Brother Hans Nilsen in all difficulties and temptations. I have thought, if it seems good to you, that we might meet up at the farm on Saturday afternoon, and, after having examined the accounts, we might have a little conversation with him."

"Let us be careful what we do," said the old man; "we know nothing for certain."

"No; I never meant that we should act indiscreetly—"

"I know that you are very prudent, Sivert Jespersen; but let us not forget that he is the most considerable man in our community, and that we must not lose him."

The Saturday when they met at the farm, according to agreement, was the last day of September. They had, therefore, to go into all the accounts of the farm, the dye-house, and the mill.

The accounts were in good order, and everything had been well managed. They thanked Hans Nilsen with the utmost friendliness.

When the books were closed and arrangements had been made for the future, they seated themselves round the room. Fennefos, who sat in the middle by the table with the account-books, raised his head, and looked calmly from one to the other.

No one failed to remark that his old expression had returned; the downcast, unsettled look which at one time they had observed was entirely gone. Sunburnt and vigorous, as he stood there among the pale-faced townsmen, he seemed more than ever full of power.

The old dyer, therefore, made signs to Sivert Jespersen, and began to move, as if he would depart.

But Sivert Jespersen had made up his mind to fathom Hans Nilsen's secret, or, at all events, to secure, for himself and the elders some hold upon the overbearing young man.

"We have been talking among ourselves," he began. "We have been talking about you, dear Hans Nilsen; yes, we have, indeed. We are all of opinion that you made use of very strong expressions that day—you remember, no doubt—at my house."

"I spoke with warmth, and if my words were too severe, I beg of you all to forgive me. I thought it necessary; but there was no want of charity in my heart."

"There is not one of us who supposes that there was, Hans Nilsen,' said the old dyer.

"No that there was not," continued Sivert Jespersen; "but what makes us anxious is the look of dejection which we have observed in you ever since. You are still young, Hans Nilsen, and we are old—at all events, we are all your seniors. We know full well to what temptations young blood is exposed, and if you have met with a downfall at the hands of Satan, we would willingly endeavour to raise you up again."

Hans Nilsen Fennefos looked from one to the other with a piercing glance, and it seemed to them that it rested for a painfully long time upon Endre Egeland.

"I thank you all, but God has been merciful. I require no such aid as that which you offer."

"How glad I am to hear it!" said Sivert Jespersen, with effusion. "But—do not be angry with me, dear friend—if we are outwardly preserved from falling, we should never forget what has been written about thoughts, words, and passions."

"Will any of you, I wonder, cast the first stone?" said Hans Nilsen, looking calmly round.

No one responded, and Sivert Jespersen's next neighbour touched him with his foot as a hint to stop. But it was too late. Fennefos had made up his mind, and, rising quickly, spoke thus—

"Dear brothers and friends, I did indeed use hard words the last time I addressed you. I came from scenes of poverty and found prosperity. I came from affliction, and found ease. I came from hunger and want, and I found myself at the rich man's table.

"I therefore remembered the rule which Hauge had left for our guidance:

" 'The elders must not connive at any depravity among themselves, but must duly rebuke it. Those who have acquired the respect of the believers, and would be exemplary Christians, must take heed lest they accustom themselves to flattery and luxury; they must even submit to sharp admonitions and to hard fare.'

"I spoke to you as my duty constrained me; but since that day the Lord's hand has fallen heavily on me, and, in my grievous sinfulness, I thought I should never again dare to stand forth and speak a word of rebuke to any one.

"That was the time when you saw me wandering amongst you, bowed down and forsaken. But God be praised, who has lifted me up. I will dare to hope that He will not cast me entirely aside as an unworthy instrument; but, dear friends, among you I can no longer tarry."

All looked uneasily at him.

"Surely you will not separate from the Brethren?" said the old man.

"No, that I will not do; but I must leave this place, both on account of my own infirmity, and because I fear that after this I cannot warn and admonish you with sufficient power; for, dear friends, I am of opinion that in many respects you go sadly astray."

"Will you travel northward again?" inquired one. "Or, perchance, the Lord has turned your heart towards the poor heathen in Africa?" said another.

Hans Nilsen looked up at him, and said: "I am grateful to you for the suggestion. I will think over it, and will pray the Spirit to guide me aright."

This seemed to bring relief to everybody. The mission was their own, originated and established by the Herrnhutters and Haugians. If Hans Nilsen entered upon the mission, he would remain with them, and they would not lose him. They now felt, for the first time, how great a support he was to their cause.

Sivert Jespersen began at once to exhort him to allow himself to be sent on a mission to the heathen lands lying in darkness.

Whether it was the expression, "allow himself to be sent," or whether Hans Nilsen could not on this occasion tolerate Sivert, it is sufficient to say that he answered him rather sharply. "If I do go, there is but one who will send me forth—the Lord."

"Take great heed to your missions, dear friends; you should

remember how the unbelievers, and not less the clergy, derided you when you began them.

"Already the fire you kindled has spread over the land, and help and funds pour in abundantly. See how these same clergy hasten like ravens attracted by the scent of prey. They will not suffer laymen to keep such Christian work in their control, whilst there is life and vigour in it; but would subject it to the rule of the Church, as they call it; that is to say, they will spoil your work and introduce their pride, strife, and intolerance. So long as all goes well, they will thrust themselves forward, exclaiming 'Behold us!' but if anything should go amiss, they will draw back, protesting that it must always be so when the people act upon their own judgment."

The old fire now came over him, and the elders looked round sadly one at another, grieving that they should lose such a brother. At last one said:

"But where will you go, if you do not accept the mission at our hands?"

"I imagine," said Hans Nilsen, "that I shall have little difficulty in finding heathens everywhere. But let us now separate for the present, and may the God who enlightened our forefathers be with us all, so that we may do His will."

Upon this he gave his hand to them all, one by one, and took his departure.

It was a still, oppressive autumn afternoon, and the little gathering broke up, the Brethren strolling across the fields towards the town.

The Haugian farm, as it was called, looked well in the evening light, with its solid, well-kept buildings.

The soil was poor, but well cultivated; and small groups of trees stood here and there, by the well-ordered stone fences.

When the little company of elders reached the gateway in the road leading to the town, the old dyer stopped, and burst into tears; the others gathered round him.

"Here stood I," said he, "in the spring of 1804, with my father and Hans Nilsen Hauge; at that time, wherever you looked, it was all heather and broken ground.

"My father and Hauge had been talking of purchasing the moorland here, as was soon done. Hauge had given his advice and instructions as to the improvements and the work he considered necessary, very much those that have since been carried out.

"When we were about to return home, my father said: 'Yes, if God will but give His blessing to it.' I suppose he thought most of the things of this world, did father.

"It was a hazardous undertaking, and the Haugians had but little capital at that time.

"Hauge smiled, and said, cheerfully: 'I am not in the least anxious on that score, Ingebret, if you are alluding to worldly prosperity. I would rather pray that those who come after us may be protected against too great success and facility in the business of this world. You must bear in mind,' said he, 'you who are still young, that it requires a strong back to bear prosperity.'

"I can picture him now before me, standing just there. He was young himself in those days, and not so very much older than myself. Nevertheless, I was conscious that I stood in the exalted presence of one who was worthy of all honour, before whom I would fain bow myself.

"Something of the same feeling came over me to-day, when he spoke—young Hans Nilsen Fennefos. It is of no use denying it; it is he who is in the right, and it is we who are backsliders and lukewarm."

The old man, shaking his head sadly, turned towards the town, the others accompanying him in silence.

Madame Torvestad aged very much under the vexations which now beset her. The Brethren had taken Hans Nilsen from her, and continued to act without consulting her. Moreover, the Gnadau system of treatment seemed to bear no fruit.

Henrietta, indeed, grew pale and thin, owing to much fasting and confinement; but, on the other hand, a defiant look appeared in her eyes.

One day her mother heard her singing a popular nautical ballad, on the devotion of a sailor's bride to her betrothed. Upon this, Madame Torvestad's patience broke down, and, losing her usual self-control, she went into the room, and gave Henrietta a box on each ear, saying: "I will soon teach you a very different song."

Henrietta sat as if petrified. She had often seen her mother in a state of irritation, and had received many a sharp blow in her younger days, but she had never seen her like this before. She did not expect much forbearance, but it never occurred to her that things could come to such a terrible pass.

In the course of an hour, Henrietta was called down into the sitting-room, where she found Madame Endre Egeland. The stout sallow-complexioned dame kissed her, and it was now broken to her that she was betrothed to Erik Pontoppidan Egeland, the most objectionable person under the sun.

When Sarah heard of this engagement, she went across to her mother. They shut themselves up in the parlour, but the interview was of brief duration. Madame Torvestad soon got the better of her daughter, and when it came to the point, and Sarah found herself seated opposite to her mother in the old room, she could not muster courage enough for a decisive attack.

Besides, what could she say? Could she divulge her own shame and sorrow?

Sarah went upstairs to Henrietta, who made no answer to what she said, except, "I will not, I will not. I have sworn it." She was ill and feverish.

Sarah undressed her and put her to bed, but her mother wished to nurse her herself, and Sarah was obliged to leave, even more depressed and unhappy than before.

As the weeks passed on, her heart became more and more hardened.

Fennefos recovered his clear, pure looks, and, when in her company, seemed to ignore her presence.

One day it was rumoured that he was about to become a missionary. Sarah heard of it, and she grew more and more gloomy. She hated her mother, and detested her husband, comporting herself, however, with such calmness that no one could have imagined what thoughts were surging through her brain.

Jacob Worse had now entered upon an earnest struggle with the devil. By degrees it became evident to him that the evil one was always at work, both inside and outside his innermost heart.

They strove together, the devil and Worse, from morning until evening, and at night when he dreamt. Generally the captain got the worst of it.

When he became aware of his snares in time, he occasionally outwitted the crafty fiend. Thus it occurred one day, when he was with Skipper Randulf, who had induced him to take a turn through the town, talking and leading him farther and farther towards the wharves, that he suddenly discovered his danger. He heard a couple of boys who passed him say that a ship was about to be launched, and it was easy to perceive in this a stratagem of the evil one. It was an old trick of the devil to lead his thoughts to the sins of his early life, by means of things pertaining to ships and the sea.

He had, therefore, long since laid aside the half-finished model of the *Hope* up in the garret; and when he saw that the devil tempted him through Thomas Randulf, he turned round suddenly, and hastened home to Sarah. Randulf grieved over his friend, and, in the evening at the club, said "It is all up with Jacob Worse; take my word for it, he is not long for this world. I saw it to-day."

"I don't think so," said another; "he looks a little pale and poorly, but—"

"Yes, I tell you I saw it to-day, by his trousers."

"What rubbish you talk, Randulf!" said the chief pilot, who was seated at the card-table.

"Rubbish!" said Randulf, pugnaciously. "Your word is better than mine, is it? I tell you that when a man is doomed, his trousers hang loosely about him."

They all laughed, and some one suggested that when people are ill they grow thin.

"No, no," cried Randulf, with much warmth; "what I allude to has its own peculiar appearance. The trousers look so heavy, so empty, and so long, that they seem as if they would slip down, and three heavy folds rest upon the feet. When I see this, I know that a man has not long to live. You may take this as a fact."

When the bad weather began in October, Jacob Worse went

out but seldom; he had grown chilly, and kept much to his room.

He read the small books as much as he could, but they did not avail to bring him that spiritual comfort for which he strove so hard.

At the meeting it was strange to see, amidst the peaceful, benignant faces, this woe-begone old man, with his thick white hair and his deeply furrowed placid cheeks, looking wistfully from one to the other, and listening anxiously, hoping some day to hear the words which should bring peace to his soul.

But from old times the devil had too secure a hold upon him, placing oaths upon his tongue and evil thoughts in his heart.

At the meeting, when Sivert Jespersen was reading out a sermon, the devil would lug in those two hundred barrels of salt, or so distorted his vision that Endre Egeland would seem to be staring at the girls with his small green eyes.

At night, when the wind howled around his house, it seemed to him that the devil would take him out on the sea on board the *Hope;* and he experienced a pleasure in lying and thinking how well he used to sail the good ship, and how grand she looked in a heavy sea.

Sometimes Satan tempted him to pride when Garman and Worse did a good stroke of business, or to wrath and indignation when Romarino came and asked for money or endorsements.

The devil even made use of Thomas Randulf to corrupt him. One day, when Worse met him in the market-place, opposite his street door, he hurried back into his house; for it seemed to him as if Randulf had long, crooked claws.

It was best to be at home, especially if Sarah was there. There, if he was very vigilant, he was able to keep the devil at arms' length.

All this time, however, his malady was gaining ground; he slept badly, and his appetite failed him. The only thing he relished was pea-soup and salt pork, such as he had been accustomed to at sea, and he brightened up every morning when he smelt the peas in the kitchen.

One day, however, it occurred to him that this, too, might be one of the temptations of the evil one, leading his thoughts away from the one thing needful, and back to the sinful recollections of his past life.

The next time the pea-soup was placed on the table, he could scarcely touch it.

The devil was in the peas, too.

CHAPTER XIV

"My dear Christian Frederik,

"Since your lamented mother's death, whose too early demise we ever deplore, I do not know when I have felt myself more contented or in such good spirits.

"In every man's life there is a certain point where his character and inner nature undergo a change and become altered. His interests continue as before, the amount of energy with which he approaches his work need not lessen; and yet when he arrives at the turning-point, he sees with other eyes, and is, in some respects, actuated by other feelings.

"This transition, of which I can here give but a very imperfect description, is the inevitable result of the change from youth to old age, and this it is which of late years, ever since your mother's death, has slowly and gradually manifested itself in me.

"With feelings of gratitude to a merciful Providence, I am able to say that I feel happy in having become an old man.

"But my heart is chiefly filled with gratitude when I consider how much bodily health and strength, and especially mental vigour, I still retain, so that nothing of what has hitherto occupied my thoughts has yet become alien or indifferent to me.

"I enjoy more peace of mind, the brain, undisturbed by passion, is better fitted to perform its functions, and the somewhat precipitate ardour of youth has given place to the circumspection of mature age.

"I write to you to-day, my dear son, more explicitly, and upon subjects different from those on which we usually correspond. I am led to do so, partly with a desire to inform you of what you are about to undertake, and partly because this letter may be one of the last which we shall exchange at a distance; for it is now my wish, and my paternal injunction, that you, in conformity with our prearranged understanding, should return home in the ensuing spring.

"I leave it to your choice to decide whether you will return from Paris by Copenhagen, or whether you will go to England, and come thence in one of the lobster-smacks.

"It will be a great joy to me to see you at home again, and in good health. I hope also that you, on your part, will be contented and happy, and prepared to take a part in the business.

"I have never forgotten that when I, in my youth, returned from a long absence in foreign parts, Sandsgaard seemed to me an out-of-the-way and neglected corner of the great world.

"But the experience of life has taught me that a man who is endowed with a philosophical spirit and high principles, will easily accommodate himself to whatever fate has prepared for him.

"I venture to hope that even if you should come direct from Paris, you will not deem Sandsgaard an entirely unworthy residence; for of late I have renovated and decorated the mansion, so that it seems only to want a throng of young and happy people to conjure up those times on which my memory loves to dwell, although clouded by bereavement and sorrow.

"However, why should I again recall a grief which must always cast its shadow on my life?

"Let us look forward to the future, which, for you younger people at all events, seems likely to bring happier days.

"Perhaps, also, in the contemplation of your felicity, I may find some compensation, and solace for many tears.

"Without doubt, you will have remarked that in our recent correspondence I have, with a definite purpose, endeavoured to impart to you such a general knowledge of our business as was practicable, without being too prolix.

"I look upon you already as my fellow-worker and associate in labours, for which your letters, and the accounts you have sent me, as well as the reports of your superiors during your residence abroad, encourage me to believe that you are not unfitted and still less unworthy.

"You are aware that the firm has prospered, a matter which a merchant does not care to talk of, but between us two, I may say that the firm has met with extraordinary success.

"You will, therefore, find—to your agreeable surprise, I trust—that many branches of the business which hitherto I had been unable to develop adequately, by reason of the want of funds, have now, like plants under a fertilizing shower, made auspicious growth, owing to the abundance of ready money.

"You will, therefore, on your arrival, find a wide field for your young energies, and you will be spared the anxiety and care which I, for many years, unknown to you or to any other person, have undergone.

"I now come to that point in my letter which may be termed the chief or cardinal point, namely, our relations with Worse.

"In our correspondence we have never treated particularly of this affair; nevertheless, I seem to have observed that it was only your filial respect which restrained you from criticising my conduct in admitting Jacob Worse into the firm.

"For this reason, my dear Christian Frederik, I will speak out once for all, and say that it was neither more nor less than the salvation of the firm.

"It may be that there is something humiliating in this avowal; but, for my part, I can only say that it would have been far more humiliating and more injurious to our credit to have secretly accepted a subvention from one of our own *employés*.

"It was I, therefore, who proposed the change in the firm; for I considered such an open proceeding, not only more in consonance with our reputation, but also with the highest commercial principles. I will not deny, however, that the change of the firm's name cost me a struggle, and I am not blind to the complications to which it may lead.

"I have of late carefully considered all this, and it is my purpose to inform you in this letter of the present condition of affairs, and briefly to confide to you the plan which I propose to follow, and which I hope to carry out in the future.

"Our old Jacob Worse is very ill, and, after a visit which I paid to his sick-bed a few days since, I can have but little doubt—I regret to say—that his days are numbered. His marriage, as I both thought and predicted, has brought him little happiness.

"His wife, as you know, is one of the religious enthusiasts, and of late years she, in conjunction with her mother and the rest of the pious folks, have succeeded in spoiling our old Worse to such an extent that I do not care to sully this paper by a description of his lamentable decadence. I shall, therefore, restrain my grief and anger, and will confine myself to business matters.

"When Jacob Worse dies—and, considering his present condition, one can only wish him a speedy and painless departure—it will be necessary to divide his property between his widow and the son of his first marriage, which may entail complications as regards the firm.

"In order to avoid this as much as possible, I have made up my mind to offer to young Romarino Worse, when the time arrives, a sum of money in lieu of a position in the firm. I am inclined to think that he will acquiesce, partly because, according to my slight knowledge of his character, a considerable sum, either in cash or convertible security, will be much appreciated by him.

"As I have already said, I know but little of the young man, still I have formed an impression that young Worse is not a person with whom we should like to work.

"Although I believe that so long as Providence vouchsafes to me strength to continue at the head of the firm, we should know how to manage him, yet I would not embarrass you with a companion in whom we could not place entire confidence.

"I hope to accomplish this change by the time you arrive, and I hope, moreover, that it will meet with your approval.

"On the one hand, there is no doubt something decidedly unpleasant in our recent alliance with Worse, but, on the other, we must never forget that it was old Jacob Worse's money that saved us, and I enjoin you herewith to keep an eye on the family; we ought to stand by them, both by word and deed.

"When this affair is arranged, my mind will be at ease; and I hope that we have yet before us a fair number of years in which to work together in the firm of Garman and Worse.

"If, as I suppose from your last letter, you have already reached Paris, you will, no doubt, have enjoyed the pleasure of meeting with your brother Richard at our legation, whither I send this letter.

"I am convinced that you will mutually derive much benefit and satisfaction from each other's society in the great city.

"Your brother Richard, by reason of his connections, will be able to introduce you to circles which would otherwise be inaccessible to a stranger. On the other hand, I do not doubt that your presence may, in many respects, be advantageous to your younger brother.

"The career which Richard has adopted entails much greater expense and a more luxurious mode of life than is necessary or becoming to a merchant. Nevertheless, I would put it to you, whether you could not, by means of brotherly counsels impress upon Richard the propriety of greater economy. Do not misunderstand me, or suppose that it is my desire that you should mar your brief intercourse by lecturing him, nor do I wish that your communications should lead him to think that I am dissatisfied with him.

"On the contrary, I wish that you may both employ your time in Paris in acquiring those pleasant impressions for which that city affords such an excellent opportunity, to such an extent and with such moderation as befits gentlemen in our position, avoiding that useless extravagance which only testifies to a vain desire for ostentation unsuitable to persons of refinement.

"As your brother's stay in Paris will apparently be of longer duration than yours, I will cause the letter of credit, which the firm sends by this post, to be made out in his name; and whilst I am on the subject of your younger brother, I will make a confidential announcement to you.

"After my death, you will find no reference to Richard in my accounts. His education has, for many reasons, been far more expensive than yours. Nevertheless, it is my desire that, like good brothers, you should share and share alike. I enjoin you, however, to deal out to your brother by degrees the portion which may appertain to him.

"For your brother Richard, with all his talents and excellent qualities, has, I fear, but little aptitude for acquiring and retaining this world's goods. You, my dear Christian Frederik, who have been endowed with this facility, must, therefore, act as a guardian to your brother. Remember me kindly to the dear boy, and ask him to seek some musical friends who will assist you to purchase a good piano of Erard's, which you will see carefully packed and sent off, or, perhaps, you can bring it with you in the spring, when you return home.

"Our old piano does not satisfy modern requirements, and, moreover, ever since your mother's death it is painful to hear tones which too sadly remind me of my great loss.

"For several weeks we have experienced severe and continuous storms, and we have heard of many wrecks and disasters along the coast. Happily none of our own vessels are in these waters; but people are anxiously awaiting news of many ships belonging to this town, which are on their way from the Baltic.

"You will be surprised to find how much the trade and shipping of the good town has increased during these last few years, and I fancy that much of what happens, or is attempted here, will seem as strange to you as it does to me.

"That which especially excites my wonder and anxiety is the religious enthusiasm which, in my youth, was confined to peasants and uneducated people.

"So far from disappearing or being cured, as one would expect and hope, it seems rather to expand, and to gain adherents amongst those whose intelligence should protect them from such folly.

"I have also heard that some of the younger clergy have approved of--nay, have actually joined—this absurd and hurtful revival. Every true patriot must greatly deplore this; for just as a judicious enlightenment is beneficial to the common people, so, on the other hand, is it injurious when hypocrites and ignorant persons devote themselves to the Holy Scriptures, which they can neither understand nor apply rightly.

"And if it really should happen—though I can scarcely credit it—that the clergy allow themselves to be dragged down by ignorance and enthusiasm, I should greatly fear that it will be to the detriment of our dear fatherland.

"In the meantime, you will understand that, in a certain sense, there is a great distance between Sandsgaard and the town, and I trust that you will find the atmosphere here as fresh and pure as ever.

"And now, my dear son, I will conclude with an affectionate salutation from myself and your two aunts. The good ladies are in 'court mourning,' as Jacob Worse used to term it in the old days; nevertheless, they are looking forward to the pleasure of seeing you once more.

"I have a suspicion that they are planning a marriage for you, for they are devoted to small children.

"I, too, to speak plainly, have a great wish that new life, laughter, and the sound of tiny footsteps should be heard once more in the old house.

"Your loving father,
"MORTEN W. GARMAN."

CHAPTER XV

A STORM can be endured, however severe it be, if one is safe on the land.

But when it rages week after week, day after day, and night after night, so that no one can declare when one storm ends and the next begins, there are few who are exempt from an oppressive nervous feeling of anxiety, especially if, under such circumstances, they happen to live in a small town built of wood, close down by the open fjord, with the sea in front of them.

Then the heavens lower, so that the clouds course along the earth, and rain and spray drift far inland. Rifts in the leaden sky show fiery storm-streaks during the day, and the night is dark as death.

But the worst is when one lies helpless in bed, and the tempest rages in the small crooked streets, shaking the eaves and tearing off the tiles.

When one has not slept well, too, for many nights, and the day has been spent looking from the barometer up at the grey sky, or out on the deserted streets; when here and there a red spot on the mud marks a broken tile; when one hears tales of misfortune in the town and in the harbour, or of how narrow an escape from fire there was last night—fire in such a storm—then it is that one doubts whether the world is not out of course, whether everything will not fall asunder or be upheaved, and the sea pour in over the low reefs, sweeping churches, houses, and all out into the fjord like chips.

"The wrath of God is upon the land," said the Haugians, as they held on their hats on the way to the meeting.

In the entrance passage, the wind lifted the ends of the women's shawls over their heads, so that they entered the low, half-lit meeting-hall in a somewhat dishevelled state. Here they sat, packed close together, while the reader had either to raise his voice or to cease for a time altogether, when the wind shook the doors and windows, and wrestled with the ash trees outside.

In the pause which followed, he began to read again, but without life or freedom. Uneasiness prevailed as they looked one at another, the women crept together as each blast struck the house, and the men had much to think about.

Many ships owned by the Haugians were on their way home from the Baltic and St. Ubes. People waited and waited, but nothing arrived; whilst the tempest grew worse and worse with ever-increasing gales, between south-west and north-west. If they have not found a harbour of refuge in time, God have mercy both on them and us.

Even Sivert Jespersen was without a smile on his countenance, sitting still, and pushing his hands up his coat sleeves until they reached the elbows; he seemed as if clutching at and grasping something.

Madame Torvestad, with an austere and imperious aspect, sat in her place; many gazed at her, but she maintained her composure. He, however, whom all wished to see among them, was absent.

Eight days before, Fennefos had quietly taken leave of the Brethren, and had embarked for England in a Dutch ship, which had been lying in the harbour. It was his intention to proceed from England to India. He had not, however, left the country; for the Dutchman had been compelled to take shelter from the storm, and Fennefos lay weather-bound at Smörvigen, a few miles from the town. He had even visited it two days since on some business.

The tempest had been somewhat moderated during the forenoon, but in the evening the wind went to north-west, and blew harder than ever.

Heavy seas came into the bay, causing the vessels and lighters to roll, and breaking on the open stone foundations under the wooden storehouses, here and there even washing up through the floors above, on account of the unusually high tide.

The wind whistled terribly through the rigging of the great ships, and the moorings and fenders creaked and grated.

Along the gallery of Jacob Worse's warehouse, a slender white form groped its way down the steps, and stood on the ground floor, which seemed to rock every time the sea rolled in underneath.

Mustering all her strength, she contrived to draw aside so much of the hanging door of the warehouse that she could squeeze herself through the opening.

Supporting herself with one hand, as she leant over the dark water, she repeated once more her oath before she let go:

"I promise and swear to love you faithfully in life and death, and never to marry any other person, Lauritz—my own Lauritz."

Saying this, she loosed her hold, a heavy sea swept her under a lighter, and she sank.

Later in the evening, some seafaring folk, who had been on board a vessel to look after its moorings, saw something white, which surged up and down by the stone steps at the market quay.

From the quay the news spread over the whole town, even more quickly than such news generally travels; for all were in such a state of consternation and excitement, owing to the long-continued tempest, that the report of a corpse seemed to chime in with the general feeling, and the tidings swept over the town as if borne upon the wings of the tempest.

Children who were going to bed heard the servant girls in the kitchen wringing their hands, and crying "God preserve us!" but when they inquired of their mothers what it was all about, they were told that it was something with which small children could have no concern, and, believing that it must be something very terrible, they crept trembling under the blankets.

Many versions of the story were circulated. Some said that she had left her bed in a fit of madness—she was ill of a nervous fever—whilst Madame Torvestad was at the meeting and the servant girl away.

Some only muttered and shook their heads, and these latter gradually formed the majority.

Others thought that it was another instance of what went on among the Haugians.

Henrietta Torvestad had committed suicide; of this no doubts were entertained. Perhaps her mother had tried to force her to marry Erik Pontoppidan. Yes, the overbearing Madame Torvestad was blamed, she and the Haugians, the gloomy, deceitful Haugians who grudged any joy, either to themselves or others. It was they who had caused the death of the poor girl; it was they who were the evil genius of the town, which seemed as if a curse rested upon it.

Corpses floated in the bay, and tempest followed tempest incessantly, as if the day of judgment were at hand.

In spite of the weather, many people were abroad in the streets, in order to procure further information, and they found a group with a couple of lanterns down by the market-place.

The Haugians heard the news just as they came home from the meeting. Sivert Jespersen put on his greatcoat again, turned up the collar, and hurried off through the dark streets to Madame Torvestad.

Many others besides him had ventured out. Men and women of the Haugians were afraid to stay at home alone with this terrible news, which, in some measure, caused them to feel conscience-stricken.

They went out in order to ascertain the truth, and to learn how the elders received it. They met many persons in the streets near the market-place, and a number of people bearing lanterns, who had collected near Madame Torvestad's house.

Whenever any of the Haugians approached, they threw a light on their faces, calling out their names with scornful and opprobrious words. In order to enter, the Haugians were obliged to take a circuitous route, and when they reached the door, a couple of the Brethren opened it when the voice was recognized, shutting it quickly again.

Indoors they felt more secure, for Worse's premises were built in a square, with a court-yard in the centre, like a fortress. But here, too, there was distraction and terror. Madame Torvestad was said to have gone out of her senses. She sat upright by the side of the bed, watching the water as it dripped from the corpse, and would not allow any one to touch it.

The old dyer was the only person she would suffer to be with her.

In the chief part of the house Jacob Worse lay, and fought his last fight with the devil. He was in a room looking upon the court-yard, for in the rooms towards the market-place they did not dare show lights, in order not to excite the crowd, which was increasing, and from which menacing utterances broke forth at times.

In a short time the principal men and women of the Haugian community assembled. They went about with pale faces, in anxiety and bewilderment, and no one was capable of taking the lead. In the meantime the storm raged on, and the house shook to its foundations.

Jacob Worse lay on his death-bed, his features pale and drawn. For many days he had suffered great pain, which was now gradually leaving him, and both the doctor and the nurse declared that it was his last night.

But the struggle was not yet over; one could see this by the anxious way in which his eyes were turned from one to the other, when Sarah was out of the room.

Sometimes he seemed to lapse into deep terror, throwing himself from one side to the other, muttering something which they could not understand, and rubbing his hands together.

"He is possessed by Satan," said one of the women.

This was the general opinion, and some searched in the Bible or in one of the many little books for texts or hymns applicable to persons possessed by the evil one.

But the majority were occupied with the terrible fate of Henrietta, or were watching the tumultuous crowd outside.

Sarah moved among them with a distracted air; she seemed, indeed, as if petrified with grief. It was not grief, however, that distracted her. The separation from Fennefos, and Henrietta's death conjoined, inflicted a stunning blow, which both chilled and hardened her.

Her dying husband yonder in his bed, the frightened men and women, the uproar in the street, were matters of indifference to her, and she could almost have smiled at them.

Out of doors things grew worse. A couple of boys began to batter the wall; others, approaching the windows, climbed up and pressed their faces against the panes.

The Haugians crept away into corners, and Sivert Jespersen lay almost under the table.

"Some one must go out and speak to the crowd," said one of the older women.

Sivert Jespersen was the man to do it, as he was the oldest of them, but he would not venture forth; he knew only too well that his presence would only make bad worse.

The old dyer was with Madame Torvestad; it would be better to ask him to make the attempt.

It never occurred to any of them to apply to the police, for no one in the town, and least of all the Haugians, was accustomed to seek help in that quarter.

There must also have been some of the better class in the crowd that filled the street and the greater part of the market-place, in front of Skipper Worse's street door; for some of the lanterns were of the expensive hexagonal sort, and of polished brass.

While they were debating whether they should fetch the old dyer, the people outside ceased their uproar, and nothing was heard but the hasty footsteps of people leaving the street and hurrying to the market-place, where they crowded round somebody; and the lanterns being directed on the central spot, it was comparatively light.

Here, taller than all the rest, the Haugians recognized their own Hans Nilsen Fennefos.

He was speaking to the people. The tempest drowned his words, but they knew his power over the wills of men; and whilst they all, both men and women, pressed to the windows, they thanked God for this succour, and congratulated one another, as if their lives had hung on a thread.

Sarah remained alone in the sick room. She was absorbed with the idea that she would see Fennefos again. She was terrified; she almost trembled, and thought she would be unable to bear it.

Worse gazed at her, but finding no consolation in her distracted looks, he shut his eyes, and seemed as if dozing.

Fennefos, entering by the street door, was received in the unlighted passage by many friendly hands and affectionate greetings.

The first thing he said was: "Why do you sit here in the dark; are you afraid of the light?"

After the whispering which had hitherto prevailed, it sounded as if he spoke in a loud voice.

Two women went for lights, and the blinds were drawn down.

"You have come just at the right moment, Hans Nilsen," said Sivert Jespersen, clapping him on the shoulder.

"How pleasant are the feet of those who bring glad tidings!" said Nicolai Egeland.

"I come rather with evil tidings," said Hans Nilsen, looking gravely from one to the other; "although I see that there is grief enough already in this house. We heard yesterday at Smörvig that your ship *Ebenezer* is cast away to the South of Bratvold. Not a man was saved. I, therefore, came here that you might make provision for the widows and the fatherless.

"The Lord gave, and the Lord has taken away, praised be His Name," said Nicolai Egeland.

Sivert Jespersen turned away, and went out into another room. He seemed to be occupied with some calculation.

In the street the people had begun to disperse. Fennefos was known and, in a measure, respected.

That one whom all knew to have departed as a missionary to India had now suddenly reappeared, produced also a certain effect; there was, moreover, something about the man which enthralled all his hearers. He spoke a few impressive words as to how ill it became them to add to the burden when the Lord's hand fell heavily on a brother's house.

The better sort of lanterns disappeared, and the ordinary ones soon followed; indeed, there was no temptation to remain in the market-place on such a night.

Gradually the crowd broke up, some of them venting their feelings by hammering at the wall as they passed Madame Torvestad's corner.

Fennefos had seated himself among the Haugians in the sick chamber, and addressed them again.

Henrietta's death had moved him deeply, and every word he uttered thrilled with emotion and pity, finding its way to all the sorrowing hearts.

All listened. Some wept in silence. Sarah alone sat with half-averted face and unmoved features. Sometimes she turned towards him; but he looked at her as he looked at the others, frankly and openly.

Her deep-set eyes penetrated him, as if with a wail of the deepest despair. Now that she was about to be free, all was lost. Would he not help her?

He would not; not as she wished.

He spoke to them as if he were already far away, and it seemed to them as if they heard the much-loved preacher speaking words of peace from distant lands. After this, he rose, and bid them "Good night" and "Farewell."

A great and painful surprise ensued. Was he about to leave them again? Would he deprive them of that peace of which he had just been the messenger?

They gathered round him with entreaties and endearments, talked of the storm and of the dreadful weather, adding: "You will hardly find the way, Hans Nilsen, this pitch dark night."

But he answered them gently, with his mother's hymn.

"For He who stills the tempest
And calms the rolling sea,
Will lead thy footsteps safely,
And smooth a way for thee."

At the door he turned once more, looking affectionately on them all. Coming lastly to Sarah, who stood close by him, he reached out his hand to her for the last farewell. The old innocent friendship of their youth reappeared in his look —at once so kindly and so frank, yet full of sorrow and of heartfelt sympathy.

When the others followed him out in the passage, Sarah turned back, took a light, and went upstairs. Here she broke down, weeping for poor Henrietta, for herself, and for all the misery around her.

Nothing remained to her but that bright, pure look, in the remembrance of which her grief lost the hardness which had beset her, and her thoughts reverted to the old times, when she and Fennefos were as brother and sister.

In this condition a couple of women found her, by the linen closet, weeping; and one said to the other: "See how she loved him!"

She started up in a confused manner, but quieted herself again when she found that they alluded to her husband.

Several women who had small children at home now left, as the streets were empty; but the majority of the company preferred to remain in the house all night, in order to watch and pray with poor Skipper Worse, and to be at hand in case of need.

From time to time one would go across the yard to listen at the door of Madame Torvestad's apartments, and they were comforted by hearing the voice of the old dyer, which proved that Madame Torvestad had come to herself again.

At midnight coffee was brought into the room, and they took it in turns to go in and drink a cup, in order to keep awake.

In the room of the dying man some sat reading good books, or one of them would offer up a prayer for the sufferer, that the Lord might soon release him and mitigate the pangs of death.

Jacob Worse had been lying perfectly still for a couple of hours, and they could not tell whether he was conscious. Sarah sat by the bedside, and took his hand in hers. It was the first time she had shown anything like spontaneous affection; but it was now too late, he was too far gone to observe it.

As the night drew on, the tempest abated, and the reading and prayers lessened. All had undergone so much mental fatigue, that weariness asserted itself, now that the storm was on the wane, and the sick man was lying calm and still.

One and then another fell into a doze; Sivert Jespersen also closed his eyes, but not in sleep. He was busied with calculations.

The reading now ceased, and all was perfectly silent. Suddenly they all sprang up, for yonder, from his death-bed Jacob Worse cried out:

"Lauritz, you young scamp, go aloft and clear the dog-vane!"

They hastened to his bedside, bringing lights; pale and terrified, they gazed on the dying man, thinking it was the devil himself who spoke through him.

Sarah had cast herself down by the bedside in prayer.

Jacob Worse was completely changed; his glazed eyes were half open, and the look of pain had departed from his face; he seemed to be the self-possessed Skipper Worse of old days. The thick white hair was arranged in seemly order, and his hands lay upon the coverlet as if he had finished something.

At this, the last moment, the devil had relaxed his hold; and whilst the malady wrestled for the last time with the strong limbs of the dying man, and his brain made its last effort, a crowd of ill-defined recollections and bewildered thoughts whirled past, and a sudden vision brightened the last moments of the sufferer.

It was the vision of that celebrated return from Rio, the proudest moment of his life.

He was standing again on the deck of the *Hope*, a fresh north wind was blowing in the fjord, and the old brig was gliding in under easy sail.

He opened his eyes, but did not see the wan faces which had gathered around him. He saw the sun shining over Sandsgaard Bay, where the summer ripples hastened towards the shore, with the news that Jacob Worse was in the fjord.

He tried to raise his head, in order to see the better; but, sinking back upon the pillows, he muttered with a happy and contented smile:

"We come late, Herr Consul, but we come safely." And, so saying, old Skipper Worse sailed out of the world.

INDEX OF AUTHORS

The volume number is given in Roman numerals

INDEX OF TITLES